Friday Night with the Girls

Shari Low

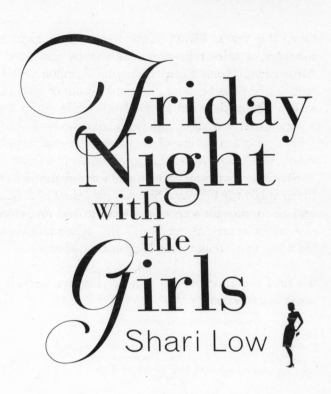

piatkus

PIATKUS

First published in Great Britain as a paperback original in 2011 by Piatkus

Copyright © Shari Low 2011

The moral right of the author has been asserted.

A CIP catalogue record for this book
is available from the British Library.

ISBN 978-0-7499-5216-7

Typeset in Baskerville MT by Palimpsest Book Production Limited,
Falkirk, Stirlingshire
Printed and bound in Great Britain by Clays Ltd, St Ives plc

Papers used by Piatkus are from well-managed forests
and other responsible sources.

MIX
Paper from
responsible sources
FSC® C104740
www.fsc.org

Piatkus
An imprint of
Little, Brown Book Group
100 Victoria Embankment
London EC4Y 0DY

An Hachette UK Company
www.hachette.co.uk

www.piatkus.co.uk

Praise for Shari Low:

'More fun than a girls' night out!'
OK!

'There are only two words for Shari Low: utterly hilarious'
Carmen Reid

'Totally captivating and it felt like I'd lost a new best friend
when it came to the end'
Closer

'Shari Low writes with humour and skill about the
complicated subtleties of adult relationships. A gentle
warning to smug marrieds everywhere'
Dorothy Koomson

'Great fun from start to finish'
Jenny Colgan

'Compulsive . . . This is a hilarious read'
Sun

'Absolutely hilarious. A brilliant read that keeps your
attention right up until the end'
Bookbag

Over the years, **Shari Low** has been a nightclub manager, a sales rep, run health clubs and lived in Amsterdam, Hong Kong, Shanghai, London and Los Angeles. She has been fat, thin, in love, out of love, back in love again, then out of love (this could go on for a while), a wife, a mother, good at reading bedtime stories, rubbish at football, obsessed with travelling, addicted to eBay and blessed with a group of fantastic friends.

Shari now lives with her lovely husband and two very funny sons near Glasgow. She has published nine novels and also writes for screen, newspapers and magazines.

And she's currently medium-sized, in love and looking for a bargain break to the Maldives or Monaco.

To find out more about Shari, visit her website at www.sharilow.com

Also by Shari Low:

What If?
Why Not?
Double Trouble
The Motherhood Walk of Fame
My Best Friend's Life
A Brand New Me
Temptation Street

To John, Callan and Brad. Everything. Always.

One

2008

The St Kentigern Hotel, Glasgow. Friday night, 8 pm

'. . . and the study concluded that the majority of women prefer to have a lunch or night out with their girlfriends than a night of hubba hubba with their partner.'

Puffed up with the thrill of having delivered this little nugget of anthropological interest, Ginger took a large slug of her Jack Daniel's and Coke and waited for a response.

Next to me, Lizzy was nodding thoughtfully. 'Well, there are definitely advantages. And by the way, you're far too old to be referring to sex as hubba hubba.'

I jumped in before Ginger had a chance to come over all lingo-defensive. 'Actually I think I agree with the survey. At least when you're out with the girls you don't have to suck your stomach in and spend the whole time trying to keep your arse in a flattering light.'

'I can't believe you do that.' Lizzy looked shocked. I understood her surprise. It was ridiculous that I felt that way. Surely I should be able to exhale at least once during sex? On the one

1

hand, I was sure I could win a medal for Olympic-standard lung capacity, but on the other hand shouldn't I be comfortable enough to be honest, open and slightly spongy in the abdominal area?

'You're right,' I agreed, 'I should just let it all hang out.'

Now she looked even more shocked. 'No you shouldn't – you should just switch the light off!'

Ginger and I dissolved into giggles but Lizzy was unrepentant. 'I haven't had sex with the light on since nineteen eighty-seven.'

We tried to regain a touch of decorum as a very pretty waitress placed a new round of drinks on the table. Ginger groaned as soon as she was out of earshot. 'What does it say about me that she looks way too young to work here? God, I'm old. Old. A haggard old crumbling specimen of womanhood.'

'And shallow. You forgot to mention shallow.' I picked up my large glass of red wine, careful not to spill a drop on my brand-new white chiffon tunic. It had been a spontaneous buy from Zara that afternoon and I'd swept caution to the wind by wearing it despite the potential hazard created by tonight's triple threat of red wine, soup and a chocolate sponge dripping with butterscotch ice cream.

This weekend had been Ginger's idea. Her treat. Three nights in the St Kentigern Hotel, a five-star spa hotel in the centre of Glasgow. It was hugely indulgent given that I only lived fifteen minutes away and there is a perfectly good salon on the High Street that does a special on gel nails, eyebrow threads and a Brazilian for fifty quid, with a free paracetamol thrown in to numb the pain. However Ginger insisted that we merited a joint treat to celebrate our birthdays, all of them within a few weeks of each other. Given everything that had happened over the last few months, I'd thought about cancelling but I was glad now that I'd come.

I needed this. I needed a break from . . . Nope, I wasn't going to go there. I was just going to be thankful that I'd been here three hours and had so far managed not to give any thought to anything more important than the minibar. And of course . . .

'I hope Cassie has this. You know, friends like this, that she'll go through life with and share all the good stuff.'

Cassie. My daughter. A seven-year-old with a personality that was reminiscent of tropical weather – sunny, warm, adorable, good for the soul, but with occasional hurricanes and tornados which necessitated boarding up the windows and hiding under a bed until they passed.

Ginger was shaking her head so furiously that she didn't even notice that strands of her wild mane of red corkscrew curls had caught in her drink and were sprinkling Jack Daniel's back and forward across a Gucci top that had cost what I make in a month.

'No way. Friends, yes. Friends like us?'

'Speak for yourself, I'm a great friend.' Lizzy was speaking just a little louder than usual. I believe the official decibel rating was 'Four glasses of cava and a pre-dinner cosmo'.

'You are,' I agreed, speaking just a little quieter than normal in the hope that Lizzy would follow suit.

Ginger was busy looking suitably incredulous. 'I know, but come on – do you remember nothing? Do you seriously want Cassie to repeat history? We've been friends for how long?'

'Since we were eleven.'

'Eleven. That's . . .' Ginger put on her 'doing calculations' face, then switched straight to horror. 'Oh my God, that's almost thirty years. Thirty! I'm still telling people I'm only twenty-nine! I really need to start avoiding you two and get younger friends.'

'We can only hope,' I said to Lizzy, with a wink. She grinned, and for the first time I noticed the tiredness around her eyes. Not that anyone else would see it. Strangers would notice the stunning taupe satin strapless dress, the incredible figure and the poker-straight, Demi Moore black hair. They wouldn't see the slight shading under her eyes or the smile that stopped just short of full beam because she hadn't had a decent sleep in months.

'Thirty years,' Lizzy repeated. 'It's hard to believe that we've fitted it all in, yet it seems like only yesterday that we were getting ready in your bedroom on a Saturday night and getting up to absolutely no good.'

'That's my point,' Ginger said. 'We've had so much drama, so many disasters – do you want her to do all the things that we did? Make all the same mistakes?'

'Yes! I wouldn't change a single thing about anything we did.'

As soon as it was out I realised that wasn't true and so did the others.

'OK, apart from the obvious,' I conceded. 'But nothing else. Not the dramas, not the disasters, not the dodgy boyfriends . . .'

Lizzy collapsed into giggles and blurted, 'Gary Collins!'

The shrieks that followed almost derailed a waiter carrying a silver tray the size of a small island.

'You see – this is what I mean. We've shared everything and we've had some fantastic times. That's what I want for Cassie. I want her to know about all the stuff that happened to us, and then when she makes her own mistakes I want her to have great friends that will dig her out of every mess she gets into and she'll do the same for them.'

I surreptitiously opened the top button of my black crepe trousers. Chocolate cake remorse was alive and well at my side of the table.

'It might be time to start making some selective choices with her friends then.' There was a plopping noise as Ginger transferred the remaining ice lingering at the bottom of her otherwise empty glass into her next drink.

'Why?' I asked puzzled.

'Because it would really help if one of them was related to a good lawyer.'

'Because . . . ?' Lizzy asked.

Ginger was laughing hard now. 'Harry's Bar.'

'Oh my God, do you remember?' Lizzy's smile made it to full beam this time. 'One day we have to tell Cassie about that!'

'Definitely,' I agreed. 'But not until I've hired a legal team and put a padlock on the drinks cabinet.' A scene from the past flipped out of my memory and I could see it all like it was yesterday. 'That all started in my bedroom too. Lizzy, you were dancing to Wham! and, Ginger, you were . . .'

Two

Lou

1986 – Aged 16

'Turn it up, turn it up, I love this song!'

Lizzy jumped up onto the bed and started to dance around in only her pink polka-dot bra and knickers. If the old bloke across the street was looking through his telescope he'd have a stroke. Sure, he said it was for his astronomy but I was pretty sure he couldn't tell Jupiter from one of Saturn's rings.

The boys (and girls) from Wham! were belting out 'I'm Your Man' and Lizzy was shaking her hips into a near frenzy. 'God, I still can't believe they've split up. Apparently George Michael wanted to be taken more seriously as a song writer. Like "Wake Me Up Before You Go Go" wasn't a classic,' she gasped between shimmies. I made a mental note to remind her to take her asthma inhaler tonight.

Just in time, the DJ on Radio Clyde announced that he was taking the pace down and we all simultaneously groaned. We liked 'pace up'. Getting ready to go out on Saturday night had to be done to a throbbing beat with the one exception being,

'Aaaaaaaaaaaaaaahhhhh!'

Cue exception. 'Take My Breath Away' by Berlin. *Top Gun.* Goosebumps. Heart racing. And a deep certainty that I knew without any doubt the identity of my future husband. I flopped back on the pink candlewick and joined in, reminding everyone within earshot why I wasn't a member of Bananarama.

Just before the high bit that made me sound like I was having my fingers amputated without anaesthetic, I switched back to conversation. 'D'you think Tom will sing that to me when we're married?'

From her semi-concealed position of hanging out of the side window, smoking a ciggie, Ginger said, 'Yeah, right. Think again there, Loopy Lou, because Tom is mine. You can have that Iceman bloke. Or the one that copped it.' I would have argued, but I knew Ginger would probably win on account of her obvious anatomical advantages.

Me: short, 32B, a face that veered towards unremarkable and before the head stylist at my Saturday job in the hair-dressers came over all experimental-punk and ran amok with a blue semi-permanent colour, my crowning glory was a vibrant shade of mouse.

Ginger: 5 feet 8 inches, 34DD, athletically toned, with a mane of stunning red corkscrew curls that made her look like the West of Scotland version of Diana Ross.

On aesthetics, it was a clear victory for Motown.

'Anyway.' Ginger said it in two syllables, popping out a smoke ring in the middle. 'I'll be Tom's obvious choice because he'll be far more comfortable with someone who has the same level of fame.'

Lizzy and I howled with laughter. Despite having no discernible talent or marketable skill whatsoever, Ginger had been telling us that she was going to be famous since we were six. We reminded her often that there was only one success story from our town who had ever gone on to achieve a level of national fame and that was a horse born on McCormack's farm that won the Grand National. She was determined though. She was going to act. Or model. Or perform. Or marry Tom Cruise. What did it say about our lives that the last one seemed like the best idea of the bunch?

I turned my focus to things that were slightly closer to home than Tom's Beverly Hills mansion – my friend who was now pretending to waltz up the other side of my bed. 'Lizzy, will you stop dancing up there. Last time you did that I had to get a new mattress and my mother is still docking my wages two pounds a week,' I said.

'Where is your mum anyway? Thought she'd have been in doing fag patrol before now.'

I looked at my watch. 'I'm guessing, er . . .' Quick calculation. 'On the M74 somewhere around Lanark.'

'Why?'

'Because my dad fell asleep on the train on the way home from the football and missed his stop. Again. A train guard phoned from Waverley Station to say that they'd found him when the train reached the end of the line, but they're refusing to send him back the way because he's too pissed. Apparently they had to try twenty-six different telephone numbers because he's so incoherent they couldn't make out what he was saying. Do you think Tom Crui— I mean, *Val Kilmer* will end up a drunken arse and have me driving around the country looking for him every Saturday?'

'Definitely,' Ginger replied, stubbing her cigarette out on the windowsill and then flushing away the ash with a splash from her green plastic beaker of vodka and fresh orange. Some bright spark – I think it was Ginger's older brother, Red (his name was actually Ronald, but the follicular pre-disposition to ginger was a family trait) – had once told us always to drink vodka because it didn't leave a smell on your breath and therefore no one would know that you were drinking alcohol. It was a great theory even if it was cancelled out by the fact that the last time the very accident-prone Lizzy consumed one too many odourless vodkas, she attempted – in a drunken overestimation of her super-powers – to leap-frog a bollard, fell right over it and cracked her front two teeth. Thankfully her uncle is the local dentist so he sorted out the physical damage. The mental trauma of being grounded for three months, with daily rollickings from her mother, Saint Carla of the Holy Screech, may never heal. Nor will the indignity suffered when it became public knowledge five minutes after it happened. That's the thing about living in a small town. Weirbank may be less than twenty miles from the throbbing metropolis of Glasgow, but everyone knows everyone and even a minor humiliation is considered entertainment for the whole town.

'Take My Breath Away' ended and the cheesy DJ on Radio Clyde made an even cheesier link to 'Notorious'. I don't get the fuss over Simon Le Bon but I'd give my entire stock of Silk Cut Menthol, my Avon lipstick collection, all my mixed tapes and a kidney for a night with the guitarist John Taylor. I think it's the emaciated look and the way his fringe falls in his face. I could be good for that man. I could feed him my signature dish (there's nothing wrong with fish finger sandwiches), give him a good haircut and then snog him giddy. But only if Tom Cruise and Val Kilmer were unavailable.

I stood up and smoothed out the creases on my purple taffeta puffball skirt. It (and the matching boob tube and bolero) had taken two weeks' wages to buy but it was so worth it. Even Ginger was jealous and she'd made enough cash from her Saturday job in the fish shop to buy a new pair of green suede tukka boots, shocking-pink leg warmers and a white fake leather skirt that looked like a small pelmet for her nethers. If my Auntie Josie were here she'd be warning Ginger about life-threatening chills and losing her virginity just by bending over in male company.

My Aunt Josie is my dad's sister. Three years older than him, she is loud, opinionated and doesn't put up with any of his crap. He hates her almost as much as I love her. I can't tell you how many times I've wished there was a slight reshuffle in the gene pool when God was giving out offspring and I'd been given to Auntie Josie. Instead, Josie had my cousins Michael and Avril and I got Dave and Della Cairney – the poster couple for 'co-dependent relationships'. I heard that term on an old *Dallas* repeat. Mary Crosby used it some time before she lost the plot and shot JR. It fits my mum and dad perfectly. He's arrogant, egotistical and completely self-absorbed and demands to be the centre of her world at all times, and she adores him so much that she's happy to oblige.

'Bugger, these jeans must have shrunk in the bath.'

Ginger and I both just stared at Lizzy, neither of us quite prepared to ask the obvious question.

After a few moments she registered our confusion. 'That's how I got this design on them,' she explained, gesturing downwards to the random white blotches in the denim. 'You take normal jeans, twist them tightly, put them in the bath, pour bleach over them and leave them overnight. Next morning this is what you get. God, you two know nothing about fashion.'

'Yeah, but at least my legs don't look like they've got a fungal infection,' Ginger replied.

Lizzy ignored the dig. 'Look, can you just come and pull this up for me?' She was lying flat on her back on the floor now, with the hook of a coat hanger threaded through the little hole on the zipper of her apparently very-fashionable jeans. The exertion of trying to pull it up was turning her face pink and threatening to spoil the matt finish of her Revlon pressed powder foundation cover. Ginger and I took our positions – she fell to her knees and straddled Lizzy's hips, grabbed both sides of the open zipper and prepared to pull them together, while I clenched the hanger and adopted a 'tug of war' stance for maximum leverage. 'Pull!' Ginger shouted, as she squeezed the denim together, giving me a small moment of opportunity to yank on the coat hanger. Success! The zip went up first time with only a small hesitation halfway. The two of us then got into our next position, one on either side of the prone Lizzy, took an arm each, and pulled her up to a standing position without bending her body in any direction. 'A pound says that zip gives out before the end of the night,' Ginger said.

'Nope, I reckon it'll be the buttock seam again,' I replied. Lizzy groaned. Public humiliation number thirty-four of the year – shortly after the bollard situation and right before she set her hair on fire by forgetting to take a cigarette out of her mouth when she was spraying hairspray at the youth club disco – was when her new black cords split right up the back while she was dancing in her usual vigorous style to 'Suspicious Minds' by the Fine Young Cannibals. We called it the *Flashdance* incident.

I checked my watch. 'Right, let's get going – don't want to miss Harry's tea break.'

Harry was the owner of the local pub, called – in a moment of wild originality – Harry's Bar. It was our regular Saturday night hang-out despite the fact that we were almost two years too young to be there. However, licensing laws didn't take into account that when Harry took his 7 pm, 15-minute break from overseeing the door, we sprung into action. With the help of seven layers of Maybelline mascara (Lizzy), a cocky swagger (Ginger) and a padded bra (me), we could flirt our

11

way past the leery bouncer and keep a low profile in the furthest corner from Harry's eagle eye.

One enhanced bosom and serious flirt later, we made our way into the smoke-filled bar. It was heaving as always, but my boyfriend alert was on full beam and it only took me a few seconds to spot him. There he was, leaning against a pod in the far corner, bottle of Grolsch in front of him, with a Haircut 100 jumper and a hair flick that was so sharp we could use it to cut a hole in the windows if we found ourselves in an emergency exit situation.

That's my boyfriend. Mine. I still can't quite believe it. I'd have sworn he would have fancied Lizzy or Ginger, but no, he asked me out first. Actually, when I say 'out', what I really mean is that he once volunteered to walk me home and I ended up kissing the face off him in a bus stop even though it was so cold I lost the feeling in my feet. Ever since, I've been madly in love with him and always pack a spare pair of socks when we go out. He's the love of my life. Actually the third one, but number one doesn't count because I was twelve and number two doesn't count because he chucked me first. Therefore, for the sake of self-preservation, I've deleted them from my romantic history.

I did my very best strut over to the boyfriend and watched his face break into a grin when he saw me. 'Hey, babe,' he drawled, tossing his arm around my shoulder and stooping down to kiss me. I ignored the sound of Ginger pretending to retch behind me. She dislikes public displays of affection even more than she dislikes double trigonometry and *Hart To Hart*.

But back to the gorgeous bloke who was now slipping his hand up the back of my boob tube.

Gary Collins. Pros: He's nineteen, the best-looking guy in our whole town, he plays guitar, and he told me he loved me after our third date. Cons: Who cares? He's nineteen and the best-looking guy in our whole town.

OK, so putting the fact that I'm madly in love with him to one side for a moment, if I had to highlight one slight blemish on his personality profile, I'd have to admit that he is partial to the odd liberty with the truth. Already this week he's told me that he has an audition for a band, is getting his own car and is moving into a place of his own after Christmas. Firstly, there's no way he's auditioning for a band because he can only do four chords properly. I know he's failed his driving test three times (I found this out because my Aunt Josie heard that on his last test he met with disaster when the old crazy lady who lives at the end of Main Street let her Alsatian off the leash and it ran out in front of his car. The dog survived, but he took out a traffic island and the driving examiner hasn't been back in a car since). And he won't be getting his own place because a) he can't afford it and b) he knows he's got a good thing going living at home with a mum and three sisters looking after him.

Oh, and, incidentally, I know he only told me he loved me because he likes a bit of emotional drama and he's also – as Ginger kindly pointed out – desperate to get into my knickers. So far, the combination of my iron will and strong pants elastic have been an impenetrable force. It's not that I'm prudish, but . . . I don't know. It's kind of a big deal really, isn't it? Ginger lost her virginity to one of Red's mates six months ago and now he's joined the army so she'll probably never see him again. I'm not entirely sure whether having sex with Ginger had anything to do with him taking a job that involves leaving home and comes with the possibility of getting shot. But since I'd like Gary to stick around and avoid life-threatening situations for a while, I've decided it will take more than being able to sing 'Holding Back the Years' almost as good as Mick Hucknall to move from energetic groping to full-on penetration.

Unfortunately, Gary doesn't seem to appreciate my concern

regarding his mortality. Last week he asked me if we'll be dry humping until the end of time. Eurgh, even the thought of that makes my buttocks clench. I pointed out that there are other options (with my fingers crossed behind my back that he wouldn't take the bait). Option number one: cold baths. Option number two: that whole masturbation thing. Aren't teenage guys supposed to do that every ten minutes? Isn't that what posters of Samantha Fox are for? That girl is so stunning she is definitely going to end up married to some famous movie star. As long as it isn't my Tom. Although they would make a perfect couple. Anyway, back to option number three: Rosaline Harper. She has had sex with half of the boys in our year and the only reason she hasn't satisfied the other half is because she's been suspended for the last two months after she got caught giving Alfie McGuinness a blow job in the Home Economics store cupboard.

Anyway, what it comes down to is that I'm not having sex with Gary yet. And it's not just because my Auntie Josie thinks he's a tit. Speaking of which . . . that hand up the back of my boob tube is starting to cause a reaction in the nipple area.

'You look gorgeous,' he whispered. See what I mean about the lies? I'm not gorgeous. Maybe cute, possibly funny, but not gorgeous. I mean, come on – my hair is navy blue and styled like I'm the third member of the Thomson Twins. He, on the other hand, looks like a young Elvis – all black hair, chiselled cheekbones and piercing eyes. If you overlook the decidedly un-Elvis hair flick. I should really call him out on the bullshit but, hey, maybe love really is blind. Or at least capable of serious distortion.

'So . . . my mum and sisters are out tonight – you wanna come back to mine?'

I replied by kissing him again. Thank God Ginger had headed to the bar for drinks or she'd have taken me out with a flying beer mat for tonsil-wrestling in public. I was buying time while I weighed up my answer. I didn't want to go home. Guaranteed, my mum would appear back from Edinburgh with the wandering arse, and at some point he'd sober up long enough to blame her for everything and she'd end up in floods of tears. Or else he'd fall asleep and snore so loudly that Mrs Smith next door will batter on the wall with her Zimmer and threaten to report him to the council. Just another normal Saturday night. The thought made me shudder and suddenly a night at Gary's had distinct appeal. I could just phone Mum and tell her that I'm staying the night at Lizzy's – although I'd have to go outside to find a payphone because she thinks I'm at the chapel youth club and this pub does not sound like a meeting place for teenagers run by a group of guitar-playing nuns. On the other hand, did I really want yet another night of simulated sex on his single bed with 'Fa-a-ntastic Day' blaring in the background? I was wearing my new puffball, for God's sake. Although . . . oh, he is so cool. And nineteen. And the best-looking guy in the town. And I love him. I might have mentioned these things before. Maybe I'd just go. Maybe I'd spend the night there. Hell, maybe the boob tube would come off and I'd let him graduate to dry humping with perks. It wasn't like Tom Cruise/Val Kilmer was going to come and sweep me off to a life of glitz and glamour any time soon.

'French Kissin' in the USA' came on and, at the sound of Debbie Harry's voice, Lizzy jumped up and started dancing on the table. Great way to keep a low profile. Could she never just dance on the floor like normal people?

'You didn't answer me – are you coming home with me?' He was nibbling my ear now, the sensation of his hot breath on my neck kicking the nipple-tingling up to pelvic-stirring lust. I'm sure I read that terminology in a magazine in the doctor's surgery waiting room.

'Urgh, if you lick her ear one more time I'm going to vomit,'

Ginger promised as she returned clutching three drinks, all heavily adorned with paper umbrellas and swizzle sticks. The guy behind the bar thought she was nineteen and he'd been trying to get off with her for months. Nothing says 'I fancy you' more than a selection of paper and plastic cocktail tat.

I leaned in close to his ear and whispered, 'Sure.' The hand that was up the back of my boob tube gave me a squeeze. To hell with it, why not? But if he crushed, mangled or pulled a thread in my puffball I might have to go into mourning.

Despite the daggers, boring into the back of my head from the ginger direction, we slipped into a long, slow kiss that had that lust ramping up with every passing second. Behind me, I was vaguely aware of an increase in the noise level. Then a few shouts and hollers. Nothing new there. It wasn't a Saturday night in Harry's Bar without a fight or six. Oooh, this was nice. Really nice. Perhaps . . . perhaps it was time for me to start overlooking the fact that he was a compulsive exaggerator and my aunt thought he was a tit. Oooh, I could hear 'Holding Back the Years' . . . Get ye behind me, Mick Hucknall. I'm sixteen. It's legal. And surely if you're going to lose it to anyone then it should definitely be someone who looks like Gary and who is not – as far as I'm aware – planning to choose a career involving military weapons.

'Excuse me!' Another vague sound in the background, but I was too busy being surgically attached to my boyfriend's lips to pay attention. Only when the music stopped, the lights came on and the sound level suddenly plunged, did I break off and pay any attention. The first thing I saw was a black shiny jacket with silver studs. Unfortunately, it wasn't an Adam and the Ants tribute act.

'Miss, would you mind lining up against that wall.' Despite the phrasing, it wasn't a request.

I unpuckered and did what he said, my heart beginning

to thud in a way that not even kissing the best-looking man in the town could achieve.

Ginger and Lizzy were already there, Lizzy looking like she was about to cry, Ginger looking like she was about to punch someone. Hopefully not Shiny Buttons.

'Right!' another officer of the law bellowed. 'In case you haven't caught on yet, this is a police raid. We have reason to believe that underage drinking is occurring on these premises. Therefore we would like to see full identification from each of you, and anyone who doesn't have ID with them will be getting a nice little ride in one of those white cars with the blue flashing lights down to the station.'

Bloody hell, a comedian. We were being apprehended by a really bad Billy Connolly impersonator with a smug grin and a truncheon.

In the next two hours, during our involuntary trip to our local police station, Ginger, Lizzy and I tried every excuse and tactic bar claiming we were undercover members of the A-Team. Actually we might have tried that too. In the end, they formally arrested us, then relented and let us off with a caution. The good news was that we wouldn't be left with a criminal record. The bad news was that they phoned our parents to come collect us. The next morning my dad had the hypocrisy to go mental and accuse me of blackening the family name. This from the man who'd been drunk and disorderly while travelling through almost every city and town in Scotland – albeit without knowing where he was on at least ninety per cent of occasions.

Arrested. In trouble. Lost out on a night at Gary's house. Probably dumped in favour of Rosaline Harper. Fed up. Humiliated.

And my parents are threatening to disown me.

Well, every cloud . . .

Three

'Hey! It's our very own answer to the Kray twins,' came the greeting from my Aunt Josie. 'I've spent the last week practising baking a Victoria sponge with a nail-file filling for next time you get banged up.'

I rolled my eyes and tossed my denim jacket over one of her kitchen chairs. Auntie Josie's house is only a few streets away from ours, but they are a million miles apart in every other way. In our new cul-de-sac semi, everything is perfectly in place. The floors are spotless, there isn't so much as a crumb on the kitchen worktop and the toilets look like they've never been used. Even the cushions on the couch have to be kept at a particular angle, in case of such monumental occurrence like a visit from the local MP or Armageddon. Can't have those Russians pressing that big red button and us being blown to smithereens with haphazard soft furnishings. Auntie Josie's house, on the other hand, is an exercise in chaos. Every room is a mishmash of furniture. Nothing matches, everything is well used, and she has ducks on the wall of her kitchen. Ducks. In a diagonal row. As if nature intended them to be made in a Taiwanese factory, then nailed to a partition wall before soaring towards the sun. She says they match the ceramic hen she keeps her eggs in and the red china cock that sits on the windowsill. It's a whole big nature-fest. But it's also the most welcoming house you could ever encounter. It's got that lived-in look that makes you want to kick off your shoes, curl up on a chair and dip digestives in your tea – which is why it's the human equivalent of an animal rescue centre. Whenever anyone is in-between houses, has been thrown out by their partner, disowned by their parents, has burst pipes, is having their front room decorated or for some other miscellaneous reason has found themselves homeless, Auntie Josie takes them in. Currently, two of Michael's friends have spent the last week on her brown Dralon couches and she has an Indian gentleman in the spare room who has come here with the intention of teaching yoga. Yeah, like all that bendy, chanting stuff will ever catch on. On top of that, whenever anyone within a two-mile radius has a problem, a dilemma or some gossip, this becomes the nerve centre of the situation, providing a shoulder to cry on, beverages and sustenance. Auntie Josie has three jobs and I'm fairly sure one of them is just to pay for her massive weekly bill for tea bags and biscuits.

The real reason so many people come here though is that Auntie Josie has a heart of gold, she's funny and she's always, always honest – even when the truth hurts . . . like right around now.

'What the hell were you thinking? That was the most stupid thing to do!'

However, her honesty invariably came with a slightly skewed perspective.

'I can't believe you would go into that pub without some decent fake ID.'

And that, in a nutshell, is why I love Josie. She is all about enjoying life and getting away with it.

'Right here's the kit and the kettle's on. There are caramel wafers in the cupboard.' Caramel wafers. The Scottish working-class antidepressant.

I picked up the box containing the home perming kit and pulled out the contents. All through my childhood I'd watched Josie and her friends perming each other's hair into tiny tight curls. The day she finally announced that my Saturday job in the hairdresser's qualified me to take over the role felt like a rite of passage. Yes, that day I became a woman. One that smelled of really, really strong ammonia.

I picked up a comb, laid out the tiny rollers and passed Josie the little pad of tissue papers, to be handed to me one at a time as I wound every individual curl. I had the whole process down pat now. Take small section of hair. Saturate with lotion. Wrap in tissue. Wind onto roller. Secure with band. Try to finish whole head before the fumes cause permanent damage to my lungs. Depending on luck, the result varied somewhere between Shirley Bassey (the intended outcome) and the weird science guy out of *Back to the Future* (a look we tried to avoid).

'So what's with the slumped shoulders? Oh dear God no. You've slept with him, haven't you? You have. And now he's done a runner. And you're pregnant. I'll kill that little fecker. Just wait till . . .'

All that before I'd even wound the first curl. If I didn't stop her she'd have continued to escalate the story until Gary had an amputated penis and she was doing time for grievous bodily harm.

'I didn't sleep with him.'

'Oh. Do you want a caramel wafer?'

'No, I'm fine, thanks.'

I managed to get a few rollers in on the crown of her head before she regrouped.

'So what's with the slouched shoulders then? Look, don't

worry about the police thing. We've all done it. And I won't tell you what I had to do to get off with it back in my day.'

I decided not to ask and focus instead on the general situation. 'It's not that,' I said, with a shrug of the slouched shoulders. 'It's just that . . . I've been offered full time at the salon.'

'And are you going to take it?' she asked. I could detect an edge of wariness in her voice. Josie always hesitated like that – it gave me time to consider the options, think things through, come to a considered opinion, make my own mind up . . . then she'd storm in like some SWAT team guidance counsellor and tell me exactly what she thought I should do.

I'd been working at the salon on Saturdays and after school since the day of my fourteenth birthday. Even though I was the youngest, the rest of the girls who worked there treated me like I was just like them. I loved it. I loved the gossip, I loved that there was never a dull moment and I loved that we played loud music except when old Mrs Welsh was in because the vibrations set off her seizures.

For a while I thought about other jobs. Perhaps a translator (overlooking the fact that I barely scraped through O level French). Or a nurse (overlooking the fact that anything remotely gory made me faint). Or a journalist. Although, I didn't think I'd be able to bang on people's doors after they'd lost their whole family in a six-car pile-up and beg for an interview. And anyway, that would mean going to college for four years, where I'd have to drink cider and wear black eyeliner out to my ears and that's a look I could never carry off. Besides, the reality was that university and college were definitely out because my parents had made it quite clear that they wouldn't be supporting any of that further education stuff and to be honest, the sooner I got a job, the sooner I could get out of that house and get on with living my life.

But then, earning £35 a week for standing all day, every day, for the duration of the mandatory three-year apprenticeship, inhaling the giddy scent of perming lotion probably had its drawbacks too. The hours were long. The pay, let's face it, was rubbish.

'And on those wages I won't be able to afford to leave the house for years.' It was a few seconds before I realised that I'd said that part out loud.

That was the crux of it. For years all I'd looked forward to was the day that I could move out and if I took this job with such paltry wages then there was a chance that day would be a long, long way off.

'You know that you can always come and live here, love. Of course, you might have to share with Mr Patel in the spare room but I'm sure he wouldn't mind. He's always chanting with his eyes shut so he probably wouldn't notice. He says he's got super-human flexibility. There are worse things in a room-mate.' Her laughter was cut short when she popped a Benson & Hedges in her mouth and lit up. Great. Between the nicotine and the perm lotion chemicals, I'd be lucky if I made it out before my cardiovascular system collapsed.

Josie had been offering to put me up for years but I loved her too much to be such an imposition. She already had her hands full and the last thing she needed was yet another person to look after.

So back to my options. The way I saw it I could take the apprenticeship in the salon, earn £35 per week plus tips for three years until I made it to junior stylist and the rewards grew.

Or I could stay on at school for another year, get some highers and hope that would lead to a better paid job – maybe in an office or something – that would get me out of Dodge sooner and give me an outside chance of getting a head start on a really good career.

Or . . . 'You could go on the game.'

That was Josie's contribution. I hoped she was joking. I was on to the second half of her head now and she was looking vaguely like something Doctor Who would fight to the death for attacking the tardis.

'Or I could go on the game,' I repeated with a rueful grin. 'Yes, I want to be a high-class hooker when I grow up.'

Auntie Josie clutched her heart dramatically and adopted the disposition of an overemotional Oscar winner.

'My darling, you make me so proud!' she solemnly declared, before her trademark laughter snapped her back to normal and she yelled, 'Mr Patel, there's a cup of tea on the side here for you.'

I've no idea where he came from but he immediately appeared in the doorway and thanked Josie before disappearing again.

'He doesn't look very bendy,' I couldn't help commenting as he shuffled off.

'Oh he is. Last night he took a banana out of his mouth with his toes.' My raised eyebrow provoked an indignant response. 'What? Look, telly was rubbish, we were just passing the time.'

Again, some things were just better left un-probed. I rolled in the last perming rod, squirted what was left of the lotion over Josie's head, and put the cellophane cover over the entire operation, tying it in a knot at the base of her neck. Naturally, she complemented this avant-garde look by lighting up another ciggy, flicking the kettle on and launching into an account of neighbourhood gossip so outlandish and scandalous that it was like listening to an audio version of the *News of the World*.

'Look, love, I'm not going to preach to you, but money isn't the most important thing in life. What do you really want to do?'

This I knew. I'd spent hours daydreaming about what I wanted out of life. Hours. I'd contemplated my hopes, my dreams, my desires and the attainable goals. Then I discarded the 'attainable' bit.

'Travel. See the world. Go surfing in Hawaii. Live in a penthouse in New York. Have an international, phenomenally successful career. Get in to size ten jeans. Join Bananarama. Marry Tom Cruise. Then when I'm old, like thirty, I want to have a great career, a gorgeous international superstar husband that adores me, four kids and a car like the one out of *Starsky and Hutch*. I want to have it all.'

It was the truth. In an ideal world, if I was, say, junior royalty or a character from a Jackie Collins novel or drunk on Malibu and optimism, then that's what I'd want. Unfortunately, the only thing I was drunk on was perming fluids and reality.

Josie mentally absorbed my revelation, took it all on board and processed it in a meaningful and profound way then reached the obvious conclusion. 'So you're going to end up working in hairdresser's for the rest of your life then?'

'Pretty much,' I confirmed. Yep, 'attainable' was back. 'But look on the bright side, Aunt Josie – if I take the full time job at the salon, you'll get your hair done there for free.'

She ignored my attempt at highlighting the silver lining.

'Just promise me you won't have unprotected sex with that twat you're seeing, then get knocked up and marry him. I honestly don't think I could spend a lifetime of Christmases listening to how he was going to join the next Duran Duran just as soon as he gets the hang of a few more chords on the guitar.'

'I promise.'

'Do you mean that?'

'Almost completely.'

And as I contemplated her warning while unravelling sixty-eight perm rods, I realised that sometimes you just have to go with the flow. Roll with the punches.

24

Like Mr Patel's party trick with the banana, sometimes life just requires a little bit of flexibility.

When I got home Della and Dave were lying intertwined on the couch, a Rod Stewart album playing on the stereo, with one of the corner lamps providing the only illumination on their romantic evening. They both looked less than impressed when I spoiled the moment by arriving home. I was used to it.

You would think having two parents that were totally loved up was a good thing. A couple of the girls at school had parents who were divorcing and they hated every minute of it so I suppose I was lucky – there were no fights, no arguments, no sulks or threats. There was no need for any of those things in a relationship that was built on adoration and obedience.

'I've been thinking about what I should do. You know, about school and work and stuff.'

Awkward. Why did I always feel like I was five and in the way when I was speaking to them? Neither of them spoke, so I just carried on.

'I thought I'd stay on at school for one more year and just keep working in the salon at nights and weekends.' I was starting to squirm now. 'Thought it would be smarter to get some more qualifications and then decide after that what I want to do.'

My mother immediately looked at my dad for his reaction. It was the law in her world – find out what he thought and then agree.

'What's the point of that?' he asked.

'Because . . . because . . . if I go full time in the salon just now then that'll be it and I don't know if that's what I want to do yet. I was thinking I could wait a year, get some more qualifications, see how it goes.'

'Really?' Oh, crap he was annoyed and my mother was

beginning to get that slightly panicked look around the eyes. 'What do you think this is – a hotel? You think you can just stay here and have everything laid on a plate for you and act like Lady Muck until you get around to deciding what you want to do? Nope, doesn't work that way. We're not just here, working our arses off to finance you, while you float around doing sod all.'

Here we go. I could point out that I hadn't had a penny off them since I was fourteen and started working Saturdays. I bought my own clothes, my own make-up, my own books. I could mention that most parents would be delighted that their kid wanted to focus on education, get a better job, do something that would deliver a good long-term career. I could say that a few of my teachers thought I had a pretty good chance of getting good results.

But . . .

'Lou, this isn't a free ride. You should be bloody thrilled that you got offered a job and I'm disappointed that you're even thinking about refusing it. You're sixteen – time you started acting like it.'

'I don't know if it's what I want to do though and . . .'

'Lou, discussion over. You want to live here, you'll pay fifteen quid rent a week from now on. I'm not here to support you and your delusions of grandeur, lady.'

'Mum . . . ?'

'Your dad's right, Lou.'

Of course he was. Of course. Wasn't he always? Wasn't he almost fucking papal when it came to infallibility? Nope, scratch that – he was a god. A god who decreed on high to his congregation of one – Della Cairney, chief apostle and worshipper.

So that was that then. Decision made. I was leaving school, going to work in the salon whether I liked it or not. God said so and the only option was obedience.

'No.'

It took me a moment to realise that it was me who'd said it. It took me another moment to realise that my dad was looking at me with a mixture of disbelief and mounting rage.

Shite. This wasn't going to go anywhere good.

'Actually, forget that.' I shrugged. 'You know what, I'll take the job. But my rent money? I think I'll spend that elsewhere.'

With that I turned and stormed out, attempting to add drama with a door slam but the draught excluder got in the way and instead I tripped, lunged forwards and my forehead met with the banister in the hall.

'What happened to your head?' were Josie's first words when she answered the door.

'Had a fight with the banister,' I replied. 'Aunt Josie, I need a favour.'

'Anything, my ladyship,' she replied with a jokey bow.

I took one step to the side to reveal a black bin bag containing all my worldly goods. 'Any chance you can ask Mr Patel to budge up and make room for me?'

Four

'You smell kinda strange.' Gary did his best not to sneer when he said it. He learned that lesson a few months ago when I declared my boobs a no-go area after he commented on a previous pungent aroma. How was I to know that the combination of Tic-Tacs and Eau De Charlie would fail to trump that other heady combination of Silk Cut Menthols and a tuna and onion baked potato?

'Perming lotion. I did Josie's hair today.' I flicked my navy-blue asymmetric fringe out of my face.

'You're really good at stuff like that,' he said casually.

'She looks like the weird science guy out of *Back to the Future*.'

'Right.' The resulting silence was broken by the drumming of his hand on the steering wheel of the car. Yes, in a resounding kick in the balls to my powers of judgement, he'd actually gone and passed his driving test.

So now he was the best-looking man in our town with a car.

He was officially the Weirbank equivalent of a Sex God. One that should clearly be with the Weirbank equivalent of a Sex Goddess, not the Weirbank equivalent of the lead singer of Siouxsie and the Banshees.

Actually, now I thought about it . . . What was going on? He was usually all over me by now, desperate to get from the statutory kissing stage, to the groping, to the optimistic probing in the nether area. This was invariably followed by my apologetic rejection and then he'd pretend not to mind before rushing me home in case my parents discovered I was gone and phoned the police. Maybe he was even more anxious than usual now that I 'had form'. Ooh, yes, after that bust for underage drinking I was practically a seasoned hood.

'So you passed your test then?' Lou Cairney, winning the Olympic gold in the category of 'stating the obvious'.

'Yeah.' He shrugged, oozing nonchalance. 'What do you think of the car?'

'It's, er . . . green. And really cool.' I hadn't gone out with him this long without learning a thing or two about exaggeration. In truth, it was a bit of a battered old banger in a screaming shade of Kermit, but at least it worked most of the time (he'd already sussed that parking it on a downward slope made jump-starting it easier).

I flicked on the radio to break the unusual subdued mood that had descended and got on with the business of feeling entirely awkward. Gary was definitely acting strange. Maybe now that he had a car he was going to chuck me for someone more flash. Maybe he'd finally hooked up with Rosaline Harper. Maybe he . . . aaah, stomach churning, mouth now drier than the ancient pine tree air freshener that was dangling from the rear-view mirror. God, I was hopeless in situations like this. I was hesitant to speak because I knew that I was guaranteed to come out with something highly stupid/ridiculous/inappropriate/inane. I would then delete as applicable. Nervous situations had that effect on me. I couldn't even pretend to be rapt with the view around us because the sleeting rain drumming off the windows reduced the vision to zero. That wasn't necessarily a bad thing. We were sitting in the Car Park in the Sky, a local snogging spot on the outskirts of the nearby town of Paisley. The area we were parked in had been given its name because it was halfway up a ruddy great hill and it allowed a stunning view over the whole of the town. It was especially beautiful at night when it really did feel like you were floating in the sky surrounded by stars . . . until inevitably an overenthusiastic coupling in the next car caused a violent rocking commotion that detracted from the beauty of it all. Despite the scenic vista, I was quite glad the windows were so steamed up we were now in a zero-visibility situation because a) the car next to ours looked scarily like the one owned by my biology teacher Mrs Tucker and b) there was less chance of anyone spotting me and – given my criminal status – reporting me to Interpol.

So . . . No view, weird atmosphere, risk of stupid/ridiculous/inappropriate/inane outburst. There was only one thing to do: I stared at Gary instead. He was looking particularly cute tonight. The black leather trousers were almost identical to the ones that John Taylor wore – it didn't even matter that Gary's were PVC and the heat rash would last way into next week. On the top he was wearing a string vest, with a white shirt over it, the buttons undone down to the waist. And his jet-black hair had been cut over his ears, was spiky at the top and then fell down really long at the back. Deadly. Totally hubba hubba. Me, on the other hand? Pink pyjamas. I hadn't wanted to risk Josie hearing the midnight rustle of my black bin bag, so I'd just thrown on a long petrol-blue jumper and a pair of legwarmers over my fleecy pink night-time fashion statement and pulled on my purple suede tukka boots. I could have cried when I misjudged the drop from the box-room window and my right foot scraped all the way down the pebble dash. I was going to have to come up with a really good explanation as to why one of the boots was now missing a toe. But I'd worry about that later. Right here, right now, I was sitting with my gorgeous, beautiful, sexy boyfriend, and even his weird mood couldn't spoil it. In fact, there was nothing on earth that could detract from how lovely this was. Nothing. Noth— Aaaaargh! The bars of a familiar song started on the radio and I immediately snapped it off before it made my skin itch and my teeth hurt. If only that female who met Chris de Burgh had dressed in bloody purple then we might all have been spared the agony.

Where was I? Oh yep, even his weird mood wasn't going to spoil this. In fact, he'd actually climbed up the scale of my estimation given that he'd defied my Auntie Josie's predictions (OK, I'd thought it too) about his driving capabilities. I could now strike his boast that he was buying a car off the 'exaggeration/big fat porkie' list. The fact that it still technically belonged to his Uncle Cyril and he was paying it up at £10 a week didn't matter. What a breakthrough. I didn't care that he'd never get his own place or sing in a real band – I loved him. We were simply meant to be. Destined.

'Lou, I've been thinking . . .'

I recognised that tone. It was the one that they used in the *Godfather* movies right before someone got whacked. Oh no, that wasn't going to happen here. There could *not* be a bullet here with my name on it.

'I've been thinking that . . .' he continued.

Instinct kicked in. This wasn't a time for fear or hesitation. Gary Collins was not going to tell me anything I didn't want to hear. I had to fight this because a) he was nineteen b) he was the best-looking guy in the town (yes, I know I'm repeating myself again) and c) I realised that maybe, just maybe, he wasn't lying about how he felt about me. Maybe he did love me. Maybe this was it. The One. And if I let him go now over some stupid doubts and the instincts of a woman with questionable hair, I would never forgive myself. Noooo, I'd already had a bad day: I'd had a career choice foisted on me, I'd left home and I was living in a room so small that it necessitated sleeping in the foetal position. This guy was one of the few good things in my life and I damn well wasn't going to let him go.

This called for tact, assertive action using the first weapons that came to hand.

And that is how, on a rainy night in Paisley, Gary Collins finally got to see my nipples.

As I prepared to say goodbye to my virginity in a bright green Mini Metro I realised that when something feels right then it usually is . . .

. . . except when it's not.

Five

Lou

The St Kentigern Hotel, Glasgow. Friday night, 9 pm

'Is my face burning? Is it? Oh my God, I'd forgotten about the car. For years after that I'd get a nervous twitch every time I saw a green Metro.'

If we weren't in the middle of a very classy restaurant I'd have put my head on the table for a minute to recover. 'I'm locking Cassie up until she's eighteen. And banning her from speaking to any boy with access to a car. Why didn't you stop me? Why?'

'I was too busy trying to work out how to get behind enemy lines to give Jason Walsh a piece of my mind for running out on me,' Ginger said. 'Did I ever tell you that I bumped into him at a concert a few years ago? Fat. Bald. Total cliché. Said he was on his third divorce and he should have stuck with me all along. I told him I was glad he hadn't – that I'd gone on to bigger things. Emphasis on the "bigger".'

An older couple a few tables away eyed us with blatant disapproval as our cackles interrupted their romantic ambiance.

I gave what I hoped was an apologetic smile and was rewarded with a furious glare from the woman.

'Girls, I think we'd better keep it down. That lady is looking mighty displeased and she has a steak knife in her hand. Shall we move through to the bar?'

We asked for the bill to be charged to our room, left a tip and moved through into the very glamorous bar. Four young, very stylish guys in shiny, skinny-legged suits vacated a table at the window just as we arrived so we slid in and took their places.

'Oh no,' Lizzy groaned as she plopped herself down. 'Do I just look like a floating head?'

We immediately grasped her point. Her gorgeous, chiffon tunic dress was exactly the same shade of soft purple as the high-backed chairs.

I thought again how glad I was that I'd come. If I was at home I'd just be thinking about it all. Wondering. Regretting. This was filling all that headspace with laughter and warmth.

The problems were still there and we all knew that but for now it was enough to cover them up with a shiny layer of nostalgia. Ginger and Lizzy had been around for every single important thing that had ever happened to me, from losing my virginity to leaving home . . . to . . .

'Oh. My. God. Those girls are the same shade as my garden fence,' the floating head whispered, her gaze resting somewhere behind me. 'Don't turn around,' she hissed. 'Do not turn around – they're looking!'

So of course I turned around.

Three girls, must have been eighteen or nineteen, all of them in unfeasibly high heels, outrageously short skirts and fake-tanned complexions which sat somewhere between mahogany and dark oak on the woodstain chart. One of them caught my eye and glared, before her gaze went to Ginger and her expression completely changed. That always happened. There were consequences of being friends with someone as notorious as my large-haired friend.

'Who do those three remind you of?'

An answer wasn't required. The tans, the dresses, the shoes, the aura of being absolutely indestructibly young and fearless . . .

'So which one is which then?' the floating head asked, amused at the theory.

'It'll be easy to spot which one is a younger version of Lou,' replied Ginger, a distinct note of teasing in her voice. 'That'll be whichever one buggers off first to meet her boyfriend.'

Six

Lou

1988 – Aged 18

'Miss Cairney, if you'd like to follow me.'

Just by looking at the guy in front of me I could tell several things:

He was married (ring on finger).

His wife probably hadn't spoken to him since the seventies (dated clothes, scary demeanour, cruel face and he hadn't even looked at me or smiled).

He was evil. Pure evil. The kind of man who enjoyed inflicting pain on others (just a hunch).

This was about to be one of the most tortuous episodes of my life.

I did as he said, despite the fact that every single synapse in my brain (thank you, Mrs Tucker – those anatomy modules did leave some residual information) was screaming at me to run. Run like the wind. But I was wearing my favourite white high heels and I knew I'd never make it to the end of the street without a free pass to several weeks in traction.

I was trapped. Cornered. And I couldn't do anything other than give in to his demands and hope I survived. He stopped suddenly, opened the door of a black car and stood there, waiting for me to climb in. I searched around frantically looking for an escape, heart beating out of my chest. I tried to calm myself down by picturing my favourite place of safety, an image I conjured up whenever I was feeling upset, or down, or scared. Nope, it wouldn't come. I wasn't sitting in the corner of that American dance hall and Patrick Swayze wasn't just about to come rescue me and make me do thrusting pelvic dance moves all the way up the centre aisle, culminating in a high jump into mid-air from which he would catch me.

Nobody was going to rescue Lou from this corner.

I climbed into the seat and, hands shaking, resigned myself to my fate. As he climbed in next to me I could smell the evil coming from his breath. Or it might have been tuna.

'So, Miss Cairney, shall we begin?'

'Oh, my God! Oh my God! I cannot believe it!' Lizzy screamed. 'Here! Drink this then tell me exactly what happened.'

She handed me a Malibu and pineapple and grabbed a bottle of Grolsch for herself. It was more of a fashion choice than a particular liking for the beverage. As soon as she popped the top off the bottle, she bent over and threaded it through the top of her Reebok trainers. Matt and Luke Goss had started the trend and, as the head of the Scottish chapter of the Bros devotees club, Lizzy slavishly followed – despite the fact that one had come loose the week before when she was taking her shoe off, she'd then stood on it, punctured the sole of her foot and had to go to A&E for a tetanus injection.

'Every detail!' she demanded, her screech level ramping up by the minute. She'd inherited more than her mother's jet-black

37

hair and DD bosoms. I was just about to open my mouth when the door slammed and Ginger stormed in, gob blazing.

'I swear if I ever see another set of old lady feet again it'll be too soon. Corns. Bunions. When I get to sixty, just shoot me. I swear I mean it. Just. Fucking. Shoot me. Because if the rest of the body is anything like the feet, then life will not be worth living.'

Neither Lizzy nor I chose to point out that since she was doing a Youth Training Scheme in a chiropodist's practice, the chances of her encountering future foot deformities were – like her hair – exceptionally high.

'On a scale of one to ten, how happy are you?' Lizzy asked her.

Ginger regarded her with open hostility. I had a feeling PMT was in play here, taking her general agitated demeanour up a notch to downright irritation.

'Lizzy,' she sighed, 'it's Friday night. I want to be doing something glamorous, something that would top off a week of excitement and thrills, possibly spent in the company of a rock star. Instead, I'm knackered and contemplating going to bed early after a week working with old lady feet. I'm a one, Lizzy – the only thing that'll push me up to a two is if you magic up a vodka and pineapple from somewhere.'

There was a pause as she slumped down on the one free chair in the room. Actually it was the only chair in the room. Lizzy and I were both on bean bags. When Ginger realised we were still sitting there with huge grins despite her rant, the perception skills of Cagney and Lacey kicked in and she eventually clocked that something was afoot. Pardon the pun.

'What? What's going on?'

'Tell her!' Lizzy prompted. 'Tell her!'

'Well, I . . .'

'Sod it, I'll tell her.' Her impatience cut me dead. 'Lou passed her driving test! Can you believe it?'

Ginger didn't reply for a moment.

'Did you hear me?' Lizzy wailed.

I thought it best not to tell her that the passengers on overhead jets en route to nearby Glasgow airport could hear her. Ginger's gorgeous face suddenly broke into a grin and she gestured in my direction. 'Did you go dressed like that?'

Instinctively, I quickly glanced downwards. White spandex dress, highly clingy to my size 12/14 body, due to having been purchased for Ginger's size 10 body. The below-the-knee hemline would have brought a bit of modesty to the ensemble if it wasn't for the fact that my boobs were spilling out of the top. Three sunbeds that week had left my legs a deep shade of mahogany and the white stilettos completed the look.

I nodded.

'Then I believe it,' she said, her words topped with a resounding edge of pride. 'Did he by any chance notice that you can't actually drive?'

I screwed up my nose as I shook my head. 'Not so much.'

Three identical hairstyles rocked backwards and forwards as we dissolved into laughter. The coiffures were my handiwork. After two years of training, with one afternoon a week at the local college, I'd finally been allowed near a pair of scissors. So far, I was concentrating on getting really good at the most popular hairstyle around: cut over the ears at the side, the top feathered backwards with a little quiff pulled down at the front, the back cut in long layers and sprayed so that every strand was almost horizontal. Between the hair and the shoulder pads that we'd inserted in every jacket we owned (my favourite blazer now gave me a silhouette that was the approximate width of a sunlounger), getting in and out of confined spaces was a squeeze. Every week I was allowed to take one model into training night, so slowly but surely everyone I knew was being inflicted with the same haircut.

It looked fab on Lizzy, Ginger, her brother Red and Josie, but Mr Patel was getting strange looks at his yoga classes down at the community centre.

'The driving instructor looked like a serial killer but he didn't take his eyes off my boobs the whole time. Not even when I mounted the pavement outside the fruit and veg shop in the High Street. The rest of it was perfect though. Except for the parking bit at the end, but I got it on the third try.'

'Oh my God. Oh my God. This is so fantastic.' Lizzy frequently repeated herself in times of excitement. 'We have a flat, we have a car—'

'Hold on!' Ginger interrupted. 'You passed your test this morning and already you have a car?'

I nodded, trying really, *really* hard not to seem too pleased with myself. 'When I lived with Josie she insisted that I give her an extra five pounds every week to save for me. She said it was in case I ever needed a good lawyer. Anyway, when I told her I passed my test she gave it back to me so I bought Red's car off him for two hundred and ninety pounds.'

'That car is a wreck!' Ginger was clearly unhappy with this development and, to be honest, I was a little put out that she was adding any kind of downer into the situation, especially since it involved her own brother. But I didn't let her reaction bother me. I already loved my new Ford Cortina. Even if it was ancient, there was a hole in the passenger side floor, a strange smell coming from the boot and, if you pulled back the upholstery on the inside of the door, there was an Irn Bru bottle wedged inside to hold the window up.

'I know. But those brand-new Jaguars are slightly out of my price range, so unless they'll give me one for say, flashing my arse at the showroom, then I'll have to make do with what I can afford. And besides, the Cortina has just passed its MOT and Red says it's completely road worthy, so it'll be fine.'

Lizzy butted in, completely disregarding the bickering, always eager to diffuse any confrontation. 'So, as I was saying, we have a house, a car and it's payday! Where are we going tonight, girls? I'm not working until ten o'clock so we've got hours yet.' Lizzy was funding her way through college by working in a nightclub called Tijuana Junction in Glasgow. There was nothing Mexican about it. Nothing. If they wanted to call it something that truly evoked the atmosphere and qualities of the place, they'd have named it Dodgy Plumbing and Feet Stuck to the Carpet. But it was cheap to get in and always mobbed, thanks to the bouncers' policy of admitting all female clients as long as they wore short skirts or revealed at least three inches of cleavage. We'd realised very early on in our socialising careers that this was a common theme with the door staff of licensed premises.

'Come on, let's go for it,' Lizzy exclaimed in her usual state of overexcitement, suddenly reminding me that one of the customers in the salon had told me that coffee could make a person hyperactive. That couldn't be right, could it? Otherwise, why would it be called Mellow Birds? But Lizzy did drink at least ten cups a day and had more nervous energy than anyone I'd ever met so maybe there was something to it.

I could see that Lizzy's idea appealed to Ginger. She and I made eye contact and she got that look – the one that usually ended with us in trouble, lost or naked in public. OK, that was just the once and, to be fair, she didn't know those French exchange students would nick our clothes while we were swimming naked in Loch Lomond.

'I say we head up to Glasgow, go to a couple of bars. I've got twenty quid – that'll get us a few cocktails in the West End,' she said.

I wanted to. I really did. There was nothing that I loved more than going out on the town with Lizzy and Ginger. We'd been living together for a year now and apart from the occasional minor disagreement about clothes, make-up and the artistic integrity of Terence Trent D'Arby, apart from the slight compromise of privacy because we all shared one huge bedroom and apart from the drilling noises that came from Lizzy's uncle's dentist surgery down below (he owned the flat and had agreed to rent it to us for minimum rent because it breached just about every safety regulation and was therefore unfit to rent out on the open market), I was loving every minute of it.

There were only five rules that governed our existence:

No men allowed, except in event of communal parties, in which case, the more the better.

Friday night was Girls' Night Out.

Sunday nights were 'clean up and tidy' nights. Unless there was a decent happy hour on somewhere in which case any efforts to 'clean and tidy' were deferred until the next available Sunday. I think we'd actually managed to get the Jif out twice in the last six months.

All bills were split three ways. Unless someone was skint in which case the others chipped in the deficit.

No Phil Collins music. (That one was Ginger's. She claimed she suffered from a rare psychotic condition whereby 'A Groovy Kind of Love' invoked homicidal tendencies. We were too scared to put it to the test.)

I pondered the offer. I did want to go up to town in my new, not so shiny Cortina. I did. I wanted to drive down busy streets with the windows down and let Lizzy stick her head out of the sun roof and whistle at cute guys. But there was something else I wanted to do even more.

'I . . . I . . . can't. I have to go pick up Charlie at the airport.'

Charlie. My boyfriend of one month, three weeks and two days. I'm too embarrassed to give it in hours and minutes but I do actually know. Oh OK – one month, three weeks, two days, ten hours and thirty-six minutes. We met when he came into the salon one Saturday afternoon and we were so busy that I was the only one available to cut his hair. I expected him to say no when I revealed that he would be only my third paid client and the other two were a five-year-old and Mrs Conchenta's red setter, but strangely he agreed. I won't tell you what his hair looks like but let's just say that from the back it's difficult to tell the difference between him, Lizzy and Mr Patel.

He'd asked me out that night and we'd been together ever since. It was fate. We'd just clicked straight away and I knew, just knew, that he was special. I was about to launch into full-scale daydream when I realised that the temperature in the room had dropped and Ginger and Lizzy were staring at me with shocked expressions.

'But . . . it's Friday night!'

'I know, I'm sorry! But he's flying into Prestwick Airport tonight at nine o'clock.'

Which was three hours, fourteen minutes and twenty-seven seconds from now.

Right up until the last minute, I'd prayed that he'd manage to get out of the fortnight at his aunt's house in New Jersey, but he'd explained that his mum had her heart set on seeing her sister for the first time in thirty years and he couldn't let her down. That was the kind of guy that Charlie was – loyal, dependable, reliable. And the fact that he looked a bit like Rick Astley was a bonus too.

'So you're going to drive all the way to Prestwick to pick him up? On the motorway?'

'It's only an hour and a half away. It's not like a different country,' I added defensively.

'Lou, you haven't been further than the sports centre in Merrylee Road. How are you going to get all the way to Prestwick?'

Lizzy had a point. But I was determined that I wasn't going to lose another moment that I could be with Charlie and, OK, yes, perhaps I wanted to show off a little by swooping in to collect him from his flight.

'Look.' I narrowed my brow and squinted in what I hoped was an expression of steely determination.

'Have you got conjunctivitis?' Ginger interrupted. 'Your eyes look weird.'

Maybe steely determination wasn't my thing.

'My serial killer driving instructor certified me as being fit to drive this morning. I really want to see Charlie, I've been missing him like crazy, and there's no point waiting until tomorrow morning when I could drive down, collect him and his mum, take them home and be with him tonight. *We* can go out tomorrow night. Besides, don't you think that's a great way to meet my future mother-in-law for the first time?'

'Nope, I think it's a great way to waste twenty quid on petrol.'

'That's why you're single,' I told her, throwing a cushion in her direction.

I didn't care what they said. This was going to be like one of those final scenes from movies featuring Meg Ryan. And like a great romantic-comedy heroine, I was on the way to get the bloke and the happy ending.

Seven

Did any of the great romcom heroines ever get a puncture?

Did the great Shakespearean love stories end with the requirement of breakdown assistance?

I wasn't even out of the end of our street when I stopped, gave in to curiosity and checked why the car was driving like it was pulling a train.

Going back home and facing Ginger's 'I told you so's' wasn't an option, so instead I nipped into a phone box and called Red. Fifteen minutes later he was there, with the good grace to look slightly sheepish.

'I'm really sorry, Lou. I had no idea this would happen.'

I shrugged. 'Don't worry, I think it was my fault. Someone smashed up the bus stop outside the flat last night and I parked next to it. I was so excited about getting the new car that I didn't even notice I'd stopped on top of glass.'

Oh, common sense, common sense – wherefore art thou?

Red opened the boot of his new white Toyota Carina, took out some tool-shaped thingies and got to work on removing the tyre. Ginger swears he's gay, but I'm not so sure. He's the least camp man on the planet and I've never seen him wear the Boy George hat we got him for Christmas last year. He always wears beat-up jeans, white or grey T-shirts and black boots. And they're not even suede. The only time I've ever seen him in anything else is when he's on his way to work on a Saturday. He's a photography assistant for the place down the shopping precinct and when he's covering a wedding he has to wear a suit.

Nope, he's definitely not gay. I mean, he always wears Aramis aftershave and, according to an interview I read somewhere, that's George Michael's favourite too.

'So where are you off to then?' he asked as he started winding up a tool thingy that was attached to my deflated tyre.

'Collect my boyfriend from Prestwick Airport. He's flying in tonight at nine pm.' I checked my watch – still two hours and thirty-nine minutes until he landed. Thank God I'd left myself some extra time.

'Are you sure you want to do that? It's a fair drive and you've only just—'

'I'm sure.' I cut him off with a smile. There was nothing else he could say on the matter that his sister and Lizzy hadn't already mentioned. I was going. Case closed.

'Didn't you used to go out with Gary Collins?' he asked casually. 'He was in my year at school. Dunno what happened to him.'

Dear God, as if this night couldn't get any worse. My flatmates were in big fat huffs because I'd cancelled the hallowed Friday Night with the Girls. I had a flat tyre. I was freezing cold. My white five-inch stilettos were killing me and I was in danger of missing the most romantic episode of my life. And now . . .

'He took off with Rosaline Harper. To London.'

'That's right! I remember hearing something about that now. About two years ago?'

November sixteenth, 1986. The night after I'd tossed my virginity in his direction in the back of his car. He didn't even leave a note. Despite the fact that, unlike Ginger's first love, Gary hadn't taken off to a war zone, I still hoped that someone would shoot the bastard. Josie was all for tracking him down and removing his genitals but I hid all sharp instruments until she eventually calmed down.

'Yeah, something like that,' I said casually. It had taken me a long, long time to master nonchalance when it came to Gary's betrayal. Not that I ever considered revenge, but for a while I actually felt some kind of kinship with that psycho woman from *Fatal Attraction*.

With a sharp heave, Red pulled off the damaged wheel and slid on the spare and put the screw thingies back on. I made a mental note to brush up on my vehicular technical terms.

'So how are things at the photography, er, place? Must be quite cool with all those, er, wedding films that people are doing now.'

And perhaps a crash course on photographic terminology too.

'Yeah, it's great. It's just part-time while I'm at uni, but it gives me some experience and some dosh. Right, there you go. Perfect. Take it into a garage on Monday just to check the wheel balance, but it should be OK to use in the meantime.'

'Thanks, Red.' I gave him a big hug, careful not to let any form of grease get near the baby-pink skirt and white T-shirt I'd borrowed from Lizzy. She'd agreed to lend them to me before I trampled all over her social plans for the night.

'No problem. And hope it works out with Charles.'

'Charlie.'

'Sorry, *Charlie*. Anyway, hope it works out . . .' he repeated, throwing his tools in the back of his car. It was difficult to believe that he and Ginger came from the same gene pool.

47

He was so nice, so thoughtful and civil, whereas Ginger could set a new world record for brutal bluntness. '. . . 'cause Ginger says your taste in men is chronic.'

Actually, I was beginning to see a slight similarity.

'Red, can I ask a huge favour? I mean, apart from dragging you out here at night and taking advantage of your tyre-changing capabilities.'

'Sure.'

'Don't tell Ginger about this. I don't think I can handle hearing "I told you so" every day until the end of time.'

I tore into the terminal building and checked the huge arrivals screen. Half an hour! The flight landed half an hour ago! Shit! Shit! Shit! But surely he wouldn't be through yet? I mean, he had to get off the plane, then collect his baggage, then go through customs. Damn that bloody combine harvester. I'd been stuck behind it for twenty miles coming down the A77, too terrified to overtake in case I got squashed by a bloody great big lorry coming the other way.

Crowds of people were streaming towards me from the same direction, so, fighting against the heaving masses, I headed in the direction of what I hoped was the arrivals area, scanning the faces with periscope motions as I went. Where was he? Had I missed him? Was he gone? He'd be here, he had to be. I tried to tell myself that this always happens to Meg Ryan – ten minutes from the end of every film she suffers some kind of unavoidable setback, then at the very last moment destiny gets its act together and sorts out the problem. Well, if destiny would care to intervene it would be useful right about now. And doing something about my feet would be a good place to start. These shoes had been selected on the basis of standing stationary, looking deadly, waiting on the second (OK, fourth, maybe fifth) love of my life to storm through the doors into my waiting arms. At no point had I taken on board a contingency that involved me abandoning my car outside the terminal building and then doing a two hundred metre sprint through a crowded terminal building. I was praying that the nerve endings would die soon and that the resulting numbness would be a blessed relief from the pain.

I was slowing to a speed that allowed me to decipher some of the accents around me. Predominately West of Scotland with the occasional smattering of American. This was Charlie's flight, I could feel it. He was here! Somewhere. I just had to . . .

Aaaaaaaaaaaaaaargh.

I went down like I'd been shot by a sniper. Full frontal, face first, traitorous heel of shoe skidding off into the distance. Splat.

'Are you all right there, love?' A concerned elderly gentleman with a talent for being oblivious to the obvious was first on the scene.

'Mufth. Ma. Mfose.'

Yes, indeed I had. Burst my nose. Red liquid oozed through the fingers that were desperately trying to stem the flow before it reached Lizzy's white T-shirt.

It was like trying to contain an oil slick with a bucket. Oh holy crap, she was going to kill me.

'There you go, love, just keep it steady, keep it steady.' I had no idea who was speaking but I didn't have a choice. The elderly gentleman had launched an attack, pinching his fingers around the bridge of my nose. 'Don't worry, love, they taught us how to do this in the war.'

A small crowd started to form around me and, suddenly, a very sombre policeman, who looked like he was way over the weight limit for any kind of public service action role, crouched at my side.

'The first aid team are on the way,' he announced with, I

have to say, not much compassion in his voice. 'Happens all the time,' he told Sir William Haig, who was still reliving his war years courtesy of my facial contusions. 'They drink too much on the plane and then we have to sort it out at this end. I'd bloody ban alcohol on flights if it was up to me.'

'Ah wothnt dwinkin!' I spat, outraged.

'Is she Polish?' asked someone in the crowd.

To Sir William's obvious disappointment, the first-aiders – visibly irritated at having their tea break disturbed for anything less than a full cardiac arrest – arrived and took over. Despite my vehement objections, they manhandled me into a wheelchair and while one took my pulse, the other eyed up his defibrillation paddles with solemn regret.

Slowly, the crowd began to disperse when it became clear they weren't witnessing a scene that would require their presence on a *Crimewatch* reconstruction. Then . . . it was just a glimmer at first. A passing flicker of recognition, one that was then blocked by a large lady with a Dundonian accent.

'Owthi way! Owthi way!'

'She's getting aggressive,' shouted one paramedic.

'Aye, that's definitely Polish she's speaking,' said the lady from Dundee.

I pushed all of the hands off me and stood up, sending another projectile globule of blood shooting from my nose.

Charlie! It was him. It definitely was. And look, he had his arm around his mother, helping her across the terminal building. Except . . . He was laughing. And that arm thrown around that female's shoulders was more of a casual, loving gesture than a maternal guidance aid. They were close enough for me to get a good look now. Yep, I could see all too clearly. And unless his mother was approximately twenty-one and sported a natty line in denim miniskirts and boob tubes, then this wasn't the happy picture of motherly support I'd been expecting.

He leaned over and kissed her as they walked, too engrossed in each other to even notice the small crowd and the cast of *General Hospital* still attempting to attend to a distraught Polish woman with a bleeding nose and one shoe.

Giggling now, they passed us right by, staring into each other's eyes, not even looking at where they were going. Never in my life have I ever prayed more for a bloody great big pillar to suddenly materialise out of thin air.

He'd lied. The second love of my life (OK, so who's actually counting?) had pulled the same stunt as the last one and buggered off with someone else.

I briefly considered giving chase, but given that I looked like an extra from a scene of mass destruction in *Alien*, I decided not to bother. Instead, I thanked my audience for their participation, hobbled out to my car, took the parking ticket off the front window, got in and drove off using my one good foot. As I headed up the road, I almost wished there was a combine harvester in front of me as it would delay the inevitable. Lizzy's huff would escalate to devastation when she realised that I'd wrecked her favourite clothes. Ginger's huff would escalate to unbearable smugness that my rejection of a night with the girls had landed me on my arse. Literally. I could only hope that both situations would be diluted by love and sympathy when they saw that my face looked like it had done ten rounds with Muhammad Ali.

What a disaster. When was I ever going to learn? Josie was always telling me that my common sense took a bus to Pathetic Central whenever there was a man involved (I knew her honesty came from a place of love so I didn't take offence). Given that it was Friday night and I'd dumped my pals for a bloke who was probably right now licking his duty free vodka off some blonde's buttocks, I had to concede that she probably had a point.

I flicked up the indicator lever to signal that I was pulling out to overtake a caravan doing twenty miles an hour in the inside lane.

Bollocks. Bloody bollocks. Friday night, almost midnight and look at me: I could have been drinking cocktails and having a great time with my pals right now and instead I was driving in the dark, in the middle of bloody bollocking nowhere and all because of a bloke who was definitely not worth it.

A terrifying thought suddenly came into my head: I'd done exactly what I'd spent my life watching my mum do. All those nights spent driving to get my dad, leveraging her happiness because of a man, putting him first above everything else, caught up in some stupid messed-up fantasy where all that mattered was making him happy.

Woe.

I'd turned into my mother – the one person whose life I'd always sworn I would never have.

Well, enough. No more. Never again was I going to allow a guy to mess me around, take me for a ride, break my heart. Fuck Meg Ryan. Life wasn't like the movies and I had to stop expecting Tom Hanks/Billy Crystal/Richard Gere/Tom Cruise to wander in and save me. I might have been Della Cairney's daughter but I was Josie Cairney's niece and I was pretty sure that if there was a fight for supremacy in the genetic pool of life, Della's genes would need David Hasselhoff to resuscitate them.

As I passed the Hillman Imp that was pulling the caravan, I caught the smiling expressions on the faces of the middle-aged couple in the front seats. Dear God. Caravan-pulling tourists were happier than me. Could this night get any worse?

The cosmos answered by sending a sudden torrent of hailstones against my windshield. I gripped the steering wheel a little tighter, desperately trying to keep calm. It was a bit late to wish I had more practise at driving in the rain. And in the dark. And while sporting a broken nose and eyes like a puffer fish. And . . .

Bang. Blackness. Silence.

In answer to my question, my night just got about as bad as it could be.

Eight

Lou

The St Kentigern Hotel, Glasgow. Friday night, 11 pm

'Getting arrested, leaving school, leaving home, losing virginity . . .'

Ginger shrieked. 'Eeeeew, I have no wish to think of you in that way! Clear the mind. Clear the mind. Uuuuuummmmmmmmm.' She clipped together her middle fingers and thumbs, closed her eyes and went for it.

'Lizzy, make her stop. We've paid for three nights here and I don't want to get ejected after one,' I begged.

Lizzy nudged Ginger in the shoulder. No reaction. She poked her in the ribs. Still the mock meditative chanting continued.

'Ginger, that jacket is stunning. Is it Prada?'

'Gucci. Limited edition. Couldn't resist it.'

'There you go,' I told Lizzy. 'A prod to the ego always works.'

Ginger grinned and signalled to the waitress for another round of drinks.

'So go on then, smart one – what would you consider the landmark events in our lives?' I asked her.

'In my life or yours?'

'Either.'

She thought for a moment and then let out a shriek that was almost other-worldly, before pausing to compose herself then starting to whistle.

Yep, whistle.

A tune.

Oh. Dear. God. No.

'Lizzy, make her stop again,' I pleaded. 'Quick, ask her if the handbag is Chanel!'

But this time Lizzy was otherwise engaged. It was hard to help a friend in need when you were harmonising to the soundtrack of the most mortifying moment of her life.

Nine

Lou

1991 – Aged 21

> *Baby, I know what it meant to you*
> *I wanted it so bad and the words I spoke were true*
> *Under the stars you offered your soul forever*
> *But it didn't feel right, so goodbye, my lover*
> *Oh, oh, oh, oh Sue, I'm sorry it could never be you . . .*

'Switch it off! Quick!' Angie hissed. 'The last time she heard it she almost took out the speaker with a flying hair-dryer!' Down at the reception desk, Rosie, the sixteen-year-old junior lunged towards the sound system and flicked it from 'radio' to 'cassette'. Chesney Hawkes 'The One and Only' cut Radio Clyde dead.

Rosie and Angie, the salon juniors, were now watching me, eyes wide, ready to duck should another hairdressing implement be used in an act of random violence.

'Aw that's a shame, hen, I was enjoying that! I love that

song,' moaned Mrs Marshall, my regular Friday afternoon, 5 pm shampoo and set. 'I mean, we should be dead proud of him, shouldn't we? It's like *Local Hero* but without the football and that lassie with the chunky legs.'

Do not speak. Do not speak. Do not. I was talking to myself and, apparently, Mrs Marshall's much lauded psychic powers (for three years she's been telling me about her weekly conversations with her sister Patsy, who has been dead since 1988) were switched off, because she didn't pick up on my reticence to discuss the matter further.

'I mean, who'd have thought wee Gary Collins would turn out to be a star? I knew him when he was a toddler running about in the nuddy and now that lovely Ross King on the radio says he's going to be bigger than Jason Donovan.'

Yep, who'd have bloody thought it? Stardom. Fortune. Fame. And now he had a number one hit with a song he told *Smash Hits* that he wrote after 'a night with an old girl-friend, when he realised that they weren't physically compatible and he would have to break her heart'.

I could feel the familiar anxiety twisting my guts and it was all I could do not to pepper the walls of the shop with a dozen heated rollers. Getting 'humped and dumped' on the night you lose your virginity was bad enough, but to have someone actually write an international hit that basically accused you of being a terrible shag? My dignity had officially battered itself to death with a rolled-up teenage music magazine.

Our whole town knew that he never went out with anyone called Sue and, let's face it, it's not exactly a leap of artistic creativity from 'Sue' to 'Lou'. Oh, the humiliation. It was painful enough when only my nearest and dearest knew that he'd got his way then buggered off before daybreak, but now? Public shame. People laughed at me in queue at the post office. The ladies in the baker's couldn't look at me with a straight face. And if one more teenage boy rattled the window of the salon and made rude gestures at me there was going to be carnage. The only small consolation was that I'd heard he dumped Rosaline Harper the minute the money started coming in and now she had a flourishing career in a Glasgow massage parlour called Wandering Hands.

I suddenly realised that I'd stopped backcombing Mrs Marshall's curls and was now rubbing the side of my hip.

'Are you OK there dear?'

I snapped back to the present. 'I'm fine thanks, Mrs Marshall. Just an old injury. It plays up when I've been on my feet too long.' Deep breaths. Deep breaths. And let the tension go. Mr Patel had been teaching me how to take calming breaths but I had a feeling that I was too far up the stress scale to be cured by inhalation and exhalation alone.

'OK, you two, you can relax.' I attempted a calming, carefree smile in the direction of Rosie and Angie. 'And if you've finished clearing up, you can head off. The girls are coming in so . . .'

'Hellooooooooooooooo!'

Mrs Marshall's psychic powers may have been tuned out but it seemed like Lizzy's were right on form as she charged in the door at that exact moment carrying multiple garment bags aloft in each hand. 'Hi, Mrs Marshall, you're looking deadly,' she announced with a grin. 'The men won't be able to keep their hands off you at the bingo tonight.'

Mrs Marshall blushed furiously. Her husband had died in the seventies but she'd reliably informed me that last year he'd finally given her paranormal permission to move on and find a replacement to share her twilight gambling years. Thus the weekly hair appointments and the interest in songs about matters of the heart by local bloody heroes.

Lizzy hung her baggage on the nearby coat stand, kissed me on the cheek, then plonked herself down on the next chair, ignoring the fact that a large strip of gaffer tape was the only thing stopping the foam stuffing from escaping the red leatherette covering.

There was no denying the shop was getting shabby. And, if I'm honest, that was the biggest reason for my general dissatisfaction with life these days. The Gary Collins episode was just my cherry on top.

The salon was owned by Donna Maria, an eccentric Italian lady who had lost all interest since she married the bloke who owned the town's mattress warehouse a few years before. They now lived in permanently rested bliss and spent all day counting his considerable fortune. Apparently there was big money in mattresses – and not just in the way Rosaline Harper made it.

Donna Maria had more or less given up on the salon now and left me and two other stylists, Wendy and Pamela, to run it. There were definitely pluses to the situation – flexible hours, long tea breaks and free hair maintenance for family and friends. But the cons outweighed the pros. The salon was getting tired. Every day was more or less exactly like the one before. And as long as I stayed here nothing was going to change. Lately, I'd been beginning to think it was time to move on. I had ideas. Plans. Ambition. Things I wanted to achieve. And I would . . . just as soon as I'd stopped daydreaming about getting my own salon and rising to stardom in the hairdressing world and took steps to actually achieving it. Quitting a dead-end job in Weirbank would be a start, but apart from the teenagers making filthy signs at me through the window I was comfortable here. Happy. Content. Some of the time.

I gave Mrs Marshall's coiffure a final spray and used a hand mirror to show her the back of the style. She acted like it was a delightful surprise despite the fact that I'd been styling it exactly the same way since the first day she sat in my chair.

'Right we're off then,' Angie said, as she and Rosie headed for the door. 'G'night, girls – don't forget your share of the tips. I've left it in an envelope on the desk.' It wasn't compulsory to share tips but the memory of surviving on thirty-five quid a week was too fresh to keep the perks to myself.

'Doing anything nice tonight?' I asked, praying that whatever Angie was doing, she'd be accompanied by a responsible adult. She reminded me so much of Lizzy at that age: dippy, accident prone, funny, naive, with a fractured relationship with reality.

'Yeah, we're going to see *Silence of the Lambs*,' Rosie replied.

'I hate nature films,' Angie said, pouting.

'Me too,' Lizzy interjected. It was like looking at two kindred spirits, separated at birth.

The bell on the door trilled as the girls left, passing Ginger on the way in. We heard the clanging of the bottles before we saw her. One vodka, one gin, one tonic, accompanied by two large cartons of fresh orange. And, by the looks of things, she had a head start on us.

She did something between a stagger and a lunge towards the first available seat and then forgot to keep her feet on the floor so spun around three times before coming to a halt. Thankfully, dizziness prevented her from catching the look that passed between Lizzy and me.

'And what about you girls then? Are you off to the cinema tonight too?' Mrs Marshall asked as I helped her on with her coat. If she really had psychic powers, wouldn't she know this already?

'Nope, we've got a hen night tonight,' I replied.

'Oooh, lovely! Whose is it? Anyone I know.'

I made a practised effort to inject excitement and enthusiasm into my expression and tone, then gestured to one of my lifelong best friends.

'As a matter of fact, it's . . .'

Ten

'Marry me?' he repeated.

Despite the streams of tears that were flowing down her face, his breathless girlfriend sniffed loudly, then, after an excruciatingly long pause, broke into a beaming grin.

It was the third proposal in La Fiora that Valentine's night, but thankfully, the only one at our table. Walking into the restaurant had been like entering the land that decorative restraint forgot. Pink walls. Pink streamers. Pink table covers. Pink balloons. And smack, bang in the middle of it, three guys with very pink faces looking about as comfortable as my posterior in my too-tight pink pants.

It took several rounds of unidentifiable pink cocktails before the mood completely relaxed and the laughter at our table rose to our normal level, much to the irritation of the earnest couples attempting to have a poignant romantic experience at the surrounding tables.

Admittedly, I'm slightly biased against the traditional celebration of pink tinfoil tat.

Valentine's night is my least favourite night of the year. A lifetime trapped in the sycophantic love fantasy of Dave and

Della Cairney, topped off with the romantic success of, say, a celibate hostage in a siege situation, had left me with a severe aversion to the day of fluffy pink hearts and flowers. I'd decided that should I ever meet Saint Valentine, I'd have no option but to lock him in a room with a three-foot padded card that belted out 'I Just Called to Say I Love You', on a repetitive loop.

Since the disaster with Charlie it had been strictly short-term relationship stints for me. A few weeks here and there, and the minute they started to act like the relationship was going to get any deeper than a meaningless fling, I'd give him the 'It's not you, it's me' speech and move on to the next one. It was safe. Easier. Less complicated. And, actually, more fun. I had the occasional man for formal functions, movies, weekend breaks and bendy activities and my girls for nights out and carefree jollies and adventure. And as far as I was concerned that's the way it was going to stay. We were like Thelma and Louise, but with an extra passenger and without that cute cowboy. What was his name? Brad something. Bound to be a one-hit wonder, but in the name of the clitoral shakes, he was gorgeous.

Where was I? Right – girls, together for ever, no man could come between us.

'You know, I've got a feeling Dominic is going to pop the question tonight,' Ginger had announced in the taxi on our way to meet our respective dates.

'What – fancy a shag? He pops that question every night,' Lizzy joked. 'Don't think I don't hear you two at it in the bathroom. And I don't even want to know why my loofah has disappeared.'

While the taxi driver had a choking fit in the front, Ginger leaned over and ruffled Lizzy's newly styled hair. It was pulled up and tied on top of her head and then spiked up with a can and a half of fast-set hairspray. She looked like a cross between Pebbles from *The Flintstones* and Cher after an altercation with a live electrical socket.

'So what would you say?' I asked Ginger after I pulled them apart and leaned over to thump the driver between the shoulder blades. Thankfully we were stopped at a set of traffic lights. He gasped out a thanks as the lights turned to green.

'About what?' Ginger asked.

'If he asked you to marry him.'

She thought about it for a moment, her face flushed to a shade close to her hair colour. 'You know what, I think I'd say yes.'

'No way!' And there was Lizzy's familiar screech. 'We're much too young for all that marriage stuff.'

'No we're not. Half the girls we went to school with are already married and Stacey O'Conner has four children.'

She was right. But, in fairness, she had married on her sixteenth birthday and her 'miracle twins' were born six and a half months later. The priest maintained they were premature and it was an act of God, despite the bouncing babes weighing eight and a half pounds each. Her next set of twins were born two years later and I don't think she's been out of the house since.

Determined to avoid an argument, and pretty sure Ginger was being deliberately provocative, I steered the conversation on to safer ground – the merits of Kevin Costner – and kept it there all the way to the restaurant. Ginger getting married? No way. She'd only been seeing Dominic the Draughtsman for a year and she'd only just qualified as a podiatrist – and yes, she still hated the sight of feet. And no (although she only admitted it in times of severe intoxication), she still hadn't lost hope that there was more to life than growing old in Weirbank. Ginger was destined for bigger things than a small town could ever give her – she just hadn't found the escape route that led to a different life yet. However, if I had to put money on anyone flying from here it was Ginger. As soon as she had a few months of experience in the clinic, I reckoned she would head off to work in Glasgow, meet some wild rocker who was having issues with his corns, and never be seen again.

When we reached La Fiora the bloke at the door told us that our partners were already seated. We let him take our coats and then converged on the foyer mirror, dabbing down the shine with Elizabeth Arden powder and sharing a Max Factor lip gloss.

'What about you and Sam, Lou? Any chance this one will last longer than a week?' Lizzy probed.

Sam was my sympathy date. He worked for the same huge construction company as Ginger's boyfriend Dominic the Draughtsman and Lizzy's man, Adam the Accountant. There would have been a nice poetic balance if he was Sam the Surveyor or Sam the solicitor. Unfortunately, he did something in some department called AT. Or was it ET? Or IT? To be honest, over the half a dozen times or so that the other guys had dragged him along with us to even up the numbers, he'd talked about work so much that I'd started switching off as soon as he spoke about anything office-related.

'Nope, don't think this one's going anywhere,' I answered. 'He's a bit too geeky for me. He claims that one day we'll all have computers in our houses and communicate with each other by talking to the screen. I think he's on drugs.'

I made a final check that my hair was flowing down across the right side of my face. The scar was barely visible now, but that didn't make me any less self-conscious. A broken pelvis, a broken leg, a fractured shoulder, a cracked nose and a face full of glass that required fifty-six stitches – that was the going rate for a relationship disaster these days. But I wasn't bitter. I really wasn't. I'd woken up in hospital eighteen hours after the crash and spent the next day calming Josie down, persuading Red that it wasn't his fault and just feeling oh so thankful to be alive and in (almost) one piece. Surprisingly, the Cortina hadn't been to blame. Turns out that in a tragic twist of fate, at the exact moment I drew alongside the Hillman Imp, the driver – Mr Bert McTavish from Kelso – had suffered a fatal heart attack while laughing at a joke his wife told him, causing him to swerve across the road and force my car into the central reservation. Kind of put splitting up with a boyfriend into perspective. I prefer not to contemplate why I've never bumped into Charlie since then, but Josie does look a bit shifty when I mention his name.

I've learned my lesson – overblown romantic gestures are not for me.

The conversation we'd had at the flat was completely forgotten, until a slightly sheepish guy stood up as the pudding plates were taken away and cleared his throat, before lunging down to a one-legged kneeling position and pulling a small red box out of his pocket.

'Babe,' he said to his startled girlfriend in front of a startled audience. 'I know we're young and I know we haven't been together for, you know, years or anything like that . . .'

An appropriately startled opening, I'd say.

'But the thing is, I . . . I, er, love you so much and would be . . . it would be great if . . . do you want to marry me?'

'Open the box. Open the box,' I whispered, still stunned but recovered enough to appreciate the sweetness of this and to understand that he needed a helpful prompt.

'Oh, right, I'll erm, open . . .'

The ring was perfect. A small but beautiful solitaire on a white gold band.

'Marry me?' he repeated.

Despite the streams of tears that were flowing down her face, his breathless girlfriend sniffed loudly, then after an excruciatingly long pause, broke into a beaming grin.

'I will,' shrieked Lizzy. 'Oh bloody hell, I definitely will!'

No one except me noticed that Ginger lifted her glass and downed her pink champagne in one large gulp.

Eleven

Lizzy

The St Kentigern Hotel, Glasgow. Friday night, 11 pm

'Oh God, I'm filling up. Don't let me drink any more. I had no idea he was going to ask me. That was definitely a land-mark moment for me. I can remember every minute of that night. Every single minute.'

'Do you remember me thumping Dominic on the way home with the brand-new furry muff I'd bought from C&A that afternoon?' Ginger asked. 'I mean, a pink furry muff. Is it any wonder the guy didn't propose to me?'

My eyes were really watering now but I wasn't sure if they were happy tears, sad tears, nostalgic tears or too much wine tears. 'And I remember the getting ready for my hen night in the salon too. After you told Mrs Marshall it was my hen night, she went quiet for a minute and then told me that her dead husband had just informed her that I was marrying my lifelong soulmate.'

'Do you think they have crack in heaven?' Lou joked.

I feigned dramatic petulance. 'I can't believe you said

that! Adam is my lifelong soulmate. He is. It's just that . . .' Another memory hit me and I back-pedalled furiously. 'I remember being so thrilled that day. I remember saying "I can't believe that this time tomorrow I'll be married!" And then you said . . .'

Lou took up her part of the story. '"I can't believe you've been engaged for eight months already. It seems like only yesterday he proposed."'

Ginger got in on the act. 'And I said, "I can't believe we're having a hen night the night before the wedding. It's madness."'

It was so vivid I could almost hear the conversation in my head. 'And I told you that we hadn't missed a Friday Girls' Night in years and we weren't going to start now. Then I assured you that we'd just have a couple of drinks and then head home for an early night.'

Lou held up her glass. 'A toast,' she announced. 'To youth and foolish optimism.'

Twelve

Lou

Still 1991 – Aged 21

'Why? Why did we ever think it would be a good idea to have a hen night on the actual eve of the wedding?' Lizzy groaned.

'Because we had four hen nights and we were running out of time to squeeze in another.'

It was true. We hadn't so much had a hen night as a hen month and it had almost been a relief to get to the swapping of the 'I do's bit.

Now, sitting in the toilets at the reception, I was glad I'd sworn off any form of alcoholic beverage all day, given that the hangover from last night was still lingering. Lizzy was clearly suffering the same after-effects of overindulgence. She was sitting on the sink unit, in full wedding dress and veil, holding an ice pack to her forehead with one hand, clutching a cigarette in the other, while steeping her feet in a basin of cold water. The only blessing was that after having sunbeds every day for the last month, we were all so tanned that it disguised what would undoubtedly be our nauseatingly grey pallor.

'Where's Ginger?' she asked.

'Still sulking because you made us wear these bloody peach meringues,' I retorted. 'I can't believe you sprung these on us this morning.'

'Look, it was my gran's dying wish to see me married in her dress with my friends in the same bridesmaid dresses that her two best friends wore.'

'Lizzy, your gran is still alive.'

'Yeah, well, she won't be if Ginger finds her. Peach is definitely not her colour scheme.'

She winced as our laughter made her head hurt all over again.

'It was OK, though, wasn't it? The wedding?' she asked.

'Lizzy it was beautiful.' I wasn't lying. The sun had shone, the guests were enthusiastic, the priest threw in a few jokes and the vows were beautiful. Despite the fact that I still felt my friend was far too young to be marching up the aisle, I couldn't deny that the day had been breathtaking.

I'd almost shed a tear at the church, until I got distracted by Ginger throwing evil glances at Dominic the Draughtsman. She hadn't seen him since she resolutely thumped him then dumped him on Valentine's night and I'm sure the poor bloke had absolutely no idea what he'd ever done wrong.

None of us, especially Lizzy, had seen the proposal coming, but in hindsight it was meant to be. Lizzy and Adam were completely devoted to each other. He adored everything about her, relished her quirky ways and didn't mind taking regular trips to A&E when she inadvertently injured herself after falling off bar tops, dancing on tables, or wearing shoes with eight-inch stiletto heels.

'God, I love him so much,' Lizzy said with a wistful sigh.

'I know. But we'll miss you.'

'I'm only moving next door and you can still hear every word I say.'

As a wedding present, her uncle, the dentist, had gifted her the other flat above the surgery and the walls were so thin we could speak to each other without raising our voices.

'True. But I'll still miss you. And so will Ginger.'

'You think?'

Much as Ginger knew that our version of the St Valentine's Day Massacre wasn't Lizzy's fault, there was no denying that it had caused an unspoken tension between them.

Just at that, the door flew open and in strolled Ginger, carrying a glass in one hand and a wine bucket, complete with ice and full bottle of champagne, in the other.

'Hey, there you are! Please tell me I can get out of this dress now. Seriously. I look like a consumption victim from the nineteenth century.'

'Wow, that history O level wasn't wasted,' I teased, grateful that Ginger's alcohol level hadn't tipped her from 'happy-go-lucky' to 'brooding and maudlin'. Lately, it had been a crapshoot as to which version we ended up with at the end of any given night.

With much negotiation of frills and bustles, Ginger leaned over and enveloped Lizzy in a huge hug. 'Sorry I've been a cow sometimes lately,' she said. Oh bugger, here it comes. 'It's not your fault, I swear. It's just that . . . Do you ever get the feeling that there must be more to life than this?'

Well, hello maudlin, we've been expecting you.

'Do you ever think that something has to happen to get you out of the life you have? I mean, I look at feet all day. Feet. Why did I do that? That careers guidance woman who talked me into a career in feet should be sacked. Or shot.'

Yet, I empathised. I did. Neither of our current paths were setting the world alight and only twenty-four hours before I'd been having the same thoughts.

Before anyone could reply, a piecing shriek cut through the conversation.

'Oh fuck, no! No!' Lizzy jumped down from the sink top and dashed towards the door. 'I warned them! I told the guy in the band that if he let my mother sing he wasn't getting paid. Oh fuck, Adam will have this marriage annulled before she gets to the end of the song.'

Out in the smoky function suite, Lizzy's worst nightmare was indeed coming true. There was Saint Carla of the Holy Screech up on stage, resplendent in a blue and gold sequinned frock that may have been borrowed from the wardrobe of Shirley Bassey for the occasion, murdering 'I Never Promised You a Rose Garden'. With actions.

'Tell me this isn't happening,' Lizzy gasped, just as the band, looking traumatised, launched into a big finish. Carla lapped up the claps from the few members of the audience who weren't frozen by the trauma of what they'd just been subjected to. 'Oh, no – she's going to do another one. Ginger you've got to get her off of there before . . . Before . . .'

'"Jolene"?' I gasped with horror.

Lizzy nodded, eyes wide with terror.

Noooooooooooo. We'd had 'Jolene' at Lizzy's twenty-first party and it was no coincidence that there was a snippet on the news the next day saying that the RSPCA had reported a sudden leap in the number of dog fatalities in our area.

'OK, I'm going in,' Ginger announced, taking a deep breath and then launching into a manoeuvre that can only be described as storming the stage. In a smooth yet determined motion, she managed to subtly wrestle the microphone from Carla's hands, and then escort her to the side of the platform, whispering in her ear the whole time. Carla then slapped her hand to her mouth in horror and made a mad dash to the fire exit.

'Car on fire?' I asked Lizzy.

'Yep,' she replied.

It was Ginger's fallback ruse for getting rid of anyone causing us problems in a crowded situation. Over the years, dozens of innocent men, three pub managers, twelve bouncers and a stripogram dressed as Elvis had been advised that their vehicle was on fire, forcing them to make a swift departure.

Meanwhile, Ginger returned to the centre of the stage to hand the microphone back over to the lead guitarist.

'Give us a song, doll!' someone shouted from the audience.

This wasn't unusual. Even at weddings in posh venues like this Glasgow hotel, the singer in the band generally took a break in the set, and was frequently replaced by family members keen to 'do a turn'.

'Yeah, go on, give us a wee tune!'

The crowd were getting into it now and even a deafening blast of feedback from the speakers didn't dampen their enthusiasm.

'Go on, love – do you know any Lulu?' shouted someone else.

Well, they were barking up the wrong tree. I'd been with Ginger almost every day of her life since we were toddlers and I'd never, ever heard her sing. Never. She'd be out of there in a flash, over to the bar for a top up and then back to deliberating the general shiteness of life.

'We-e-e-e-e-e-e-e-e-e-e-e-e-e-e-e-ll!'

If Saint Carla of the Holy Shriek had at that very moment walked back into the room dragging Lulu behind her, I couldn't have been more astonished.

Ginger. On stage. And that noise, that absolutely fantastic, incredible sound was coming directly from her lungs. As she launched into the first line of 'Shout' the band quickly got their act together and caught up with her, the crowd jumped to their feet, Lizzy and I removed our chins from the floor

72

and the whole place went completely, absolutely and resolutely mental.

She was brilliant. Magnificent. The most stunning voice I had ever heard.

And as Lizzy and I roared with laughter while doing a wild approximation of our very best sixties dance moves, we didn't notice that over at the entrance to the function suite, a man had stopped, leaned against the door frame and was now staring at Ginger, transfixed at the sight of a consumption victim from the 1800s, wearing a peach meringue, giving the performance of a lifetime.

That man, and what he was about to do next, would change everything.

Thirteen

Ginger

The St Kentigern Hotel, Glasgow. Friday night, midnight

Now it was my turn to trot out the 'feels like yesterday' clichés. But it really did. 'I thought it was a wind-up, you know. I thought that at any minute one of those camera crews would appear from behind a plant pot and the bloke claiming to be Ike Stranger from Edge Records would actually be Cedric Veal, a bit part actor from Slough. Then they'd all laugh and disappear and I'd see my face on *You've Been Framed* one Saturday night.'

'When did you actually start to believe it?' Lou asked. I struggled to absorb the question because I suddenly realised how exhausted she looked. Shattered. But then, I suppose it would be more surprising if she looked any other way. That was why I'd dug my heels in and refused to cancel this trip. She needed it. I made a mental note to tell her at some point this weekend how damn, fucking incredible I think she is. I know she'll be mortified and she won't believe it but that's just Lou. She doesn't have a single clue how amazing she is.

Oh, bloody hell, I couldn't get maudlin again now. I just couldn't. I had to fight my natural urges and keep this weekend upbeat.

'Somewhere after the first blow job and before the first gig,' I announced, sending the mood soaring back to hilarity. 'I don't know if I've ever told you this, but I offered to have sex with him that night and he refused. Refused! He was a middle-aged bloke confronted with a drunk, lustful virgin . . .'

Lizzy and Lou howled with laughter and I had the self-awareness to switch to slightly sheepish. 'OK, well I was drunk and lustful – and he refused. I think I probably suspected then that he meant business. God, could you imagine if Cassie came home and said some guy wanted to take her to London and make her a star? He'd have to get through the three of us first.'

The others nodded. It was true. Perish the thought. We'd have her chaperoned on a twenty-four hour basis by the three of us and several large men with weapons.

'Back then though,' I continued, 'it was different. My parents were OK about me going and they were right. Ike did everything by the book at the start. Got me vocal lessons, booked small gigs, helped me put a cool image together, brought in a PR team, worked on getting me some brilliant songs. It really was a dream come true.'

I suddenly realised that this was the kind of stuff that magazines used to pay me good money for – AN INTERVIEW WITH GINGER – THE EARLY YEARS.

'And do you know what the best thing about that whole early period was?' I asked.

Lizzy and Lou were hanging on every word. Oh yes, *Rolling Stone* magazine, shake in your rock star boots because they were about to get an exclusive. Something hot. Juicy. A stunning revelation.

'The fact that I'd never have to look at a pair of old lady feet ever again.'

Still laughing, Lou nipped off to go to the loo.

'How do you think she's holding up?' I asked Lizzy. Her brow immediately furrowed in the middle, sending another mental note to my cerebral diary to remind me it was time for my Botox top up. I sometimes have difficulty focusing on one thing at a time. Yes, I'm a little self-absorbed. I blame having fame at an early age and I've come to terms with the fact that this means my chances of getting to heaven are slim.

'I think she's feeling like crap and determined not to show it,' Lizzy replied. As she spoke, she reached across the table and put her hand on mine. 'This was a good thing that you did, Ginger. A really good thing.'

Maybe there's an outside chance of a day pass to heaven after all.

I'd only just composed myself when Lou slipped back into the seat beside Lizzy.

'I was just thinking . . .' she said.

'While you were on the loo?' I asked her.

She smiled as she nodded. 'Yes, while I was on the loo . . .'

'Another mental picture for the recycle bin.'

She ignored the jibe.

'I was just thinking that was probably the most pivotal time in all our lives and we each found what we'd dreamed of when we were growing up. Lizzy, you got married. Ginger, you found fame. And I . . .'

I couldn't help but put a tiny pinprick in her bubble of perfect logic. 'You almost earned yourself six to twelve months at Her Majesty's Pleasure.'

Fourteen

Lou

1994 – Aged 24

'OK, it's time to get serious,' Lizzy announced. 'You know, like philosophical and all deep and stuff.'

'Who are you and what have you done with my friend Lizzy?' I asked her. Not that she wasn't always deep. Compared to, say, the fluid in my contact lens pods.

She didn't even look up from the magazine in front of her.

'All right. So you have to choose one bloke to shag, one to marry, one to avoid – the choices are Gary Barlow, Michael Hutchence or Marti Pellow.'

'And welcome back, Lizzy. I'd avoid Marti Pellow, shag Gary Barlow and marry Michael Hutchence.'

Lizzy required further clarification. 'Why would you avoid Marti Pellow?'

'Because I've already had one local superstar singing about me being a crap shag, I couldn't risk a second one. And the ten thousand three hundred and forty-nine times that I've heard "Love Is All Around" this summer has driven me to the bloody brink of madness.'

Nancy Drew had the decency not to comment on either point as she continued her interrogation. 'Shag Gary Barlow?'

'Even if I really am rubbish he'd be too nice to say.'

As Lizzy pondered this, I tried not to roll my eyes, but they slipped on to a spin cycle anyway. 'Are we really having this conversation? It's six thirty, everyone will be here by seven, and we're not even nearly ready. Don't know if you noticed but it's getting just a little frantic around here,' I said, with a definite overtone of 'frantic' thrown in to demonstrate my point.

'But that's why I'm asking you philosophical questions – to take your mind off the stress. Ouch! Bloody hell, that was almost an *Aliens* moment there – you know the bit where the creature bursts out of that bald woman's stomach?' She took a deep breath, placed a hand on top of one side of the space hopper she appeared to be concealing under her silver, off-the-shoulder, lurex jumper-dress, paused for a few seconds, then smiled and carried on like nothing had happened.

'OK, so why do you want to marry Michael Hutchence?'

'Gorgeous, sexy, bit dangerous and I reckon we're the same size so I could borrow his leather trousers.'

'Great basis for a lifelong commitment.' Lizzy's thoughtful nod was cut short by a painful wince. I was caught between concern, worry and the residue of frantic from a few moments before. 'Babe, I love you. But if you give birth tonight I will eradicate you from my life and deny ever having known you. I'll walk past you in the street. I'll remove your number from my Rolodex. I'll . . .'

As she giggled, two hands went round the belly again and she crossed her legs at the knees. 'Don't make me laugh, Lou – honestly, my bladder is not to be trusted.'

The very obvious reality of this situation didn't escape me.

I bet this never bloody happened to Vidal Sassoon. I could almost categorically assert that when he was opening his first salon, Twiggy wasn't there, heaving around a large stomach, threatening to pee on his floor.

Yep, I was definitely living the high life. But not even the threat of a brush with incontinence could suppress my excitement. My own salon! I was all dressed up in a gorgeous orange, spandex minidress, set off to a Mediterranean tee by the copper head-to-toe tan that had taken a week of exposure to UV tubes to achieve, and I was about to embark on the most exciting night of my life. The opening of my own salon. Mine! And for the purposes of this moment of thrilled, giddy glee, I would overlook the fact that it was actually owned by the bank and obtaining their co-operation and funding may have involved a very, very slight manipulation of the truth, which could loosely be interpreted as fraudulent activity.

You see, here's the thing. All those bloody yuppies from the eighties are now away rejecting capitalism and finding themselves banging on bongo drums and meditating in spirituality camps in the Outer Hebrides – easy to do when you have squillions of cash to fall back on – and all that's left from the decade of excess are some very nervous bank managers who only want to give out loans to people who don't actually need them. So when I went to sixteen different banks with my business plan to take over the salon they all rejected me, because, according to sixteen different gentlemen in suits, I'm skint.

Well, yes, Mr Bank Manager, that's why I'm in need of your services. If I wasn't impoverished then I wouldn't be asking for a fecking loan.

In the end, the equivalent of my own personal superhero saved the day.

'I'll be the guarantor on your loan,' Aunt Josie offered. I knew she was only doing it because I'd been sitting with my

79

head on her kitchen table for an hour and she wanted to get the dinner out.

I slowly prised my head up and squinted in her direction. 'Thanks, Aunt Josie, I appreciate it. I do. But they don't accept repayments in caramel logs.'

She took advantage of my brief head levity to slide a plate of fish fingers and chips under my chin.

'Look, don't you worry about a thing. Just set up the appointment and I'll sign to guarantee the payments.'

'But you're even poorer than me. And anyway, the guarantor has to be a property owner so thank you, really, but that won't work.'

A bread basket in the shape of a chicken hit the table and I absent-mindedly pulled at the French loaf that was inserted where no God-fearing chicken would allow.

'Just set up the meeting and I'll sort it out,' she promised.

There was no point in arguing, so I carried out her instructions and set us up for an episode of ritual humiliation, figuring that at least she'd then hear the limitations of the situation from the man in the suit. And that's why, the following Monday, in the outfit normally only reserved for funerals and public events featuring the attendance of a minor member of the royal family, Josie thanked the manager at the Royal Bank of Tight Bastards for seeing us, and proceeded to offer to co-sign my loan. She filled out 194 forms, showed him her bank book, handed over her birth certificate as ID, and then gave him her very best grin. I waited for him to laugh us all the way out of his office, with a security escort to ensure that we left the premises. But no.

'That all seems to be perfectly in order there, Mrs Cairney. And Miss Cairney,' he said, turning to me, 'I will of course have to refer the application to head office, but I don't see any reason that we can't proceed. The funds will be available in your account before the end of next week.'

'But . . .'

The word was barely out of my mouth when Josie stood up, shook his hand and, in her very best and poshest voice (also normally reserved for funerals and events featuring the attendance of a minor member of the royal family), thanked him profusely then practically manhandled me out of the door.

'Oh my God, we did it. I mean, you did it! We got the money. Oh I love, love, love you!' I told her as I spun her around, almost taking out the old drunk bloke who permanently resided on a tyre outside the butchers in the High Street.

'How lucky were we?' I ranted on, fuelled by 100 per cent pure joy. 'I mean, they must have changed the rules or . . . something. Have you secretly got a massive stash of cash in your account?' I joked, and then clapped my hand over my mouth as realisation dawned. 'You won! You won the jackpot up at the bingo!'

There was sudden activity from the poster boy for Michelin. He shot bolt upright and slurred, 'Gonnae lend us a tenner then, doll?'

Josie surreptitiously glanced around her in the manner of a nervous criminal from *Murder, She Wrote*. 'No, I did not win the bingo jackpot. Although, that old boot Minnie Brown did and she didn't even buy a drink for the table. Shocking way to behave.'

She threw a pound in the tyre guy's direction, ignored his disapproval and then pulled me by the hand down the street. 'C'mon, love, we've got things to do.'

'Celebrate?' I prompted, thinking that even though the loan wasn't actually in my account yet, I could probably stretch to a couple of cocktails at the new wine bar across the road.

'Definitely!' Josie agreed. 'Then we have to go let Donna know that we can take her up on the offer of the lease, we have to go get cracking with the plans for the shop . . .' She pulled me across the road, and waited until we were at the central reservation before finishing, 'And then I have to get this birth certificate and bank book back into your mother's drawer before she notices that they're gone.'

'Do Take That know about Mr Patel?' Red asked, gesturing in the direction of the small but flexible Indian gentleman pulling some pretty impressive moves to 'Everything Changes But You'.

The salon was filling up now and my nervous anxiety that no one would show up had now transferred itself to a nervous anxiety that there wouldn't be enough booze/food/space. Not even the reassuring presence of a highly amused Red and Mr Patel's impersonation of Robbie Williams could calm me down from borderline hyperventilation to mildly manic. It did help though that everyone's first reaction as they walked in the door seemed to be impressed approval.

Obviously I was biased, but I really did think that the place looked great. Outside the huge neon sign lit up the street announcing that CUT was now open for business. Inside, the tacky old lino floor was gone, replaced by matt black ceramic tiles with a metal-effect finish. Both of the long walls that ran from the front of the shop to the staffroom at the back were mirrored, making the room look twice as big. I'd struck lucky and picked up gorgeous, brand-new red leather swivel chairs from a Glasgow hotel that had gone into receivership before it opened. And my cousin Michael's best friend had put his carpentry skills to outstanding use by knocking up ten gorgeous work-space units, which were then painted gloss black, attached to the walls, each one adorned with a dryer and a set of curling tongs. On the back wall next to two rows of gleaming white basins, hung twenty gorgeous red gowns that Josie had run up on her old 1940s pedal-powered Singer sewing machine. Now she was standing in the middle of the salon directing everyone to admire her handiwork, while dressed in the style of an eighties diva. Any minute now the costume director of *Dynasty* would be on the phone asking for their outfit back. Her black herringbone pencil skirt was nipped in at the waist by a six-inch wide red belt and a scarlet silk shirt – complete with enhancement the size of a park bench across the shoulder area – topped off the look. It was good of her to co-ordinate her clothes to the salon colour scheme.

She caught my eye and winked, aping one of the photographs on the wall behind her. They were the most stunning aspect of the room – huge black and white canvases, hung at ten foot intervals along every wall. Those had been Red's idea. He'd been passing one night and spotted us inside decorating so popped in with half a dozen fish suppers and a crate of Diet Coke. Before he left, he suggested taking some 'arty' photos then blowing them up into massive prints. The following night I rounded up all the usual victims and they were all forced to subject themselves to a haircut (although thankfully I now had the skills to risk more than one style) while Red snapped around them. I've absolutely no idea how he got from that to the resulting grainy silhouettes which now wowed everyone as soon as they crossed the threshold. I'd never been prone to cockiness but I had a feeling even Vidal Sassoon would be a smidgeon impressed. Josie had asked for a copy of hers – a gorgeous image of her laughing as she winked – and had hung it up on the only space in the house that didn't have flying wildlife. No one had the heart to tell her that it was slightly disconcerting having her stare down from the wall while we were in the bath.

I broke the easy silence. 'Thanks for everything, Red, I really do appreciate it.'

He shrugged. 'No problem, the prints are great for my portfolio too.'

I checked the time on my Day-Glo Swatch. 'Have you heard from Ginger? She was supposed to be here an hour ago.'

Red shook his head, his rueful grin reminding me of that bit at the end of *Grease* when John Travolta comes over all goofy. If John Travolta had red hair. And was Glaswegian. And standing in a hairdresser's wearing black jeans and a Bowie T-shirt. OK, he was nothing like John Travolta at all. I blame the nerves and the alcohol.

'Haven't heard from her, but you know what she's like. She was an unpredictable nightmare before all the singing stuff, but now that she's the second coming of Debbie Harry she's impossible to track down.'

He said it without malice or bitterness, just a matter-of-fact air of truth. He was right. In the biggest surprise since Gary Collins' band released its last single, 'You Never Turned Me On', (I get it – I'm a crap shag – was he ever going to bloody get over it and move on?), Ginger had swapped a career in feet for a future in music. Turns out that the bloke who'd wandered into Lizzy's wedding in the hotel that night was Ike Stranger, an A&R guy from Edge Records, up checking out the Glasgow clubs on the lookout for the next big Glasgow band. Instead he found Ginger – pissed, cantankerous and dressed in a meringue, and realised that she was something special. I think it was the voice and the Doc Martins that she was wearing under her dress that did it. Anyway, my chum wasn't in the stellar level of Gary Wanker Collins yet, but after a couple of years of touring pubs and playing smallish gigs, she'd released her first single – 'Numb' – and was starting to get a bit of recognition. Swallow diving off the stage during last week's live edition of *Top of the Pops* had definitely helped the buzz. Hopefully, the three blokes from Maidenhead that she landed on would be out of hospital soon.

Where was she? She promised that she'd be here, so she definitely would. Definitely. She wouldn't let me down. On a personal level, I really wanted everyone I loved here tonight, and, on an admittedly shallow professional level, having a minor celebrity like Ginger here would guarantee that the local paper ran a photograph of the salon opening on the front page this week. No, I'm not proud of my motivations, but I had to make as much money as quickly as possible. I had to make this business work, I had to support myself and you never knew when I'd have to slip Josie a few grand to help her flee the country if the fraud squad rumbled her.

I suddenly became acutely aware of Lizzy gesticulating to me from over near the door and slid over to join her, leaving Red to chat up one of the models that I'd wooed here (with promises of free haircuts) to add a bit of glamour.

'OK, don't freak out,' she hissed, immediately setting my demeanour to 'imminent freak out', 'but Dan has just arrived.'

'No. No. No. No.'

'Yep. And he's . . .'

I felt the hand coming round my waist, closely followed by a meeting between my nostrils and a detectable whiff of Ralf Lauren's Polo.

'Right behind me?'

Lizzy nodded.

'Hey, baby,' he whispered in my ear. 'Place looks great.'

OK, this wasn't part of the plan. I'd been seeing Dan for about six months but hadn't expected him tonight because . . . 'I thought you were in London this week,' I stuttered, hoping the accompanying cheesy grin said 'but I'm glad you're not' instead of 'bloody bugger, you're the last person I wanted to see!'

Dan and I had a good thing going. I'd met him when I did his blond highlights, before he took up his position as the only straight flight attendant on Air Alba – one of Scotland's national airlines. Actually, the term 'airline' might be an exaggeration. Eight puddle jumpers and a dozen 747s bought second hand from Aeroflot are not exactly going worry the board of British Airways.

The girls in the salon had debated Dan's sexual orientation for months. Never, in all my West of Scotland butch male experience had I ever encountered a straight guy who moisturised. And cooked. And kept his flat pristine. And . . . and . . . (OK, this one really freaked me out) *waxed*. He did. There wasn't a hair to be found on his chest or under his arms. And on top of that he dressed like he was straight out of a Burton advert and was obsessed with flash gadgets. Why, in God's name does anyone need a mobile phone? Why? What could possibly be so important that you couldn't wait until you got home to tell someone? They'll never catch on.

Anyway, on average he was home three days every week so we never fell into the whole blasé/taking each other for granted thing because we didn't live in each other's pockets. Which was great. Fantastic. Especially because . . .

'Vic!' Everyone within ten yards craned to see what had caused Lizzy to go into full screech mode.

I, on the other hand, was wondering if this would be the only salon opening in history where the owner was caught commando crawling out of the door.

There was no stopping my high-pitched pal. 'Oh, Vic, thank God you're here!'

Really? Had she lost her mind? I met Lizzy's startled gaze with my completely confused one, then watched in awe as she grabbed the newcomer's hand and pulled him towards the staffroom, screeching 'I'm having a weird pain and I need you to check me out.'

With that she dragged him off into the crowd, turning to throw me a wink as she left. God, she was good.

'Who's that guy?' Dan asked.

My other boyfriend.

'Oh, just some friend of hers,' I replied, grateful that the heat in the room gave me an excuse for my flushed face.

'He looks kinda familiar. Do you know him too?' Dan probed.

Yes, because he's my other boyfriend.

'Just through Lizzy.'

'Cool. You should drag him out with us some night. Wouldn't mind having a look at that Tag Heuer he's wearing.'

It's not real. It's a fake that his sister brought him from Benidorm. I know that because he's my other boyfriend.

'Sure, I will.'

When hell freezes over. Because . . . well, you know.

Please don't judge me. The whole two-timing thing had come about completely by accident. Dan was away for a few days and I'd gone out with the girls, had a few cocktails, broke a heel on my shoe, accepted a lift home from a cute guy and the next thing I knew I was leading a double life, seeing two lovely blokes, neither of which would ever be more than a casual thing. I was going to sort it out. I was. Eventually. But they were just both so nice and I wasn't sure which one I liked best and if I was being really deep and getting in touch with my deepest psychological issues I'd say that I liked seeing both of them because that way neither relationship could ever become serious and we've already ascertained that that's a good thing. In my experience, serious relationships either end up in the seventh circle of co-dependent hell (i.e. my parents) or with one party (usually the one with bollocks) going off into the sunset with someone else. Nope, casual was good. Great, even. A perfect solution. Except when both turned up on the same night.

I untangled myself from Dan. 'Just need to go check Lizzy's OK. You grab a drink and mingle and I'll catch up later.'

Just as soon as I've had a cosy tête-à-tête with my other boyfriend.

Maintaining a beaming grin on my face the whole time, I ploughed through the crowd, throwing out hellos, thanking people for coming and adding in a few 'great to see you!'s here and there. By the time I burst into the staffroom Lizzy was lying on the purple sofa looking pained.

'Oh thank God. Where've you been?' she hissed. 'Another few minutes and I was going to have to whip up my skirt and ask him to have a rummage round my cervix.'

'Where's Vic?'

'Through in the kitchen getting me some water.'

See. That's the kind of nice guy that he was. My taste in blokes was great. Just a little too inclusive.

'I owe you one, doll. Thanks. Talk about thinking on your feet.'

'You're welcome. But when Vic gets over the sheer terror of me dragging him in here, you're going to have to convince him that I'm not a complete loon. The poor man is traumatised. He just kept saying, "But I'm a plasterer! A plasterer!" while standing with his back against the wall, ready to dive low and catch if the baby shot out in front of him.'

The door opened and a sheepish Vic poked his head round. The look of relief on his face was palpable. 'Lou! You're here! Great. So I'll . . . I'll . . . just go and get a drink then. You'll be OK here, won't you? Oh, and the shop looks brilliant. Well done.'

With that, his gloriously toned, gym-buffed body disappeared out of the door and back into the main throng.

'Do you think he looks a bit like Tom Cruise?' I asked Lizzy.

She groaned. 'Really? It's the biggest night of your life, there are a hundred people out there, you narrowly avoided a Dodge City moment between your two men, I just threatened to show one of them my inners and all you can think about is whether or not he resembles Tom bloody Cruise? No! He looks like a bloke from Glasgow who is now traumatised and will never again go within a hundred yards of a pregnant woman.'

'But a bit like Tom Cruise?'

A black pillow with an image of Phil Collins on it came hurtling in my direction as she cracked and succumbed to the giggles. 'Oh God, bladder alert! I'm just nipping to the loo.'

'Lizzy, I hate to break it to you but these days you don't "nip" anywhere. You lumber. You waddle. You . . .'

'Can I remind you that I just saved your arse?'

'You're as graceful as a gazelle,' I told her, opening the door and holding it while she glided past. In the manner of a penguin-like gazelle.

I left her to it and headed back into the crowd, trying desperately not to let the 'three's a crowd' romantic issue spoil the night. I'd worry about it later. Dan had a couple of mates in tow, so no doubt they'd soon head off to a club, meanwhile Vic would be working next morning so he'd probably head off early too. And what were the chances of them meeting each other? Slim. This place was packed and neither were the type to mingle and strike up conversations with strangers. It would be fine. Fine. I took a deep breath and tried to calm myself with positive thoughts. Mr Patel swore by the power of a focused, positive mind. And anything that could make a 57-year-old man from deepest Bangladesh think he was Robbie Williams had to have something going for it.

So I told myself that the whole Vic/Dan thing was just a small hitch. Everything was going according to plan. All we needed now was Ginger to arrive. Snap. Snap. Photo for the press. A few more drinks. Then, hopefully, everyone would toddle off into the night raving about how CUT was the trendiest salon in town. The phones would be red hot. The appointment book would overload. I'd pay back the bank and all would be just fabulous. Fantastic.

The volume in the room turned up a little and I realised that people were getting a little more animated and there was a definite buzz going round the crowd. My heart throbbed just a little faster as I realised there could be several reasons for this.

The excitement about the salon was building to frenzied levels.

Mr Patel was now break-dancing in the manner of MC Hammer.

Dan and Vic had bumped into each other, had a quick chat, and were now duking it out over my honour.

A celebrity had arrived.

It was hard to miss the huge ginger mass that was heading this way from the door. Either someone had Dougal from *The Magic Roundabout* on their head or my other best friend had arrived.

'LOULOU BABY!!!!!!'

That would be my other best friend then. And holy Mariah Carey, she looked stunning.

Her hair fell down her back to her waist and was as wide as it was long. And hello boys, her boobs had come courtesy of either a plastic surgeon or one of those new Wonderbras, because they formed a gloriously sexy shelf which you could perch a pint on. They were barely contained by a chain-mail strapless, skintight minidress, which jangled as she walked. She looked every inch the star. A huge surge of pride welled up as I threw my arms around her and, at that moment, I wouldn't have minded if everyone else evaporated and just Lizzy, Ginger and I could kick off our sparkly high heels, kick back on the staffroom sofas and catch up properly for the first time in . . . Bloody hell, had it really been months since we spent any proper time together? Lizzy and I had travelled to all of Ginger's gigs when work/life/transport/dosh would allow, but an hour or so of snatched conversation before she got back in her van and headed off to the next venue just didn't cut it. Maybe after everyone had left we could head back home and have an all-night gossip catch-up.

A shriek came from behind me and I swayed to one side to avoid being trampled by an oncoming gazelle on a mission to hug the new arrival. There was no doubt that premature deafness and spending my senior years using the most powerful hearing aids on earth would be the price I would pay for being friends with Lizzy.

'Listen, I can't stay long because we have to be in Edinburgh by midnight. I've got a PA at Stomp!' Ginger blurted, grabbing two glasses of champagne from a nearby counter.

'PA?' I could almost hear Lizzy's mind whirring.

'Personal appearance,' Ginger clarified.

So much for our Friday Girls' Night in. But hey, she was here now and that's all that was important.

'So what do you want me to do?' she asked, placing an empty glass on the nearby counter.

'Do? Nothing. I just want you here, and maybe get a pic taken for the local paper.'

'So who's giving the speeches?'

No, no, no, no. No speeches. People came, saw the salon, had a drink, maybe a wee dance to the music, left. No speeches. Definitely no speeches. The thought of a room full of people all staring at me waiting for me to say something wonderfully witty filled me with horror. I even got nervous reading out jokes from Christmas crackers.

My blank expression obviously registered with her.

'Lou, you have to make this a night to remember. Give people something to talk about.'

'She's right,' Lizzy concurred. 'There should definitely be speeches.'

'Hang on, let me sort it.' Ginger spun on her six-inch steel heels, with only a slight wobble, and headed off in the direction of the DJ.

OK, I could handle this. If Ginger wanted to give a short speech to thank everyone for coming that was fine. Great. It would even raise the 'trendy' level a little, having a rising star officially opening the business. Yep, a speech could work. A short, light-hearted, dignified few words would be . . . oh bugger.

'Excuse me everyone!' A set of silver knickers flashed the whole salon as Ginger, the DJ's microphone in hand, clambered up on to the top of the reception desk. The crowd expressed their approval with a round of applause and a chorus of wolf whistles.

Ginger found her footing and gave a small bow, sending the audience into another round of appreciation.

'Thank you, thank you!' She grinned, completely unaware that the small bow had slightly dislodged the mighty bosoms and they were now making their own personal appearance.

Out of the corner of my eye I spotted Vic, utterly transfixed at the sight in front of him. I even had the cheek to be mildly irked by his reaction. I know. Pot. Kettle. Other boyfriend standing thirty feet away.

'I'd just like to say a few words on behalf of my gorgeous pal and owner of this lovely place, LouLouLouLouLou, because, er, she's a bit shy and I've always been the mouthy one.'

Everyone laughed as they warmed to her self-deprecating charm. OK, this would be fine. It would be.

'First of all, thank you all for coming.'

More whoops and hollers.

'On behalf of Lou –' she paused to give me an exaggerated wink '– I'd like to thank everyone who worked on CUT.'

Aw, that's nice. OK, stop there.

'So that means huge thanks to Josie!' Dear Lord, don't let her mention the loan.

Over at the window Josie took a bow before, mercifully, Ginger moved on.

'And my big shag of a brother – not to me, obviously 'cause that would be weird – Red!'

Out of the corner of my eye I could see that Red's face now matched his hair.

'And who else do I need to mention?' Ginger looked over to me. 'Parents? Boyfriend?' she said in an exaggerated stage whisper. I tried to shake my head with as little movement as possible, just enough to make her stop. All at once I had a horrible feeling that this was not going to end well.

Another stage whisper. 'What? Just boyfriend?'

Nooooooo. But clearly, I didn't have the bottle to say that out loud so she charged on regardless. 'Dan? Where are you Dan? Take a bow, you big suave devil.' Ginger tottered on her heels as she bent down, grabbed her glass and drained it.

Behind me Lizzy whispered, 'Oh shit.'

I, meanwhile, was a little preoccupied watching my life flashing in front of my eyes. Vic! Where was Vic? Dear God, please make him be in the toilet. Or outside recovering from his near brush with Lizzy's genital area. Or . . .

'Lou?'

Right next to me.

I slowly turned my head to the right to see a stricken face that definitely now looked absolutely nothing like Tom Cruise.

'I'm . . . I'm . . . sorry, Vic, but . . .'

He didn't even stop to hear the rest and I didn't blame him. Even I could hear that guilt oozed from every word.

The only blessing was that Dan was at the other end of the salon, down nearer the door, and was oblivious to the drama. Vic moved through the crowd, all of whom were still staring at Ginger, who had moved on to an impromptu a cappella rendition of her new song.

The shop. The gathering. My best friend up there belting her heart out. Sure, the half-visible knockers detracted slightly from the ambience but nevertheless this would have been a truly special moment in my life if it wasn't for the fact that my stomach was now somewhere around my knees and I felt like a complete cow. Suddenly the whole double-date thing didn't seem like quite the great idea that it had been an hour ago.

'I should go after . . .' Lizzy's arm shot out and grabbed mine, holding me back. 'No, Lizzy, I should. I need to explain to him.'

I had to get to him before he left. Right now he was probably shocked, but perhaps anger hadn't set in yet and there was still time to explain and talk to him before he escalated to completely furious or irrevocably hurt.

He was twenty feet from the door now. Fifteen. I could still get to him. The whole scene was playing out like slow motion as he got to ten feet, eight . . .

Now he was right next to Dan. Right next to Dan. Oh shit, he was right next to Dan.

The push took everyone by surprise, most of all Dan who was now moving speedily in an unexpected direction with an expression that sat somewhere between stunned, confused and totally pissed off.

Drinks flew. The people that Dan crashed into shouted their outrage. Some pushed back. Dan's friends stepped in. The jostling escalated. Oh crap, this couldn't get any worse. The only blessing was that Vic hadn't stuck around and was now out of the door.

Like a rabbit in the headlights, I completely froze. Rushing towards the mêlée wouldn't solve anything, but someone had to stop it. It was getting worse now, more and more people getting involved, while Ginger carried on singing, one glass of champagne past the point of oblivion.

My whole night was going to hell in an elevator and it was all my fault and I had no idea how to stop it. Suddenly, like a red flash of middle-aged superhero, Josie realised what was going on behind her and turned, inserted two fingers in her mouth and gave out the most deafening whistle I'd ever heard. The result was twofold. On the floor, the jostling and fighting stopped. On top of the reception desk, Ginger, momentarily disorientated by the interruption swayed precariously forwards. Red reached out to steady her, saving her from a repeat performance of the body surfing from *Top of the Pops*.

Meanwhile, Josie grabbed Dan and one of his pals and pushed them towards the door. Dan knew better than to argue. He didn't even turn around, just stormed out, no doubt furious that his impeccably pressed suit was now sporting a large purple damp patch after a meeting with a Dubonnet and blackcurrant.

As he went through the door, I saw him turn to the side. He'd changed his mind. He was going to come back and look for me, object to being huckled out for something that clearly wasn't his fault.

I'd apologise, we'd laugh, it would all be forgotten and he would never find out who the weird guy that sent him sprawling was. It would all blow over. But . . .

No. Just when the gods had obviously decided that this wasn't enough of a roaring fuck-up for one night, I realised that Dan had paused to let in two new attendees to the soiree.

Maw and Paw Cairney had joined the party. I felt Lizzy's hand tighten even more around mine, her support clear with just that little gesture.

'What are my parents doing here? How did they even know about this?' Not telling them had been deliberate. Not particularly charitable, but deliberate. For a start, neither of them had been in the least interested in what I was doing. And, on top of that, the combination of my dad and free drink could only lead to disaster and, let's face it, I was managing to attract that without any help. Oh fuck, this night definitely could not get any worse now. It couldn't.

It could. My mum and dad were making a beeline for me and there was nowhere to hide. Not that there was any huge amount of bad feeling between us. In fact, the opposite was true. Whereas some parents might have been devastated that their sixteen-year-old had moved out, it transpired that mine were actually pretty pleased. My dad was thrilled that he had my mother's complete devotion, he didn't have to fork out a penny on supporting his pesky offspring and they had complete freedom to up sticks and go for all the romantic weekends they could muster. My mother was now free to devote herself entirely to her husband and didn't have to deal with another female who patently disapproved of how she chose to live her life. And me? Well, at least I wasn't hanging around where I wasn't wanted. I occasionally popped back for birthdays and the occasional impromptu visit – although that backfired at Christmas because they rented a chalet in the Alps and took off for a week and forgot to tell me. I only got back to Josie's in time for a handful of Brussels sprouts and three chipolatas.

'Well done, Lou. You've done a fantastic job here.' Oh shit, was she being sarcastic? Did she know we'd committed fraud with her bank book? Was she about to deliver a sucker punch and call in the serious crime squad?

'Thanks, Mum.' I gave her an uncomfortable hug, before something blatantly obvious convinced me she was serious – my dad looked completely pissed off. God, he hated not being the centre of attention. As quickly as I realised it, my mum spotted it too.

'I think,' she blurted, 'that you definitely got your dad's creativity and entrepreneurial side.'

And there it was. Of course. All this was down to his brilliance. It had to be. I should have realised it before now.

I'll never know how I would have reacted because right at that moment events were taken out of my hands.

'Della, good manners has always stopped me saying this, but you're a complete arse to that girl.' Yes, Josie had something to say and she wouldn't be stopped. 'And, as for you, sunshine –' she gave my dad her stare of death '– this has absolutely fuck all to do with you. Nothing. That girl hasn't inherited a single one of your genes because if she had she'd be a selfish, self-centred cow with an ego the size of the roundabout at the end of the High Street. Everyone clear? Good. Now, Lou, I believe Lizzy needs a wee sit down in the staffroom because – sorry, Liz, don't take offence – she's looking a bit strange.'

Just as Josie said it, I felt Lizzy's hand tighten even more on mine.

Thank you, God, for giving me pregnant pals to act as decoys in time of family strife.

'Lou, I'm . . .' Lizzy stuttered.

Here for you? Coming with you? Ready and waiting with love and support in your hour of need? Well, this was definitely one of those and . . . Ouch! The hand that held mine suddenly spun me round and there was a dramatic shriek to go with it.

Lizzy was bent over double now, clutching her side, her face disturbingly close to the shade of Josie's salon gowns.

'Lizzy!' I gasped, falling to my knees in front of her, automatically pushing her hair back from her face. 'What is it? Oh shit, are you OK?'

In hindsight, it wasn't one of my more intelligent moments.

'No, you daft boot,' she half wailed, half screeched. 'Get. Me. To. The. Hospital. Or. I'm Giving. Birth. On. Your. New. Floor.'

As I screamed for help in a manner that would make my

97

sweating, heavy-breathing friend incredibly proud, I realised that there was one inescapable conclusion.

People were definitely going to have something to talk about tomorrow.

Fifteen

Lou

The St Kentigern Hotel, Glasgow. Saturday morning, 1 am

'Sometimes I wish I could go right back to that moment,' Lizzy said wistfully.

I recoiled in horror. 'What? When your waters broke all over my floor and you managed – by a stroke of sheer genius – to ruin my dad's new canvas shoes?'

'Don't know what he was thinking – fucking espadrilles at his age,' Ginger mused, quite correctly.

'No, just to that time in general,' Lizzy said and, despite the fact that we were over a decade down the line, there was still a sadness in her voice. 'When I knew nothing about what was going to happen. I was clueless, I really was. There hadn't been any signs. Adam was behaving completely normally. Nothing made me suspicious at all. I know you find that hard to believe but I honestly didn't see it coming.'

'Don't beat yourself up, honey,' I told her. 'None of us did.'

'Well—' Ginger spoke and I cut her off with a swift 'Shut up or I'll tell the barman to stop serving you.'

And as if by magic, she was silent.

'OK, you're forgiven,' I told her. 'Order up another round and I'll be back in a minute. Just need to phone home and check in.'

'Give them our love,' Ginger said as I slipped out of the booth.

As I stepped outside the front doors, the cold air and silence were a relief after the heat and noise of the bar. The concierge asked if I wanted a cab. 'Thanks, but I'm just out to make a quick call,' I said, holding up my phone as evidence and earning another friendly smile in response.

I held down the H key on my BlackBerry and it rang almost immediately. One ring. Two rings. Three. I realised exactly how tonight had played out at home. Cassie had begged her dad to let her watch a movie on the TV in our room, they'd snuggled up and before they'd got to the bit where the large green ogre won the day, they'd both fallen asleep and were now cuddled up, snoring peacefully. I had a sudden longing to be there with them.

'Hi.' I heard my own voice. 'Sorry we can't answer. Please leave a message and we'll get back to you.'

'Hey, it's just me. I miss you guys. Hope—'

A couple of clicks cut into my message, followed by a sleepy 'Hello.'

'I'm guessing you fell asleep. *Shrek 2*?' I asked softly. He would hear the smile in my voice.

'*The Princess Diaries*. It's my choice tomorrow night and I've got *Monsters, Inc.* all lined up and ready. How you doing? Having a good night?'

'Really good. Reminiscing.'

'Oh God, drunk women reminiscing. Suddenly *The Princess Diaries* seems like the better deal. I thought you lot only talked about celebrities and shopping.'

'Nope, we just tell you that so you won't get insecure and think we're talking about you.'

He laughed, setting off another pang of homesickness. I knew it was ridiculous. I was the very woman who would shout at the telly when reality TV contestants cried because they missed their mothers after they'd been away from home for an hour and a half.

'I miss you,' he murmured.

'I miss you too.'

There was a pause. 'Have you asked them yet?'

'No, not yet. Hasn't been the right moment. But I will . . .'

'OK, honey. Sure you're OK?'

'I'm sure.'

'Then, go back to the party. I'll tell Cassie you called in the morning.'

'Tell her I love her.'

'I will.'

Sixteen

Lou

1996 – Aged 26

'Avril, can you do Stacey's shampoo up at the basins, then go clear up the staffroom, then come back and sort out the roller drawers, please?'

My little cousin adopted the kind of sneer that lead singer from Oasis would be proud of as she turned on her bright-pink, rubber-soled platforms, flicked back her black, bottom-skimming ponytail and strutted off in her leopard-print Lycra leggings.

Up at the sinks, I heard her greet one of our regulars with the kind of superior customer service I'd come to expect. 'Right, Fatty, budge up and tip your head back and, no, I don't care if you've got any holidays booked.'

'Sorry, Stacey!' I yelled. 'I fire her every week but she just keeps coming back.'

'Fatty' was actually a 6-foot, 130lb model who wore a size 8 and was one of my regular band of customers.

'Don't worry, Lou, I'm kind of getting used to her. And

having her wash my hair saves me on tips because she gets nothing.' Stacey's giggle at the end of the sentence was cut short by the sound of a blast of running water and a short yelp. That would be Avril's revenge then.

There were definitely pros and cons to employing a relative. Josie's daughter, Avril, had come to work for me the day after she'd been asked to leave school, after pointing out to the headmaster that he was a tosser. I think the exact words she used were, 'baldy, idiotic, sexist, misogynistic, narcissistic tosser'. Which, on the bright side, at least showed that she'd been paying attention in English and had a vocabulary that consisted of impressive words that could be thrown out while in the midst of an antagonistic confrontation.

In the three months that she'd been here the cons had been many. She was irreverent, moody, ungrateful, rude and dressed like the sixth member of that new band, the Spice Girls – Stroppy Spice.

But strangely, on the pros side, the regulars had come to think her dry bitchiness was hilarious and I hadn't lost a client yet. And much as she moaned, she also worked harder than any other member of staff and was – to her horror – starting to show a talent for make-up at the weekly model nights we ran as part of the staff training schedule. Only the week before, she'd given Stacey a retro, Bowie-inspired glamour look, using metallics on her eyes, cheeks and lips. The result had been stunning.

Plus, Josie was really grateful that I'd given her daughter a break and I figured that it was the least I could do, especially when Avril announced that her back-up career plan was 'missionary work in Amazon region or having a boob job and becoming a stripper'.

I picked up a round brush and turned my attention back to Mrs Marshall. I felt eternally lucky to have kept all my clients from the old days and, on top of that, our late-night and Sunday opening, student discounts, press adverts, and a leaflet campaign, which wore out my favourite trainers delivering flyers to every house and business in the town, had resulted in a full appointment book and an eclectic new clientele that crossed the demographics. So far today we'd had four senior citizens who were going off to Magaluf for a fortnight, a wedding party, a menagerie of other females aged from twelve to eighty, a local vicar and the entire under-nineteens town football team. For the purposes of staff morale, I chose to overlook the fact that I caught Avril snogging one of them in the fire escape just after they arrived, and another in the gents' toilets just before they left. I was hardly in a position to judge. The debacle of the opening night had left indelible scars on my soul (and at least a dozen heel imprints on the reception desk from Ginger's stilettos).

'Right we're off then. Are you sure you don't want us to keep you a seat at the pub?' Angie asked as she trooped towards the door with Wendy, Pam, Rosie and the juniors we'd taken on when Rosie and Angie got promoted to stylists.

'No, I'm fine, honestly. I've got plans for tonight.'

'She's lying,' Avril shouted from the basins. 'She's going to go home alone, eat a microwave meal and spend all night watching tapes of Bruce Willis movies. She needs help.'

'Have you got a staple gun?' Mrs Marshall interrupted.

'Erm, somewhere. Why?'

'Because you should use it on that lassie's mouth,' she replied with an indignant purse of the lips. That was loyalty for you.

As the others left, I turned my attention back to my client. 'Are you sure you want to stick with the Rachel, Mrs Marshall?'

A year before, she had claimed that Mr Marshall had visited from the afterlife, told her she should watch *Friends*, adopt Rachel's hairstyle and visit New York to find his replacement. He'd been proven right when she came back with a 74-year-old retired sailor called Hank. They now had a poodle called Jennifer Aniston in tribute to the woman who helped bring them together.

By the time Stacey and Mrs Marshall had been dispatched off with gleaming bouncy locks, it was after eight when Avril and I pulled the door closed behind us.

'You coming over to our house?' she asked without looking up from the notes that she was counting out of her pay packet.

'Are you asking because you want my company for the night or because you want a lift home?'

'Lift home.'

And the Oscar for the best act of brutal honesty goes to Avril Cairney.

'What were you doing when God gave out tact and diplomacy?' I asked, trying my hardest not to grin as I fiddled with the lock on my silver Mazda 626. It was my one indulgence. I may live in a flat with paper-thin walls in a building that smelled of dental fluids, but at least I had a snazzy car.

'I was in the queue for good looks and superior wit,' she said with a flash of perfect white teeth. I was still grinning when I hugged her ten minutes later and watched as she clambered out of the passenger seat and levitated up the garden path on those platforms.

Josie appeared at the window and waved and I blew her a kiss. As I slipped into first gear and pulled away, I realised that all I wanted to do was go home, pull the TV into the bathroom, and lie in the bath watching educational documentaries. Oh OK, watching Bruce Willis movies. So the truth in Avril's comment had stung a little but there was no denying that *Die Hard 2* was a classic.

And anyway, what did I care? I was a grown woman, I'd built up a successful business, and sure, the work/life balance might be a little off at the moment but that wasn't a priority.

What did it matter if the most important things in my life were a shop and an action hero with a receding hairline? There would be plenty of time for a social life and other stuff later.

I parked outside my flat and started up the stairs. I'd phone Ginger. I'd prove I wasn't completely antisocial by phoning a friend. On a Friday night. While I was in the bath. With a movie on in the background. Not that I thought for a moment that she'd be home. Since she married Ike her schedule had got busier than ever, especially since she was now living in London, had semi-retired from the music industry and diversified into band management. She claimed that she didn't mind that she'd never achieved super-stardom but I wasn't sure that was true. Bluff and bravado had always been the mainstays of Ginger's personality.

I missed her.

However, I'd be forever grateful that her last official act as a rock star had been to approach Gary Collins at the televised BRIT Awards just as his name was called out as a nominee in the category of band of the year and proceed to pour a Jack Daniel's and Coke over his head. As far as I was concerned that was an act of heroism and solidarity that warranted the government declaring a National Ginger Day.

I parked the car outside the flat, ignoring the posse of teenagers sitting on the wall at the corner of the street belting out a drunken chorus of 'Don't Look Back in Anger'. The cider bottles they used as percussion instruments to accompany the chorus was a nice touch.

Lugging my weary body up the stairs, I had only three things on my mind. Bath. Bruce. Bed. Bath. Bruce. Bed. Bath. Bruce . . .

As quietly as possible, I slid my key in the lock, turned it, pushed the door. Almost there. Almost. But not quite.

The door to the flat next door swung open and there stood

Lizzy, balancing a sleeping two-year-old on the large bump that once again protruded from her shocking-pink jumper and lime-green jeans. If we had our time again I'd have made her pay attention back in social sciences class when the teacher explained the concept of contraception. And colour co-ordination.

'When was the last time you had sex?' she blurted.

Out of all the things I could possibly have expected her to say at that moment, I must confess that wasn't one of them.

'Can I have a multiple choice?' I asked hopefully.

'I'm serious, Lou. When was the last time you had an earth-shattering experience with a male?'

I knew the answer. I did. 'Erm, it was . . .'

'A male that wasn't Bruce Willis.'

I slumped as the wind was removed from my sails. 'Oh. Dunno.'

'Then we're going out tonight. Me and you. Adam will babysit and you and I are going to hit the town!'

I was torn between horror at the prospect of my cosy night in being ruined, and horror that a six-month pregnant mother of a toddler had more energy than I.

'Lizzy, I'm knackered and I just want to . . .'

'I don't care. This is for your own good. It's Friday night, Lou, and we haven't been out in months. What happened to Girls' Night? Much as I love the idea that since you are likely to stay single for the rest of your life, you'll probably die rich and leave your entire fortune to your god-daughter –' she motioned to the sleeping bundle in her arms '– I refuse to let you neglect your social needs any longer. So we're going out and arguments are futile. Be ready in half an hour or I'm breaking the door down.'

'But you've got a key,' I replied for reasons that seemed important in that moment.

'I was going for drama,' she said with a grin. 'Too much?'

I nodded. Lizzy on the rampage and dragging me out against my will on a Friday night was definitely too much. There had to be a way out of this. I needed a decoy. Or an excuse. Or someone to rescue me.

Where was Bruce bloody Willis when I needed him?

Seventeen

'Is there anyone in here over twenty-one?' I shouted into Lizzy's ear as we crossed the crowded floor at the Spotlight. I could see where the name came from. The dark walls were carved and painted to give the impression of chiselled granite, which glinted as the massive lighting rigs bounced different colours off the surface. It was a fairly new nightclub in the neighbouring town of Paisley and appeared to be populated solely by boys who looked like that Australian singer Peter Andre, and girls who looked like Avril. In my black jeans and shirt I felt decidedly overaged and under-Lycra'd.

'S'cuse me, are you a bouncer?' an obviously inebriated young lady with a broad Glaswegian accent slurred in my direction. 'Because that guy over there is acting like a fanny and I want him put oot.'

Right then. 'Bad to worse' was the moment's cliché of choice.

'I'll get to him in a minute,' I told her. 'I just have to go talk to two fannies over there first.'

'Aye, right then,' she slurred and tottered off on her white high heels in the direction of the toilets.

Great. Smashing. Couldn't be having a better time.

The Spotlight had been open for about six months and this was the first time we'd actually made it there. How things change. There was a time when there wasn't a nightclub within a thirty-mile radius that we weren't intimately familiar with. Lizzy and I made it to the bar and I ordered a Bloody Mary and a Virgin Mary and wondered how long I'd have to stay there before Lizzy would concede that now I'd been out socialising, so was therefore no longer in danger of ending my life as a decrepit old lady whose only friend was the bloke behind the counter in the Blockbuster video store.

I knocked back a healthy measure of my deep red cocktail and felt the icy buzz send tingles to my brain. Maybe I needed this. Maybe it wouldn't be too bad after all. Just at that – in what had to be the most radical music mix in documented history – the DJ slid from 'Firestarter' by the Prodigy to Gina G's 'Ooh Aah, Just a Little Bit'. Something inside me died.

'Oh, I love this song,' Lizzy screeched. 'Come on, let's dance.'

She pulled me by the hand and whipped me over to the dance floor, where I edged into the darkest corner. There are just some things that no one else should ever see and a female bouncer and a six-month pregnant woman in a neon-green dress, dancing to the most irritating song of 1996 is one of them.

It was a giddy relief when there was no more and we could slink back to where we'd left our drinks. I was just grateful that she hadn't felt her usual non-pregnancy urge to dance on a raised surface. Sensible, mature Lizzy may be less outrageous than young, crazy, accident-prone Lizzy, but at least we were less likely to end the night in A&E.

I downed my Bloody Mary and ordered another, just as Lizzy was possessed by the spirit of some demented God of match-making.

110

'What about him over there?' she asked, pointing at a tall, grey-haired guy standing at the other end of the bar.

'Too old. And I think he's the toilet attendant so he'll work nights and we'd never get to see each other. Stop trying to fix me up.'

I honestly meant it. There was not one iota of me that had any desire for a relationship. Not one. I truly couldn't see the point. I'd learned my lesson. When I was a teenager, I'd accepted the fact that I was the most inflexible gymnast of modern times, so I gave up gymnastics. A few years later, I realised that my paintings looked like a cat had vomited on my canvas, so I gave up art. Several wrecked relationships and a national hit record that paid testimony to my general crapness in romantic relationships with the opposite sex had taught me a lesson that I couldn't ignore.

Unfortunately Lizzy hadn't got the memo.

Like a submarine periscope surveying the horizon, her head swivelled in the other direction.

'He's cute. What about that guy there? The one in the black shirt?'

'Lizzy, will you stop! I've already told you that the last thing I need right now is a boyfriend. And even if I did, there's far more chance of me meeting a guy in the salon than there is of me picking up anyone decent in a nightclub. Meeting anything more than a one-night stand in a club never happens. Never. So stop . . . Actually he is quite cute.'

My body automatically detached from my brain as I involuntarily straightened up, shook out my hair and yes, I'm ashamed to say, the breasts did swell slightly in his direction. Traitors.

So much for learning lessons.

'Go chat or wait till he spots us?' Lizzy asked in the voice of a secret agent.

'Wait,' I answered. I may be out of practice but I wasn't

about to risk serial humiliation by charging on over there and striking up a conversation until I'd observed him for a little longer. First impressions were impressive though.

Expensive-looking black shirt. Dark jeans. Brown hair, short at the back, spiked up on top. No wedding ring. Broad shoulders. A little on the short side, maybe five foot ten, but I could live without high heels. It worked for Nicole Kidman and Tom Cruise.

Definitely a possible.

Just as I concluded my in-depth analysis of the subject, he laughed at something his friend said and, as he turned his head, caught my eye and made no move to look away.

'Shit, he can see me looking!' I hissed, to a yelp of hilarity from my alleged friend.

'Oh no! Now he might realise that you actually like the look of him and he might even come over here and ask you to dance and that would be the worst possible outcome!' The amused sarcasm dripped from every word.

'You're not helping me here,' I replied tersely, feeling my toes curl with the discomfort. Stick me behind any seated guy and put a comb and scissors in my hand and I feel absolutely at ease. Stick me in a Wonderbra in a nightclub and put a Bloody Mary in my hand and I ding the bell at the very top of the self-conscious scale.

This was excruciating.

The guy leaned over and whispered something to his friend, who followed his gaze over to Lizzy and me, then started towards us.

'Lizzy, don't turn around but they're on their way over.'

'Why can't I turn around?'

'Because they'll see that bump and head for the hills.'

'Good point. I'll keep it out of the way until it's too late for him to change course.'

'Excuse me, haven't we met?'

I was momentarily confused by the situation. Mr Cute Dark Shirt was still at least twenty feet away and yet I was hearing the oldest chat-up line in the book.

'Behind you.' Lizzy gesticulated over my shoulder and I turned to see a tall guy in a sharp black suit and white shirt, left open at the neck. His blond hair fell just past his collar at the back, shorter and swept back at the sides, framing a square jaw with a hint of stubble which took the edge off his smoothness.

'Pardon?' I said, trying and failing not to show irritation at the interruption.

'Haven't we . . .'

'Actually I got that bit. No, I don't think so.'

Dear God, was that the best he could do? Any minute now he'd follow it up with 'Do you come here often?' and we'd have to report him for crimes against chat-up originality.

'We have,' he continued. I felt my irritation rise as, out of the corner of my eye I saw the bloke from the other side of the bar spot me speaking to another guy and halt in his tracks. Nooooo. Don't stop. Come over. Please don't stop.

'You're the girl from the hairdresser's.'

I vaguely registered that perhaps this wasn't just an empty chat-up speech, but I was too busy focusing on the lost opportunity to respond. Right on cue, the other guy shrugged, turned and headed back off in the other direction.

Great. The first time in many months that my ovaries have shown the smallest sign of a flutter and the operation was hijacked before it could even get off the ground.

'The hair salon in Weirbank.'

Was he still talking? Really?

There was no other option but to engage.

'Sorry? I mean, yes, I work there but I don't think we've ever met.'

Even in the dim lights of the club I could see that his eyes had a cute glint. Blue. No, wait, green. No, blue. Green. Could someone not switch off those bloody disco lights so that I could get a decent look at him? He was leaning in closer now. Not in a creepy invasion of the personal space way but friendly. Casual.

'I was at the opening night of CUT. It was . . . er . . . eventful.' At that his face broke into what might just have been the most irresistibly contagious grin I'd ever encountered.

Two things happened. The breasts got on board and subtly re-swelled in this new direction and inside my head I heard a definite voice saying, 'Oh, you're so mine.' Houston, we have take-off.

'I was with Dan. Dan Hodges.'

Mission abort! Mission abort!

'Ah,' was my considered, eloquent reply.

'I think you were seeing him at the time,' he continued

There was no point in sugar-coating or backtracking.

'I was. Right up until the part where he got thumped. I look forward to living down the humiliation somewhere around middle age. Or if I get hit by a truck and develop amnesia.'

What was I talking about? Mouth, desist and disengage immediately! Being caught off guard or pushed into a nervous situation always led to an outpouring of verbal tosh.

'Poor guy never recovered. He became a Buddhist and went to find himself in Nepal,' cute guy added.

I was momentarily speechless again, until the grin reappeared and I realised he was joking.

'Actually he moved to Thomas Cook and works the charter service from Manchester to Malaga.'

It was hard not to laugh, especially with Lizzy giggling away beside me.

'I'm glad. He'd never have been able to keep up his blond highlights in Nepal.'

114

It was his turn to laugh, then, 'Sorry, I should have introduced myself. I'm Marc Cheyne. And you're Lou?'

His expression made it clear that he was raking up information from the past.

I nodded. 'And this is Lizzy.' In a gesture that seemed a bit out of place given the surroundings, he reached out and shook her hand.

'When's the baby due?'

'Twelve weeks.'

'Excellent. Didn't you go into labour that night just after the fight broke up? I remember the paramedics carting you out.'

Lizzy nodded. 'Yep, it was an evening of dignity all round.'

It suddenly struck me that this guy, cute though he was, was here alone. Wasn't that a bit creepy? Even more so since he looked like he was in his early thirties and therefore a good decade older than the club's regular clientele.

Urgh, he was obviously a lounge lizard, out on the pull, looking to get his leg over. In fact he was probably married too. Just because he didn't wear a ring didn't mean he was single. He probably took it off. Oh, I had him sussed, yet I was slightly disconcerted to realise that as far as my lust genes were concerned, none of these facts outweighed the cute grin and the twinkly eyes. Thank God I was sober enough to read this situation and make sensible decisions. Lust or no lust, I wasn't going anywhere with a creepy guy who stalked out nightclubs alone looking for action.

'Are you here with friends?' I heard Lizzy asking.

Damn, why hadn't I thought of that?

'No . . .'

Hah! I was right! A lounge lizard on the prowl! He was probably a walking mass of STDs.

'I'm the manager here. That's how I knew Dan. He used to come in here with his mates and they invited me along that night.'

'I just have to nip to the loo,' Lizzy interjected. 'It's the bladder. Mind of its own.'

At that moment the music did a complete change of direction yet again and suddenly the Spice Girls were telling me what I really, really wanted. I didn't need a description.

'So are you still with that other guy?'

I shook my head. 'No. Public humiliation has a bit of a vanishing effect on some people.'

He nodded with mock seriousness. 'Yeah, some folk are just oversensitive like that.'

There was a pause as we both stood and stared at each other with borderline stupid grins on our faces.

'So . . .' he repeated.

I waited for what I dearly hoped was coming.

'Would you like to have dinner with me next night I have off?'

Bingo!

'No.' I shook my head regretfully. 'I'm really sorry but I can't.'

Somewhere deep inside me, parts of my anatomy were threatening to form a picket line for improved working conditions.

The poor guy looked mortified. 'OK. Well. It was good to see you again.' He started to back away, but he only made it about six inches before I blurted, 'Sorry, but I had an argument with Lizzy earlier and my point was that you never meet anyone decent in a club. But if you come to the shop one day and ask me nicely, I might say yes,' I said.

'You might say yes?' he repeated archly.

'I might.'

Oh, the eyes were crinkling again and there were teeth – gorgeous, straight, white perfect teeth.

'Then I might just do that.'

Eighteen

Lou

The St Kentigern Hotel, Glasgow. Saturday morning, 1.30 am

'Commitment, compatibility and trust,' Lizzy was saying as I slid back into my chair.

Ginger groaned. 'Jesus, you sound like an advert for Hallmark.'

'What have I missed?' I asked, puzzled.

'I just made the fatal mistake of asking Barbara Cartland here what she thought were the most important things in a relationship. She didn't mention sex once so I've disowned her. She's dead to me now.'

'Ignore her, Lou,' Lizzy said dismissively. 'OK, it's your turn. What do you think?'

'Luck,' I said. I really believed that good relationships were all down to luck. I knew too many couples who seemed perfect for each other, yet had ended up in a screaming match with a divorce lawyer on speed-dial.

'What else. Come on. What advice would you give Cassie about finding the right relationship?'

117

I tried to ignore the twisting sensation in my gut. Her question threw up a whole new spectrum of discussion but I wasn't going to go there. Not now. Not at 2 am, in a crowded bar in the middle of Glasgow. Instead I took a deep breath and thought about my answer. I was pretty sure that luck made a good relationship, but after growing up with Dave and Della, I had a good idea on how to avoid the bad. I ticked the points off on my fingers as I said them.

'Right then – not that I've given this much thought but . . .'

1. *Never forget who you are.*
2. *Compromise is a good thing. Agreeing to everything he says/ wants/does is not.*
3. *Never be so blinded by adoration that you allow yourself to be treated badly or used as a doormat/chauffeur/ housekeeper.*
4. *If he doesn't want you to have friends or interests outside of your relationship, this doesn't mean he adores you so much that he wants you all to himself. It means he's a narcissistic control freak who should be chucked.*
5. *Your opinion is just as valid as his.*
6. *He's not always right.*
7. *Or in charge.*
8. *When you have children, they become the most important thing in your life. If he disagrees with being demoted, that's his problem not yours.*
9. *Negative behaviour can never be justified by him swearing undying devotion and repeatedly telling you that you're the love of his life. People also swear undying love for cars/ money/pets/serial killers on death row.*
10. *If any of these behaviour patterns ring a bell, it's time to leave.*

Ginger and Lizzy sat open mouthed for a few moments as they absorbed this.

'Glad you haven't given it much thought then,' Ginger eventually said with playful sarcasm.

Thought? I'd given it plenty over the years. Just a shame I didn't always practise what I preached.

Nineteen

Lou

1997 – Aged 27

'Hi, honey, I'm home!' My sing-song joviality was borrowed for the occasion from American sitcoms of the 1950s. Or anything starring Doris Day.

The truth was that I was exhausted. Knackered. Fit for lying down and slipping into a self-imposed coma until it was time to get up on Monday morning and do it all again. And strictly speaking I wasn't actually home.

'Home' was still a flat above the dentist's next to a familiar mother of two whose children had inherited her capacity for shrieking. It had taken a bit of persuasion for me to accept Marc's key and agree to move in with him for most of the week. Actually, all of the week. I couldn't remember the last time that I'd stayed over at my own home, but that didn't mean that I was ready to give it up. Not yet. Despite the fact that Marc had been saying for months that it made absolutely no sense for both of us to be paying rent, the very thought of giving up the flat made my teeth grind. I still hadn't cut the umbilical cord to my single, independent life, but I'd stretched it a bit and was working on a full-scale detachment.

And besides, not only was Marc's apartment quiet and free from the heady aroma of disinfectant and mouthwash, but it was in a gorgeous Georgian townhouse in the West End of Glasgow, with huge sash windows and the swankiest kitchen I'd ever seen. The white voile curtains fell from just below the ornate coving to the deep mahogany floor and, continuing the theme, the bedroom was a light, enticing collision of mirrored furniture, a huge white wooden bed, a solid wood floor and a stereo system that took up one whole wall. But the best thing about it was that it was across the road from a cinema so there wasn't a new release in the last year that I hadn't seen. Four times, in the case of *The Full Monty*. And me and my bag of Pick 'n' Mix had practically taken up residence when *Armageddon* came out. No, I didn't want to miss a thing.

'Hey. Good day?' Marc came towards me with two glasses of white wine in his hand. The whole wine drinking thing was new to me but I was doing my best to acquire a taste for it. According to Marc and all his nightclub buddies, it was more sophisticated than double vodkas and orange with a splash of lime and a decorative feast of cherries, lemons and a plastic monkey hanging off the side. Personally, I wasn't convinced. As far as I was concerned, if a bottle didn't come with a screwtop then it wasn't worth having.

'Yeah, it was fine. Busy. Knackered now though. Just want to slouch out, order in Chinese and watch *The X-files*. What time are you going out to work?'

He shook his head and broke into a languid grin. 'I'm not.'

'What?' My eyebrows rose straight up to their 'suspicious' setting. Marc always went to work on a Friday night. Always. In fact, other than last year when we went to Ibiza for a fortnight, I'd never known him to take a weekend night off.

Thursday to Sunday was when the club was busiest so he had to make sure he was there. On top of that, he was always in the club on those afternoons too, clearing up from the night before and getting ready to reopen. I'd come to realise that the job of a nightclub manager may seem glamorous, but in reality it was eighty-five per cent slog, ten per cent danger, and five per cent strolling around like you were the dog's bollocks.

In a strange way, the conflicting work schedules were one of the reasons why our relationship worked so well. By the time I closed up the shop on a Friday or Saturday night all I wanted to do was come home and crash out (or lately, nip over to the Cinemax for a solo encounter with *Titanic*, but I kept that act of solitary saddo behaviour to myself).

Tonight was one of those Fridays and the only thing I wanted to party with was a large bag of cheese and onion crisps and the remote control for the TV. Lizzy and I kept promising to reinstate our weekly meeting but to be honest I was glad that her two toddlers were keeping her too busy to get out. The last thing I felt like was hitting the town these days. If there was such a thing as a work/life balance I was wobbling like a workaholic elephant standing on one leg. On a skateboard.

I dropped my bag and waited for him to explain why he wasn't going to work. Was it my imagination, or was he looking a bit sheepish? Bloody hell, he'd been fired. Or he was having an affair. Or he was sick. That was it! He had succumbed to the recent wave of mad cow disease! But then he looked perfectly healthy, so maybe not. There was definitely something suspicious going on though. I made a silent vow to deploy tactics learned from watching the finest legal brains on *L.A. Law* to get to the bottom of it. Or I could just forget my propensity for drama and panic and wait until he explained.

122

As if reading my mind, he leaned over, slid one arm around my waist and murmured in my ear, 'Since it's your birthday tomorrow I just thought I'd take the night off and take you out somewhere special.'

Thankfully, my groan was halted by the tongue that was exploring the depths of my tonsil area. Eventually he came up for breath.

'I like you, do you know that?' he whispered as his hand went up the back of my T-shirt and he unhooked my bra like a pro.

'Like?' I murmured, buying into a dialogue we often played with – usually right before foreplay or right after a disagreement. I was thinking this was definitely the former. Was it wrong that even right at that moment I'd still swap this encounter for a cheesy snack and an episode of *The X-Files*? It had been a long week.

'OK, maybe more than like,' he replied.

There was a pause while he pulled my T-shirt over my head and tossed it over the back of the couch. Must retrieve it before it's found by the cleaning lady who comes in for two hours every Monday morning. She already finds it difficult to disguise her blatant resentment that a woman has moved into what she considers to be Marc's bachelor pad. If it wasn't for an age difference of thirty-five years, I'd suspect she was there to perform duties that were definitely outwith her job description.

'Just maybe?' I still played along, my hand tugging on his belt. I felt like I had to go with it. The guy had taken the night off just for me, we were alone, he was clearly horny. Whether I felt like a bout of the naked hokey-cokey or not, to refuse would have been rude given that he had obviously planned this surprise for me. And besides, he seemed to think I was OK in the sex department and the scars from my first encounter made me eternally grateful for the approval and

123

keen to show that I could maintain these standards of orgasmic adequacy.

The cheesy puffs, *L.A. Law*, Mulder and Scully would just have to wait. I pushed my hands deeper into his hair and pulled his face towards me.

'OK, I love you,' he whispered, before sliding further downwards and flicking his tongue against an erect nipple.

'Then you can carry on doing that for at least another ten minutes,' I told him in my very best provocative voice. 'Because I love you too.'

We had been four weeks into the relationship when he had completely astounded me by telling me that he loved me. It should have seemed strange but it didn't – especially because I knew even then that I was crazy-ass in love with him too.

This put everything that had come before it into perspective. This was what love felt like.

With an impressive display of athletic strength, he lifted me up, carried me over to the couch, and – without breaking mouth-to-nipple contact – followed me down and proceeded to ravish me.

Oh, and it took a lot longer than ten minutes.

If only Gary Wanker Collins could see me now.

Twenty

I pulled at the skirt of my little black dress as we climbed the steps to the restaurant, trying my best to avoid flashing my knickers, while ignoring the internal screams of my swollen feet. I had pulled out a pair of jeans and my favourite smart-but-comfy boots, but Marc had used his power of veto and persuaded me to dress up a little. Six-inch high studded sandals were not designed for optimum comfort at the end of a six-day working week spent almost entirely in a standing position. Urgh, how I wanted to be home on the couch with my tender toes in a bucket of bubbles.

Marc had won the 'going out vs. staying in' battle and, after a quick shower and some crucial cosmetic coverage, we'd headed to Santangelos, my favourite restaurant. Located in the basement of a glorious old building in the city centre, it was all brass and wood and reminded me of the interior of *Cheers* – without the resident shrink, ex-sports star, the gobby waitress and the postman who never left the bar stool long enough to deliver any mail.

Rico, the far too good-looking Italian manager, shook Marc's hand and then did that hug/back thump thing that macho blokes do. They'd been friends since they were in their early twenties, when both of them worked as barmen in the same nightclub and shared rat-infested student digs. The pub/restaurant/club world was a small one and most of the managers and owners knew each other and traded off information, hospitality and girlfriends. Myself being the exception. Although if Rico asked nicely I don't know that I could be responsible for my actions. I blushed as he leaned over to kiss both of my cheeks. If that man ever developed mind-reading skills I'd be done for.

Of course, I didn't actually mean it. I was happy with Marc. We had a good thing going. A settled routine. With none of that intensely claustrophobic stuff. He loved me. I loved him. It worked.

He was easy and uncomplicated and, OK, so we might not spend every waking moment locked in a frenzy of romance but all that mushy passion was seriously overrated. My mind flicked back to the memory of a huge suitcase under my mother's bed that contained all the cards that my dad had ever sent her. Hundreds of overblown declarations of devotion that she pored over whenever he disappeared off the face of the earth on one of his benders. If that's what hearts and flowers got you, I'd rather stick to easy and uncomplicated.

We followed Rico as he headed down to the rear of the restaurant and were almost at the private dining area at the back of the room when I heard the unmistakable sound of nails scraping down a blackboard. Since there was no blackboard and no nails, that could only mean one thing.

I looked at Marc questioningly and he responded with a wink, as Rico pulled back the curtain that guarded the privacy of the back booth to reveal the excited faces of Ginger, Ike, Lizzy, Adam, Josie and Avril.

Now they were all shrieking. I just hoped no one in the

main restaurant had a pacemaker or we could have a medical emergency on our hands.

'What are you all doing here?' I asked, to be rewarded with a raucous impromptu chorus of 'Happy Birthday', led by Ginger.

God, she looked great. Thin, but great. It was so good to see her. For the last year, every time Lizzy and I had a few drinks we'd vow to book a trip down to London, only for sobriety, work, children and commitments to put the knackers on it.

'Babe, you look amazing,' I told her as I slipped into the leather studded sofa and gave her a huge squeeze.

Oh, this was fantastic. Really, really fantastic. So much for Marc avoiding grand, sweeping romantic gestures – there was no way I was swapping him for Rico now. At the other side of the table, Marc slid beside Josie and Ike, while Avril ignored them all by chatting to someone on her new mobile phone.

'Who's she talking to?' I mouthed to Josie.

'Perverts. She's got a part-time job on one of those new sex lines to earn a bit of extra cash.' She accompanied the revelation with two thumbs-up.

Deciding this was one of those occasions in life where there was such a thing as too much information, I took a quick slug from the champagne glass that had materialised in front of me and – much to her discomfort – gave Ginger another hug. Public displays of affection were still not her thing.

Four waiters descended on the table with huge slabs of antipasti and baskets of assorted bread that smelled incredible.

'So tell me everything. How's work? How's life?' By my reckoning we had a few hours to catch up on months of gossip and I didn't want to waste a minute.

'All good,' Ginger replied.

Was it just me, or did her grin not reach her eyes? 'I'm

looking after a new boy band and I swear they're going to be a cross between Oasis and Take That. The lead singer already has anger issues and a weight problem. S'cuse me.' She gestured to one of the waiters. 'Can we have another bottle of champagne and I'll have a Jack Daniel's and Coke too.'

Over beside Marc, I noticed Ike's head shake and his lips tighten. His day-old sexy stubble was a stark contrast to the suave cut of his suit and the perfectly groomed hair. It struck me as bizarre that I barely knew the husband of one of my closest lifelong friends, but since almost the day that they met they'd lived in London and when Ginger did come back up she often came alone. Despite the age difference though, Ike seemed to be good for her. The stereotype of the sleazy music-industry guy getting his money-making claws into the female talent and controlling their lives definitely didn't seem to apply here. He was more of a protector, a carer, a balance for her roller-coaster personality and inherent volatility. And let's face it, after doing his apprenticeship looking after Ginger, the guy was a shoo-in for a role with a UN Peacekeeping Force.

I snapped out of my reverie when I realised that Lizzy had weighed in on the conversation too. 'Did you do the test?' I heard her whisper to Ginger. What test? What's going on? Oh God she was sick. My best friend was sick and I didn't even know about it. Memo to self – that would be the propensity for panic and drama taking over again.

Ginger glanced around to make sure that everyone else was engaged in their own conversations.

'Three stabbings and an indecent exposure . . .' Marc was saying to Ike.

'. . . the year end. Difficult to predict the stock situation . . .' Adam was telling Josie, unaware that she had completely glazed over and was staring vacantly at Rico's passing arse.

'Go on, big boy, grab it tight.' That was Avril. And I didn't want to know.

Yep, coast was clear for Ginger to continue. 'Pregnancy test,' she half whispered/half mouthed.

I bit my tongue to stop myself from uttering an exclamatory yelp. Pregnancy! Ginger had never, in all the years I'd known her, ever expressed the slightest notion for a baby and now she was doing tests?

'Negative,' she told Lizzy, her voice oozing relief. Bloody hell, she looked rattled. This was clearly some burst condom/forgotten pill/senseless on Jack Daniel's scenario that left the possibility that Ginger was up the duff. Why didn't I know about this? Why? Lizzy clearly knew. Ginger obviously knew. Therefore . . .

'Why don't I know about this?' It was out before I realised it.

Lizzy's turn to whisper now. 'It's new. And you haven't been around for a while and –' she switched her focus back to Ginger '– oh hon, those prayers worked. Are you relieved?'

Ginger nodded. 'You've no idea. I've never been so terrified in my life.'

I reached under the table and took her hand. She was obviously drained with the stress of it all because such an act of tactile affection in Ginger's direction usually resulted in rolling eyes and a response stating, 'No, I do not need a hug so fuck off and stop coming over all American.'

This time she just did nothing. No retraction of the hand, no reassuring squeeze, just nothing.

Where had I been? Ginger was obviously in the middle of an important, emotional time in her life and I had been completely oblivious. There was no way this was going to happen again.

With a flicker of surprise, I realised that Lizzy had been right – I hadn't been around much at all. The last few times she'd called me to arrange a Friday night out, I'd made excuses. I used to see her when I was right next door, but now I rarely stayed at my flat because Marc preferred to crash at his. Sure, it was bigger. And cleaner. And didn't come with the sound of screaming children during the day. But maybe we could stay there one or two nights a week just to even things up? I'd run that past him tomorrow.

'So how come you haven't told her about all this?' Ginger asked Lizzy, with a head toss in my direction.

'We haven't had a chance to gab properly in ages.' Lizzy sounded just a little defensive and . . . was that a little hurt too? That was ridiculous! We'd had a night in and a long gab only . . . only . . . Shit, when was the last time that we had a night in and a long gab?

'And I've not had a chance to pop into the shop. You know, with my broken ankle.'

She had a broken ankle? Several pounds of white plaster completed a circular ascent that started on the floor and ended with a thump on the table. Irrevocable proof that my other best friend did indeed have a broken ankle.

My mouth was opening and closing like an overwrought haddock before I managed, 'How did you break it?'

'I fell . . .' There was a split second of relief as I realised that she'd had an innocuous, everyday stumble and I hadn't missed something crucial in her life like, say, an ascent of the north face of the Eiger or her first solo swim of the Channel.

'. . . off a podium. In a nightclub. When we were in Las Vegas.'

What?

Had I been in a coma? Or a time warp? Or prison? Hang on. The last time I spoke to Lizzy she was bawling her eyes out because Princess Diana had just died and that was August. We were now in October. Two months!

130

How had I ever managed to let two months pass without anything more than a few five-minute conversations?

But then it was difficult to juggle everything because, you know, I, erm, worked long hours. And on nights off I liked to crash out. Or if Marc was off we liked to do things together, just get quality time and . . .

A memory flooded back of me standing in the rain, ten years before, wearing an obscene white dress while I waited for Red to come change my tyre. I'd pushed my pals to one side for a boyfriend then and I'd just realised that I'd been doing it all over again. What. A. Tit.

Well, that was going to change right now. I felt a shift of priorities wash over me. Or that might just have been a dip in my blood sugar because I was drinking champagne on an empty stomach.

The point was I'd caught it in time. I just had to make a bit more effort to stay in touch with the girls and I also had to stand my ground where Marc was concerned. Dinner parties, that was the answer. Wasn't that what 'almost thirty-somethings' did these days? Even if Marc hated them and I had the culinary skills of, say, a cheese plant, that was no excuse. I'd have my friends over and show an active interest in their lives while trying not to kill them with insufficiently cooked food.

I was in charge of my life and it was time that I acted like it. This was my life. Mine. And I was going to reassess my priorities and take back control.

A loud, repetitive ding cut through my thoughts and I realised that Marc was banging his spoon on the side of his glass.

'A bit of warning might have helped there,' Avril hissed. 'You just scared that bloke shitless and he hung up just when he was getting to the tickly bit.'

'Sometimes it's hard to hide my pride in my children,' Josie deadpanned, to a thunderous glare from her daughter.

Marc cleared his throat and stood up, earning a chorus of applause and whistles. 'First, thank you all for coming out to celebrate Lou's birthday.' More whistles. 'And, Josie, well done for keeping tonight a secret.'

Josie performed a mock bow in recognition of her achievement. For a gossip-aficionado like Josie to refrain from spilling the details must have been torture.

First thing tomorrow morning when I turned over my newly revised leaf and re-entered into society, I was going to nip over there with croissants, coffee and a bulk box of caramel logs. We had serious catching up to do.

'And I'd just like to say a few words about Lou.'

Aaaaw, so sweet. But he could stop now because everyone was staring at me and I hated being the centre of attention. Hated it. Almost as much as Ginger hated public displays of affection. He should stop now before one of us snapped.

'We've been together now for just over a year and it's honestly been the best year of my life.'

'Oh my God, I'm filling up.' That was Josie. Beside me, Ginger just tutted.

'Lou, you are beautiful and kind, and the best friend anyone could ever have . . .'

No, I'm not! I'm not! Lizzy was almost up the bloody Eiger and I knew nothing about it!

'. . . and I love you.'

I mean, I've been crap lately. Really, really crap. But now I was going to fix it.

'So Lou . . .' Bugger, he was still talking. I thought he'd finished.

'Lou Cairney . . .' What? What is it? My mind was running its own commentary on the situation and I'd lost the capacity to switch it off. Champagne always had that effect on me.

'Happy birthday, darling.'

Oh, right. Thank you. That's so sweet. Now sit down before Ginger takes you out with a bread stick.

Rico appeared at his side with a large shoe-sized box and Marc took it then nudged it across the table.

A present! I knew exactly what it was. For weeks I'd been hinting about the silver strappy sandals that we'd seen one day when we were passing the window of House of Fraser and he'd obviously been listening.

Maybe this being the centre of attention thing wasn't so bad after all. I peeled back the pink foil paper, lifted the lid and gasped. I couldn't help it. OK, so it wasn't the silver ones but it was the black ones that were exactly the same and Marc had been right when he'd said that they would go with far more outfits than the silver.

Oh, they were gorgeous! I was so, so lucky. In fact, I was going to put them on right now. Everyone was still staring at me so perhaps if I ducked under the table to change my shoes it would take the heat off for a few moments.

I surreptitiously slipped my shoes off then pulled the other sandal from the box. I was just about to go low, when I spotted the charm. The ankle strap was threaded through an adorable silver charm with a gleaming crystal stone in the . . .

'Lou.' Marc's voice sounded distinctly more tense than usual. Had Ginger booted him under the table? And would everyone please stop looking at me?

'Lou,' he repeated and this time I saw his eyes move to the sandal that I was holding, before settling on the charm, then flicking up to meet my gaze. The charm. Me. The charm. Me.

The realisation took me much longer than everyone else at the table. It wasn't a charm. It was bigger than that. It was more of a . . .

'Lou, will you marry me?'

133

Twenty-one

Lou

The St Kentigern Hotel, Glasgow. Saturday morning, 2 am

'Were you guys pissed off with me when all that was going on?'

They both spoke at exactly the same moment.

'No,' replied Ginger.

'Yes,' replied Lizzy.

We'd discussed it a few times over the years but not in any great detail. It was tough to get Ginger to discuss anything emotionally deeper than the latest release on iTunes. So the conversation I was working up to having with them this weekend would probably leave her requiring therapy. Tomorrow. We would talk about the tough stuff tomorrow.

'I felt it too, but I don't think I realised it at the time. I just kind of thought everyone was busy doing their own stuff. You were away.' I looked at Ginger. 'Lizzy, you were so busy with the kids.

'And I was . . . somewhere between knackered and torn. I so wanted the salon to succeed, yet I wanted to make Marc happy too. I guess everything else got put on hold for a while. I'm a crap friend. Look, I'm bowing my head in shame.'

I took it too far and cracked my forehead off the dark wood table. The three permatanned teens from a few tables away watched and giggled. They hadn't taken their eyes off us all night. They were either trying to pluck up the courage to come speak to Ginger, or wondering why we were in a trendy nightspot instead of spending the weekend on a Saga tour.

'Ouch, that hurt.' I wasn't sure if I was talking about my head or the fact that Lizzy admitted she'd been upset with me. I couldn't really blame her because somewhere inside I knew I was messing up . . . and what happened next proved it.

Twenty-two

Lou

1999 – Aged 29

'I'm not looking down. I'm not. No way. I'm not looking down. I'm . . . oh, fuck I'm looking down.'

I sent up a silent prayer to the patron saint of bloody great heights that none of the twelve Japanese tourists standing to my right understood English. By the way a couple of them were looking at me in amusement, I had a feeling the prayer was going unanswered.

It didn't help that Marc also seemed to find this whole scene highly amusing. He reached his hand out to me. 'Come on, I've got you. Trust me.'

I shook my head and managed to spit some words out through gritted teeth. 'That's what they always say in the movies right before someone goes "splat".'

On this breezy, cloudy New York November afternoon, we were standing on the Observation Deck on the eighty-sixth floor of the Empire State Building, 1,050 feet up, and I was scared out of my wits. It had taken twenty minutes just to

136

get me into the elevator and even then I only did it because Marc had promised me we'd stay inside. He'd lied.

'Babe, come on, you'll be fine. It won't kill you.'

'They always say that in the movies too. When the paramedics come, can you tell them it was a heart attack? And tell Josie I love her and she can have all my worldly goods except the salon. Avril can have that, but only if she doesn't go through with her promise to rename it "Cut the Crap".'

I felt a slight swaying motion and automatically grabbed the first thing that came to hand. To his credit, the small Japanese man smiled kindly when he peeled my fingers off his arm one by one.

Marc was starting to look slightly irritated now. What did he expect? After three years together, he was fully aware that I was phobic about having my feet a large distance from the ground. I didn't do tall roller coasters. High bridges were the work of the devil. And if I went within fifty yards of a bungee rope I had to sit down and put my head between my knees until the urge to faint subsided.

This wasn't *Sleepless In bloody Seattle*. Tom Hanks wasn't standing by with a twinkle in his eye ready to make me his and whisk me off to live happily ever after in an unfeasible romantic comedy plot. In my head, this was more *Die Hard 1, 2* or *3* – the bit where someone freezes in a moment of peril and John McClane has to drag them from a burning/ airport terminal/subway system to save their life. It was not possible to be any more scared than this.

As Marc finally took the hint and stepped back over to my side, he let out a long sigh. I'd have punched him if my hands weren't too busy gripping on to the wall.

'Can we go down now?'

No answer.

'Marc, can we—'

'This isn't working out how I thought it would,' he interrupted me.

Really? Actually it wasn't working out how I thought either. I was pretty sure I'd be requiring resuscitation by now.

'Look, Marc, I'm sorry but it's the height . . .'

'I don't mean the sightseeing,' he countered. 'I mean us. Now.'

Oh bloody hell. A relationship chat at 1,050 feet. Great. Somebody shoot me.

'Marc, what do you want from me? And whatever it is, can you tell me when we get back onto solid ground?'

I was sweating. Actual rivulets of sweat were running down my face.

What was going on with him? He wasn't usually this insensitive. I mean, sure he was definitely an Alpha male and it was highly unlikely that he was going to get in touch with his inner light of emotional empathy any time soon, but this was getting somewhere close to psychological torture.

'It's just that I kind of had a vision of how this was going to go up here.' He rummaged in the pocket of his cream chinos. Terror aside, I'd thought his choice of dress was cute today. A little formal – and it didn't exactly co-ordinate with my skinny jeans, Guns and Roses T-shirt and Uggs – but the preppy trousers and the white polo shirt on those broad shoulders and perfectly toned arse made him look like an American jock. If I wasn't close to death, I'd consider nipping back to the hotel for a siesta with perks.

'I brought you this.' As he pulled the ring box out of his pocket, twelve Japanese tourists burst into applause and suddenly the clouds were alive with the sound of clicking cameras.

Dear God, I was hallucinating. I was seeing Marc standing there in front of me and he was holding out a ring. This was how madness started, but I wasn't sure if it was him or me that had lost the plot.

I eyed him warily. 'But haven't we already done this bit?'

'You say yes. It is good ring. You say yes.' A small Oriental lady who was blatantly invading my personal space took the time to offer life-changing advice.

Marc grabbed my hand and half escorted, half pulled me back inside the building. My heart rate dropped from 'explosive' to 'faintly hysterical'.

'Lou, it's not an engagement ring.'

Oh. So it's just a present. A gift. A little token of his affection for the last two years of love and devotion.

'It's a wedding ring.'

It's a wedding ring. Right then. A wedding. The heart rate returned to 'explosive'.

'I thought we could get married while we were here. To be honest, I was going to plan the whole thing as a huge surprise . . .'

That part of the sentence was contributed by the Fucking Great Big Understatement Association.

'. . . but when I looked into it I discovered that we have to register and then wait twenty-four hours before we actually get hitched. We have to produce birth certificates and passports too.'

It was a few seconds before I realised that my mouth was opening and closing and words were coming out in a crazed babble. 'Oh well, it was a nice idea, but I don't have my birth certificate so we couldn't possibly get married and it's just as well really because none of our friends are here so it wouldn't be the same as getting married at home and it would be quite weird really and . . .'

The last word just kind of faded into the ether as I ran out of breath.

Marc was staring at me now, really intensely. Why did I get the feeling that I was saying something wrong? What had I missed? And did that little Japanese woman really think I couldn't see her loitering behind a sales rack of I Heart NYC T-shirts, trying to eavesdrop on our conversation?

'I brought your birth certificate.'

How the hell did he get that?

'Josie got it for me.'

Ah, the kleptomania queen strikes again.

'And I thought that we could go register today, then get married down at the Boathouse in Central Park tomorrow. I've booked a slot.'

He'd booked a slot. Yes, I was aware that I was repeating things while my brain tried desperately to process this.

'Lou, I want to marry you. I know that you're scared . . .'

Terrified.

'But I know that you love me and that we're meant to be together. There's no reason to keep putting this off. Marry me. Tomorrow. At the Boathouse.'

Now I knew how people in a siege situation felt right before the cops burst in and wiped out the bad guys. I had a feeling I was about to get taken down by friendly fire.

He was right of course. For two years he'd been casually suggesting that we name a date and get down to the whole business of planning the nuptials and I'd just as casually been avoiding it.

The truth was that the whole prospect of a wedding day terrified me almost as much as standing on the eighty-sixth floor of a New York tourist attraction. I loved Marc, I really did. He was funny and smart and not to mention eminently shaggable. The guy was a catch. Yet . . . Yet, what? What the hell was wrong with me? Why did the very thought of marrying him, marrying anyone, fill me with dread? He should have saved the money he'd spent on the wedding ring and bought me therapy sessions instead.

My gaze shifted from my feet to his face: his gorgeous, hopeful, perfect face. 'Well?' he asked.

I couldn't do this. It was too soon. I hated surprises. I felt out of my depth. Out of control. I needed time to think this over and consider what he wanted us to do. How could I get married in twenty-four hours? I didn't have a dress. Or shoes. And my nails! My nails looked like they'd been gnawed by small rodents. I could not get married with gerbil nails. And I definitely couldn't get married without the people I loved here. There was no way Marc could have told Josie why he wanted my birth certificate because if she knew there was even the slightest possibility of me getting married she'd be standing over behind that T-shirt rack in a frenzied state of anticipation with her new Japanese best friend.

No, there was no way I could do it. I had to say no. It was going to disappoint him but we'd get over it. Maybe we could start planning it when we got home? Work up to it. Take it step by step. Ease into it gently.

'Lou,' he started, and I could hear a trace of exasperation creeping into his voice now. He ran one hand through his hair without even realising that he was doing it. It was one of the little quirky mannerisms that I loved. 'Lou, let's do this. Let's just do it.'

Something in my heart snapped, sending tears shooting to my eyes. He was right. I loved him. He loved me. I didn't want to be with anyone else. And OK, it might not feel exactly right but I was self-aware enough to realise that was down to my inbred aversion to marriage as opposed to any doubts about Marc. Maybe it was time to get over it and take the plunge. Marriage could work. Some people could do it. Lizzy and Adam were doing great. Ginger and Ike seemed happy.

Marc and I would be happy too. This meant a lot to him. He was a traditional kind of guy and he wanted a traditional married life. Even if he had to talk his bride-to-be down from a great height on the day before the nuptials.

Maybe this was what I needed. Maybe it was best to have this sprung upon me because who was I kidding? Ease into it gently? I'd never do it. I'd keep finding excuses to put it off and he would lose patience eventually. A stomach-churning realisation hit me – I would lose him. One day he would have enough of my procrastination and he would leave and I couldn't blame him. He wanted proof that I was in this for the long haul.

He wanted commitment.

I wiped away a tear that was falling down my cheek.

Commitment.

I may never parachute out of a plane or abseil down a cliff, but maybe it was time for me to tackle this fear head on.

Marc was right. I just had to do it. I just had to commit. It would be just like when I decided to take the plunge and open the salon, only without the possibility of action by the fraud squad.

'OK.' I exhaled and nodded simultaneously. I suspected that wasn't how most people accepted a marriage proposition but I was taking baby steps. His expression changed; a glimmer of relief lit up his eyes as he realised where I was going with this.

'OK, Mr Cheyne, let's do it.'

A few moments ago, out there on that ledge, I didn't think it was possible to be more scared.

I was wrong.

Twenty-three

I woke up thinking about Mrs Marshall and wondering what time she'd booked in for her shampoo and set and whether she would be channelling Baby Spice, Dolly Parton or the blonde one out of *L.A. Law* today. Then I realised that there were a couple of bigger issues requiring some priority attention.

This was it. The big day. The moment that little girls dream about and practise for and plan down to the last detail.

'Lou, we need to leave in five minutes.'

'Isn't it unlucky for you to see me in my dress before the ceremony?' I yelled from the bathroom. He heard me without a problem because the walls in the hotel were paper thin. We'd ascertained that the night before when the people in the next suite were conversing. Apparently 'Oh yes, baby, oh yes, baby, oh yes,' was 'So big. Oh, so big. Ooooooh, so fucking big.' It went on. And on. And on. We finally got to sleep at 4 am, safe in the knowledge that we were sleeping only feet away from the biggest penis in the free world.

I paused in my efforts to pull up the zip on my dress as I waited for his reply. 'Yeah, but I'm not taking a separate taxi in case you head straight back to the airport and leave me standing.' He laughed.

As if. What a ridiculous notion. That would be entirely crazy. I hadn't even thought of that . . . OK, I had, but not for at least ten minutes. A final tug got the zip right up to the top and my eyes watered a little when a stray lock of hair was removed from my scalp in the process.

Standing back, I checked out my reflection in the bathroom mirror, reeling a little as I realised that the woman in the ivory dress was me.

Marc had chosen well. When we got back to the hotel from the Empire State Building yesterday, he'd called down to reception and asked them to bring up 'the package'. I just hoped that the FBI weren't listening in on the call, given that he sounded like a Columbian drug dealer.

Ten minutes later, a concierge appeared at the door carrying a huge box with a Saks Fifth Avenue crest. Marc had scoured the internet for a dress he thought I'd love, bought it and had it sent over to the hotel before we arrived. Now, as I performed a slow, careful turn, I could see why he'd picked it. There were two layers to the off-white shift creation, the inner one a beautifully soft, satin-back crêpe, the outer one made of the most delicate lace. The round neck was caught in the back with tiny crystal buttons, then the fabrics glided downwards, gently curving in at the waist, skimming the hips, before falling to just below the knee. The long fitted sleeves completed the classic cut, giving it a retro forties feel. It was like something Holly Golightly would wear in *Breakfast at Tiffany's*. But then Holly Golightly was a size eight, whereas I was a size fourteen with a stomach that had fallen foul of a deep pan Hawaiian from room service the night before.

I took a deep breath and sucked in my stomach. Mr Organisation may have thought he'd covered all the bases, but there was a definite deficit in the magic knicker field. The dress was stunning, and I was so touched that he'd gone to all that trouble. Urgh, there's a 'but' coming. It's just that there was no denying that I'd have chosen something a little less classic and a little more forgiving.

I reminded myself that this wasn't what it was all about. We'd just get the vicar (was it a vicar? Or a priest? Or some government chap? Was it weird that I had absolutely no idea who was going to be officiating at my own wedding?), or the priest or whoever, to change the vows.

'Do you Marc, take Lou, in sickness, health and carbohydrate-related bloat . . .'

There was a knock at the door. 'Almost ready!' I replied, then clutched on to the vanity unit as a wave of anxiety took hold. For the hundredth time that morning I wished that Josie were here. And Ginger and Lizzy. And Avril – even though she'd say that I looked like I'd dressed for the day by rolling in a set of Josie's kitchen curtains. She might have a point. I definitely wasn't sure all this lace was really me.

But what did that matter? What mattered was that I was marrying Marc and we were going to have an amazing day and then we'd go home and tell everyone and – after Josie had battered Marc around the head with a boot for not inviting her – we'd have a wonderful life together. I had a sudden urge to phone home, to talk to someone I loved, but instead I picked up the posy of white roses that lay on the vanity counter, took one last look in the mirror and unlocked the door.

'God, you look beautiful.' Marc's grin made him look like one of those models on the Ralph Lauren posters that we'd seen on the walls of Bloomingdale's. How had I ever managed to snag a man this gorgeous? His navy suit was impeccably cut, his white shirt was immaculate, right down to the mother-of-pearl cufflinks at his wrists, and the light-blue tie set off the outfit perfectly. It was all just so . . . Marc. If I'd ever taken the time to imagine what he'd wear on his wedding day, this would be exactly what I'd have come up with. Formal. Smart. Grown-up. In the wardrobe mirror I could see the image of the two of us standing next to each other. Grown-ups. Oh, dear Lord, we were grown-ups. Don't panic. Do not panic.

He reached out and took my hand. 'Ready?'

I nodded. I was ready. It was time. I just had to remember that this was going to be amazing, that after it I'd spend the rest of my life with the man I loved and . . . breathe. Remember to breathe.

No one from the reception desk even looked up as we passed. No one in the whole world knew that I was on my way to get married. Not a soul. It suddenly struck me that I could get hit by a bus in two hours' time and the name on the death certificate would be Lou Cheyne. Who was that?

That wasn't me. And if Marc was killed too then Josie would come looking for me but she'd never track down my body because it would have been given the wrong name and despite the best efforts of a crack team of forensic investigators I'd never be identified so I'd rot in an unmarked grave, never claimed, without a single soul knowing I was there.

I had a hunch this wasn't what most brides pondered on the way to their wedding.

The New York late-afternoon traffic was thick and slow, but of course Marc had anticipated that and left plenty of time to get there. 'Didn't want to give you anything to fret about,' he told me.

Great. Nothing to fret about then. All I had to do was sit back, relax, enjoy this journey through the most exciting city on earth, and make my way to an oasis in the middle of all the chaos to say my vows. The steady stream of chatter from the cab driver added to the ambience. By the time we turned on to Madison Avenue we had already ascertained that he had two wives, seven children and he sent money back to his family in Turkestan every month.

I let Marc chat to him as I watched the people go by on the street, an eclectic mix of tourists, suits and the odd female who looked like she'd stepped off the set of that new show about New York women. What was it called? Something and *the City*, or *City Sex* or . . . nope, it was gone. Lizzy kept raving about how great it was but it was on when I was working late and since I'd yet to master how to tape anything on Marc's VHS I hadn't seen it yet.

Jesus, this car was taking for ever. We stopped at a set of traffic lights and as I listened to the driver fill Marc in on his educational background from the ages of eleven to sixteen, a sudden cacophony of noise made me jump. The bells on St Patrick's Cathedral. They rang out loud and clear, each one making my nerves in the spinal area tingle. It was so quintessentially New York, so bloody wonderfully atmospheric that a picture of Josie hijacked my brain. She would love this. For years she'd talked about coming here and if she'd made it she would love every glamorous, emotional, crazy minute of this adventure.

She should be here. She. Should. Be. Here. And so should Lizzy. And Ginger.

'What day is it?' I blurted out. Since we'd arrived in New York I'd completely lost track of the days.

'Friday,' the driver replied.

Friday. I should be with the girls. It was the law.

I could hear the driver getting more and more animated as he spoke. 'Lady, what are you doing? Lady, you can't get . . .'

Marc joined in now too. 'Lou, what the hell . . .!'

I didn't hear what came next. I was out of the door and I was too busy running, not an easy task in four-inch heels that were a half-size too big, but I was running and nothing was going to stop me.

Nothing except . . .

'Oh shit, sorry!'

Several large plastic sauce bottles and a dozen bags of potato chips went crashing to the ground and the vendor at the hot dog stand stood open-mouthed in shock. Normally I'd have been a gibbering mass of apologies, but I just kept on running. Actually I was hobbling now because one of the shoes was back there in a puddle of miscellaneous sausage dressings.

I limped on, bumping into people, dodging prams, crossing puddles and narrowly missing being lassoed by a large man holding leads attached to a menagerie of dogs.

Eventually I saw a doorway and stumbled inside, ignoring the puzzled glances of the people behind the counter. 'Slice or full?' one of them asked, gesturing to the array of pizzas in the glass display shelf in front of him.

Did I look like a woman who'd just popped out for a quick bite to eat? It was bloody November in the city centre of New York and I was sweating, my face was a vibrant shade of puce, I was wearing an off-white lace frock and one shoe.

'Erm, just coffee, please,' I stuttered and slid into the booth right at the very back of the shop. I'm fairly sure it was pay-at-the-counter, but the nice man brought the coffee over to the table, and gently placed it down right next to my forehead before tentatively backing away.

Eventually, when my breathing returned to somewhere near normal, I lifted up my head, took a slug from the cup and pulled out my mobile phone.

My thumb had pressed speed-dial 1 before I had a chance to consider the implications. It rang. And rang. And rang. Come on, Aunt Josie, pick up. Pick up. Eventually it clicked to answering machine and my favourite voice rang out. 'I'm not here because I'm away doing sordid things to that bloke out of *Taggart*. Leave a message and I'll phone when I get the feeling back in my bad hip.'

I hung up. It was probably just as well. There was nothing that Josie could do and she would just come over all protective, raid the Christmas fund and be on the next flight over to collect me.

Speed-dial 2. It was answered almost immediately. 'Hello?'

'Lizzy, it's me.'

Cue ear-shattering shriek.

'Oh my God! Are you having a great time? Have you done all the sights? Did you go roller-blading in Central Park? And please tell me you've seen at least one of the cast of *Friends*. Matthew Perry! Always liked him the best. Or Joey! How you doing?' The last bit was said in the voice of a twenty-something Italian American male.

'Lizzy, Marc planned a wedding.'

'What? When?'

'Here. Today. In Central Park.'

Cue another, 'Oh. My. God!' This time said in the voice of Chandler's girlfriend Janice.

'That's so amazing! And romantic! Oh Lou, I wish I was there. I think that's the most beautiful thing I've ever heard. It's so—'

I hung up.

I know, I'm a terrible friend. But right there, right then, I couldn't listen to any more. I needed . . .

Speed Dial 3.

'What?' The voice was deadpan and decidedly irritated.

'Ginger, it's me.'

'Aren't you in New York?'

'Yes.'

'OK, I just forgave you for calling at midnight then. Whassup?'

'Marc planned a wedding here.'

'That's so cool. For when?'

'Now. Today.'

'WHAT???? What the fuck was he thinking?' This was more like it.

'He wanted to surprise me.'

'Wanted to bloody take charge, you mean. Why would he think you wanted to get married over there with none of us with you? That's crazy.' She paused for a moment, obviously realising that her stance could be perceived as a tad inflammatory. 'I mean, unless you want to do it in which case, you know, I suppose it's OK. Do you want to get married there?'

'No.'

There was another momentary pause before she blurted, 'Oh thank fuck. In that case he's a tit because he should have known that you'd hate it. And Josie will kill him. Does she know?'

'No.'

'Wow, there's going to be blood. So what time are you doing it and where are you now?'

She obviously hadn't quite grasped the full extent of the debacle that was the current situation.

'In an hour and I'm sitting in a pizza joint. We were on our way there and I jumped out of the taxi at St Patrick's Cathedral and bolted. And I lost –' a sob caught in my throat '– a shoe.'

'Bloody hell, I can't believe I'm missing this. So what are you going to do?'

'I don't know. I love him, Ginger, but I just got spooked and freaked out and I . . . What have I done? Lizzy says it's the most romantic thing that she's ever heard.'

'You're taking relationship input from the woman who still watches *Dirty Dancing* every week and then calls her husband Johnny when she bangs him afterwards?'

'Lizzy does that?'

'I've no idea but it's a great rumour so I think we should spread it. But anyway, don't you dare beat yourself up about this. He should have known it was insane to spring it on you. You're far too fucked up for that kind of thing.'

'Thanks. I think.' I sighed, and not just because my dress had just snagged on the underside of the table. 'What am I going to do?'

Ginger was obviously struggling to summon up the sympathetic and logical side of her personality.

'It's up to you, honey. Do you want to marry him?'

'Yes. Definitely. No. I mean, I do, but it's just all so sudden.'

It was obvious from her voice that she was trying to be reasonable. Not one of Ginger's normal traits. 'Is it Marc that's the problem or the wedding?'

Impressive. Perception wasn't one of her normal traits either.

'The wedding. I love Marc and we're, you know, happy. Or at least we were until half an hour ago. I don't think he's going to be too chipper now.'

'Then maybe it's a good thing. Like pulling a plaster off. It'll be over and done and then you can just get on with your life. If you don't go through with it over there then you'll end up coming back here, planning a huge big ceremony that will stress you out and cost you a fortune. Then we'll all start avoiding you because all you'll talk about will be dresses and cars and whether or not you should invite the old lady who lived next door to you when you were six.'

'She was lovely.'

'I know but I think she's probably dead so that solves that problem.'

For the first time in the last twenty-four hours, I laughed. And meant it.

This is what I needed. I just needed to have a pal by my

151

side, even if it was via phone and she was 1,764 miles away. I'd looked that up before I came.

'You know, maybe Lizzy was right, Lou. Maybe this is romantic.'

I had no idea what to say so I chewed on my bottom lip instead.

She had a point.

'Ginger, I . . .'

The hairs on the back of my neck stood up as Marc materialised in front of me, his face flushed, his tie pulled open at the neck, one hand clutching two hundred dollars' worth of Jimmy Choo. The servers behind the counter were now nudging each other and pointing in our direction. For someone who hated being the centre of attention, I seemed to be playing the starring role on a regular basis these days.

'What the hell was that all about?' Despite the fact that he'd probably run the whole way, he was barely out of breath. That's the kind of fine physical specimen that he was.

'Lou? Lou! What's going on?' Ginger sounded as agitated as I felt.

'I'll phone you back.'

Slowly, I took the phone down from my ear and placed it on the table, never once losing eye contact with Marc. How could I do this to him? I loved him and he was standing there, nope, sitting now, and he looked so . . . wounded.

'Lou? Who are you phoning?'

'Ginger.'

His expression darkened. 'Great. She's always sensible in a crisis.'

'I'm . . . I'm sorry. About the whole running thing. I kinda freaked out.'

'You think?' The words were sarcastic but his face softened and there was a hint of a rueful smile.

God, I loved him. I did. What was I playing at? He reached

152

across the table and took my hand – a pretty compassionate gesture given the circumstances. If the roles had been reversed I had a feeling that Marc would be sitting there wearing a thin crust, extra-large meat feast by now.

'Babe, I love you. But I can't keep doing this. I want to get married, have children, grow old with you but you're still acting like this is some kind of student romance that means nothing.'

'It doesn't mean nothing!' I was horrified that he thought that. But then, given today's course of events it probably wasn't exactly a stretch. 'I want all those things too.'

'Then prove it, Lou. Marry me today. Because if we don't do it right now then I don't think we ever will.'

Twenty-four

Lou

The St Kentigern Hotel, Glasgow. Saturday morning, 2.30 am

'Nightcap or bed?' Ginger asked. 'And by that I mean, let's have a nightcap.'

The bar was much quieter now, and a very smart man in a suit had already checked that we were residents and therefore still entitled to order drinks without contravening licensing laws.

I was already feeling slightly queasy – I'm not sure if it was the wine or the memory of Marc's face as he waited on my answer.

'Do you ever regret your decision?' Lizzy asked.

I didn't even need to think about it. On the scale of 'most pivotal and scary moments of my life' it rated pretty high, yet when I'd calmed down the answer was obvious. 'No. I just regret—'

'Well, now what are three gorgeous ladies like yourselves doing sitting here alone at this time of night?'

A tourist. Obviously American. Obviously wealthy.

Obviously about to feel the wrath of Ginger if he didn't cut the cheesy patter and move on.

I decided to intervene, for all our sakes. 'We're just leaving actually,' I told him, picking up my handbag and gesturing to the others.

'We are?' replied Ginger, clearly not impressed with my sleaze-avoidance tactics.

'We are.' God bless Lizzy for reinforcing my point.

'Now, now, don't be so hasty. Champagne. How about I buy you girls a bottle of champagne and you can tell me all about Glasgow?'

Ginger knew when she was beat. Slightly unsteadily, she leaned over, picked up her bag and stood up.

'Sorry, as my friends said, we're just leaving.'

Texan Tourist wasn't impressed. He, unlike us, obviously hadn't quite mastered the art of cutting his losses.

Twenty-five

Lou

2001 – Aged 31

There was no doubt about it, Marc was definitely getting even more handsome as he aged. As I watched his reflection in the mirror, I could see that there were changes. A few more lines around the eyes. A few grey hairs. An easiness to his posture that conveyed that this was a guy who was happy with his lot. As the light glistened off the three diamonds studded into his platinum wedding ring, I felt a surge of relief. I'd done the right thing. Thank goodness I'd had the strength to go with my feelings.

I pushed his fringe back from his face and softly ran my fingers across the back of his head.

'So how's Emily?' I asked, as I lifted up the first section and started to cut.

'She's good.' His smile said it all. Actually, not quite all. 'She's erm . . . we're . . . pregnant.'

I stopped cutting as the surprise took over. 'You're kidding! That's amazing! Is it weird that for the first time in a long time I want to give you a huge hug and kiss you? Without tongues.'

His laughter filled the salon. 'Not weird. I think it's compulsory.'

'OK I'll pencil it in for before you leave. Is Emily thrilled? And when's the baby due?'

'She's over the moon. It's due next summer, beginning of June. We're only beginning to tell people now that she's just passed the three-month stage.'

'I'm happy for you both, Marc, I really am. You'll make great parents. So . . . names. I suppose Lou is out of the question?'

'I'm guessing it is,' he laughed. 'Especially if it's a boy.'

I had a vision of Marc, a few years from now, standing on a touchline watching a little mini-Marc playing football, a gorgeous tall, willowy blonde Emily standing beside him. They'd be like an advert for vitamins or shampoo or the latest healthy family cereal.

I paused to do a quick check . . . Nope, no stray little nuggets of regret or sorrow for what might have been. In the two years since that disastrous trip to New York we'd come to terms with everything that had happened. Sure, at first it had been tough. Moving my stuff out and saying goodbye had felt like the end of the world, but too many doubts and insecurities had been thrown up for us to carry on. We just wanted different things. He wanted the picture perfect family life and I wanted . . . I've no idea. All I knew was that the prospect of the picture perfect family life terrified me. So I said goodbye, went back to Mouthwash Towers and got on with my life, focusing all my energies primarily on the salon but also on spending more time with the important people in my life: Ginger, Josie, Lizzy and Bruce Willis. There had been flings – enough for me to still feel that there was a glimmer of hope in the happy-ever-after department, but not enough to gain a slapper badge. No one had made it past three dates and on to a deeper relationship yet. I just wanted to have a good time: no strings, no ties, no promises of undying devotion while my bruised heart recovered from Marc.

He took a slightly different approach to relationship recovery. Only weeks later he met Emily and they were married within six months, and suddenly my meltdown in New York went from being a devastating kick in the bollocks to a lucky escape for both of us. Emily was perfect for him. The love of his life. After years of trying to make me fit his image of perfection, she was the round peg in the round hole and, although he'd never be so brutal as to say it to me, I could see that they were happier than we'd ever been. Now we were friends. Without perks. I cut his hair, I kept Emily blonde and glossy and we all got along just fine. It was all very civilised and mature, but I drew the line at holidays and anything else that would compel me to be around her when she was wearing a bikini. There was only so much my ego could take.

'So what about you? Met someone yet?'

I nodded and his eyebrows raised in surprise. I used to be able to do that before I overloaded on the Botox. I blame Lizzy. Her dentist uncle started doing cosmetic treatments out of the surgery downstairs and she persuaded me to try it. According to the upper half of my face, I'd been in a permanent state of shock and awe ever since. I couldn't even wreak revenge by banging on her wall at obscene hours because she had finally moved out of the flat next door and into a lovely detached cottage on one of the picture-postcard lanes on the edge of the town. However, sometimes in my sleep I could still hear the shrieks.

'It's new though, so I'm not sure about it yet.'

'How new?'

'Third date tonight.'

I may have gushed and screeched just a little when I said that, but if dates one and two were anything to go by this one had promise of outlasting my three-date limit. He was . . . wait for it . . . a pilot. Now I know that shouldn't matter but it does. It falls into the same category of sexy-occupation-desire as firemen and rock stars (with the exception of Gary Collins who was still both a rock star and a wanker).

'Third date! Wow, that's almost a long-term commitment for you these days.'

I smacked my non-paying customer across the back of the head with a vent brush. If I wanted to hear brutal truths I'd call Ginger.

'So where are you going tonight then?' Marc pressed on playfully. 'Paris? New York? Milan? London?'

'Glasgow. We're having dinner with Peter's parents.'

'Peter? Peter the pilot?'

I laughed. 'I know. Lizzy and Adam the Accountant thought that was hilarious too. Lizzy thinks it's a cosmic sign that we're destined to be together. But then she also thought that about Dennis the Doctor and that one lasted a fortnight. I'm still sure he was self-medicating – no psychiatrist should be that happy all the time.'

'How are Lizzy and Adam?' Marc asked. Now to anyone else that would seem like a completely innocuous question and I might have thought so too if he hadn't broken eye contact with me and run his hand through his hair right before he said it. Marc only does that when he's excited, sad, stressed or perturbed.

The answer was that Lizzy was great. Her life had turned out so perfectly: gorgeous husband, gorgeous kids, gorgeous home. She was happy. Contented. But I sensed that he'd asked for a reason and I wasn't disclosing any information until I knew what it was.

I clicked off the hairdryer and caught his eye in the mirror again.

'Why did you ask like that?'

'Like what?'

'Like there was something going on and you don't want to tell me.'

'I didn't,' he said in his very best 'that's ridiculous' tone. Caught! He only used his 'that's ridiculous' tone when he was lying. And he was the worst liar in the world.

'Marc? Is there something going on that you don't want to tell me?'

He rolled his eyes. 'I bloody hate it when you do that. Look, it's nothing . . .'

'But?'

'But Adam was in the club the other night.'

'Adam! No way. Adam hasn't been in a club for the last decade. It must have been someone else.'

'Nope, it was definitely him.'

That was bizarre. Of our crowd, Adam was always the one who went home when the rest of us crossed the alcohol threshold that transformed us from responsible adults to the highly embarrassing 'let's hit a dance floor and show those youngsters how it's done'. Which invariably was renamed the following morning, 'For fuck's sake what were we thinking, someone's playing drums inside my skull and I'm pretty sure I've pulled a hamstring.'

The dryer was still perched in mid-air while I pondered a new disturbing thought. 'He wasn't doing anything he shouldn't have been was he?'

'No,' Marc answered. 'He was in with another guy and they left alone. I promise. I saw them go and they didn't have a bevy of half-naked females hanging off their arms. Not even one fully clothed one.'

I waited for any obvious signs of lying. None. OK then. Thank God. Panic averted. I shrugged it off. 'Must have been a work night out or something. Strange Lizzy never mentioned it though.'

But hey, it was a free world. Adam could do anything he wanted. Lizzy probably knew all about it. There was no point in making a drama about it. None. Nothing to see here. Please move away and go back to what you were doing.

'So anyway.' I flashed one huge, gleeful grin. 'Have I told you that I'm dating a pilot?'

Twenty-six

Butterflies! I actually had butterflies in my stomach. That hadn't happened since I charged out of a New York taxi in the marital version of *The Great Escape*.

'OK, tell me again how nice your parents are and how your mother isn't going to stab me with a steak knife for trying to steal her son.'

'Do you want me to do it in my pilot's voice or my normal one?'

I thought about that for a moment. Yes, to my eternal naffness, I'd been making Peter the Pilot say things in his 'Hello, this is your captain speaking' voice since we'd met. Even though we weren't on a plane. Nor was he a captain. Thankfully, he still thought it was cute. I had absolutely no doubt that the novelty would wear off, he'd start to see me as some kind of demented bunny boiler and he'd be out of there quicker than you could say 'One way Easyjet to Luton'.

'Normal. No, captain. No, normal. Definitely normal.' I had a feeling this vocal tussle wasn't building my case for long-term girlfriend potential.

He pulled on the handbrake and leaned over and kissed

me. 'It'll be fine, I promise. My mother's been much better since the anger management classes. She hasn't killed a single person this year.'

Did I mention that he could sometimes be quite funny? And he was a pilot?

We both got out of the car, met on the pavement and I leaned down to return the snog.

Yes, he was short. In my heels I was just over six feet tall. He was five foot six. We were Tom Cruise and Nicole Kidman – without the weird religious beliefs and the multi million-pound divorce settlement.

The height difference didn't bother me in the least. Not at all. OK, it did feel a little bit odd. I just kept telling myself that we're all the same size lying down. Size doesn't matter. Good things come in small packages. Lizzy and I had come up with at least half a dozen other similar clichés the other night but imminent in-law fear was now affecting my powers of recollection.

The doorman at the Carriage Club opened the huge bronze door to let us through and my excitement/trepidation level slid up another notch. The Carriage Club was the most exclusive restaurant venue in Glasgow, a four-storey building that contained a stunning, Gothic designed restaurant, several bars and a nightclub which was frequented by the trendiest people in the city. It attracted an eclectic mix of the wealthy, the celebrity and the successful. Er, and me. Who was none of the above. This might explain why I'd only been twice, both times with Ginger, who practically lived here when she was in town. Tonight we were here courtesy of Peter's father who was something big in banking. I made a mental note to warn Josie to keep her career in financial fraud quiet if she ever met him.

We made our way up one of the sweeping gilt staircases, across the huge mezzanine area at the top and through the imposing doorway that led to the restaurant. At 9 pm it was already busy, with almost every table taken. We were shown to our booth, in the far corner of the room, beside the entrance to a private dining area that – from the volume of the revelry within it – was obviously being used. My curiosity was immediately piqued. This place was a legendary destination for touring celebrities and bands. Who was playing in the city this weekend? I was sure I'd read somewhere that Atomic Kitten were in Glasgow. And Kylie. Two gents in suits appeared from the room and walked past us and I caught a hint of an Irish accent.

Westlife! Oh my fecking God, it must be Westlife. Lizzy would have a freaky if she were here. She was the only married woman I knew with a picture of a boy band on her fridge. She'd drawn a heart around Mark's face and always broke into 'Uptown Girl' as soon as she started Hoovering. Apparently murdering a cover of a Billy Joel classic relieved the monotony.

I'd just slugged back my first glass of Dutch courage when I spotted the maitre d' heading our way, escorting a couple who were possibly the most perfectly matched people I'd ever seen. Same height, same hair colour, same tans, same style of dress. Great. Now, instead of thinking, Lovely to meet you, I was thinking *Flowers in the Attic*. Do not say that out loud. Do not.

I surreptitiously clocked the positions of all table knives just in case.

'Lou, this is my mum and dad, Jack and Penelope. Mum and Dad, this is Lou.'

Very formal. And no, it wasn't in his captain's voice. Smile. Be gracious. Make a good impression. A wave of heat rose up from my chest, with the effect of sucking my silk blouse against my skin. If a damp patch appeared I was out of there. This was ludicrous. What was wrong with me?

We all shook hands and sat down. This was going to be fine. It was. I was not sixteen. I was a successful business woman, a cosmopolitan woman of the world and I would not be intimidated by a couple who may or may not have been brother and sister in a past life. Or Thunderbirds. I couldn't help notice that they were both gifted in the shiny face and generous eyebrow department.

Be cool. Be calm. Don't get flustered.

'So, Lorna,' Penelope began, in Margaret Thatcher's voice. Not a good start. 'Peter tells me that you have a little salon in the suburbs. Quite right, dear. I mean what's the point of coming into the city? Too much top-notch competition here.'

I had a horrible feeling this wasn't going to go well.

By the time desserts were served, I'd lost my fear of her stabbing me, primarily because if I had to stay there any longer I was going to take matters into my own hands and kill myself. She was snooty, she was rude, she was relentlessly self-involved and she was a master of the backhanded compliment. She'd talked about herself, the charity work, herself, her holidays, herself, and Peter's achievements from 1967 until the present day. And how she influenced them. Oh and apparently my hair was lovely and the perfect style for someone with a plump face. To make matters worse, his father was practically monosyllabic and Peter seemed to have reverted to being twelve. Just before pudding was served, he'd allowed her to lean over, straighten his tie and rearrange his hair flick.

Somewhere between the crab starter and the sticky toffee pudding, my opinion of him had plummeted so far that he could have recited the *Karma Sutra* in his captain's voice and not a nipple would have been piqued. What had I seen in him other than . . . OK, so he was a pilot. If this was what having a shallow personality did for you, then I was really going to have to get in touch with my spiritual side.

165

The noise from the private dining room interrupted my thoughts. Westlife were now singing something about being in a world of their own, and it was getting a raucous response. How much did I want to be in there instead of out here with the Glums? Dear God, get me out of here. I promise I'll be good. I'll help old ladies across the street. I'll do voluntary work. I'll pray every night. I'll stop Josie from giving heavy breathing phone calls to people she doesn't like. Just save me. Save me please.

'LouLouLouLouLou!'

It was hard not to laugh. Staggering out of the private dining area, like a severely intoxicated Glaswegian version of an archangel sent from heaven, was Ginger. I leaped up to hug her, ignoring the horrified sneer on Penelope's face as a bush-sized mass of ginger frizz descended on her table.

'Baby!' she hollered.

'Ginger! What are you doing here?'

'I'm here with my boys. They're playing at the Concert Hall tomorrow night. Did you not hear them?' She gestured to the room she'd just appeared from. 'They're in there just now taking the piss out of Westlife.'

Her boys. They were the new big boy band in the making – a collection of hair gel, testosterone and overdeveloped pectoral muscles called Stud.

'Anyway, what are *you* doing here?' she said, scanning the table, waiting for explanations and introductions.

I made sure that I was enveloped in a hug and that only she could hear my reply.

'Being held hostage by pure evil. Save me.'

She pulled back and winked. 'I need you to come with me right now!' she said loudly.

'You do?' I asked, feigning disappointment.

'I do! Because . . . because . . .'

No, don't let me down now. Come on girl, you can do this.

166

'Because . . . tampon emergency!' she announced with gusto.

Penelope looked like she was about to have a stroke but I didn't wait to find out. I grabbed my bag and made rapid apologies to Peter and his parents, then bolted as fast as decorum and my unfeasibly uncomfortable shoes would allow me. We only stopped for breath when we reached the safety of the mezzanine.

People tried not to look at the two giggling women who were acting in a far too uncool manner for an establishment of this calibre.

'A tampon emergency?'

A shrug accompanied her very wellied, rueful grin. 'I was under pressure. And fifteen, apparently.'

'Seems to be contagious. My boyfriend's been stuck in adolescence since his mother sat down.'

'Boyfriend?'

'Three dates.'

'He looked tiny.'

'He's a pilot.'

'Aaaaah. Good enough.' She pulled a cigarette out from between her boobs, followed by a lighter, and lit up, while I tried not to be jealous that her size eight arse was encapsulated in the most amazing pair of leather trousers I'd ever seen. She looked deadly. Over the trousers were thigh-high leather boots with heels that were not a fraction under seven inches, and the outfit was topped off by a black blouse, which was left open to reveal a cleavage designed by God. One that doubled as a storage device for smoking paraphernalia.

'Thanks for saving me, hon, I owe you.'

'Don't be crazy. You're coming back in with me. We'll sneak you past their table. It's so busy now they'll never notice.'

I shook my head. Much as that sounded like the best idea I'd heard in a long time, I wasn't going back into the lion's den for anyone. Better to just take off, call it a night and be thankful that I met the family before I did anything stupid – like go past five dates and actually get attached to a guy who let his mother rearrange his flick.

She was right though. People were swarming across the mezzanine and from where we stood we could see that the downstairs entrance was busy too. I wanted to suggest that she come on home with me but there was no point. Ginger the party animal hadn't been to bed before dawn in years and she wouldn't start now . . . not while there was still Jack Daniel's in the bar and cigarettes in her bosom.

I gave her another spontaneous hug and she tried not to squirm. 'I missed you, Ginger. I feel like we haven't caught up properly for ages. How about we spend the weekend together – we'll descend on Lizzy and spend the next two days in pyjamas drinking coffee and trying not to let the kids hear that we're talking about inappropriate subjects.'

I could tell she was about to give me the reasons why that wasn't possible, when suddenly she paused, thought, then, 'Fuck it. That sounds brilliant. You're right, we need to catch up. Let's do that. I need to go to the guys' gig but you and Liz could come with me. We can be eighteen again for two hours, as long as we don't scare any members of the public.'

I laughed.

'Let's go find a phone and call . . .' She paused as something down below caught her eye. 'Fuck me dead, there's Red! Reeeeeeeeeeeeeeeeeeedddddddddd!'

I leaned over the balcony, looking in the direction of the door and, sure enough, there was Ginger's brother arriving with a crowd of very trendy-looking people. Hell, how long had it been? Five years? More? Last I heard he'd moved to London and was working as a photographer for a music magazine. Or a newspaper. Or . . . something.

'Reeeeeeeeeddddddddddd,' she hollered, but it was no use.

We were too high up and it was too busy down below. 'Don't worry, he's coming up that other stairway,' I told her. 'I'll just nip over and—'

'Reeeee . . !'

It was a weird sound. Like someone going through a tunnel or going off into the distance. Already facing the other way, I snapped my head back to see . . . Several things registered. Ginger was no longer standing beside me. A movement just below. A black shape. Falling. Falling. People looking up. The horror. And the screams.

Oh God, the screams.

Twenty-seven

Headline: the *Daily Record*, 18 November 2001: MUSIC
MANAGER IN SERIOUS CONDITION AFTER FALL IN TOP
GLASGOW NIGHTSPOT.

The paper had lain on the table in the corner of the room
for twelve days. The twelve longest days ever. The first forty-
eight hours had been a tornado of activity, with doctors and
nurses and specialists racing in and out of the room in the
ICU.

At first there was so much to say, so much activity, so many
questions, so many tears, but for the last few days only the
beep of the machine that monitored her heart.

Now we took it in turns – Ike, Red, Ginger's mum Moira,
me. Lizzy came as often as she could, for at least a few hours
at night when Adam was home to look after the children.
Only two were allowed to be with her at any time so we
worked in shifts. Ike and Moira. Red and me. One of us
taking off for a shower and a couple of hours' sleep in the
family room when Lizzy was there.

The doctors didn't say so much now. Two broken legs. A
fractured arm. A smashed pelvis. Internal bleeding. A swelling

on the brain that had forced them to put her into a medical coma to relieve the pressure and give her body a fighting chance to heal. They'd stopped administering the drugs to keep her asleep the day before. Now it was a waiting game. A medical crapshoot as to when she would wake up, *if* she would wake up.

A sob stuck in my throat and I forced it back down. I would not give in to thoughts like that. She was going to be OK. She'd come back. She had to.

A million times I'd replayed that moment in my head. If only I'd been closer to her. If only I hadn't looked away. If only she hadn't been wearing those crazy boots. If only she hadn't seen Red. If only she hadn't leaned over. If only . . . If only she wasn't lying there somewhere between life and death and if only we could do something to fix her.

The door opened behind me and, for a few moments, the aroma of coffee prevailed over the smell of cleaning products. Moira, like most women of her generation, cleaned when she was distraught. There wasn't a square inch of the room that hadn't been disinfected, polished or buffed.

I took the drink from Red and he managed a faint smile. 'Anything?'

I shook my head. 'Nothing. The doctor came in on rounds about ten minutes ago. Still saying the same thing: the fractures are healing but it's all about the head and they just don't know.'

There was a long sigh as he pulled up the chair across at the other side of the bed and sat down. Almost two weeks we'd been sitting like this and, bizarrely, it was starting to take on some kind of weird normality. At first we'd just stared at Ginger, immersed in fear, looking for every little sign of hope. Then we talked. Sometimes about stupid stuff, sometimes about the things that were important. We took turns to read to her, to play music that she loved, to tell her

171

ridiculous stories that would make her laugh. But mostly we were just there and moving through the moments.

Without letting go of her hand, I put my head on the bed and closed my eyes. Exhaustion hit in waves. I'd stayed round the clock that first weekend, but since then I'd been working at the salon every day, then coming straight to the hospital at night. The regular clients all knew Ginger so it was the main topic of conversation at CUT. 'How is she?' 'Any progress?' 'No news?' I spent all day every day wishing I was at the hospital, and all night at the hospital wishing Ginger would get better. Life had turned into one big exhausting wish-fest.

It was even tougher for Red because he was so far away from home. For the last five years he'd been living in Notting Hill and working for a London newspaper as chief photographer. His office had been very understanding about his leave of absence to take care of his sister, but staying with his parents, hundreds of miles away from his home and job, had to be hard.

'Hey.' As I lifted my head I realised that Red was wearing a different T-shirt from a moment ago. 'You fell asleep,' he said softly. Why did we all speak like that in the hospital? We were in the presence of Ginger – we should argue, raise our voices, bitch about stuff. We'd already joked that she wasn't waking up because she was bored rigid with all of us just sitting there doing nothing. The gallows humour got us through the worst bits.

I spotted the clock. Midnight. Bugger, I'd been sleeping for two hours. Some support system I was. I stretched and shook the magazine I'd been leaning on off my face, fairly sure that I had the text from the front cover of *Heat* imprinted on my cheek. I leaned over, took his mug of coffee from his hand and glugged some back. He didn't object.

The door opened behind us and Lizzy came in looking as

172

exhausted as I felt. 'Hey, babe, you're not on duty tonight,' I said softly, torn between being pleased to see her and worried that she was pushing herself too hard.

She shrugged. 'I know, but . . .' Tears. Huge big fat ones, rivers of them.

I flew out of my seat and put my arms around her. 'Lizzy, don't, she's going to be OK. She'll get through this. She will.' It was the same stuff all of us had been trotting out for twelve days but we had to keep believing it.

'I know, it's not that it's just . . . I couldn't stay home, Lou. I just worry about her and Adam, he doesn't understand. It's like he just doesn't understand anything any more.'

I was so stunned I could have budged Ginger across the bed and lay down beside her to recover. Lizzy and Adam had always been so solid. If there was one couple, other than Dave and Della, who were totally meant for each other it was them.

'What's wrong? What's been happening?'

'You know what, I'm just going to go have a run around the block and come back in half an hour,' Red said gently.

Despite the tension, Lizzy and I laughed. 'And there goes the West of Scotland male – first sign of emotion and he heads for the nearest exit.'

Grinning, Red gave a deep bow and then bolted for the door.

'So tell me,' I prompted. 'What's been going on?'

Lizzy grabbed a handful of tissues from the box on the bedside table and dried her face, then blew her nose so loudly that several coma patients in adjoining rooms probably stirred.

'I don't know, Lou. It's been like this for months.'

Months. My friend had been having problems for months and this was the first I knew of it. 'Why didn't you say?'

She shrugged. 'Because it was all small stuff. Little things. Nothing I could put my finger on. And you know me, I just like to sally along and hope everything sorts itself out.'

There was no arguing with that. In our little trio, Ginger had 70 per cent of the confrontational quota, I had 29 per cent, and Lizzy was left with 1 per cent that she used only when returning unsuitable goods to Marks & Spencer. Even then it took her weeks to pluck up the courage.

'And what with you working all the time and me juggling the kids, whenever we have seen each other I've just wanted to have a good time and escape the stress for a while.'

I reached over and stroked her hair.' Oh, Lizzy, you know I'd have taken time off, come over to see you, done anything to help.'

'I know, but it's just been . . .' More tears. Only when they stopped did she tell me about how Adam had been distant, moody. How he still had time for the kids, but not for her. How they hadn't had sex for months. How she sometimes caught him looking at her like she was a stranger he barely knew.

'Do you think . . .' I hated to ask but it had to be broached. 'Has he met another woman?'

'No!' Her reply was emphatic. 'He swore that he hasn't and I believe him. You know Adam, Lou, he's so sweet, so caring – I honestly don't think he'd do that to us.'

She was right. There was no way he was out on the town on the pull. Absolutely not. A memory suddenly niggled – something that Marc had told me months ago. That he'd seen—

'Is the coast clear yet?' Red's head popped back in the door and Lizzy dried her face again, put on a huge smile and nodded. 'Absolutely. We've now reverted to our default position of flippant humour and false bravado.'

'Excellent. Although, you know if you ever need anything I'm here for you, Liz.' Aw, so lovely. But, aware that he was straying into that dangerous minefield of female touchy feely territory, Red still looked mildly terrified.

'OK, so I've got an idea,' I said, more out of a need to

cheer us all up than anything else. 'I think we're going down the wrong track with the music. I'm bringing in a Westlife CD tomorrow. Or Celine Dion. She bloody hates her.'

Red smiled. 'Mariah Carey. Or New Kids on the Block. Or who's that guy with the really bad hair?'

'Michael Bolton!' Lizzy cried. 'You're right. That would do it. Sheer bloody outrage would make her wake up.'

We lapsed into comfortable silence again, as I gently stroked my finger along Ginger's arm, lost in the hypnotic motion of the movement, just wishing for change, for something . . . Beside me, Lizzy was singing the chorus of 'Time, Love and Tenderness'.

'Lou,' Red said, a little louder than normal. Suddenly the steady beep of the heart monitor increased pace. 'Lou, I think . . . Get a doctor! Quick, get someone!'

He jumped up and shot to her side, his hand instinctively going to her shoulder, holding her.

I was already at the door and had thrown it open by the time he finished speaking.

'I think she's waking up, Lou. Michael fucking Bolton, I think she's waking up!'

There was a flurry of activity as doctors and nurses flocked around her and we retreated outside to let them work, praying the whole time. It was a couple of hours before they let us back in again and the sight in front of us was incredible. Sure, she was pale, and skinny and her hair had taken on hedge-like proportions, but she was awake.

'So,' she murmured questioningly while staring intently at us. I was prepared for this. Maybe she wouldn't remember us. Maybe she would be altered, confused. She might even be frustrated or angry. We had to be ready to handle whatever changes had occurred and we would do it. If the last couple of weeks had reinforced anything, it was how much we loved each other and needed to pull together, be there for each other, provide a solid support system – and many more of those touchy feely phrases that made Red and Ginger deeply uncomfortable. It was obviously something in their genetic make-up.

OK, Ginger, hit us with it. Whatever you need, we're here. Anything.

'So,' she repeated. 'What did I miss?'

Twenty-eight

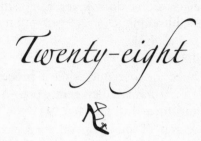

'Hey, how's the patient today?' I asked as I breezed in, carrying a huge bunch of bright yellow sunflowers which I knew would put everyone in a happy mood.

Ginger practically growled her reply. 'About to hunt down whoever makes the food in this place and stick their mash potato scoop where it hurts.'

It would seem that I'd vastly underestimated the power of the sunflower. 'So let's see: rude, aggressive, impatient, volatile – honey, I think you're almost back to normal.'

Despite herself, she smiled. 'Almost?'

I nodded to the pink, flannelette Spandau Ballet nightgown that Moira had retrieved from the box in her loft containing Ginger's teenage bedwear. 'Yep, your tits aren't hanging out of a Wonderbra yet.'

I moved quickly to dodge the flying pillow.

'Any word on when you're getting out of here? I think Ike is desperate to get you home.'

'Hopefully the weekend. The sight of these four walls is driving me insane.'

Three weeks and four days she'd been in hospital and

despite being unconscious for almost the first fortnight, the staff, her family and everyone within a hundred feet had been informed in no uncertain terms that she was going a little stir crazy. Ginger didn't do solitary. She didn't do hospital food. And she didn't do . . .

'Urgh, I need a drink.'

. . . teetotal.

'What?' I froze for a second while I processed this latest little nugget of information, then gently placed the sunflowers on the table and turned to face her. 'Are you kidding me?'

Without a scrap of make-up on, her ivory skin looked almost alabaster and for a moment I got a flashback of the girl who used to hang out of my bedroom window with her menthol cigarette dangling from her bottom lip, vodka and fresh orange in hand, thinking she was the coolest chick ever. If this was a movie scene, I'd pine for the sweet, un-jaded child of yesteryear. But the reality was that Ginger had never been sweet or un-jaded. She'd been born fierce and argumentative and I had a hunch that was why no one had ever said what I was about to say now.

'Ginger, you have got to cut back on the booze. I'm sorry, honey, but come on, you would never have fallen if you hadn't been completely pissed.'

Her Spandau Ballet nightgown inflated as indignation made her sit up straighter and take a deep breath.

'Pardon?'

Oh God, she had hurt and anger written all over her face. This wasn't going to end well. But I'd done a whole lot of thinking during all those hours that I'd sat by her bedside and I'd come to a realisation that horrified me. It was time to share it, because if something like this happened again for the same reasons I'd never forgive myself. 'Ginger, I'm sorry – and I'm only saying this because I really care about you – but I can't remember a single night out that we've ever had

178

that you haven't been pissed. Every night, every special occasion, every birthday, every Christmas . . . It has to stop.' I was crying now. And not just because I was terrified that each word could be my last because I could see from her expression that she was about to unleash the wrath of Ginge.

'Lou is right.' The voice came from the doorway and we both turned to see Red standing there clutching a large box from KFC. 'She is. Don't look at me like that, sis. You can kill me, but if you do I'm taking the chicken down with me.'

It was the perfect thing to say to diffuse the situation and although I'm sure a SWAT tactical team would have advised against it, I dived towards the source of danger and clutched the one arm that wasn't in bandages.

'Look, I'm not going to give you some big lecture, but just think about it OK?'

It must have been a trick of the light but I was sure I could see tears welling up in her eyes. She immediately switched attention to Red. Or rather, to the package he was carrying. 'Eight pieces and fries?'

He nodded as he pulled a can of Irn-Bru from his pocket. Scotland's other national drink. If we were a tribe, this was the potion that we truly believed could cure everything from hangovers to broken hearts.

She withdrew her good arm. 'I hear what you're saying, Lou, but I'm fine, honestly.' Her gaze locked on to mine and I could see that she'd listened. I also knew to quit while I was ahead because if she was backed into a corner or a confrontation she'd come out fighting. I'd raised the subject, now it was time to leave her to think about what I'd said.

The vase of sunflowers had been arranged and half a chicken drumstick had been devoured before she sat back and hit us with her most infectious smile. I said a silent prayer of thanks that she hadn't gone down the fury and retribution route.

'So since we're on the subject of home truths and long-term issues . . .' she started. Her stare was levelled directly at me and my heart sank. Bloody spoke too soon. OK, what was it? The fact that I'd stolen a tenner from my mother's purse when I was nine? The uncomfortable truth that I'd once shagged Marc in a toilet on board the Glasgow to London shuttle? My secret fear of clowns?

Just as I was about to tell her to get it out and put me out of my misery, her eyes went to Red.

'Are you ever going to tell Lou your little secret?'

I swear his face turned the colour of his hair, which you would think would be quite disturbing in a 'too long in a sauna' kind of way, but it actually looked endearingly cute.

Oooh, this was obviously going to be good. Ginger's wicked smile and his uncomfortable squirm combined to give this the promise of a spectacular piece of gossip or scandal. I folded my arms and looked at him expectantly, glad that for once the heat wasn't directed at me.

'Shut up,' he told her, his voice uncommonly low and thick with warning.

'Why? Not the right moment? I could give you a quick chorus of "Endless Love" if that will help set the mood.'

Her raucous cackle made it obvious that she was loving every second of this.

Ginger inhaled dramatically, tossed her hair back in the divaesque fashion of Diana Ross and let rip with 'My lov—' The perfectly pitched notes rang out and Red snapped.

'OK! Enough! Fine.'

I felt sorry for him, I did. But the compassion was being battered to death by an insatiable curiosity as to what the big secret was.

'The thing is . . . The thing . . . It's just that . . .'

Bloody hell, he couldn't even look either of us in the eye. I'd never seen him like this before. Red was normally the most laid-back guy you could ever meet, the antithesis of his sister and proof that – other than in the area of the hair follicle – genetics meant nothing.

'OK, so the thing is . . . it's . . .'

It's what? What?

Ginger looked at her bucket, back to Red, then back to her bucket again. 'Would you hurry up? My chicken's getting cold. Och, never mind, I'll do it. You men are bloody hopeless.'

'Ginger, don't . . .'

'What my big hunk of inarticulate brother is trying to say,' she told me, 'is that he's totally had a thing for you for years. Now can someone open my Irn-Bru because I can't do it with only one bloody hand?'

'You have a "thing" for me? What kind of "thing"? And can you put the bucket down because I can't have this conversation when you're holding chicken.'

'Give me the bloody chicken!' Ginger demanded.

Red put it down on the wheelie table and slid it across Ginger's bed, then took a step towards me.

Ginger sighed. 'I can't look. Honestly, how is someone in their sickbed supposed to eat when this kind of mush is going on?'

'Ginger, shut up or I'm having the doctor put you back in a coma,' I warned.

'The thing is . . . I kind of . . . love you.'

'You do? Since when?' My heart was actually hammering now. Hammering. Like in the romcoms, right at the end when there's a big fat happy ending.

'Since I changed your tyre that night. You were wearing a white dress and a . . .'

I racked my brain. Tyre. When? Then, in a retrotastic, shoulder-padded flashback, it came to me . . .

'Oh my God, we were eighteen!' My hands flew to my

181

face as the memories returned. That was the night I caught Charlie at the airport with another girl, crashed my car and my heart. 'That was one of the worst nights of my life.'

'Cheers.'

'I don't mean you. That was the night that . . . oh, bloody hell let's not go there. Were you ever going to do anything about it?'

'Erm, sure. One day. Ginger, shut up, we can hear you groaning,' he said, his voice full of nervous anxiety.

'You've seriously been in love with me since we were eighteen? Ginger, did you know about this?'

'Don't be ridiculous,' she said while masticating a chicken wing. 'I'd never have been able to keep that quiet. I just realised because he's been like a pathetic poodle, hanging on your every word since I woke up.'

'Sis, you're not helping my case here,' Red told her.

'Sorry,' she replied. 'I'll just stick to my lunch. You two carry on.'

'So, do you think we can maybe try this out? Us? Would that work?' he asked.

I didn't even have to think about it because I'd realised a few home truths in the last couple of weeks too. I'd been a workaholic for far too long. I loved every single thing about my salon. It was who I was. It was my life. But it was time to start making time for other stuff too. I had to devote more time to my friends and family. It was time to find a balance between my work and my personal life. Sure, I'd contemplated it and made token gestures over the years, but now it was time to really do something about making personal stuff a priority. And Red?

That was one priority I didn't even have to think twice about adopting because somewhere in the last month I'd realised that he was the single, most incredible guy I'd ever known.

'I definitely think we could try it out,' I told him as I leaned over to kiss him.

'Nurse!' came a voice from the bed. 'Do you have anything for spontaneous gagging?'

We left the hospital and headed to the car park, both of us suddenly too stunned to speak. He fancied me? Really? So much for my perception skills. I honestly had no idea. When we reached the car park, he walked me to my car and I suddenly got a completely pubescent dose of nerves. What did we do now? Was he already regretting what he'd said? Had Ginger forced a hand he wouldn't otherwise have played?

Don't say anything, I warned myself. Do. Not. Speak.

The sight in front of me was such a paradox. On the outside, butch West of Scotland male. Handsome, incredibly wide shoulders, flat abs, wearing a T-shirt, black jeans and boots. His style hadn't changed very much in the last decade – only the cut of the jeans and the style of the boots had altered in line with fashion trends and income. Gone were the flares and the drainpipes of the last couple of decades, now he wore biker boots and straight-legged denims with a subtle Armani insignia on the back. I'd noticed. But back to my point. The outside was all macho, together, man of the moment, but on the inside I still saw Red, Ginger's big brother, the teenager who covered for us when we were kids in trouble and who was far too cool to want anything to do with us screaming adolescents.

'Are you sure about this?' I blurted. So much for the whole 'do not speak' resolution.

'Yeah.' Did I mention that he'd always been a man of few words?

'So why didn't you say anything before?'

He shrugged. 'I was kinda busy. And far away.'

'But you're here now,' I stated the obvious. Where did that come from? He lived hundreds of miles away. There was a

183

good chance Ginger would kill me and feast on my organs. It didn't work on any level. And yet . . .

'I am,' he agreed, moving now towards me. Oh crap. Oh crap. Oooooh crap. I could run. I could laugh and claim that I was joking. We'd laugh. He'd say goodbye. I'd go back to seeing him at weddings, funerals and prolonged comas. Or I could . . .

Twenty-nine

'I almost got married here once,' I told Red, as we sat in a tiny wooden boat in the middle of the lake in Central Park. I tried to ignore the swirling feeling in my stomach. I was sure I'd once heard an old tale that you couldn't get seasick as long as you could see land. They lied. I was feeling decidedly dodgy despite the fact that I could see land, dozens of tourists, and 350 revellers celebrating a bar mitzvah in the Boathouse Restaurant to our left. Red had no idea what a bad idea it was to be lying with his head on my lap, potentially in direct line of fire.

Red removed the hat that was shielding his face from the sun and looked up at me. 'So what happened?'

'I jumped out of the cab at St Patrick's Cathedral and hid in an Armenian pizza restaurant.'

'That's crazy,' he laughed.

'I know.'

'I'd no idea that Armenians specialised in pizza.'

I snatched the hat and pushed it back down over his face, then stretched my neck back and soaked up the sun. Cheeky bugger boyfriend and possible vomit situation aside, this was bliss. Bliss. And so, so different from the last time I was here.

Only three months into Red's new job at the *Daily World*, he'd been sent to New York to cover Tartan Week, a celebration of all things Scottish culminating in a parade that saw hundreds of pipers march through the streets. I'd been thrilled when he asked me to tag along. To be honest, my giddy highlight of the trip so far was getting a look at Sean Connery as he kicked off the ceremonies. Although, I was only now getting over my disappointment that Red refused my request for a mantra of 'shaken not stirred' in bed that night.

Yep, in bed. Me. And Ginger's big brother. I still wasn't anywhere even close to getting used to it and neither was Ginger, who – despite igniting the fire – claimed the very thought of me and her brother together still made her retch.

Thinking about that first night outside the hospital still brought on the most delicious hormonal surge. From the moment he'd kissed me it was a done deal for both of us. He'd quit his job the following week, secured a new position with the company's sister newspaper in Glasgow, and moved in with me at Mouthwash Towers. I'm not sure we even discussed any of it in advance, but every single thing about it just felt, well, right. Perfect. And not in a Mills and Boon way, but in a comfortable, no pressure, be exactly who you are kind of way. I never had to dress up and go out. Or pretend to like things that I didn't. Or act brave when I was terrified. Red just let me be. No demands, no stress, just . . . bliss.

It was a bit of a recurring theme these days.

Two huge Spanish ladies in a canoe inadvertently nudged our boat, snapping me back to the present, to this crisp but sunny March day in New York.

'How long have I put up with you now?' I asked him. Without removing the hat this time, he stretched up and, by some freaky power of cognisance, managed to flick me smack bang in the middle of the forehead.

'That takes true skill,' I giggled. 'You could be a superhero with powers like that. Flickman: Brings Criminals Down with Just One Hand.'

I said the last bit in the voice of the guy who used to narrate the old Batman cartoons. The hat came off and he flashed one of his lazy grins, the ones that still made my knees turn to mush.

'Four months tomorrow,' he answered my original question.

'No way! Is it that long already? Only another decade or so and Ginger will begin to get used to the idea.'

'You think?' he replied, still smiling.

'Nope. Better give her a bit longer.'

I leaned down and kissed him, thinking that it just didn't get any more amazing than this. It didn't get any sweeter than feeling his hand move through my hair and his flick-finger stroke the side of my face. However, after a few moments, I was forced to give in to the pain emerging from the unnatural spinal curvature, straighten up and confine myself to returning his gesture by tracing the contours of his face with my fingers.

'Mmm, I like that,' he murmured. 'But you didn't finish your story.'

'What story?'

'About almost getting married. So why didn't you go through with it?'

I thought about it for the first time in years. 'I couldn't. Don't get me wrong, I can't think of anything more beautiful than getting married here, but he just wasn't the right guy. Marc had this image of how he saw me and I always felt it didn't match who I was. Does that make sense?'

He squinted up, his hand shielding his eyes from the sun.

'Of course it does. My last girlfriend saw me as Brad Pitt. She was gutted when she realised the truth.'

Did I mention that Flickman had his limitations? We were going to have to work on his capacity for emotional depth and appropriate responses in situations that required insight and sensitivity. I went back to my story and this time went for the practical. He was better in that area.

'OK, well apart from that, Josie, Lizzy and Ginger weren't here and I couldn't even contemplate getting married without them.'

He was silent for so long that I thought he'd nodded off again.

'So if they were here then you'd, say, marry me?'

Always the comedian. Well, two could play at that game.

'Of course. I've always wanted to marry a superhero and Spiderman's always sneaking out at night. No telling what he gets up to.'

'He's shagging Wonder Woman.'

'That explains it.'

The two large Spanish ladies performed a turning movement that resulted in a full-scale ramming of our boat, making it rock violently from side to side. It didn't help that one of them was getting hysterical.

'I told her, we need man to do this. Two fat ladies in boat no good,' one of them yelled. 'One hour going round and round. Blessed Jesus and the Virgin Mary!'

'Do you want to go back into the side?' I asked.

'Of course!' the hysterical one screeched.

Red sat up and took charge. 'Give me one end of your oar,' he told them. When they pushed it over, he grabbed it, then used his scarf to tie it to the rope hook on the end of our boat. Then he took our oar and paddled us all to dry land.

Yep, that was the kind of guy I'd fallen in love with and

188

for the first time I knew . . . I knew that he'd never hurt me. I knew that he would never try to change me. I knew that we had an equal relationship. I knew that he'd never lie to me.

I had no idea that only a few days later, I'd realise that one of those assumptions was wrong.

Thirty

The noise of the door slamming woke me and I pushed myself up and rubbed my eyes.

'Morning, babe. Where have you been?'

'Running,' Red replied. Actually the answer was fairly obvious. There was a towel slung around his neck and his pale-blue T-shirt was stuck to his finely toned torso.

'But you ran last night too. Are you having an affair?' I eyed him with mock suspicion.

'Yep. Those women from the boat lake the other day. They're using me as the filling in their sandwich.' I put the duvet back over my head for a few moments to give my brain the chance to dispose of that mental image.

'I was thinking we could to go to Yankee Stadium today,' he announced. 'There's a daily tour and the concierge can get us tickets. Is there anything you'd rather do?'

'Stay in bed, order room service and watch reruns of *Cheers*.'

From my position under the duvet, I reached for the remote control and started flicking through the channels. American TV was beamed direct from heaven. At home we had four channels of predominately doom and gloom. Here there were so many options, with a completely addictive mix of genres, old reruns and new shows. *Cheers*, *NYPD Blue*, *Cagney & Lacey*, *The Late Show*, *The Tonight Show*, *Nightline*, *MASH*, *Friends*, *Frasier*, *Twin Peaks*, *Seinfeld* . . . And don't even get me started on the talk shows. Between Rosie O'Donnell, Oprah, Maury Povich and the other dozen shows just like them, I had no idea why anyone even left the house. So far today I'd been involved in a violent custody battle, an alcoholic intervention, two confessions of adultery and a lesson in clog dancing and I hadn't even left the comfort of my duvet. We only had two days left of our fortnight holiday and much as I loved every single moment of the New York experience, I was perfectly happy where I was right then and there.

Red jumped on the bed beside me and snogged me while attempting to remove the remote control from my grasp. I slipped it under my buttocks and he laughed. 'I'm not scared to go in there after it, you know.'

'Oh really?' I asked archly. 'Well, make it quick because Ricki Lake is back on in three minutes and she's got a female who's been screwing her twin sister's husband. And his dad. I can't tell you how much I want to come and live here.'

'Three minutes?'

'Three minutes. OK, ready, set, GO!'

He catapulted himself up on top of me and suddenly Ricki's slapper lost all appeal. I'd just re-evaluated what I wanted to do that day. All day. Many times. So deliciously intoxicating were the things that my boyfriend was now doing that it took me a moment to register the sound of the doorbell.

'Room service!' shouted the voice.

'Did you order anything?'

'Just some breakfast. Omelettes. Hash browns. Toast. Juice.'

I contemplated the options. Sex. Food. Sex. Food.

My ravenous appetite took over. I would go on a diet

the minute I got home but right now my body seemed genetically predisposed to sampling every dish that New York had to offer.

Red got up, pulled his discarded shorts on while I clambered back into my T-shirt and boy-pants and dived back under the duvet. It was just as well.

'SURPRISE!!!!!'

If I had a dodgy heart I'd have been clutching my left arm and gasping at that very moment. A surprise it definitely was.

Josie. Lizzy. Ginger. The three of them stormed in the door in a flurry of shrieks, cackles and massive hugs as they launched themselves on top of me where I lay. They looked fabulous: all of them sporting large sunglasses and clutching bags from Ginger's Louis Vuitton collection.

'But . . . but . . . but . . . ?' Neither speech nor understanding were coming automatically to me at that very moment. 'What are you doing here?'

'We've come for your wedding!' Josie's voice came to us from the depths of the minibar, where she'd already located a miniature bottle of Scotch and a large Toblerone.

'For my . . . what?'

'Cheers, Josie, I hadn't actually got to that part yet,' Red told her.

'Well, hurry up, that's the best bit!'

Red fished in the pocket of his shorts then froze, an expression of utter panic crossing his face. He frantically glanced around, then lifted one side of the duvet, delved under, rummaged around next to my body, then, with a beaming smile and a huge exclamation of relief, pulled out a small square box.

'I don't even want to know where that was,' Ginger said dryly.

Actually, I was pretty curious. But there were far more pressing questions hurtling around in my head.

'OK . . .' He took a huge breath, like he was about to dive from a deadly height. 'Lou, I'm hopeless at things like this . . .' True. Even in my startled state, I could see what was coming and realised that it required a huge romantic gesture. Not one of Red's areas of expertise. 'But I love you more than anything. Marry me.'

I sat there, gobsmacked, my mouth opening and closing like a puffer fish on acid. I finally managed a strangled, 'But . . . erm . . . When?'

'Shit, I forgot that bit. Tomorrow. At the fountain in Central Park. I know you said the boat lake would be perfect but I figured that was a bit unoriginal after the whole Armenian pizza thing. So. Will You? Marry me?'

I couldn't believe I was in this situation again! What was it with men I bloody dated thinking that they could just bloody steam in and arrange things without giving me choices? What if I wanted options? What if I wanted a whole big bloody wedding palaver with the big dress and the cakes and all the old dears doing the Slosh to 'Hi Ho Silver Lining'? What if I wanted that?

But . . . I didn't. That was for people with families and parents who had been saving for years to give them a huge send-off. My dad had told me in no uncertain terms that I shouldn't come looking for any money from them for a wedding because they had better things to spend it on. I was ten. I got over it, but he repeated it often enough over the next few years for it to become ingrained in my mind.

All I wanted was me and the guy I loved, with my best friends in the most romantic setting on earth. All I wanted was this.

'Lou?'

Red was looking worried now and the others were starting to shuffle on the spot in anticipation of something either really good or really bad. Except Josie who took another slug of Scotch while staring transfixed at my face.

'I'm only doing it if I can wear my jeans and my Converse and we can go to that little deli on 75th afterwards for cake.'

This was a true test. It would determine whether I was contemplating marrying Control Freak Groom or someone who wanted me to have my idea of nuptial heaven.

'We can wear anything you like and go anywhere you choose afterwards. Just marry me.'

'Yes.'

'Yes?'

'Absolutely yes.'

He dived back on top of me and wrapped his arms around me while I deafened him with an amplified yelp of excitement.

'No tongues! No fricking tongues in front of your sister!' Ginger yelled, but even she was grinning from ear to ear.

Lizzy opened the room door, reached into the corridor and brought in an ice bucket with a very presumptive bottle of champagne.

'Oh my God, you had all of this planned?'

'I called them and wired the tickets after we'd been at the boat lake. They got on a flight three hours later. Then I arranged everything else last night and this morning.'

'While you were supposed to be out running?'

He had the grace to look sheepish.

'You lied to me?' My tone was clearly sharper than I intended as there was a sudden silence in the room as Red nodded with just a trace of apprehension.

'Well, feel free to do that again if it results in jewellery and a party,' I told him, before going in for a long, schmoozy snog.

'Urgh, I wish they wouldn't do that,' Ginger said, then consoled herself by knocking back a full glass of champagne.

I decided not to comment. I didn't want our newly imminent in-law status to get started on the wrong foot.

Suddenly Lizzy spoke up. 'Jewellery! You didn't give her the ring! Give her the ring!'

'I hope you're better at taking photographs than you are at proposing, love, otherwise you two had better get used to living on one salary.' The others laughed at Josie's wit, but I was too distracted by the little velvet box that was being opened in front of me. On the inside of the lid, I could see the words Tiffany & Co., and they headlined a simple silver-coloured band with a square diamond set into the metal. I gasped. If I had to design my own ring, that was exactly how it would look. Not big, or showy, or studded with stones that would catch on things while I worked. This was a ring that I could put on and never take off again. It was perfect.

Tears sprung to my eyes as I realised that I had never experienced happiness like this. I came here on holiday and I was going to go home as someone's wife.

'Right, I'm taking charge today,' I announced, jumping out of bed and casting aside all thoughts of a day sponsored by the television and the dysfunctional of the nation.

'Fine, but we need to go register everything at the marriage bureau this morning.'

'OK, but after that it's girls only this afternoon. We need a spa, we need lunch and we need cocktails. And then we're going shopping.'

'For what?' Red asked, aware that I'd already dragged him around every shop in Manhattan and the excess luggage charge may require a small mortgage.

'I'm bloody sick of being the one on the receiving end of the surprises around here so it's my turn. I'm going to buy you something that'll rock your world.'

My brand-new fiancé laughed. 'OK, but here's a pointer – if it comes from a soft-furnishing department it's going back.'

I made a mental note not to tell him about the four

leopard-print cushions and the gold silk bedding set that were due to be delivered to the concierge for me that day by those nice people at Bloomingdale's. There were some things he could hear about when we were in the first flush of married life and anything would be forgiven as long as I was naked when I told him.

I headed for the shower, giddy with excitement, determined to spend the day tracking down something that showed Red exactly how much he meant to me. A wedding ring. A gorgeous watch. An amazing camera.

But in the end his wedding gift was none of those. It was so much more.

Thirty-one

'Fuck, my feet are killing me. I only came for the spas and the cocktails and the wedding bit. No one said anything about strutting around Manhattan until my feet bled.' Ginger pulled off her spiky heels and let out a deafening sigh of relief as her feet were soothed by the cold floor.

'Tell me again what you think about the ring,' I squeaked, beyond excited at the prospect of seeing Red's face when he opened the box. I just hoped he would love it. It was a white gold band like mine, but instead of a diamond, there was a setting of three black sapphires. It was stunning.

A waiter appeared and positioned himself at Ginger's side. He didn't get the order he'd been expecting. 'S'cuse me, but can you please tell her that her husband-to-be will like his ring because she's been asking us every hour all day and we've now lost the will to live.'

'Certainly. My name is Justin, I'll be your waiter for tonight. The specials are corn-fed teriyaki beef on a bed of fusion soy noodles, Malaysian curried chicken with spinach and chickpea rice, and that ring is divine so if he doesn't like it then please leave it as my tip.'

God, I love New York. The only city on earth where the waiters come with a sharp line in dialogue. Justin retreated with an order for four cosmos and a beer in preparation for the arrival of my fiancé. Did I mention I now had a fiancé? I seemed to remember informing every person I'd spoken to all day. In fact I may have invited the staff of the jewellery counter in Sacks to the ceremony.

I was getting married.

Me. Lou Cairney. Was going to become Lou Jones. And the thought of that didn't scare me. For the first time I felt ready to stop basing my view of relationships on the twisted dysfunction of my parents and start believing in those who made it work. Marc was happy with Emily. Ginger was happy with Ike. Lizzy and Adam seemed to have regained their general state of contentment. It could work. Red and I could make it work.

'Back in a sec, I'm just going to the loo,' Lizzy announced, just as Josie reached over the table and squeezed my hand.

'Listen, love, you know I don't go for all the mushy stuff, but I'm really proud of you and not just because you landed a bloke who had the dosh to fly us all over here for a jolly. Although that helps.'

'The genetic source of my shallow gene, ladies and gentlemen,' I joked.

'God bless the gene pool. Seriously though, Lou, I've absolutely no idea how it happened given the idiots that raised you, but you've turned out great and I couldn't be more proud if I'd shot you out of my own uterus.'

'You should be a speech writer, Josie,' Ginger piped up. 'Politicians and heads of state need your services.'

Dear Lord, if those two ever went head to head in a battle of sarcasm, it would be a long and bloody fight to the death. Thankfully they appreciated each other's talents. Since we were children, Ginger had hung on Josie's every word. She was like a role model for the vocally disdainful and disparaging.

She was also the best aunt I could ever have hoped for. I went round to Josie's side of the table and hugged her tightly, a huge lump forming in my throat as I thanked her.

'Josie, can I ask you something?'

'As long as it's not for money.'

'You're the only parent I could ever have wanted and I can't tell you how much I love you. Would you give me away?'

Huge tears splatted on the table as Josie nodded. I hugged her again, then, despite her lifelong hatred of public displays of affection, I kissed Ginger too. 'I can never thank you enough, honey. If you hadn't taken a header off that balcony I might never have found my husband.'

'Glad to help. And if it doesn't work this time around I'll have another go. Maybe a car crash next time. Or a mountaineering accident.'

I gave her another squeeze to show that I appreciated her devotion then headed off to the loo. I expected to see Lizzy at the mirrors but she wasn't there. Strange. Must have passed her on the way.

It was only when I heard a loud sniff coming from one of the cubicles that I realised I could be wrong.

'Lizzy? Lizzy, is that you?'

'Mfffwauh.'

'Lizzy, what's wrong? What one are you in?'

I was on my knees now, searching under the doors for a pair of bright-pink leather boots. I spotted them at the end cubicle and now that I'd inspected it at close quarters, I made a mental note to congratulate the management on the spotlessness of the toilet floor.

'Lizzy, open the door. It's me.'

After a few seconds delay, she unbolted the lock and, as I pushed open the flash, brown marble-effect Formica, it was hard not to gasp at the sight before me.

199

Lizzy. Cheeks blotchy. Mascara all down her face. Clutching a white pregnancy testing stick.

'Oh shit. Are you . . . Did you . . . I mean, have you . . . ?' I seemed to have adopted the speech patterns taught at the Red Jones School of Romantic Revelations.

'I can't do it,' she sobbed.

'But why?'

'Because I can't be pregnant. I just can't.'

Crouching down on my knees I put my arms around her and hugged her tightly. The management should also be congratulated on the generous size of the cubicles.

'Come on, Liz, it can't be that bad,' I said softly, finding it difficult to process this situation. The only time I'd ever seen Lizzy like this was in the case of sad movies and severe PMT. She was our optimistic one, our chipper little bundle of fun who took everything in her stride and lived a life that oozed positive karma and monklike Zen.

'It is. It's really, really bad. Oh, Lou I'm sorry, I didn't mean you to find out any of this until you were back home. No one knows. Just me. And, oh fuck, Lou, I don't know what I'm going to do.'

The hairs on the back of my head were standing straight up now as a wave of fear descended. What the hell had happened?

'Lizzy, whatever it is, we'll deal with it. It'll be OK.'

'It won't be,' she wailed. I heard the footsteps of someone walk into the toilet, hear Lizzy's pained cry, then turn and beat a hasty retreat.

'It will. Whatever it is, we'll fix it and get through it. Having another baby wouldn't be the worst thing to happen, would it?'

She nodded, tears gushing down her face now. 'Adam has left.'

'It'll all be OK,' I murmured, stroking her hair, 'and we'll . . . What? Adam has what?'

'Left.'

'What? Why? Why would he do that? He loves you and the kids, he would never . . .'

Two huge, big, helpless eyes stared at me, waiting for me to get to the next bit where I inevitably say . . .

'He has met someone else?'

The tears had stopped now and in their place was a numb, soulless expression. I couldn't believe this. He'd sworn there wasn't another woman. Adam had lied to her? No way. He was so much better than that. I'd known him for a decade and I'd never have guessed for a minute that he was capable of such a treacherous betrayal.

'Lizzy, it has to be just a stupid one-off. A drunken mistake. Do you know who it is? Is it someone local?' I asked, thinking this was the kind of information that had to be handled with extreme care. If Josie or Ginger knew the culprit they'd be up at her door within ten minutes of landing back in the country.

Another nod.

'Who is she?'

I braced myself. After fourteen years of working in a Weirbank salon, there were very few people in the town that I hadn't encountered. If I didn't know her then I would know someone who did. Fury started to build. How could he do this on his own doorstep? The cheating, lying bastard, I'd . . .

'Alex Dunns.'

Alex Dunns. Alex Dunns. It was familiar. Hang on, yes, I knew an Alex Dunns but it couldn't be the right one because . . .

'And he didn't lie before. He hasn't fucked off with another woman. Alex Dunns is a guy.'

Noooooo. Bloody hell! Broken hearts. Disasters. Post-natal depression. Near-death experiences. We'd been through just about everything in our lives, but I definitely hadn't yet reached the page in the Friendship Crisis Rule Book that dealt with this one.

'He's gay?'

'Yes.'

'And you've known this since . . . ?'

'Last week. I know, I'm so stupid. I always read those magazine articles that say women know deep down but I didn't, Lou, I really didn't. Sex hasn't been like it used to be for the last couple of years but I thought it was just, you know, the kids, and the pregnancies and the stress and work and maybe I nagged him too much, put too much pressure on him.'

She'd switched from zombie to hyper now. I pulled her close before she worked herself into complete hysterics again.

'Shhhh, hon, shhh. This isn't your fault. It's not your fault.'

Alex Dunns. He was a solicitor at the law firm on the High Street. Came in once a month or so for a cut and blow-dry. Lovely. Cute. Funny. Openly gay. Worked out. Always great for a chat and didn't mind the juniors ogling his pecs.

Alex Dunns and Adam. A couple. I'd never have called this one. Never. Suddenly another niggling thought manifested itself and I pulled back from my friend and looked down at her lap, suddenly realising the enormity of part two of this debacle.

'Oh crap. No. No. No. You can't be.' I realised that this wasn't what someone in 'supportive friend mode' should say, so quickly added, 'But if you are, we'll deal with it, Lizzy. All of us. You'll never have to cope with any of this on your own. Have you done the test yet?'

She nodded.

A cold wave of fear consumed me.

'I haven't looked. I can't. I just can't.'

Neither could I. It was just too terrifying. The prospect of what she was going to have to deal with was bad enough, but to do it while pregnant with his child would be unbearable.

With a strength that I was completely fabricating for the sake of my friend, I slowly prised the stick from her fingers and turned it over. Beads of sweat popped from my pores as she refused to look down, staring instead at my face, waiting for the reaction that would tell her what she needed to know.

'Lizzy, it's . . .' My voice wobbled, then cracked altogether as I stuttered, 'Negative.'

'Negative?' she whispered. 'You're sure?'

I nodded and showed her the stick. One blue line. Definitely. Not even a hint of a second one.

Shattered heart? Tick. Pregnancy? Negative.

Both of us slumped with relief. 'Lou, I'm really sorry,' she stammered.

'Why? Are you crazy? *I'm* sorry. I had no idea there was anything wrong.'

'Neither did I. He only told me last weekend. But I never meant to put a downer on your wedding with all this stuff. I'm so sorry,' she repeated. 'I'm a shit friend.'

I grabbed a piece of toilet roll and used it to wipe away the tears and the worst of the mascara from her face. 'Lizzy, you're going through the worst time of your life, the most painful thing ever and yet you still came here. I love you for that and I promise you're the best friend I could ever have.'

She welled up again forcing me to head off the tears at the pass.

'But don't tell Ginger that because she thinks I love her more. Just let her believe that. Look I know it's easy to say, Liz, but we really will get through this. I promise.'

As if some force of determination had overtaken her, Lizzy pulled herself up and then yanked me up too, before giving me one last squeeze.

'OK, here's the deal. I don't want anyone else to know about this yet.'

'Lizzy, that's nuts. We're your friends, we want to support you.'

A hand came up and shushed me.

'Stop. Lou, I feel bad enough that I've landed all this on you on the day before your wedding. Don't make me feel even more guilty, which is exactly what will happen if my problems make me the focus of the trip. I need a laugh, I need some joy and I need to let my hair down and have a bloody great time while I'm here because God knows what I'm going back to. So please . . . Forget everything that just happened and let's just make this the special, beautiful occasion that it's meant to be.'

'But . . .'

'And if you don't I'll definitely tell your future sister-in-law that you love me the most,' she added with a smile.

'Ouch, that's evil.'

'It is. OK, I'm going to fix my make-up and go back out there like nothing's happened. I'll say I've been in here so long because we got chatting to . . . to . . . Cyndi Lauper. That's so random they're bound to believe it. By the way, cool bra – your knockers look sensational.'

With another kiss she was gone, and I suddenly remembered my reason for coming in here in the first place. I locked the door, plonked down on the seat and tried my best to get my resting heart rate back down to normal. Poor Lizzy. She so didn't deserve this. And the kids. There was going to be a whole lot of hurt all round.

I'd been in contemplation of developments for a few moments when something on the floor caught my eye. A white box. Lizzy must have left it there when she did the test. As I picked it up I realised that it wasn't empty. What a waste. Why did these companies put these things in packs of two? Were all pregnancy tests like that? I'd never had reason to use one so I had no idea. Weren't these things pretty reliable? Maybe Lizzy should have used this second one to make sure the result was correct, but then, the test she did couldn't have been more definite. Nope she definitely wasn't pregnant. Thanks to the gods of fertility for cutting her some slack there.

I flicked the stick around my fingers. Maybe I'd need one soon though. Or maybe it would be an idea to ask the man I was marrying tomorrow how he felt about children. How the hell had we managed to miss that? Shouldn't that be one of those things that you absolutely knew about someone before you actually committed to them for the rest of your life?

A niggle of something started to tug at my consciousness and at first I thought it was a token flicker of cold feet, but that was ridiculous. Red was who I was meant to be with. Although I did have a sudden vision of sitting in that Armenian pizza restaurant for the second time, on first-name terms with the staff and them bringing me over a coffee exactly the way I like it without even having to ask. Maybe I could make it an annual pilgrimage: come to New York every year, plan a wedding, bail out, hit the pizza joint.

The very thought set my stomach rumbling and I realised that I needed food. I really, really needed food. What was wrong with me? Since I'd got here all I'd done was eat and sleep and – wow, another wave of nausea. Perhaps I should have taken it a bit easier on those lunch-time cocktails.

My mind suddenly replayed something that Lizzy said and I glanced downwards. I could see where she was coming from, but that was easy to explain. My boobs always swelled when my period was due and it must be due around now. That was probably why I was ravenous too. Definitely. Without a doubt. It was hard to tell because my periods were never regular. I put it down to a haphazard diet, stress and a mild case of polycystic ovaries that had been diagnosed when I was a teenager. I was lucky. The only symptom I had was infrequent periods – sometimes they came six weeks apart, sometimes five, sometimes four. This time it was . . . no idea.

No. I couldn't be. I was on the Pill and I'd taken it religiously. I never missed it. Well, almost never and if I did then I doubled up the next day. I couldn't be pregnant. I just couldn't. And to prove it I should just open the cellophane and pee on this stick. It would be over in minutes and I'd know I was being ridiculous, then I could go back out there with my favourite people on earth and get on with savouring every minute of this weekend.

One pee later, I passed the time by praying. Dear Lady of the Immaculate Contraception, please make this test negative.

Twenty seconds passed and I gave up trying to hold out for the full minute and peeked. One blue line. Thank you, Lady of the Immaculate Contraception, you're a wonderful woman.

I was just about to toss it in the bin, when I realised that a shadow of moisture had now crossed over from the first window to the second one. Hang on, what was that? I thought it was done, but it was still moving, like a dark cloud crossing from one little plastic square to another, leaving behind a grey gloom and a . . . blue line. Another blue line was forming in the second window.

The Lady of the Immaculate Contraception seriously needed to rethink her job description.

I was pregnant. My future husband had probably arrived and he was sitting out there right now with absolutely no idea that he was going to be a dad. What if he didn't want a family? What if he was one of those blokes that preferred to be without the responsibility of a child?

206

What if . . . Hysteria was rising, sending my train of thoughts of in random directions. What if our relationship wasn't up to this? What if I got pregnant and he didn't want it and then I'd get fat and grumpy and the next thing I knew he was announcing that he was leaving me for one of those skinny models he had to photograph every day? Or an old girlfriend who valued freedom over fertility? Or . . . Or . . . A gay lawyer called Alex?

I pushed my forehead against the cold laminated surface of the side wall of the cubicle and tried to gain some sense of balance and rationality.

I was pregnant. I was going to have a baby. As if practising for the months to come, my hormonal pendulum swung in the other direction and a gurgle of joy shot from my stomach to my throat and then straight up to my tear ducts. I was pregnant. To a man I loved. And this could only be a good, good thing.

But, like Lizzy, I realised that this wasn't news that I wanted to share with everyone just yet. This was my secret until it became Red's too. He should definitely know before anyone else, so somehow I was going to have to pull on some semblance of normality and act like an over-excited bride-to-be instead of an overexcited mother-to-be. I'd just stick with giddy enthusiasm and hope they all bought it.

'Lou, are you in there?'

Ginger's voice shocked me back to the moment.

'Lou, are you OK?'

'I'm fine. I'll be back out in a minute. Think I must have eaten something that's playing havoc with my stomach.'

Good. Plausible. Well done.

'Yeah, right,' she retorted. 'I know exactly what's going on.'

Oh fuck. But I didn't say that out loud. 'Er, what?' I replied nervously.

'I know exactly why you're in the loo and why your stomach is giving you gip. Go on, admit it.'

Admit it? Admit what? How could she know? I didn't even bloody know until five minutes ago. Was she psychic?

'What am I supposed to admit?' I asked cagily. She couldn't know. Her first niece/nephew may be on its way into the world but how could she possibly have sensed that before me?

'You're a bag of nerves,' she replied in her very best triumphant voice, 'because you were talking to Cyndi Lauper. You've always loved her!'

'You're right, Ginger. Completely bang on.' I couldn't help laughing at the absurdity of it all. 'It was amazing. I've asked her to the wedding tomorrow and she says she'll try to come.'

Thirty-two

Red groaned as he stretched, then climbed into bed and reached out his hand to me.

'Get in here, Lou Cairney. This is the last chance I'm going to have to shag a single woman.'

'You're like one of the all-time great romantics, do you know that?' I replied, stuffing the little chocolate that had been left on the pillow into my mouth. Urgh, dark chocolate. I hated dark chocolate. It was the work of Satan. I unwrapped the one that had been left on Red's side and devoured that too. Satan obviously had a hypnotic effect on pregnant women.

'I thought you didn't like dark chocolate?' Red's face was a picture of puzzlement.

'It's growing on me.'

I ran a brush through my hair and headed towards him, realising that the pillow snack was now stuck somewhere directly above the huge knot in my stomach. I had to tell him. Right now. Before we got married. I had no idea what to say, although I was suddenly thinking that I should sugar-coat it along the lines of, 'OK, baby, I'm coming. Get ready to shag a single woman . . . who's also up the duff.'

Perhaps not. In terms of great quotes from life-defining moments, I had a hunch that would never be a classic. Go on, Lou, get this done. Where's your courage?

I sat on the edge of the bed and resisted the tug of his hand pulling me towards him. Perhaps sex first? Nope, because then he'd be all sleepy and I could be accused of using tawdry manipulation tactics. Plus there was no way I could focus on orgasmic happenings with this going around in my head.

'Baby, I've got something I need to tell you and I don't want you to freak out.'

His face turned ashen and he slumped back on the pillow. 'I knew it,' he said, his voice thick with exasperation. 'You've changed your mind. You're bailing out again. Bloody hell, Lou, I can't believe you would—'

'No! I haven't changed my mind, I promise! I still want to marry you tomorrow and . . . to be honest, I can't wait. I love you. Just remember that.'

His relief oozed out of every pore and right on cue came another tug of the hand, with an accompanying seductive grin. 'Then come here and let me show you how much I love you back.'

I pulled my hand away. If only I'd stuck to those bloody rules about not seeing the groom on the night before the wedding then I wouldn't be having to deal with this. Right. Time to tell him.

'What's up?' he asked, clearly confused now. I could understand his viewpoint – much to my embarrassment, I was usually pretty much a sure thing in the sex department. I figured I had a lot of years of abstention and dissatisfaction to make up for. Plus he made me really, really horny.

'OK, I'm just going to say this. The thing is . . . The thing is . . .'

Say it! Say it! The voices in my head had megaphones and they weren't afraid to use them.

'The thing is . . . Lizzy's Adam has left her for a bloke.'

He stared at me in stunned silence for a good ten seconds. 'Out of all the things I thought could possibly come from your mouth right then, that wasn't one of them.'

I hung my head in shame. Fuck, I was useless. I had a horrible feeling that the tiny baby inside me just slapped its hand to its forehead and muttered something about whether it was too late to change its mind.

'Who's the guy?'

'Alex Dunns. He might have been in school with you.' Get back on track. Come on, Lou, get back on track.

'The lawyer from the High Street? He *was* a mate in school. We did a duet to a Wham! song at the end of year talent show and I was Andrew Ridgeley. Some things seem so obvious in hindsight. Shit, how's Lizzy?'

'Distraught. But she doesn't want anyone to know so you can't say anything. She needs to just forget it for a few days and enjoy herself here.'

'Are you sure there's nothing we can do?'

That's why I was marrying this man. He was so caring and thoughtful and kind. He'd make a great dad. I shook my head. 'Not right now, but she'll need massive support when we get back.'

'Sure. Anything. God, poor Lizzy. OK, now that you've scared the crap out of me can you come to bed? I really thought you were about to deal out some life-shattering news there, Lou. My poor heart just about had a seizure.'

Lou Cairney, you are a total disgrace. It was the voices with the megaphones again, backed up by the disgruntled foetus. They were right.

I put my hand over his and took a huge, deep breath, before spitting out, 'Red, there's something else.'

'Oh for the love of God.' His words were softened by his laughter. 'Is it always going to be like this? One drama

211

after another, never knowing what's going to come out of your mouth next? OK, let's have it. No, no, let me guess! You have an evil twin. You're allergic to mice. You've always wanted a pony. You burned down your last boyfriend's house. You're on the Interpol most wanted list. You're pregnant—'

'I am.' I cut him off and watched as he struggled to rewind the dialogue.

'You're on the Interpol most wanted list?'

'I'm pregnant.'

It felt like the point in the movies where someone pulls a pin out of a grenade, lobs it into a crowded market, then you have to wait to see if it explodes.

'You're pregnant?'

I nodded, tears plopping from my face, stomach churning. The baby was clearly doing a lap of honour of my womb in celebration.

'You're pregnant?' he repeated, louder now. I couldn't help hoping that he'd get past this bit and move on to a more comprehensible reaction pretty soon.

I didn't have much longer to wait. Red leaped out of bed, roared with excitement, lifted me up and swung me around.

'Not a good idea! Nauseous pregnant woman!' I giggled.

He returned me to solid ground then leaned down and kissed me like he'd never kissed me before, a raw, sensual caress which made my insides flip again.

Eventually, he broke off and just stared at me for a few moments, his face just inches from mine.

'Are you happy?' he asked. 'I'm guessing this was a surprise for you too.'

'Yes and yes. I did one of Lizzy's tests in the restaurant toilet tonight.'

'Lizzy's pregnant too?' He was completely baffled again.

212

'No, but she thought she was. That's a whole other conversation. Yes, it was a surprise but I'm really happy. Terrified, but happy.'

'I'm just ecstatic. I've always wanted a kid.'

I reached up and hugged him. 'I'm so relieved, Red. I realised when I got the result that we've never talked about having children. I was so scared that maybe you didn't want them.'

He got completely carried away and swung me around again. I let him. This was so amazing. He was an incredible man and I felt like the luckiest slightly queasy bride-to-be in the world. Nothing could possibly detract from the exquisite joy of this moment.

'Are you kidding? I've always wanted children. In fact, I'd really like six.'

Thirty-three

Lou

The St Kentigern Hotel, Glasgow. Saturday morning, 3 am

'I can't believe I'm still up at this time,' Lizzy groaned. 'I'm always in bed by ten.'

'I can't believe I'm going to bed at this time,' Ginger retorted, pulling on a pair of black pyjama bottoms. 'Nocturnal World is so much more fun than this.'

The hotel suite had two bedrooms but we'd somehow settled in one. Lizzy and I had decided to share the gorgeous, black-lacquered, king-size bed and Ginger had claimed the chaise longue at the end of it. Lizzy threw a cushion and it thudded against Ginger's back. Ginger laughed as she tossed it back, then pulled on a black vest top.

'Do you have a single item of clothing that isn't black?' I asked her.

'Nope. That's why I'm always a great bet for a funeral.'

'You even wore black to my wedding,' I reminded her.

'Don't you dare get all high and mighty on me, madam.

It wasn't like you were resplendent in bias-cut Vera Wang yourself.'

'You know something, apart from the fact that I'd just discovered my husband had a gay lover, I had the best time that day. It was the most beautiful wedding I'd ever been to.'

'Thanks,' Ginger huffed.

'You didn't invite us to yours!' I pointed out. Ginger and Ike had, in true Ginger style, got married in a registry office with two strangers for witnesses and then headed off to a swanky, trendy, incredibly expensive London club to celebrate with each other. We only found out she was married months later when Ike let it slip over Christmas dinner. She said she did it that way so she wouldn't end up with a pile of toasters, fondue sets and bread makers, but I knew it was more of an avoidance of gushy sentimentality strategy.

Gushy sentimentality had been big on our day though. Not in what we wore (as promised the bridal outfit was jeans and Converse and an I Heart New York T-shirt, the brides-maids were equally casual and Josie wore a psychedelic floor-length kaftan she'd spotted in the hotel gift shop that morning), but just in the perfection of the day.

It had been cold but sunny, a perfect crisp morning, as we stood at the fountain in Central Park surrounded by tourists sporting huge cameras, joggers, nannies with children, dog-walkers clutching multiple pets and a few suspicious characters who looked like they were about to conduct a flash-robbery at any minute. Josie gave them her stare of death and, despite the fact that she looked like a circus venue, they backed away.

The official who conducted the ceremony was a jovial African American who injected full drama and spectacle into his work. 'Shall we start with a song?' he asked.

'Definitely,' I replied. I was thinking 'Ave Maria'. Maybe 'Endless Love'. Or perhaps an instrumental of the 'Wedding March'.

Instead we got a rousing, inclusive, absolutely fantastic rendition of 'Oh Happy Day'. Even the suspicious-looking gang members hummed along to the chorus.

'I think we're being married by Al Green,' Red whispered, breaking off from holding my hand to clap as per instructions from Al.

I threw my head back and laughed until tears were blinding me. This was so perfect. So absolutely perfect.

A crowd of people had formed now, complete strangers, all wearing huge grins as they watched the ceremony. Actually, not all complete strangers. Turns out that Red had put the two Spanish women from the boat lake on standby to be witnesses in case there was a problem with Ginger, Lizzy and Josie's flight.

Now they were standing beside the official, wearing co-ordinating velour tracksuits in pink and purple.

I loved it. It couldn't have been more relaxed and chilled and . . . pardon?

I realised Al Green had asked us something. 'I believe you wish to say your own vows?'

Red nodded.

We did? Did we? Really? Why had no one told me? I couldn't say vows. I was hopeless at impromptu speaking. There was a reason I'd been put out of the school debating team. I couldn't. I just . . .

'Lou, I've loved you for almost half of my life. And since the day I fell in love with you I never dared to think that you'd ever love me back. I mean, what are the chances?'

Everyone smiled and the Spanish lady in the pink let out a loud sob.

'But you do and I'll never stop being thankful. I promise that I'll never take it for granted. I'll always protect what we have. I'll never break your trust or do anything to hurt you. And even if I forget to tell you how much I love you, know that I'm thinking it. If you'll have me, I'll stay with you until the end of time.'

Oh. Dear. Lord. I frantically looked for something to wipe my tear-stained face with. Josie's sleeve was the closest option and she happily made it available.

Where had that come from? The man who was so emotionally shy and positively allergic to grand romantic declarations had just swept me off my feet. How did I follow that?

I felt the pressure of dozens of eyes, all watching me in anticipation of something equally moving. Say what you feel. Say it. Just tell him how it is. 'Red, it took me a little longer to realise it, but I did and there are no words to say how much I love you. I never thought I'd marry anyone because I didn't believe I'd ever find someone I could trust to love equally, to accept me for who I am, and who believed in my happiness as much as his own. Red, if you asked me right now to follow you anywhere I would. I never believed someone as amazing as you existed. I trust you with my heart, with my life and I'll stay with you until the end of time because there will never be a day that I don't want to be with you.'

The crowd cheered as we were declared man and wife and Red picked me up and swung me around until I was dizzy. It was perfect. Perfect. Right then, right there, I knew that it was going to last for ever. We were indestructible.

Now, eight years later, I just wished that I still felt so sure.

Thirty-four

Lou

2002 – Aged 32

'When's your baby due now?' Natalia, one of our regular cabin crew customers, eyed my bump warily, clearly concerned that either the imminent birth of my child would interfere with her grooming schedule or that I'd deliver right there in front of her and risk splashing her Jimmy Choos. OK, I might be being a little uncharitable, but I was *two weeks late!*

'Two weeks ago,' I replied, trying my best not to wince as another shooting pain travelled at warp speed from my hamstring to my right shoulder blade. I felt like I should crack a joke about the baby being happy in there, that it was obviously lying on a futon, listening to Take That's greatest hits and refusing to come out, but at that moment my sense of humour was being held hostage by my hormones.

'You OK?' That came from Josie, who was hovering around me with a brush making a bad job of sweeping the floor, endeavouring to keep up the pretence of making herself useful in a salon capacity. She'd taken the last two weeks off her six

218

cleaning jobs and the moonlight shift at the bookies to mount a twenty-four-hour surveillance on her pregnant niece. She even timed my loo breaks, clocking me in and out in case I went into the toilet, had a spontaneous delivery and gave birth on the floor. She swore that happened to her mother during the war.

Why was it that people thought the perfect time to tell birth horror stories was when you were pregnant? So far I'd learned about the woman who was in labour for a fortnight, the one who popped in front of two hundred gothic teenagers during a showing of *Bride of Chucky* up at the local cinema, the ones whose babies appeared in a taxi, on a bus, and in the frozen food aisle of Asda, helped by an elderly gent on a mobility scooter clutching a pepperoni pizza.

I had absolutely no idea why the NHS was in crisis because according to what I was hearing it seemed that no one had given birth in a hospital since the beginning of time.

The door dinged to announce a new arrival and Mrs Marshall breezed in clutching Jennifer Aniston. 'Lou, love, have you still not had that baby?'

Yes. I have. But I thought I'd wear a space hopper up my jumper just to confuse everyone.

'Two weeks late,' I told her, trying my best to go for a tone of sing-song tolerance. I think it came out more 'psycho killer on the edge'.

I should have stopped work weeks ago but in a catastrophe of timing, both my top stylists had come over all 'life's for living' and gone off to travel the world together. The last postcard we'd received came from a sun-drenched island off the coast of Thailand where they had hooked up with an Australian rugby team full of muscle-bound hunks who, they informed us, were a great laugh and kept them up partying all night. I tried to tell myself they were having a crap time and would be much happier here with my daily regimen of

219

clients, pain and haemorrhoid issues. I'd made a resolution to seek hypnotherapy to forget those when this was over. It was the only way I got through the days.

Of course, this employee exodus coincided with a boom in business caused by the imminent festive period, a time when it's notoriously difficult to recruit new staff. Instead, we'd scaled down the appointments as much as possible without upsetting our regulars, and I was still working a six-day week while carrying the weight of a small hippo-potamus around my middle area. Did I mention that I was two weeks late?

And yet . . . pain and inhuman working conditions aside, I was so excited. Beyond thrilled. Giddy with anticipation. I felt a little hormonal surge lift my mood. I still couldn't quite believe that all this was actually happening to me. Just over a year ago I'd been resolutely single with a three-date limit on all relationships. Now I was married to the loveliest man on earth (there may be a slight bias in there and I reserved the right to amend this opinion on an hourly basis due to pregnancy-related mood swings), about to become a mum and, for the first time in my life, I felt like I had a family. Red. Me. Bump. Our own little unit. Ours. I also had a business that I had built up over thirteen years and that I adored. I'd managed to pay off the credit cards. We'd moved to an old Victorian semi in a pretty tree-lined street that we'd be refurbishing for the next decade, but it was so fantastic I didn't care. It was like all the stars in the cosmos were lining up just perfectly and for the first time I understood that concept of having it all. Because I felt like I was on the cusp of having the life of my dreams: husband, baby, career, home, friends and so much love that . . . that . . .

'Josie, I'm off again.' I sniffed. So much love that I dissolved into a blubbering mess of emotion every time I thought about it. Thankfully, a box of Kleenex instantly appeared in front of me.

I threw a gown around Natalia and got to work. 'Have I just put you off the whole concept of reproduction?' I asked her with a jokey smile.

'Totally,' she replied. I don't think she was kidding.

At the next chair, one of the juniors settled Mrs Marshall after her shampoo, and began combing out her wet hair ready for me to work on next. It was like a conveyor belt that never seemed to end. 'Hey, Lou, my husband told me this morning that you're going to have a girl.'

I couldn't help grinning. 'Which husband, first or second?'

'First. The second one hasn't said a sensible word since the day I married him,' she retorted, her disgusted expression reflecting her difficulty in coming to terms with the fact that the retired sailor she married after meeting him on a three-day US mini-break wasn't in fact the stuff that fantasies were made of. Since he'd arrived in this country he'd spent every day down at the local park sailing his remote control battleship on the pond, keeping himself in shape in case he should ever be called upon to mastermind a naval assault on behalf of the nation.

Just as well, then, that she still had a full and frank dialogue with the husband who'd been dead for more than two decades. It was always good to have someone to talk to in your twilight years. A girl. A girl would be good. It would be . . .

'Josie!' I yelped. The Kleenex box reappeared and I took two. It seemed like wise forward planning.

'What's with all the crying?' asked Natalia, with a subtle frown.

'Hormones,' I replied. 'And I'm just so . . . happy.' That set off a full-scale torrent and I was beyond relieved when Rosie, one of the two remaining stylists, finished trimming a Christian fundamentalist's twelve-inch beard and appeared at my side.

'Why don't you go have five minutes, I'll take over here.'
Natalia looked like she could reach up and kiss her.

'Mrs Marshall, I'll be back in a few moments, is that OK? The girls will get you a cup of tea and a garibaldi.'

'That's fine, sweetheart, on you go.'

As soon as I'd done the twenty-metre lumber up to the staffroom, I plumped myself down on the sofa and closed my eyes. Just a few moments of peace and rejuvenation, then I'd be fine again.

The knock on the door ripped right through my attempt at express Zen meditation.

'Hello my darling oh my God you look wonderful just blooming and fat and the way a mamma should and are you not due to have that baby soon?'

Donna Maria, my lovely landlady, spoke without small technicalities like punctuation.

'I'm two weeks late,' I said for the 1,232nd time that day.

'How are you? Is it time for your colour again?'

Was it just me or did her eyes shift in a weird way just then? There was a pause that was more pregnant than my abdominal cavity.

'Lou I'm really sorry to have to do this to you especially at a time like this but I'm terminating your lease on the shop.'

'Pardon?' I waited for the bit where she laughed and told me she'd been sent by the girls outside to play a joke that would shock me into labour.

'I'm sorry, Lou,' she repeated, 'but my Chantelle Donna Maria wants to open a beauty salon and now that she's about to become eighteen we want to give her this shop as a gift. You'll understand when you have your own little one that you would give them your heart and soul if they asked for it.'

Speech proved momentarily elusive. Chantelle Bloody Donna Maria. Who last week wanted to be a glamour model, the week before a pop star, who had two convictions for shoplifting from Ann Summers shops and who lap danced at the weekends without her mother's knowledge up at Bar Muff.

'But, Donna Maria, we have a contract.'

Didn't we? We did. Surely. It had been so long ago I only had vague recollections of signing something.

'Yes but it allows either one of us to give thirty days' notice of termination.' She had the grace to look apologetic and to try to sugar-coat it. 'Maybe it'll be a good thing give you a chance to stay home with the baby I mean who needs a job like this when they've got a little one I dedicated every minute of my time to Chantelle Donna Maria and I've never regretted it because she's turned into a beautiful kind giving girl.'

It didn't seem the time to point out that the blokes up at Bar Muff were probably grateful too.

'But Donna Maria, this is my business. Please, you have to reconsider! I . . . I . . . I've spent my whole working life here.'

My heart was starting to race and my child chose that very moment to send another kick reverberating up my spine.

'I'm sorry Lou but we've already promised her that she can have it and we can't go back on that I'll go now before you get stressed . . .'

Horse bolted. Stable door shut.

'. . . and I really am sorry Lou you know I hate to give you problems but my hands are tied.'

Just like that she was gone. And so, apparently, was the business that I loved. So much for bloody having it all.

'Josie!' I tried to shout but it came out more of a pitiful blurt. 'Bring the Kleenex!'

Thirty-five

What was it about visits to doctors, dentists and lawyers' offices that always made me nervous?

'My God, you're huge. Shouldn't you have had that baby by now?' Alex asked.

'I'm two weeks late.'

'Would you punch me if I made a joke about boiling the kettle and having towels on standby?'

'Yes.'

'OK then. Let's talk about this contract.'

Don't cry. Do not cry. It was twenty-four hours since Donna had broken the news and it had passed in a complete blur of tears (from me and the rest of the staff), fury (me) and threats to sneak into Bar Muff and take incriminating photos of Chantelle Donna Maria which would rid her parents of any inclination to give her my shop (Josie).

I was devastated. Distraught. The only glimmer of hope was the man sitting right in front of me – the lover of my best friend's husband. Who was also now my best friend's tentative friend. It had taken a few months of heartbreak, talking and soul-searching, but Lizzy had finally come to

terms with Adam's new relationship and to everyone's astonishment, the two men had rented the house four doors along
from her and they were making their new family set-up work.
It helped that Adam and Alex had done everything possible
to save her feelings and make up for the shock and devastation. Now the children split their time between the two homes
and they'd all brokered some kind of working alliance. I'd
met Alex a few times now at birthdays and special occasions,
but it was Lizzy who'd dug out my original contract, faxed
it to him, brought me here to see him and who was now busy
explaining the situation.

'I've told Lou that apart from the fact that you stole my
husband and ruined my life, you're a great lawyer, so we're
praying you've come up with something.'

Alex suddenly looked slightly rattled. 'Erm, thanks. I think.
OK, so I've gone through it with a fine tooth comb . . .'

Please say we can stop this. Please.

'. . . and I'm really sorry Lou, but it's watertight. Did you
have a lawyer check it when you signed it?'

A sinking feeling plummeted from my head to my toes.

'No.' I shrugged helplessly. 'I was young and naive and
overwhelmingly thrilled to have got my own place. And I
didn't want anyone scrutinising things too closely in case they
uncovered Josie's financial, er, economies with the truth.
Everything I tell you in here is confidential, right?'

He nodded warily, clearly unused to this amount of drama
on a Tuesday afternoon in the searing metropolis of Weirbank.

'But what about all the money I've invested in it? The
place was a wreck when I took it over. I've spent thousands
on refurbishment and upkeep. Doesn't that count for
anything?'

His expression told me the answer before he spoke. 'I'm
sorry, Lou, but it doesn't. That was all down to you and they
have no liability there at all. In fact, it's written in the small

print that it must be returned to them in a perfect state of repair, so you have to make sure that any outstanding maintenance is completed before you hand it back over.'

'You are kidding me!' I couldn't believe what I was hearing. Had I even read the contract before I'd signed it? I'd obviously been so ramped up on excitement that I'd blindly agreed to all their terms. What else was in there? Did I have to give them my firstborn child and internal organs should they require them? Firstborn child. Oh no! My firstborn child was coming into the world to a mother who was completely bloody useless and who had somehow managed to give away everything she'd worked for her whole career.

I was a total failure. A total and utter hopeless case. One with a vague awareness that there were fluids spurting from my facial orifices.

Lizzy handed me a tissue from the stock Josie had given her when she collected me.

'So there's nothing she can do? Nothing?' she asked now. 'Not even anything illegal?'

Alex reddened and pulled at his Hugo Boss tie. 'Not that I could possibly give an opinion on options involving anything that would break the law, but short of bumping off Chantelle I can't see any way out of this.'

Nothing. Not a damn thing. Years of blood, sweat and tears and I was going to be left with nothing to show for it except some equipment and staff that needed to earn a living. What was I going to tell them? They all had their hopes pinned on Alex pulling a legal rabbit out of the hat and I was going to have to break it to them that there was nothing we could do. How could I have allowed this to happen?

'OK, don't panic. Do not panic.' Lizzy clutched my hand and squeezed. 'It's not all over yet. We still have time to do something. We could try to negotiate. Or . . . or . . .'

I waited to see what little nugget of brilliance my lovely

226

friend was going to come up with. 'Or we could beg them for mercy?' she finished weakly.

We were officially done for.

Alex picked up the calendar on his desk and checked the date. 'I think you're going to have to look at other options, Lou. Maybe move to another premises. Relaunch somewhere else. Try to buy out one of the other salons in town, perhaps?'

Absolutely not. I wasn't giving up that easily. I would fight this until the end. I'd worked my now-considerable arse off to build up my business, it meant the world to me and I wasn't giving it up. I bloody wasn't.

No way.

Definitely n—

Alex was still talking. 'You've got twenty-eight days left to come up with something so you still have time.'

'I don't.'

Lizzy squeezed my hand again. 'Honey, don't say that. We'll find a way out of this.'

'No time,' I repeated, although now it was more of a desperate hiss. 'Lizzy, get Red. The baby . . . It's coming.'

Thirty-six

'Push!!!!!!!!!!'

I have never come closer to killing my husband. I was borderline manic after eighteen hours of labour and several thousand people telling me that I was 'doing great'. I was not. The epidural had worn off and they'd been unable to administer another. But hey, Red said I was doing great. There's a reason they don't allow weapons in hospitals.

Now, finally, a spookily tall Asian doctor who, the nurses informed me, had once played volleyball for Malaysia in the Olympics, was telling me to push. And push. And push. Until . . .

'Waaaaaaaaaaaaaaaaaaaaaaaaaaaah.'

That one came from the baby, but Red immediately defied his macho West of Scotland roots and burst into tears too.

'It's a girl,' Dolly, the nurse, announced gleefully. She held out what looked like a set of garden shears and asked Red if he wanted to cut the cord. He nodded. If this wasn't the most pivotal moment of my life I may have informed her that he'd already cut through the lawnmower cable four times this year so probably couldn't be trusted with sharp implements.

228

'Is she OK? Please tell me she's OK!' I gasped, craning my neck to see what was going on down at the other end.

The Malaysian doctor's head appeared first, then came his absurdly long arms, and in them was the most beautiful, breathtaking mound of gooey sludge I'd ever seen. 'She's absolutely fine. And loud, very loud.' He smiled.

'Oh my God – a girl. Mrs Marshall's dead husband was right.'

The doc tried not to look concerned for my mental health as he reached over and placed my baby on my chest. In line with recent behaviour, I cried.

She was perfect in every single way. She had Red's nose, Ginger's hair and . . .

'Waaaaaaaaaaaaaaaahhhhh.'

. . . Josie's lungs. And my wrinkles, but apparently they would disappear after a couple of days.

Suddenly, she stopped crying and nuzzled in and promptly fell asleep. Was that normal? Did they do that? Was that OK?'

I searched the doctor's face but he looked unconcerned so I went back to staring at my perfect little girl.

I was a mum.

A mum.

After nine months, two weeks, eighteen hours, a million tears and several replays of Stevie Wonder's greatest hits, my baby had appeared right in the middle of 'Superstition', my favourite song of all time.

She was a class act already.

'I'll be back in five minutes to weigh her,' the doctor told us, before stooping as he went through the door to avoid concussion. I realised that Dolly had disappeared too, leaving just us. My family.

I held the baby out to Red and he just stared at her for a few seconds before looking back at me, his face solemn.

229

'I love you so much, Lou,' he began softly, 'but you realise that you come second now. She's just become the most important thing in my life.'

I nodded, my chest so tight I couldn't even speak. To anyone else, this would seem like a strange thing to say, but Red knew that there were no other words that could mean more to me. Being brought up with a couple obsessed with each other, whose child had always come second, there was nothing I wanted to hear more than confirmation that he would love his daughter more than anything else in the world, including me. He would take care of her, love her, never ever walk away. This was his girl and he was going to be the most incredible dad. Oh Lord, more tears.

'And you come second now too,' I whispered. He beamed back at me and every nerve ending in my body prickled with happiness.

How had I ever got this lucky?

Dolly breezed back into the room, followed by the unfeasibly tall doc. 'Here you go, my love,' she announced. 'Some tea and toast for you. Now hand that little bundle over and we'll take care of all our checks while you have your tea.'

Despite a valiant effort to hang on to her, Red finally passed her over and reached out and took my free hand. 'Thanks, Lou,' he said, grinning.

'You're welcome. But don't think you're getting a Christmas present because one of those new Xbox thingies would mean nothing after this.'

Wow, another wave of crashing glee swept over me. It was like suddenly my hormones were on spin cycle and throwing out little bursts of emotion on a minute-by-minute basis. I held out the plate of toast to the love of my life, to the man who had brought me the kind of bliss I'd never even imagined could be possible.

'No thanks, I've had some already,' he said nonchalantly.

'When?'

'When the doc was giving you the epidural and you told me to go outside so I wouldn't faint. Dolly made me some tea and toast and I had it in the TV room. *Friends* was on. It was the one where . . .'

'*What!* I sent you out there to pace up and down. And to fret. And worry. And reflect on how brave and heroic your wife was in the face of one of Mother Nature's trials, and you were in the TV room having tea and toast?'

Even the doc and Dolly were making a really bad attempt to act like they weren't dying to hear how he was going to get himself out of this one. Meanwhile, his horrified expression showed that he realised the gravity of his error. Half an hour with Courtney Cox had just become a demon that would haunt him for ever.

Luckily, intervention from a sympathetic medical professional and our new daughter saved the day.

'Here we go then.' Dolly whipped away my cup and plate and my baby was once again placed on my chest. 'So what is this little one's name going to be?'

Red and I stared at each other. 'It would be a bad idea for you to say Monica, Phoebe or Rachel right now,' I warned him.

Names. We'd been through every baby name book in WH Smith and we still hadn't come up with one that felt right. We'd even gone down the place of conception route (Paisley) and the place of pregnancy discovery (T, G, I or Friday). But in the end nothing seemed to fit.

There was a kerfuffle at the door and a huge mass appeared from nowhere.

'I'm sorry, but can we come in now? That militant nurse told us we had to wait until the doctor had finished.'

Thankfully, Dolly found Ginger's sense of humour 'amusing and sharp' as opposed to 'call security and remove the cheeky cow'.

231

'Come on then,' Dolly replied, 'but you'll have to keep the noise down.'

Ginger, Lizzy and Josie stormed in with a clatter of heels, trying their very best to scream quietly. That's when it happened. Something that I'd lived my whole life without seeing – Josie filled up and someone else had to pass the Kleenex to her. If ever there was a time that she needed a therapeutic caramel log, this was it. 'My first great-niece,' she whispered, awestruck.

'Wow! She's so, so, so beautiful!' Lizzy exclaimed, her voice also thick with emotion.

After a moment of temporary insanity during which the woman who despised public displays of affection smothered all of us with hugs and kisses, Ginger stared at the baby, her brow knotted with puzzlement, until she suddenly had a eureka moment.

'I've just realised who she looks like!'

'Who?'

'Our aunt,' she told Red. 'You know, the one who caused a huge scandal when she ran away with the ringmaster from the circus then surfaced years later with that bloke who'd been a roadie for the Rolling Stones.'

I was scared to ask questions. There were some things that should just be taken at face value.

'What was her name?' Red asked, clearly as confused as the rest of us.

'Cassie. Aunt Cassie. She lives in an old hippy commune somewhere near Woodstock now.'

No one spoke for a few seconds while we processed the information, then, in perfect synchronicity, we all turned to look at the baby.

'Cassie,' I said softly. 'It's perfect.'

Thirty-seven

Lou

The St Kentigern Hotel, Glasgow. Saturday morning, 11 am

My first thought was that the incessant ringing was the alarm clock at the other side of the bed. I reached down, grabbed a hotel slipper and threw it in the direction of the noise.

'Aw!'

Clearly, I missed.

'It's the phone,' Lizzy wailed, while rubbing the side of her face. 'What is it with me? I even manage to get injured when I'm sleeping.'

I leaned over, kissed her, apologised, then stretched right over her to grab the phone. 'Hello?'

'Mama, it's me.'

My smile was instantaneous. 'Who?'

'Cassie, Mama. It's Cassie.'

'Cassie who?' I joked. It was the game we played every time we spoke on the phone – and much as social services might not approve of the psychological impact of denying

233

your own child, my little sweetheart could handle it because inevitably there was a pay-off at the end.

'If you don't remember you have to bring me a present.'

'Nope, sorry, I don't remember.'

'Yaaaayyyyyyy! I get a present. I love you, Mama.'

'I love you too, sweetheart. Are you having fun with Daddy?'

'Yes. We watched *The Princess Diaries* last night. I think I'm too big for it now but it's Daddy's favourite.'

I had a sudden vision of Red vouching to have his toenails extracted rather than sit through that movie again. I decided not to share the thought.

'Is Auntie Ginger with you?'

Great. I'd been away from my child for a whole day and who did she want to talk to? The creature from the Black Lagoon that was snoring at the bottom of my bed.

I tried not to give in to the desolation that ambushed me.

I wanted them to be close. Hadn't I thought of little else lately? Ginger and Cassie's relationship had to be tight, had to be rock solid and I'd do everything I could to encourage that.

Not that it required much effort. Ginger had done so much more than I could ever thank her for.

After I managed to get her to something resembling a communicative state, she chatted to Cassie and then we all said our goodbyes.

Ginger flopped back onto the chaise and called to the universe for aspirin. I served up a breakfast cocktail of painkillers de jour, coffee and water, made tea for Lizzy and me, then climbed back into bed.

Last night's reminiscing was still playing on my mind. 'Hey, Auntie Ginger,' I said softly.

'Will you stop shouting,' came the reply.

'I was just thinking. You know how we were talking about pivotal, landmark moments last night.'

'Mmmm.'

'Well, honey, I don't know if I ever thanked you enough for what you did for me after Cassie was born. You really saved my life.'

Even though she had her eyes closed, I hoped she was getting this. I hoped she was feeling just how much gratitude I had for the fact that she was there when I needed the kind of love that only she could deliver.

'Lou,' she whispered.

Yep, her voice was chock-full of emotion. She got it. She knew. And, oh dear Lord, get the bunting out because we were about to have an exquisite moment of emotional connection.

'Yes?' I answered.

I waited. It was only natural that she would find this difficult. She struggled with stuff like this. Take your time, my darling. Don't rush it. Just let it flow.

'Lou.' Lizzy nudged me then gestured in Ginger's direction. 'Don't hold your breath for more. The snoring's a bit of a giveaway that she's fallen asleep.'

Thirty-eight

Lou

2004 – Aged 34

The doorbell rang and I jumped, causing me to splash the hot cup of tea I was holding all down my front. Door. Change. Door. Change. Another urgent ring of the doorbell made my mind up for me – no time to change. Heading down the hall, I strategically positioned my arm across the brown damp patch. Before I even had the door fully open, Ginger kissed me on the cheek as she burst in, carrying so many of those big cardboard designer shopping bags that she looked like she'd done a trolley dash up Rodeo Drive.

Halfway up the hall she turned, scanned my appearance and frowned. 'You've forgotten haven't you?'

'Forgotten what?'

'Lunch. Today. You were supposed to get a babysitter, we were going to get the glad rags on and we were . . .' She spotted the stain on the front of my T-shirt. 'Eeeew, are you lactating again?'

'No! I haven't breastfed Cassie for a year. I spilled my tea.'

I was aware that I was skirting around the main issue here. 'Ginger, I'm so sorry. I forgot all about lunch.'

With a dramatic sigh, she leaned back against the brick wall. Plastering it was somewhere on the list between finishing the roof and tiling the loo.

'Excuse?' she demanded.

'Cassie has been up all night, four nights in a row, because she's teething. Red is in Cannes with three models on a fashion shoot. I've got a house full of builders. Cassie has started calling the plumber "Daddy" – which would be fine if he was easy on the eye but he's sixty-two and no longer acquainted with his front teeth. I've done two sets of highlights and a cut and blow-dry in the kitchen this morning. My mother came to see me. She only stayed for half an hour because my dad wanted her to go out for lunch with him and I couldn't even muster up the strength to be annoyed. My sanity is slowly slipping to the point where I could curl into the foetal position and start rocking backwards and forwards at any moment. Help me. Or shoot me. I'm not sure which option I'd prefer.'

Burden unloaded, I sighed, realising we made an incongruous sight. Designer lady, in her immaculate Stella McCartney suit with a black studded vest underneath, skyscraper Louboutin shoes, a Hermès Birkin bag and me, doing my best impression of a bag lady with lactating breasts.

'Mamamamama!'

Ginger's expression immediately flipped from unamused to ecstatic.

'She's in the kitchen with a bowl of spaghetti hoops, so chatting out here for the last five minutes probably wasn't one of our better ideas.'

Heading towards the kitchen, I'm not ashamed to admit that I stayed behind Ginger in the manner of a warrior going into battle with his trusty shield. She had no idea of the danger that lurked behind that door.

'Gingingingin!' Cassie screamed with delight at seeing her favourite aunt, the one with whom she shared oh so many personality traits. At two years old, my daughter was stubborn, she was bold, she was loud, she was opinionated and she had a unique sense of fashion – as witnessed by the bowl of spaghetti hoops that she was currently wearing on her head. She was also fiercely loving and had a wicked sense of humour and unbridled energy. I now had a deep understanding of why Moira, Ginger and Red's mother, had a high-grade sherry habit and smoked twenty cigarettes a day to settle her nerves.

Ginger plumped her bags down on the floor and lifted her out of her high chair, not caring that she'd be wearing the evidence of Cassie's lunch on her silk suit for the rest of the day.

One of the biggest revelations of the last two years had been Ginger's overwhelming adoration of her new niece. She made a monthly trip from London to see her, phoned twice a week to check on her progress and had moved the entire stock of Hamleys to our back room. Who knew she could have such a soft spot for a baby? When we were eight years old, Lizzy and I would play with dolls, dressing them and feeding them, while Ginger would shave their heads and send them to war with the next-door boy's He-Man. Zero maternal instincts. None. It had been one of the ground rules when she married Ike – richer or poorer, in sickness and in health, and don't ever think about your sperm fertilising my eggs.

Ike was happy to agree. With two grown-up children from a previous marriage he was already fulfilled in the procreation department.

'Ginger, are you sure you wouldn't like a little one? Just one. You don't need to go mad and have a squad of them.'

'Don't even say it!' she cut me off. 'If my mother tells me one more time that she's said three novenas at the Chapel in the hope that the Virgin Mary will swoop in and somehow

238

impregnate me, I'm phoning ChildLine to report psychological abuse.'

'But . . .'

The death stare was beamed in my direction. 'Never gonna happen. Some people are just not meant to reproduce. Talking of which, why was your mother here?'

'She wanted to give me a hand, do some ironing and look after Cassie for a couple of hours to let me get some sleep.'

'You're kidding!'

'Of course I am. She came to remind me that it's my dad's birthday this weekend and to tell me they're going abroad for Christmas. Apparently they've wanted to do it for years but didn't because they had to stay here for my sake, which should of, course, win them some kind of heroic accolade. I was thinking the Nobel Peace Prize. Anyway, she stayed for less than an hour, long enough to say she'd seen her grand-daughter and claim she was granny of the year, then wafted off to meet my dad for lunch.'

I sighed as I ran a cloth over the kitchen wall in an attempt to begin to change the colour of the paintwork, currently listed on the Dulux shade chart as 'Heinz Spaghetti'.

To Cassie's shrieking delight, Ginger blew raspberries on Cassie's neck. 'How can she not just want to spend every little minute with this little snugglebug? Huh? Huh?' It really disconcerted me when Ginger spoke in a baby voice.

'So how long will it take you to get ready?' she asked, her voice returning to adulthood.

'I'd need a satellite navigation system to find my make-up bag and I would end up wearing something I've dragged out of the ironing basket.'

She didn't look impressed. 'And what are you wearing tomorrow?'

I was immediately gripped by panic. Tomorrow was Cassie's christening. We'd been planning to have her christened since she was born but we'd been mired in so many problems and obstacles that we were only now managing to have it done. To my horror, I felt tears prickle under my eyes. 'I've absolutely no idea. I've . . . I've . . . What's happened to me, Ginger?'

What had happened to me? I used to run a business, work long hours, manage my life and make a pretty good job of it. Now I couldn't even manage to remember lunch. It wasn't that I was unhappy, because I had nothing to be unhappy about. OK, so I still felt a desperate surge of sadness when I reflected on losing my salon. And yes, we'd had builders in the house for almost two years on and off, because on top of the full-scale renovation that the house originally required to make it habitable, we'd discovered woodworm in the joists and rot in the basement that the surveyor had failed to pick up when we bought it. Alex was suing them on our behalf for negligence, but in the meantime it had taken every penny we earned so far and it still wasn't done. I tried to tell myself that the tarpaulin covering the gap in the wall, which would eventually be patio doors to the garden, made an interesting design feature. The glass doors had been lying in the garage for months but we didn't have the money to get them fitted yet. Oh and Red worked away a lot. *A lot.* In order to finance the building work, he took every assignment going at his normal job, then topped it up with freelance work he picked up. In one week he could be in Aberdeen one day, Orkney the next, then London, then a weekend fashion shoot in Barcelona. With models. Was it wrong that the 'with models' bit really bothered me? They were all glam, and skinny, and they had arses the size of two perfectly formed grapefruits. Red was going from that to me – sporting 'dragged through a hedge chic' and smelling of hairspray from the succession of clients I'd seen in my half-built kitchen. But he never stopped telling me he loved me and I knew he wouldn't run

240

off with Katanya, aged 21, 36–22–33, likes winter sports, foreign travel and Bacardi Breezers. He wouldn't. He was a good man, I had a beautiful daughter, great friends, I was healthy and the next day we were having a gathering of all those I loved to christen my girl . . . So why was I crying in the middle of the day, when I had absolutely nothing to cry about?

'You're exhausted,' Ginger announced. 'You need sleep, you've been completely neglecting yourself, and you look like crap.'

After a deafening sniff, I wiped the palms of my hands across my cheeks. 'Was that supposed to be a comforting, motivational speech?' I asked her.

'Come on, I'm taking you out.'

'I can't go out like this, I'm lactating.' I sounded as fed up as I looked.

'Hang on.' The bags from the hall were retrieved and she pulled a gorgeous grey silk jersey T-shirt from one of them. 'Throw this on, go find a clean pair of jeans, I'll clean up Cassie and we're going out. You, my darling, are in need of some serious repair work.'

An hour later we were in the centre of Glasgow, standing outside a beauty salon I'd only ever read about in magazines, Cassie fast asleep in her buggy. 'They won't let me in there,' I told Ginger apprehensively as we approached the door. This place was seriously flash and seriously expensive. It was for the glossy and the groomed, not for women with inch-long roots and trousers with dust on the hems.

My heart sank even further when we got inside. It was like something out of a Balinese beach resort, all dark wood floors and white walls, with a huge waterfall in the middle of the room and some kind of tinkling, ethereal music playing in the background.

'Ginger! Lovely to see you. You're looking fabulous,' said

the vision of perfection behind the desk. Tall, willowy, with jet-black hair, parted in the middle and falling like a sheet of granite to her waist, she looked to be in her thirties but that was just a guess because where were her wrinkles? Where? In a rush of defensive insecurity, an internal monologue was building up resentments by the second. I bet she hadn't gone four nights on twenty minutes' sleep. I bet she didn't work twelve-hour days while looking after her child. I bet she didn't have a husband who worked away all the time. I bet she didn't have an overdraft. I bet she had four fecking walls in her kitchen!!!!!

'Are you OK?' Ginger hissed to me and I realised that while I was busy welling up and launching an internal war on this perfectly lovely woman in front of me, I'd been asked a question to which they were now waiting for a reply.

'Saskia was just asking what you'd like done?'

'Erm . . . erm . . .' Sleep. I just wanted to sleep and then wake up and be organised, and in control and not exhausted any more. 'A manicure, maybe?'

Ginger sighed in despair, gave me a disdainful glare and then took over. 'What time do you close?'

'Eight o'clock.'

I glanced at the ornate mahogany clock on the wall. It was one o'clock now.

'That gives us seven hours.' Ginger was way ahead of me. 'Hot stone massage to start, total body exfoliation, removal of all excess hair in all areas, spray tan, manicure, pedicure, eyebrows, hair colour cut, eyelash extensions and anything else you can throw at her that'll make her a goddess. Add it all to my account and –' she turned to me '– I will send a taxi at eight to collect you.'

'But I can't, I—'

A hand shot up and suddenly I was staring at an

intimidating palm. 'Stop! This isn't an optional situation.' God, she was bossy. And obstinate and stroppy and blunt. But I don't think I could ever have loved her more. Seven and a half hours later, I re-evaluated that statement.

Thirty-nine

As I waved goodbye to the taxi and opened the front door, the first thing that struck me was the smell. Real food. Not the microwave meals for one that I'd been living on while Red was away, but a mixture of aromas that could only be a simmering home-cooked meal. There was another smell too. Furniture polish and wax and . . . The floor! The oak flooring was gleaming for the first time since the day we moved in here. Properly shiny. How had that happened? I put my handbag down on the hall table, which was now so buffed it was almost reflective.

It was like a fairy with cleaning OCD had flown in and slaved away until everything was left spotless.

Opening the door to the kitchen, I wouldn't have been more gobsmacked if George Clooney was lying there naked with a rose between his teeth. The tarpaulin was gone and in its place were two glass doors, perfectly fitted, giving a beautiful view into the garden. Or what would be a garden once we did some work to elevate it from swamp status.

The rest of the room was almost unrecognisable. The bare brick walls had been plastered, the worktops had been scrubbed, all the wonky cupboard doors had been adjusted, the floor had been polished and over at the spotless table sat Cassie, in her high chair, gurgling into her toy telephone. Presumably she was calling Miracles Are Us to thank them for their contribution to my day.

'How . . . how . . . ?'

I could barely speak. 'Don't you dare cry again, those eyelash extensions will never cope,' Ginger warned.

'How did this happen?' I stammered. Without tears. Just.

'You know the one guy in Stud who is from Glasgow?'

I nodded. Of course I did. Josh. Aged nineteen. An abdomen so finely toned that it looked like a toast rack. Made females scream in the street. Number one honey in *Heat*.

'I called his brother. He owns a building company that works on corporate stuff, shopping malls and office blocks, but he brought some of his boys over and finished off some of the jobs that were needing done.'

I officially, absolutely and utterly adjusted my love for her to infinite levels, previously occupied only by Red, Cassie and John Taylor from Duran Duran.

A whirlwind suddenly arrived at my side. Josie, in my pink dressing gown, wearing a pair of Red's blue socks, hair wrapped in a Barbie beach towel, cigarette dangling from her mouth. 'I offered him sexual favours in return for his time but he passed – can you believe it?'

The giggles overwhelmed me. 'I can't. The guy is obviously unhinged.'

Grinning, Ginger carried on with her explanation of events. 'Then I called Josie who arrived with four of her pals and the floor buffing machine from the community centre . . .'

'I hope Senga gets that back in the cleaning cupboard before they notice it's gone,' Josie interjected.

'And they gave the house a spring clean from top to bottom, got all the windows and floors done for you. I know that with all the work that's still to be done, it'll be chaos again soon, but at least having those doors fitted and the walls plastered means that you'll be warm and the worst of the dust and grime is over.'

'Oh, Ginger, I can't thank you enough. We'll pay you ba—'

'Stop!' The hand of silence came up again. 'Lou, enough. I'm loaded, gorgeous and successful, with great contacts – it's the least I can do.'

'And modest, love. You forgot to mention modest,' Josie observed. 'Right, I've made a curry for dinner, Mr Patel's favourite recipe. I still miss him, you know. Who'd have thought that with all that meditation and health stuff he'd drop dead of a heart attack in the middle of Costco? Sit, sit!'

I gave Cassie a huge hug and sloppy kiss, then sat down at the table while Josie dished out our meals. Lamb rogan josh, huge doughy nan breads and saffron rice. Suddenly I was ravenous. When was the last time I'd eaten a proper meal? Somewhere between that hot stone massage and now, I'd come to the realisation that some things had to change. Having even a few hours away from the bedlam had given me time to think and I'd had some kind of flash of enlightenment.

For years my focus had been work, building the business, slogging away six days – sometimes seven – a week and, much as I'd adored it, I'd seriously neglected the other areas of my life. Then I'd married Red, already pregnant and we'd gone straight into parenthood while juggling a major renovation project that had wiped us out financially, still spending hours every day seeing clients in my kitchen, with Red working day and night too to keep our heads above water. When he did make it home, the two of us were so exhausted that we barely made it past a hello and a hug before one of us fell asleep. It was madness. Where was the quality of life? Where were the balance and the enjoyment?

Well, no more. We had to get this under control, do one last push to get the house finished, then I had to look at getting back out to work and earning a decent salary, prefer-ably part-time so that I could still have lots of time with my gorgeous girl and I wasn't spending my wages on childcare. Then my husband and I were going to get quality time together and have fun and sex. Lots of sex. I'd just had a Brazilian and I wasn't afraid to use it.

For the first time in months I felt a seed of optimism and a boost of energy and confidence that this was all going to be fine. We'd get there. I just had to find a way to get past the obstacles and tackle them one by one.

'Did I forget to tell you that you look great?' Josie asked. 'My God, girl, you definitely do. Like me in my younger days but without my killer bosom.' Usually, I would brush off the compliment, but this time I didn't because I knew that she wasn't far off the truth. I'd been preened, pummelled and plucked into a level of polished grooming that I hadn't achieved since some time in the nineties. I was about to thank her when I realised that Josie was still talking.

'None of those Wonderbras in my day. Although a pair of socks tucked in the bra did help. Anyway, I've been thinking . . .' I always got nervous when Josie said that – there were no bounds as to what could come out of her mouth next. 'Would you like me to look after Cassie a couple of days a week?'

The OCD fairy had apparently now been replaced by the Grant-Any-Wish fairy.

'But you work.' My cousin Michael had become quite the entrepreneur and opened a chain of coffee shops that were doing fantastic business. He'd wanted to make Josie the manageress of one of the shops but she'd refused, choosing to work behind the counter instead. 'What do I want to be running things for? I'll stick to chatting to the customers and having no responsibility thanks very much,' she'd told him.

'The good news is that Avril's coming home,' Josie said, confusing us with the undertone of sadness. That was great! Since Avril had gone to work in a beauty salon on a cruise liner Josie had missed her dreadfully. 'But the bad news is that Michael's shutting up shop and moving to Italy. That boot he married has finally worn him down and he's moving to the village her parents live in.' I put my hand over hers and gave it a squeeze. Even though they were adults now, Josie lived for her family and having Michael so far away would be horrible for her. I could see her struggling and only just managing to get her sadness under control.

'Anyway, they've sold the shops so if I don't manage to fatally poison the cow with doctored mince and potatoes in the next month, they'll be off and I'll have my days free again. If it suits, I'd love to have Cassie, Lou.'

'Loulouloulou,' Cassie mimicked, giving a disturbingly accurate depiction of how her Auntie Ginger greeted me when she'd had a few too many beverages. I made a mental note to check what was in Cassie's cup.

'Josie, that would be fantastic and Cassie would be in heaven.' It was true. She loved her Auntie Josie almost as much as she loved her revered Auntie Ginger.

'But only if you let me pay you for your time,' I added.

Josie laughed. 'Not the first time I've had that offer.' God, she was incorrigible. And lovable. 'But I'm not letting you pay me. I've picked up some night work down at Bar Muff.' Thankfully she added 'just a couple of cleaning shifts' before I fainted with the shock.

I still had a feeling that we were at the bottom of a very large mountain, but my two fairy godmothers had just shoved my buttocks up the first few steps.

I heard the door bang and Red wandered into the kitchen, his hair dishevelled, no doubt from sleeping on the plane and his eyes pink with tiredness. Cassie screamed in delight and he swooped on her, covering her with kisses.

'Daddydaddydaddydaddy,' she shouted gleefully and my heart melted as it always did when I saw him with her. I'd realised long ago that watching the man you love, loving your child is the most incredible thing.

Eventually, he broke off, kissed Josie, then his sister, then paused when he got to me.

'You look . . . different.' His tone was puzzled but his expression made it clear that he liked what he saw. 'Have you done something?'

There was a bang as Ginger's head thudded against the table.

'Are you sure we came from the same womb?' she groaned. 'Only, I'm way, way smarter than you.'

I took over before the moment was gone. 'Ginger treated me to a makeover. What do you think?'

He reached down and gave me a long, leisurely kiss on the lip, a proper kiss, not the quick pecks we'd become used to over the last few months. He even had the focus to ignore the nan bread that his sister slapped across the back of his head. 'Cassie, if I never teach you anything else,' she told my daughter, 'public displays of affection should be outlawed.'

'I think you look stunning,' he told me when he came up for air. 'And I can't wait until tomorrow.'

Tomorrow. My hand flew to my mouth. Tomorrow. Cassie's christening! I'd organised the church and the restaurant afterwards. I'd got Red's favourite suit back from the dry cleaners. Cassie's beautiful dress and little white ballet pumps were all ready. But as for me? The face, hair and body may have been saved from ruin, but I still hadn't got round to sorting out an outfit. 'Bugger, I need to go find something to wear,' I gasped, jumping up from the table.

Thankfully, my fairy godmothers had overlooked nothing.

Ginger smiled. 'There's something hanging on the front of your wardrobe that I think you might like.'

Forty

The minister tried really hard to hide his disapproval of our music choice, but didn't quite manage it. The sounds of Style Council singing 'You're the Best Thing' belted out from a boom box as we all took our seats, Red and I sliding into the front row with Cassie and her godparents, Lizzy and Ginger.

Immediately behind us sat Josie, Michael and The Boot, with their two delicious little dark-haired toddlers. Next to them were Lizzy's ex, Adam, and Alex the lawyer, with the late arrival of my parents – much to Josie's obvious disgust – completing the row. Red's family were lined up in the front pew across the aisle and behind them were Rosie, Angie and all the rest of the staff from my old salon. I was so touched that they'd all come, with the exception of Pamela, who had met a Tahitian rugby player when she went off to travel the world, married him, and was now running a guest house in Bora Bora.

Ginger leaned over to whisper in my ear, allowing me a whiff of the Buck's Fizz she'd had at breakfast to celebrate the occasion. Thankfully, the minister was notorious for going AWOL after one too many in the Dog and Sausage on a

Friday night, on one occasion necessitating the bishop from the next parish to stand in for him on a Sunday morning. It had been the talk of the town, but attendance grew by 20 per cent the following week so perhaps it was God's way of putting out some subliminal advertising.

'You know I don't believe in any of this, don't you?'

I nodded, then buried my face in her mane to whisper back. 'I'm not sure I do either, just covering all the bases.'

The minister beckoned us forwards to the stone font on a raised marble platform in front of us, and began the ceremony, asking each of us to pledge to care and protect our baby. As Ginger and Lizzy took their vows, even the threat of eyelash massacre couldn't stop the tears.

It had been a rough couple of years, but we'd got through it and come out of the other end, still together, still in one piece, still in love with each other and with our daughter. As the minister poured the water over our little angel's head, and was rewarded with a 'No no no no no! Bad man!' I said a silent prayer to the gods, the heavens and the Make-Any-Wish-Come-True fairy.

A fantastic life was out there for us. Now we just had to go make it happen.

Forty-one

Lizzy

The St Kentigern Hotel, Glasgow. Saturday, 1 pm

'Why do they always make these little packets of shortbread so difficult to open?' I asked Lou, no mean feat when you are trying to wrench open impenetrable plastic packaging with your teeth.

'Because they were designed by carbohydrate-hating blokes,' Lou replied. 'If a woman designed that packet it would be much larger and there would be a handy tea bag supplied for dunking.'

I finally got the packet open, took out a biscuit and picked up my magazine. We'd been due in the spa an hour ago but Ginger was still sleeping and Lou and I felt no inclination whatsoever to get out of bed. We never got this kind of time together any more and it seemed a shame to interrupt it with massages and seaweed thingies.

I stretched out, then relaxed again against the stack of pillows. 'Do you think we could just stay here for ever. I mean, who'd notice? How long do you think it would take anyone to come looking for us?'

Lou laughed. 'Lizzy, have you actually met your family? I reckon they'd be up here chapping on the door within an hour of you not showing up.'

Smiling, I acknowledged that she had a point. My brood were chaotic. Wild. Demanding. And I wouldn't have them any other way. I'd always thought it was a shame that Lou hadn't had any more. She was a great mum. A natural. And even now, with everything that she was going through, her first thought was always for Cassie.

I felt a knot of sadness stick in my throat and I swallowed it back down. This wasn't the time. This was supposed to be a light-hearted break from all the bad stuff. No stress. No pressure. No demands.

'What are you thinking?' Lou asked. I realised she was looking at me and had even put down her copy of *Cosmo* to wait for an answer.

'About kids and the stresses and chaos at home,' I replied quickly, hoping I'd pulled it off.

I think it worked as she just smiled and said, 'I don't know how you do it, Lizzy. I've only got one and I'm in a permanent state of borderline panic. Do you remember her first day at school? There was I, completely wired, and you just took everything in your stride like you didn't have a care in the world.'

'Yeah,' I said wistfully. 'I should have got an Oscar for that performance.'

Forty-two

Lou

2007 – Aged 37

The air was thick with apprehension as the crowd moved forwards, children clutching the hands of their parents, some of the parents making polite conversation, others shooting nervous glances at the strangers around them. Suddenly it was all too much.

'A peg! Look, Cassie, it's a coat peg! With your name on it!'

As the other parents took one step further away from the deranged woman screeching at an inanimate object, my daughter groaned. 'Mum, you are totally embarrassing.'

Realising that I may have been just a little highly strung, I murmured an apology. 'Sorry, honey, just got a little overexcited. But remember, I'm your mother, it's my job to embarrass you.'

Cassie gave up trying to look perturbed at this very obvious break with decorum and burst into giggles. This was the worst one yet. Worse than when I started a Mexican wave at her dance display. Worse than when I tried to make life a little easier by cutting her fringe when she was sleeping and she woke up looking like the last remaining member of an eighties techno band.

But in my defence, this was a special day – a landmark event. It was my baby's first day at school.

School!

Where had the years gone? It seemed like no time at all since I sat in that New York toilet and watched that blue line appear on the stick with only a phantom Cyndi Lauper for company.

Now she was standing there, in her smart navy pinafore, a scratchy grey blazer and very shiny shoes, her uncontrollably thick mane of ginger hair tied back in a baby-blue ribbon. Yes, she continued to mimic every aspect of her Auntie Ginger's appearance and personality. Therefore, emergency measures had been enforced to ensure that this disturbing genetic situation wouldn't lead to unfortunate circumstances.

'Now, what do you have to remember?' I asked quietly, as I kneeled down to help her hang up her coat.

'That there are cameras in the playground and you can see everything.'

'Good girl.'

I know, I know, it was wrong on every level, but the only thing I could think of to keep her on the right side of angelic was to tell her that the lamp posts and fence around the school contained invisible cameras linked to my computer, that allowed me to watch her at all times. I had a foreboding vision of her in the playground shouting, 'I didn't mean it, Mum, honest!' to a six-foot wall of chain link.

I'd tell her the truth eventually, but at the moment her fearless nature and indignant sense of justice needed a little help to constrain. Only last week a nine-year-old boy who was at least a foot taller than her had stolen her best friend's skateboard and Cassie's response had been thoughtful, concise and intelligent . . . right up until the point where she decked him.

Incidents of vigilante behaviour aside though, I knew she'd be fine. She was a sociable, extrovert little soul who made new friends in minutes and was desperately looking forward to being able to spend all day with the pals she'd already made at nursery.

Yes, there were tears, worries and small moments of panic, but they were all mine. In the unlikely event that I ever became prime minister, I was going to make it mandatory that all parents be given free therapists who specialised in separation anxiety.

Another kiss, another hug, another embarrassed mutter of, 'Mu-u-u-u-u-um,' and it was time for me to leave her to it. As she skipped off into the class – *skipped!* – I dragged myself out into the playground with the consoling thought that if she had any unbearable pangs of loneliness she could always go have a wee chat to a lamp post.

'Coping?' Lizzy asked.

'Not so much,' I replied. 'I know, I'm pathetic. Don't tell Ginger.'

Lizzy smiled and ushered a straggling group of older children through the door. Since her eldest had become a teenager and moved to high school she'd been working as a classroom assistant and absolutely loved it. She was a natural. Fun, smart, bubbly, loads of energy, with a screech that could silence a class in an instant. The fact that she'd smashed a window with a football during her first month on the job had also ensured that she entered into school legend as the coolest adult ever.

She was always calm. Never ruffled. And when it came to kids, family, school, parenthood, she could cope with absolutely anything. I was totally in awe of her.

256

On the personal front, despite many attempts to set her up, she remained resolutely single and a fan of the old three-date rule. I could see her point. She'd been married since we were so young that she was loving the chance to do all the things that the rest of us did in our twenties – with the addition of an occasional night out at a fabulous new gay nightclub in town with Adam and Alex. They were one big, unconventional family now – like *Will and Grace* but with two children and a permanent partner added to the mix. I had a hunch that she would still have preferred the whole 'happy ever after with a straight husband' scenario, but she'd come to terms with the reality of the situation and was pretty chilled about it. Content.

'So, all set for tonight?'

I nodded. Today was a landmark day for more than one reason. It was my daughter's first day at school . . . and the first day of a whole new start for me.

Forty-three

'Are you sure you're OK? You really do look like you're coming down with something,' I asked Lizzy again early that evening.

'I'm fine!' she snapped, before regaining her normal sunny disposition and saying, 'Right – shag, marry, throw off a cliff. The choices are Robbie Williams, Jon Bon Jovi or Enrique Iglesias.'

'Lizzy, come on. Everyone will be here in less than half an hour and . . . Oh my God! I've just had the strongest sense of déjà vu. This is exactly what we were doing all those years ago before the first opening night.'

'No way!'

'It was! You were reading some magazine and asking me the same question. The only difference was that you were pregnant. Hugely pregnant.'

'Wow, life's weird. If you open another one in twenty years' time, count me in.'

I rubbed the small of my back to pacify the ache that was starting there. 'Bloody hell, I hope the rest of the night doesn't follow last time. Remember? Two of my boyfriends had a fight and then Ginger was so pissed she fell off the reception desk. Thank God you went into labour and distracted everyone.'

'Glad to be of service. I'm happy to yell "Fire," and set off the sprinklers if it all goes horribly wrong tonight.'

I groaned inside at the very thought. So much was hinging on tonight. So much. Five years after the first one closed, I was opening a new CUT and, if it were possible, I was even more nervous now. Back then – other than the ever-present threat of Josie being arrested for financial fraud – I only had myself to worry about. If it failed, it failed. I was so young – if I made a huge mess of it there was plenty of time to pick myself up and get over it.

This time was different. This time is would affect Red and Cassie and our future. Not to mention all of my old staff who had quit their current jobs to come back and work with me. I had to make sure it was a success. Pressure! I'd never had a migraine in my life but I was pretty sure I had one coming on now. Or it might just be that my diamanté-studded, retro-tastic headband was pulled on a little too tight. Internal pep-talk time. I was ready for this. It would be fine. It was the culmination of years of experience and it was going to pay off.

The week after Cassie's christening, I'd gone to work in a Glasgow salon three days a week and loved every moment of it. I'd have been happy there for another few years, but then the most unexpected thing had happened. After legal action that took over three years and added at least a dozen wrinkles to my forehead, the courts had ruled in our favour and the company that had missed all the faults in our house prior to us buying it had been ordered to refund the cost of the building work plus interest.

Oh happy days!

We thought about saving it. We thought about sailing

259

around the world (in fairness, that one was Red's suggestion and I'm hoping he wasn't serious). Cassie's suggestion of buying Disneyland was given due consideration. But in the end Red decided for us – we should use it to open a new salon.

CUT (the sequel).

We'd found a fantastic site just along from the old shop (which had shut down after a month under Chantelle's management when she ran off with a suspected drug baron to Marbella). Ironically our new premises was a former bank. Yes, the very bank that I'd gone to for the original loan had fallen foul of the convenience of the internet and shut down, leaving an old sandstone shopfront just begging to be turned into something fabulous.

And thanks once again to Josie, fabulous it was. Although this time her input had been more on the concept than the dodgy funding side. She'd found a part-time job cleaning a new knicker shop in Glasgow, owned by a fantastic lady called Mel, and had invited us up for the opening night. It was like walking into Marie Antoinette's most decadent boudoir. The colour scheme was an explosion of rich, opulent, deep reds, golds and blacks, a spectacular fusion of French vintage chic and gothic seductiveness with overstuffed Louis XV-style bergère armchairs, elaborate chandeliers and gilt fixtures. Mel described it perfectly when she said it sat somewhere between an eighteenth-century Parisian whorehouse and the place where brocade came to die.

It took my breath away and I immediately saw how (with Mel's generous blessing) the theme could be applied to a salon.

As I scanned the room in front of me, the butterflies in my stomach went on spin cycle. It was exactly how I'd imagined. Using the builders that Ginger had once recruited to sort out our kitchen, we'd completely transformed the main open-plan square by laying a deep gloss ebony floor, which glinted in the light, and framed it with walls that were a dramatic, swirling blend of blood red and gold. Three of the walls featured four stations, at each one a dramatic black leather chair sat in front of a huge, gothic, gilt-edged mirror, which swooped and curved its way from floor to ceiling. In front of the window was a massive semicircular antique reception desk, with an oversized gold throne behind it.

There was a black gloss door at either side of the back wall, one leading to the staffroom, storeroom and loos, the other to a shampoo room that allowed clients to have the never-dignified process of hair washing done in a separate room, with a huge plasma TV on the wall facing the basins.

The overall result was everything I'd ever dreamed of: trendy, chic and undeniably sexy. Now I just needed it to be busy too. The butterflies in my stomach all swooped at the same time. It had to work. The key to it was a successful launch, one that would spin off into regular business. All my old clients had followed me to the Glasgow salon, and they'd been delighted that I was now back in town (Mrs Marshall was eternally grateful because she'd now left her militant sailor for one of the bus drivers who used to bring her into the city for her cut and blow-dry every Friday. As a result, she had named her new Dobermann Lou. Lou the Dobermann. I feared for him down the dog park).

So the old clients I could count on, but what I also needed were new customers, young teenagers and mums, who would love the fact that just behind reception, in what used to be the manager's office, we'd installed a little playroom for kids.

Tonight had to be a success and I was pulling no punches to make it happen, including some blatant coercion on the celebrity-appearance front. I'd had to promise Ginger that I would host the whole family for dinner every Christmas Day for the next twenty years and leave her all my handbags in

261

my will but it had been worth it. The rumour (started by me) that Stud, one of the country's top boy bands might make an appearance was true and I was counting on it.

'Come on, hon, get your lovely arse out of that chair and come help me quietly panic while I put my make-up on in the staffroom.'

Lizzy shook her head. 'Not until you answer the question.'

'What question?'

'Shag, marry, throw off a cliff. The choices are Robbie Williams, Jon Bon Jovi or Enrique Iglesias.'

'I can't believe you're still on that. You do know that we're grown-ups now, don't you?'

She pushed out her bottom lip. 'I hang out with children all day. I'm allowed to be ridiculously immature.'

Against my better judgement, I thought about it for a moment.

'OK, shag Robbie Williams, marry Jon Bon Jovi and Enrique's going off the cliff.'

Her expression was pure disbelief. 'But why?'

'Because Robbie is funny, so a night of passion would be a giggle. I'd marry Jon for the huge American estate and because I still have a secret longing for rock star leather trousers. And I wouldn't touch Enrique because he's going out with that tennis player and she looks like she could take me out in a heartbeat. Happy?'

It took her a moment to respond and, as my eyes flicked to hers, I caught her taking a long, deep breath.

'Lizzy. Are you going to tell me what's going on? Are you OK?'

Her complexion had greyed again and she was looking like she was in some kind of discomfort. 'I'm fine.'

'You're not.'

'I am.'

'Not.'

'Am.'

'Can I take you back to that bit where I reminded us that we're grown-ups?'

Her lips pursed as she rolled her eyes like a truculent teen. 'Look, it's just a bit of food poisoning OK? Dodgy lobster last night I think.'

'You're sure?'

She nodded.

'OK, but, honey, if you feel like heading home I'll understand. Don't be staying here just for me if you feel ill.'

Her hands went on to her hips and she laughed. 'I'm not staying for you, I'm staying for those lovely young men from Stud.'

We were still laughing as we went into the staffroom to get made up and dressed. As I plonked myself on the couch I sent up a silent prayer to whatever deity was responsible for the areas of hairdressing and boy bands.

'Dear God,' I whispered, 'please make this a night to remember.'

By the end of the night, I'd know for sure that he'd been listening . . .

Forty-four

There wasn't a spare inch of space in the shop. One hundred people and a Dobermann were squeezed into the salon, the music was blaring and the champagne was flowing. So far so good. All we needed now was a boy band, some great entertainment and this launch would be the talk of Weirbank for months, therefore the shop would be mobbed and my family would be saved from starvation and destitution. I may have been slightly exaggerating that last bit.

Having welcomed everyone as they arrived, I stood at reception, keeping an eye out that everyone's glasses stayed full and that no one was being left out. The mix of people was even better than I'd hoped. Just behind me there was a crowd of achingly hip, Amazonian-tall teenagers, alternating between looking quietly impressed and shrieking in anticipation every time the door opened. My long-time client Natalia had brought at least a dozen of the aircrew who were stationed at Glasgow airport. Mel, the owner of the knicker shop was there with a very glamorous woman that she'd introduced as her sister-in-law, Suze. A large gang of mums that I'd tracked down at the community centre playgroup had all taken me up on the invitation and they were flirting wildly with the super-handsome Adam and Alex. I briefly wondered if perhaps someone should give them a heads-up before my scan moved on to a group of models, both male and female, that Red was friends with through work. My worry and stress dissipated into little bubbles of happiness. The overall effect was eclectic and classy . . . if you ignored the fact that in one corner Josie and Avril (the younger of the two sporting bright-blue hair) were using hairbrushes as microphones and singing along to a song about going to rehab. Which, given their current condition, probably wasn't a bad idea.

I felt a breeze in my left ear and turned to see my husband standing there, wearing a black open-neck shirt and a wide grin. 'S'cuse me, have you seen the owner of this place? I've heard that she's a complete shag.'

'Is it ancient chat-up line night?' I asked him and he responded by groping my right buttock.

I let him, feeling my erogenous zones and reproductive system respond accordingly. Naff as it is to admit it, I still fancied him insanely. He didn't look a day older than when we got married five years ago. Still trim and broad shouldered, hair a little longer but it totally suited him, he could still make me laugh with just one of his daft facial expressions. I'd got lucky when I landed Red and I didn't plan on forgetting that.

'I'm serious, darling, you look amazing tonight.'

I did a twirl and a mock bow. 'You think so?'

Probably not the time to tell him that I'd spent the cost of a monthly mortgage payment on my dress. I just hoped the accountant would agree that it was a legitimate business expense then Red would never have to know. It was a silver, highly shimmery, sequinned sheath with a slash neck that dropped in a body-skimming, ultra-tight column that stopped just above the knee. But the really sensational feature was the back. Or rather, the lack of one. The fabric fell from the shoulders in a swooping shawl style, which ended just a fraction above my bottom, leaving my whole shoulder and back bare. If Red pulled out the folds that rested just above the buttock area, he'd have somewhere handy to park his bottle of beer.

I was just about to snog him in thanks for his compliment when the mobile phone I was clutching in my hand buzzed three times then stopped.

'That's the bat signal.' I grinned, then grabbed his hand and, as casually as possible, made my way up to the back of the salon, through the staffroom and out to the delivery entrance.

I was almost there when I stopped, my brain just having processed a recent image.

'Did I just see Lizzy sleeping on the couch in the staffroom?' I asked. Red nodded, his brow slightly furrowed with concern. 'Yeah. Wasn't sure whether to wake her or not.'

'I've got a feeling the sound of twenty screaming teenagers will take care of that in about five minutes.'

I was getting a growing sense of unease about Lizzy. Opening night or not, as soon as the band were gone I was going to ask Alex and Adam to take her home, and if they couldn't do it then I'd bail out for half an hour and take her myself.

'Loulou!' Ginger's voice was the first thing I heard as I banged open the delivery door to a blast of cold air, which gave the young boy band currently staring at my chest area somewhere very obvious to hang their jackets. Red rolled his eyes and shook his head in amusement. Did I mention that my husband was born with no discernible jealousy gene? None. Which was just as well, because I was sure the lead singer had just winked at me.

'Come in, come in!' I told them, vaguely realising that I'd only had a double 'Lou' greeting from Ginger – usually an indication that she hadn't had her evening beverage. Over the years I'd learned that the length of the greeting expanded in direct proportion to how many drinks she'd had.

I hugged her tightly as soon as she got inside. 'Thanks, babe. I think I owe you more than just a lifetime of Christmas dinners for this.'

'I know! I think we're up to two kidneys, a lung and all your worldly goods now.'

Ginger playfully punched her brother, then ushered the boys through into the staffroom. Two women, one man, several large bodyguards, and a boy band in a twelve-foot by twelve-foot room, and still Lizzy didn't wake up. The poor thing must be exhausted.

My sister-in-law was in full managerial mode now. 'Right, you shaggable big hunks of wonder, jackets off if they're coming off, pump up those pecs and get ready. Lou will kick off the backing track, there's a raised platform right outside that door, and we're doing two numbers then back out. We'll be mingling with the Sugababes up in the Carriage Club before midnight.'

Anyone else would avoid the venue where they almost fell to their death, but not Ginger. In fact, she went there even more often now that they'd awarded her free champagne for life in thanks for not attempting to sue them. An intrepid journalist had discovered that the club had admitted way too many people that night so Ginger would have had a good case to claim compensation for her fall. She chose unlimited Moët instead. I had a feeling that over the course of a few years as her free stock added up, the Carriage Club might come to wish she'd sued them for a one-off payment instead.

I slid outside the door, grabbed the wireless mike that I'd planked there earlier, winked at Angie who'd taken up position at the reception desk and who was now jumping up and down on the spot like a kid on Christmas morning.

'Ladies and gentlemen!' My voice carried right across the room and everyone turned to face me. For a moment I choked, a giddy feeling of relief and thanks being strangled by my inherent aversion to being the centre of attention. Inhaling deeply, I ploughed on with my very short but heartfelt speech.

'I just wanted to say, thank you all for coming. Thank you all so much.'

Did I mention it was short?

'And while I've got your attention, I'd like to introduce some stray blokes I just found out the back.'

Suddenly there was a buzz in the room, a swarm of whispers all speculating with disbelief about what could be about to happen.

'Ladies and gentlemen, it's Stud!'

There was a gasp then a pause. A long pause. Then I realised that like the rest of the room, Angie was frozen with anticipation, eyes fixed on the door behind me.

'Angie?' I sing-songed into the mike.

She threw her hands up in the air. 'Fuck! Fuck! The button! Where's the button?'

Almost immediately she regained control of her senses, the music thumped on, four bodyguards appeared from the back and framed the little platform area, and then they were there. Stud. In my brand-new shop. In probably the smallest town they'd ever played. I spotted the teenage girls working their way through the crowd towards the stage and anticipated that in about a minute and a half, the bouncers might have to gently dissuade them from storming the stage. That's if Adam, Alex and Josie didn't get there first. My aunt, Lizzy's ex-husband and our favourite lawyer had slid up the side of the room and were standing only feet away from us. I aimed my very best arched eyebrow at Josie and she winked in reply. God help those boys if she got near them – they were in no way a match for a woman of her talents. She followed her wink with a thumbs-up, making me dissolve into laughter.

Outrageous. Incredible. Fantastic. This night was about as good as it got. I suddenly had a massive yearning for Cassie. She would have loved tonight, but it was way too late and she had her second day of school tomorrow so leaving her with Red's mum had seemed like the most sensible thing to do.

Her absence aside though, this was . . . it was everything. Oh hell, I was welling up again and there was no way I was wiping snot on the arm of the most expensive dress I'd ever bought.

As the lead singer of Stud wiggled his pelvis only inches from my beaming face, I realised this was one of the best nights of my life, topped only by my wedding and the day Cassie was born. It was like everything had finally come together. I had the family I'd always dreamed of and the salon I'd always wanted and I had balance between the two. Life was perfect.

Perfect.

'Bloody hell, those abs should be illegal.' Lizzy was beside me now and I was thrilled to see her awake, even though she was still a mighty strange colour. That lobster must have had serious hygiene issues. 'How many of those guys make up a man of my age?'

I did a quick calculation. 'One and three quarters.'

'Well, can you make sure the three quarters includes those abs because I could look at them all night.'

I threw my arm around her and hugged her as we stood there, both of us trying to move in time with the music without looking like middle-aged aunts at a wedding.

The second song was nearing the end now, the teenage girls were starting to look slightly feverish and the bodyguards were already planning their next move. It would have been great if the boys could have stayed to sign autographs, but I couldn't possibly ask for any more. The first CUT had been built on tittle-tattle after a pop star wrote songs detailing the sexual failings of the owner. Oh the shame. CUT, the sequel, would be the top gossip subject for all good reasons now. The band had established the image of the salon and hopefully this would lead to full appointment books. I gave Lizzy another squeeze and she leaned over and kissed me on the cheek.

'Well done, Lou. This is amazing.'

The music suddenly stopped and, as the crowd gave a thunderous chorus of applause, the boys waved then shot back into the staffroom, the back two bouncers running right behind them. It was obviously a practised routine because the other two bodyguards immediately reversed back and blocked the door, preventing anyone from following them. A couple of the girls looked like they were about to attempt it then changed their minds. After a couple of minutes, the human wall folded into the room and disappeared and, as quickly as they came, the gang were gone, leaving only Ginger behind. She slid up to my side and I threw my free arm around her.

'I thought you were going too?' I asked her, puzzled.

'Decided to stick around and witness your moment of glory,' she replied, grinning. And not even her trademark, slightly pissed, wonky grin, but a completely sober, genuine one.

'Have I told you that I love you, Ginger Jones?'

'Don't you dare start with all that mushy stuff or I'm going out back to catch up with the band,' she said.

'OK, I'll just whisper sweet nothings to Lizzy instead then,' I joked. I'd barely finished the sentence when I realised that something wasn't quite right beside me. There was a weight, something heavy, something . . . There was a violent thud as Lizzy hit the floor.

The next few moments were bedlam as Adam and Alex

spotted what had happened and swooped in. Adam quickly slid his arms under Lizzy and moved her the few feet back into the staffroom and laid her on the couch.

'Call an ambulance! Call an ambulance!' Adam yelled. I snatched my phone from the coffee table and dialled 999, while Adam and Alex frantically tried to revive her. Josie dashed into the kitchen area and returned with a glass of water, meanwhile Ginger and Red stood against the door, blocking it so that no one else could come in.

After what seemed like hours, I finally got through to the operator. I answered the woman's questions about location, barely containing myself until she got to the bit where she asked why I'd called.

'I need an ambulance please, really quickly, it's my friend Lizzy Murphy. She's fainted and we can't get her to wake up. She's got food poisoning and . . . and . . . what?'

Adam was signalling to me and saying stuff at the same time but in the confusion it took me a few moments to understand what he was trying to convey. I got it on his fourth or fifth attempt and almost choked on my words as I repeated what he'd said.

'And she's pregnant,' I gasped. 'Lizzy is pregnant.'

Forty-five

'It's here! I can hear it!' We all stopped speaking and listened for the sound of the siren approaching the delivery bay at the back. Incredibly, right on the other side of the staffroom door, a hundred people were still partying away, completely oblivious to what was going on right next to them.

Red disappeared through to let the paramedics in and within seconds they were in front of Lizzy, forcing Adam and Alex to back off. They started firing questions at us as they took her pulse and attached an oxygen mask to her face.

'Did she bang her head?'

'No.'

'Did she vomit?'

'No.'

'Has she come round at all?'

'No.'

'How long has she been pregnant?'

'Almost three months.' Adam answered that one, and I couldn't help moving my eyes to meet Ginger's.

I could see that she'd had no idea either.

The questions were shooting about in my brain. Who was

the father? Was she even seeing anyone? Why didn't we know about him? And why, why, why had she not told us that she was pregnant?

I didn't understand what was happening here at all.

The paramedics lifted her from the sofa onto a stretcher, then suddenly one of them froze for a few seconds, then eased Lizzy up and looked underneath her, before looking around him, his face a picture of puzzlement.

'You said she didn't bang her head or anything else when she fell?' It was more of a question than a statement.

I shook my head. 'I don't think so. She kind of fell against me and then slid downwards.'

He looked down at his gloves and then back at me again. 'So where's the blood coming from?'

The gasp when I spotted his hands was audible. They were streaked with thin red stripes of blood. 'I don't . . . I don't know.'

I looked around me and saw little spatters of blood everywhere. But if it wasn't coming from Lizzy then where . . .

As I spun around, suddenly Red spoke up. 'Lou, it's coming from you, your back . . . holy shit.'

I craned my neck to see what he was talking about and that's when I saw it – a red stain about two inches in diameter, spreading right down one buttock of my dress.

The paramedic moved in for a closer look as his partner wheeled Lizzy out. 'Let's have a look, love, maybe just a scratch where she rubbed against you.'

I could feel a wave of irritation rising. What did it matter? It was just a cut. I barely even felt a thing. It was Lizzy that he had to take care of. Why was he wasting time with me when he should be in that ambulance and rushing her to hospital right now?

'Honestly, I'm fine,' I tried to tell him, practically shooing him away from me.

273

'Lou, let him look.' Red's voice, unusually firm and clearly not up for entering into discussion.

The paramedic crouched down and moved the fabric draped across my lower back over to one side, before reaching into his box and coming out with a gauze wipe.

There was a little prickle of pain as he cleaned off the area, but I didn't react, embarrassingly aware that Josie, Red and Ginger were right there, waiting for some kind of comment. What the hell was taking him so long? Lizzy needed to go *now*.

'How long have you had this mole on your back, love?'

The question took me by complete surprise. Sure, I was vaguely aware that there was a little mole down there but there was no way for me to see it without a mirror and I couldn't remember the last time I noticed it.

'I don't know.' I shrugged. 'All my life I think, since I was a child.'

'Has it ever bled before?'

'No,' I replied, genuinely confused. 'Never.'

Red moved forwards now for a closer look and I caught an expression on his face that I really didn't like. 'I've never seen it looking like that,' he said. 'It's normally smaller and not so . . . dark.'

The paramedic held the gauze on with one hand and, with the other, reached over and took some tape from his case. One makeshift dressing later, he got to his feet. 'Just get your doctor to have a wee look at that on Monday, love. Best to get these things checked.'

Leaving Josie to see to the end of the party, Red, Ginger and I followed the flashing blue light to the hospital, all of us struck silent with the shock of the last hour.

It was only later that I realised that night was certainly a night to remember.

But for all the heartbreakingly wrong reasons.

Forty-six

Lou

The St Kentigern Hotel, Glasgow. Saturday, 2 pm

'They didn't tell us that back then, did they?' I whispered to Lizzy.

The concern and worry was in every tear that was dropping from her face. 'I'm sorry, I wasn't going to talk about it. It's just that . . .' Her arm came around me and she hugged me close. 'It could have been any of us,' Lizzy mused, truthfully. She was right. For most of the eighties, we were permanent shades of copper, our backless, frontless, minidresses exposing acres of brown flesh. It was the done thing. Aerobics class then a sunbed. A quick sunbed in the lunch hour. A course of sunbeds before any big occasion. Any excuse.

It absolutely could have been Lizzy or Ginger.

But it wasn't.

I remember there being a vague rumour that they might cause wrinkles but no one ever mentioned cancer. Ever. Now that horrible truth is common knowledge. If there's one lesson I hope Cassie learns when she's old enough to understand all this it's that she should stay away from sunbeds. Because if she doesn't then she might wake up one morning and be faced with the most terrifying thought. I finally had it all. I had the gorgeous husband, the beautiful child, the successful business, great friends, and the sheer brilliance that was Auntie Josie. I had it all. I was a woman of the new millennium who absolutely had it all . . . and I realised it might be too late.

At the bottom of the bed, finally a stirring and Ginger's head popped up into view. The first thing she saw was Lizzy and me, cuddled up, both crying. For the second time in her life, I heard her murmur the same phrase.

'So . . . what did I miss?'

Forty-seven

Lou

2008 – Aged 38

It's strange, facing your own mortality. Perhaps 'strange' isn't the best adjective to use there. I'm also particularly fond of 'devastating', 'terrifying' and 'shite'.

I thought about it all the time. As soon as I woke up in the morning. Before I went to bed at night. When Cassie smiled at me or refused to eat her jam sandwich because I used a knife that had traces of butter on it and 'you can absolutely tell'. When she cried. When she came home and announced that someone was mean to her. When the headmistress called to say she threw toilet roll bombs in the corridor. When she was sad. When she couldn't sleep. When . . . all the time.

And it made me do strange things – like cry when I was putting the washing out. Or stand for a long time staring at something completely random that had absolutely no significance. The ten minutes I spent perusing a road cone was particularly engaging. I've no idea why it happened. It's like my brain froze, locked in position and I'd be stuck there until some kind of hope or optimism kick-started the synapses again. But the strangest things were the conversations, with Cassie, in my head. Strange because she couldn't hear them. Strange because she'd never know that when I heard that diagnosis the first thing I thought of was her.

Then came the questions.

Hundreds of questions.

The one that regularly comes at me from anyone involved in my case, the one that never fails to make me wince inside was, 'How often did you use sunbeds?'

Several times a week, for about three years. In fact, I spent the years from eighteen to twenty-one looking like I'd just stepped off the plane after a week in Benidorm. It was the fashion, you see. White minidresses. White high heels. Pink lip gloss. Bloody huge hair.

At that age, I had absolutely no idea sunbeds could harm me. Back then, if I was to hazard a guess I'd have said the biggest risk of mortal danger came from inhaling the four cans of hairspray I went through every week trying to keep my coiffure on the right side of Cindy Crawford.

But sunbeds? Nope, they were all good. Healthy, even. Made you look like you were glowing with vitality. If having skin colour that resembled the deep mahogany hue of my garden hut was wrong, then I didn't want to be right. Never gave it a second thought.

Twenty years later that casual nonchalance had come back and bit me on the non-tanned arse because since the moment the diagnosis had been delivered, *it was all I thought about.*

'Mrs Jones, we've had the results of the biopsy and I'm afraid our suspicions have been confirmed. It is a malignant melanoma.'

Skin cancer. And it was his educated guess that it had

probably been caused by overuse of sunbeds almost two decades ago.

I remember watching a programme about the space shuttle *Challenger*, which blew up on take-off, killing all of the astronauts on board. The cause? A malfunction of a seal that had been fitted on the spaceship years before, just sitting there all that time, waiting to cause carnage.

The melanoma was my dodgy seal.

And I had no idea whether I was about to crash and burn.

Forty-eight

Lizzy's sunflower-yellow kitchen was like a scene from one of those TV cookery shows that sought to recreate the perfect, traditional family environment: sumptuous aromas emanating from the impressively large Aga, a white wooded, granite-topped centre island hosting two huge baskets of fruit, a Jamie Oliver book propped on a wire stand, copper pots dangling from the ceiling, a beautifully carved dresser that stored exquisite Wedgwood crockery in vertical plate racks. No one had to know that she kept a back-up supply in the cupboard under the stairs because fine china and Lizzy's level of clumsiness did not make natural companions.

In the middle of the long, rustic pine dining table over by the wall of floor-to-ceiling windows, was a huge vase of daffodils picked from the garden that was accessed through the nearby French doors. In the corner a flowery, chintz sofa sat behind a thick oak coffee table that was strewn with books and old copies of *Good Housekeeping* magazine. Lizzy could have come from lifestyle pages. She'd aged beautifully, hardly a line on her porcelain face, her jet-black hair still tumbling in waves down her back, her figure still the size ten it had been since we were in high school.

Yes, it was the absolute picture of a traditional family home. With the exception of the baby that came courtesy of the housewife's gay ex-husband, his partner, an egg donation from an anonymous source and a test tube.

I picked Caleb up out of his bassinet and snuggled him, loving that intoxicating scent of new baby. At four weeks old he had the most adorable big eyes, honey-coloured skin, cherub mouth and a shock of light-brown hair that could have belong to either of his fathers. They'd chosen not to find out which swimmers in the fertilisation race had crossed the finish line first, so Caleb was either Adam's or Alex's biological son. It would probably come to light later depending on whether he excelled at counting or arguing in the name of justice.

'What time are the guys picking him up?' I asked, hoping that it wouldn't be anytime soon.

'Soon,' she replied.

Right then.

'But they might stay for dinner so Caleb will be here for a while yet.'

Right on cue, he gurgled and wrapped his whole hand around my little finger, making my hormones slide up another notch on the broody scale. I adored my girl and I'd been thinking more and more lately that it was time for a brother and sister. But of course that would only happen if . . . if . . .

'When's the next biopsy?' Lizzy asked.

'Next week. It's the big one. Lymph nodes.'

Two arms came from behind me and snaked around my neck, followed by a loud smacker on the cheek. 'It's going to be fine, Lou. The tests will be negative and then you can forget about it, have more babies and we'll train them young

281

how to pour cocktails so we can put our feet up and have a life of leisure and indulgence.'

'If we did that we'd never get rid of Ginger. She'd just move in and put them on a fifteen-minute schedule,' I said, laughing at the thought. 'Anyway, I'd better get home. Red is coming back tonight and the house is so untidy it looks like it's been ransacked. I know it's probably psychosomatic, but I feel permanently exhausted these days.'

'Sex. You're having too much sex – it's obviously wearing you out. Anyway, Red called when you were in the loo and I told him just to come over and have dinner here. There's a lasagne in the oven that could feed the street.'

This was why I loved my friends. They didn't let me wallow, they kept me on an even keel, they subtly helped without being overbearing and this one could cook like she was the love child of Delia Smith and Gordon Ramsay. Which, if it were true, would explain why she liked football and swore a lot. I wanted to stay in the warm comfort of Lizzy's kitchen for ever, drinking tea, chatting and plotting ways to kidnap Caleb and make him my own.

I turned my attention back to playing with the handsome little bundle in my arms. 'Still no regrets?'

It was out before tact and diplomacy could slap some gaffer tape on my gob.

Lizzy shook her head. 'Not one. OK, well, maybe not telling you lot beforehand. If you'd known then you'd probably have reminded me to eat and drink and I wouldn't have keeled over at the salon launch. I felt like such a tit when I woke up in A&E. But anyway, you know I didn't want to tell you in case you tried to talk me out of it.'

'Which I would probably have tried to do,' I said. She was so right. I've yet to find the manual that deals with dissuading your best friend from having her gay ex-husband's baby but if I'm being completely honest I would probably have tried

– not because I was in any way opposed to it on moral grounds, but because I feared for her heart. Yet, it had worked out perfectly for all of them. After seven years together, Alex and Adam had married in a civil ceremony and now they had the child they'd always dreamed of. They'd originally planned to use a surrogate, but Lizzy had offered her services and her womb, and on the second implant attempt at an Edinburgh fertility clinic they'd hit the baby-making jackpot.

Lizzy was their childminder, best friend and the third person in their marriage – and that was exactly the way they all liked it. I just worried that Lizzy was so enmeshed in her alternative family that she left no time for meeting anyone new or moving on with her life. Could someone really be happy spending their whole life taking care of other people? Didn't she need to find love again, to explore new things, new interests, have her own goals and ambitions, to have someone who adored her and wanted to grow old with her? Looking at the picture of homely contentment in front of me I could see she was fulfilled, but still. Objective number one of the year: get rid of cancer. Objective number two: find brooding big hunky sexy single doctor for Lizzy.

I just hoped that if I came across a suitable candidate, he didn't baulk at the vetting questionnaire that I'd be asking him to complete.

1. Are you single?
2. Are you open minded?
3. Are you solvent?
4. Do you have addictions to drink, drugs or any other chemical stimuli?
5. Do you have any outstanding restraining orders, criminal charges or legal actions?
6. Can you provide excellent references from at least three former girlfriends?

7. Have you ever considered a same-sex relationship or do you feel this is something you would like to experience in the future?

Only on attaining a 100 per cent pass rate, (yes, yes, yes, no, no, yes, no) would he be allowed to proceed to coffee and a bun, perhaps lunch. He'd have to be patient and be prepared to take it easy at first. Lizzy's heart had been so completely and utterly shattered first time around that I knew she was avoiding committing to anything more than temporary residence of her womb. However, she was still only thirty-eight – way too young to say goodbye to romance and the chance of another love. I was determined to find her a solid, intelligent, emotionally secure, dependable partner . . . and if that failed then maybe we could set her up with the one from Stud with the world-class abs for some rampant nocturnal activities.

I realised that Caleb had nodded off again and gently placed him back in his crib just as a cup of coffee materialised in front of me.

'Any word from the parents of the year?' Lizzy asked as she poured herself a cup of foul-smelling herbal tea.

'Yeah.'

'Really?' she asked incredulously. Lizzy was so ear-shatteringly close to her mother, Saint Carla of the Blessed Screech, that she was terminally optimistic that one day my parents would come through.

I nodded. 'Spoke to my mother yesterday. They're still in Paris. My dad won twenty grand on a horse-racing accumulator so they've decided to stay there for six months.'

'And what did she say about . . . about the cancer?'

'Are you ready for this?' I asked as I took a deep breath and did a quiet drum roll on the table so as not to wake the baby.

284

Her groan was audible. 'Oh no, what utter shit have they come out with now?'

'My mother said that she's still hurt that she wasn't the first to hear about the skin cancer, that my dad said I'd completely undermined her and thank goodness she had him because he was the only person in the world who gave her her rightful place. Lizzy, close your mouth, love.' I giggled, watching as, completely dumbfounded, she slid into the seat next to me.

It took about twenty seconds before she finally regained her powers of speech. 'They are fucking priceless. Oh my God, Lou, I'm so sorry. It's a miracle that you're not a completely messed-up emotional cripple coming for those two. Doesn't that hurt?'

I shrugged. 'God gave me Josie to compensate. And no it really doesn't hurt. Look, if this was a Lifetime movie or one of those family saga novels, then they'd realise the error of their ways and come riding in to the rescue, but, Liz, this is who they are. It's the way they've always been and I don't know that I'd want them to change now. It is what it is and I don't need them. I really don't.'

It wasn't false bravado or bluff. I'd long ago come to terms with who and what my parents were and replaced them with people who truly did care. The most important thing was that, thanks to Josie, there was no ongoing cycle. My idea of parenting was very different from Dave and Della Cairney's, because I'd had a lifetime of exposure to Josie's love and care. I'd never turn my back on my child, no matter what age she was. I'd defend her to the ends of the earth. I'd never choose anyone else above her. I would find a way to tell her every day of her life that she was loved and I'd mean it with all my heart – even when she was fifteen and sliding down a lamp post from her bedroom window so that she could do illicit things with the best-looking boy in the town. Although,

I did reserve the right to ground her until she was thirty for anything involving lamp posts, subterfuge, or physical contact with anyone of the male variety.

I heard the muffled sound of the front door opening and closing. 'If that's Cilla Black coming to reunite me with Dave and Della I'll never forgive you,' I told Lizzy.

Adam and Alex bounded in, a vision of *GQ* chic, the most un-camp guys I'd ever known. In torso-hugging T-shirts and jeans they were butch, chiselled, the kind of men that could induce a nipple erection at fifty paces. There was no doubt about it, when those two came out of the closet, that small step for mankind had definitely been the straight woman's loss.

'Is it wrong that I kinda fancy you?' I asked Alex after he'd finally released me from a bear hug.

'Nope, it's compulsory,' he said with a wink.

The two of them cooed over their sleeping child for a few minutes, before realising, with obvious disappointment, that he wasn't going to wake up to greet them. I remembered that stage. For me, it lasted until Cassie learned to walk and started tearing around the house from the minute she woke up until the minute she went back to bed. There's a whole three- or four-year period back then that I couldn't remember my buttocks ever coming into contact with a chair.

'Where's Cassie?' Adam asked, clearly put out that his favourite niece (although in fairness, since he and Lizzy were both only children, there wasn't much competition) wasn't there to greet him. 'Out in the garden, playing tennis with Holly.' Lizzy and Adam's fourteen-year-old daughter showed patience far and above the call of duty when it came to entertaining a loud, opinionated six-year-old.

Lizzy was back over at the oven now, her head down behind the door, rearranging something within it. 'Are you sure you have enough for us to stay for dinner too?' I asked, silently praying that the offer still stood.

286

There was a loud mumbling from behind the door that sounded like a confirmation of the affirmative, just as we heard more shuffling in the hall. This time it was Red whose head came around the door. He'd spent the last three days touring the country's football stadiums for a feature on . . . on . . . actually, I had no idea. None. Every week the newspaper emailed over his assignments, and I printed off the list, stapled it to the cork board in the kitchen and then planned our lives around them. He'd decided to cut back on his time away when I first discovered the cancer, but I'd overruled him. I told him I wanted him to keep working full-time because we had a daughter to bring up, a mortgage to pay, holidays to save for, but I think he knew the truth: to change the way we lived would have meant admitting that something was wrong and I wasn't ready to do that yet. Normality. We had to keep everything as normal as possible.

'For the love of God, who's that at the door now? Have you got an entertainment licence for this kitchen?' Lizzy handed me a large glass of red wine, primarily, I suspected, to shut me up.

Red plonked down on the chair next to me then pulled me onto his knee for a long, blissful snog.

'Fucking stop that, you two, or I won't be responsible for my actions.'

My first thought was that the wine must be pretty damn strong because I was now hearing voices in my head. My second thought was that I'd be pretty damn unlucky to develop an alcohol- and stress-induced psychosis that involved hearing Ginger screech at me. Johnny Depp? Fine. Brad Pitt (before he left Jennifer and ran off with Angelina and appeared to stop washing)? Absolutely. Perhaps even Jon Bon Jovi serenading me as I slurred? All perfectly acceptable forms of drunken possession. Ginger's demanding bossiness? It was enough to scare anyone sober.

I un-puckered myself from my husband and turned to see Ginger, Ike, Josie and Avril, the former in a fake fur coat that reached to her ankles and was as wide as her hair. In a dim light she'd look like a very expensive designer yeti.

My confused glance went from the yeti, to Lizzy, to the yeti, to Lizzy, who finally clarified the situation by saying, 'I know you hate surprises but we thought we'd have a little get-together.'

I was open-mouthed with shock.

'But why?'

'Because we know you're going to have a tough month ahead and there's only one way to really prepare for that, physically, mentally and spiritually.'

Oh no, what now? If this was meditation, chanting or involved any kind of nude cleansing ritual then – touching family gathering or not – I was out of there. But no, I was being uncharitable. They'd obviously put a lot of thought into this, researched the options, and then planned this whole night around an activity that would benefit me. How lucky was I to have friends like this? I braced myself to react favourably to whatever they sprung on me. I'd read somewhere that aromatherapy massages were beneficial. As was acupuncture (although Josie was getting nowhere near me with her knitting needles), hypnosis and some of the Eastern techniques like t'ai chi.

Whatever it was, I'd give it a go. Although I was still slightly dodgy on anything involving nudity and chanting.

Lizzy spoke up. 'So we decided to have a dinner and then move on to the more therapeutic activity of the night.'

Out of the corner of my eye, I realised that Josie's arm was slowly coming out from behind her back. Oh crap, the knitting needles. There was nothing else that she could be carrying that could possibly have any effect on my physical, mental and spiritual well-being.

288

I checked out the locations of the doors and prepared to make an emergency exit when Josie thrust the contents of her hand towards me. After a momentary confusion, I realised it was a large pink microphone with a diamanté grip.

'Get those lungs warmed up, doll – you're up first on the karåoke.'

Forty-nine

If Cassie was my first priority in all of this, Red was up there in second place.

To say he was in denial would be the biggest understatement since Ginger told a magazine interviewer that she occasionally liked to have a wander round Harvey Nicks.

While I'd become obsessed with practicalities and preparations, Red had taken the opposite stance. Big picture, ball park, overall situation – details not required.

We still laughed, we still acted completely normally and, despite hospital visit after hospital visit, we didn't discuss the worst outcome. Not ever. It was all about staying positive and getting on with living, refusing to allow the disease to take control of our future. No, he didn't want to know what high school I wanted Cassie to go to because I'd still be here to make that decision. No, he didn't want to discuss future events and the preparations he would have to make if the very worst happened. But it was neither of those that caused him to get seriously furious with me for the first and only time in our lives.

That moment had come the night after the last biopsy,

when I was addled with fear, lying staring at the ceiling at 4 am, gripped with a wave of terror that was sending my imagination to places that it should never have gone. 'You still not sleeping?' I heard him murmur.

'No,' I whispered.

He rolled over towards me and nuzzled into my neck. 'It's going to be OK, babe.'

Usually I'd accept his positivity and nod my head, take it on board and use his confidence to bolster my levels of optimism and hope.

But not tonight.

Tonight I was too far along the road to panic. There were things I was worrying about, questions that I needed him to answer to set my mind at ease.

'Red . . . ?'

Still semi-sleeping, he murmured something unintelligible.

'If I wasn't here would you marry again? For Cassie? Red, she'll need a mum and she'll need someone to—'

He shot bolt upright and flicked on the bedside light, then turned to face me with an expression I could only describe as aghast.

'Don't. Ever. Say. That.' His voice was low but there was no mistaking the fury and fear in his eyes. 'Nothing is going to happen to you, Lou, so I don't even need to think about it.'

I was too far gone for reason and consolation.

'How do you know that? How? And what if it's not? Are we just going to ignore it all and then it's too late to prepare if it all goes wrong? Red, I lived with parents who didn't give a fuck about me and I'm not having that for Cassie. She needs to know that I tried. That I cared about her, that I did everything I could to make sure that she was going to be OK. I need to know that if anything happens to me you'll look for someone else. Maybe Lizzy. You and Lizzy would be amazing together and . . .'

291

What the hell was I saying? On one level I knew it was insane and I could hear myself come out with this hysterical rant and yet I couldn't stop. For months I'd been trying to keep thoughts like this under control and now they'd just burst into my brain and launched a full-out assault on my rationality.

'Stop.' He didn't shout yet the sound was deafening. Low. Haunted. Pained. 'Are you seriously trying to set me up with your best friend in case you die?'

There was a long horrifying pause as some kind of reality started to sink in to my brain. Oh fuck. Oh fuck. What was I doing? Why was I saying these things? Why?

Because before I got the results I needed to know that they – Red and Cassie – would be OK, because I needed to get ready to handle whatever was thrown at me. That was my way of coping. Over-think the issues. Analyse options. Consider all the possibilities. Have solutions ready and waiting to go. That was how I dealt with problems in life. But I had no right to make him face this before he was ready. These were my worries, my fears and I was transposing them on to him, making him confront the possibility that he could lose his wife and the family he loved would be devastated. What right did I have to do that?

At exactly the same moment, we both reached to each other and clung on, silently, until our pulses returned to something like normal. He pulled back, kissed me slowly, with such tenderness that my heart ached.

'I love you, Lou. And you're not going anywhere so no more, OK?'

I knew exactly what he meant.

Whatever conversations I wanted to have, whatever solutions I needed to prepare, I knew I was going to have to do them on my own.

*   *   *

Lizzy, my husband's potential future wife knew immediately what I was going to say when I arrived on her doorstep the following morning, but she followed through with the pretence of believing that I'd just popped in for a casual coffee.

I picked my moment, right in between her latching a breast pump on to one of her boobs (she had offered to express milk for Caleb for as long as his dads wanted her to) and taking a sip out of a cup of tea (therefore avoiding the potential for a reactive, furious response from the Red Jones School of Coping With Illness).

'Lizzy, if the results are not good . . .'

She swallowed. 'They will be.'

'But if they're not, then . . .'

'Then I'll look after Cassie like she was my own and do everything and anything that I need to make sure that she grows up into a healthy, confident, incredible young woman that she's destined to be. Now don't dare ask me again, because it's not going to happen.'

She pressed the button on the battery-operated expresser and all hope of future conversation was cut dead. Probably not the best time to ask her if she'd consider marrying my husband then. I picked up a copy of *Good Housekeeping* and started to flick through it . . . and I pretended not to see the tear that slid down her face and landed in her tea.

Fifty

Josie was sitting at the Formica table in the kitchen when I opened the back door.

'Thought that was you,' she said with a smile.

'How did you know?'

A sixth sense? An inherent feel for the proximity of those she loved? An oversensitivity to the vibrations of the Earth's crust that allowed her to tune into movements around her?

'Because you're like a bloody elephant coming up that path.'

A cackle of laughter was out before I could stop it. 'Don't you sugar-coat it there, Aunt Josie. Just give it to me straight.'

She laughed too, but I didn't kid myself for a minute. Her mouth said she was amused, but her eyes were scrutinising me from head to toe and they missed nothing.

'You've had a rough night,' she said, calmly. 'What's wrong?'

I sighed. 'I'm just having a bit of a meltdown.' Grabbing a cup from the draining board, I sat down and lifted the teapot with the chicken-themed tea cosy and poured myself a cup.

'I don't know if this makes any sense, but it's almost like I have to plan for the worst eventuality. Like I have to know I've got the things that matter covered and that way I can deal with whatever happens.'

'Cassie?' This time it was that inherent instinct that was providing the insight.

'And Red,' I answered. 'I asked him last night if he would please agree to marry Lizzy if anything happened to me.'

'Oh dear Lord,' was my guru's in-depth response. 'That poor girl. The love of her life turned out to be gay, he lives next door with his boyfriend, she's just had their baby, she's terminally single and now she's in line to marry her dead pal's husband. Does she know that this magical future awaits her?'

Only Josie could get away with making fun of me at a time like this.

'No.'

'Then probably best leave it that way. Leave the poor soul some hope of a normal life. What about Red? Furious?'

'Like I'd just run over his favourite Nikon with a tank.'

After a few moments her grin morphed into something a little more thoughtful. 'Love, dealing with this in the way that you are is completely understandable.'

'Really? Because everyone else seems to think that I'm completely losing the plot.'

She shook her head, still possessed with a calm aura of knowledge. Bloody hell, she was already dressing the part but now she was developing the psychological skills of a sensei. Or that little bloke with the unfortunate voice on *Star Wars*. Carry on Master Yoda.

'Lou, it's a control thing and, without coming over all deep and profound, it doesn't take an expert to see why you do this. You've spent your whole life building an existence that only depends on you. Your own house, your own car, your own business and you achieved every single one of those things yourself.'

'Apart from an act of criminal fraud perpetrated by my aunt.'

A roar of laughter escaped her. 'Shit, I'd forgotten about that. Your mother would go ballistic if she ever found out. Stroke of genius though.'

She paused for a second, reflecting on the miracle that she never ended up in jail, before continuing. 'But the point is, with those two fuckwits you were born to, you've only ever been able to rely on yourself and you've had to solve every problem, mould your life without back-up or support. And you've done an amazing job. But now you're facing the possibility that you won't be able to fix something, won't be able to solve a huge potential problem for Cassie and that's freaking you out.'

How the hell did she get all that from 'having a bit of a meltdown'?

And how the hell did she manage to get it oh so right.

Her hand slid over mine and she gave it a squeeze. 'We'll get through this, Lou.'

'You think?'

Another nod from the sensei. 'It's just about staying strong and trying to stay positive, even though I know that you must be freaking out inside. I would be.'

'No you wouldn't,' I told her. Josie didn't do weakness. Or fear. Or anything even resembling the behaviour of a victim.

'I would, Lou. The thought of leaving Michael and Avril and you would . . .' She stopped dead, shuddered, obviously unwilling to even contemplate it, then immediately snapped back to her general disposition of in-fucking-vincible.

Reaching over, she topped up my cup and then slowly reached to the other side of the table. 'Do you know what you need?' she asked, grabbing a box and wrestling the lid off it.

Therapy? Drugs? A bit of good luck?

'A caramel log.'

Despite knowing that they could solve all of the world's problems, including famine, corruptions and war, I shook my head.

There was still one person I needed to speak to. And I had a hunch that it would be the toughest of all.

Two hours later, the maître d' showed me to a corner booth in the Carriage Club.

'I can't believe they still let you in here,' I said as I attempted to bend in tight black capri pants, which threatened to give way at the buttock seam at any moment.

As soon as this was over, I needed to drop the comfort Mars bars and get back to doing some kind of physical exercise. Just now it was hard with the six-inch square dressing that had more or less permanently been on my back for the last seven months. Now the dressing on my back had a matching partner on my groin where they'd removed the lymph node for testing.

Stop thinking about it, just stop. Keep it together. Don't freak. Calm. Stay calm.

'I ordered cocktails already,' Ginger informed me. Where did she put it all? Her booze alone must have added thousands of calories to her diet every week and yet she still poured herself into killer jeans and boned basques that women half her age couldn't carry off.

But today wasn't about fashion. I chewed the inside of my cheek and decided to wait until after lunch to broach the subject. Yep, that was the best idea. Wait. Ponder. Work out the best way to kick off the most difficult conversation we would ever have.

'Ginger, if anything happens to me, do you promise that you'll look after Cassie?' It was out loud and out of my mouth before the waiter had arrived with her slippery nipple and my cosmo.

She stared at me with an expression that was somewhere between horror and something that I didn't recognise. Oh dear Lord, it was fear. When had I turned into the Grim Reaper, programmed to travel the earth causing terror, grief and spreading doom and bloody gloom to everyone I loved?

'Of . . . of course . . . I will,' she stuttered, before recovering her composure. 'I'll visit and take her out and teach her about boys.'

'If you teach her to smoke when she's twelve I'll haunt you,' I warned her.

Pools of water formed in her eyes and I swallowed hard. This wasn't about me. It was about Ginger, and taking care of Cassie if the worst . . . God, it physically hurt just thinking about it.

'OK, I'll leave it until she's thirteen then. Lou, shouldn't you be saying all this to Lizzy? I mean, she's much better at this stuff than me and she'll be the one that Cassie will gravitate towards.'

'Especially if Red marries her,' I added.

'Red's marrying Lizzy?' she gasped, confused.

'I asked him to last night.'

There was a moment of silence while she absorbed that, then she picked up a glass of wine that had yet to be cleared from the next table and downed it in one.

'You are completely freaking nuts,' was her diagnosis. But I noticed that she didn't hit me with the platitudes and reassurances.

'Your brother shared that thought. But anyway, don't avoid the question. Ginger, I don't think you realise how much Cassie loves you and how alike you are. She will always love Lizzy, but it's you she'll need more than anyone because you'll understand her. You're going to be the one she will come looking for when she needs a mum.'

Suddenly, two big fat tears appeared and she wiped them away with the sleeve of her Dolce & Gabbana jacket. Did I mention that the Grim Reaper was sponsored by Kleenex and had a talent for grief inducement? I'd finally discovered something that terrified the life out of the very boldest of my friends – and it was six, loud, opinionated and currently planning on being either prime minister or a dog groomer when she grew up.

A highly attractive, broad-shouldered waiter arrived with our drinks and a wary expression – two upset women in the middle of the day was never a situation that could be approached without caution.

After a suitably long slug of her drink, Ginger finally spoke. 'I can't believe you would trust me with your child. Do you not remember what I did with your hamster?'

'Mmm, but on balance I think it's pretty unlikely that you'll inadvertently let Cassie escape only for her to be kidnapped by the next-door neighbour and held to ransom for three Curly Wurlies and a skateboard.'

She held her glass out to mine. 'Then I hereby promise that I will take care of my gorgeous niece until the end of time should I be required to. But you need to promise me something . . .'

'Anything.'

'Promise me that if Red and Lizzy do ever marry, I won't have to wear that fucking horrible peach dress again.'

I clinked her glass with mine. 'I promise.'

A strange wave of calm washed over me. Cassie would be fine. Red would cope. I'd spoken to everyone I needed to and I knew that even if the very worst were to happen that my family would be taken care of, because I was surrounded by the most incredible friends anyone could have.

'OK. So you know what I think we should do now?' Ginger said. 'I think we should eat lunch and then drink until we fall down. And then I think we should still go on our spa weekend.'

'What spa weekend?'

'The one we booked months ago for our birthdays.'

'Ginger, I can't.'

'You can.'

'I can't.'

'Look, Lou, you just listen to me. I know you're confused and scared and I would be too. I don't know how I'd even begin to deal with what's happened to you. But Lizzy and I are your family and we want to be with you. Please let us. We need this too.'

That's when it happened. The indefatigable warrior that was Ginger broke down and sobbed in the middle of a public place, while the moon turned blue and someone found a pot of gold at the end of a rainbow.

'What do you think?' I asked Red later.

'I think you need to go. They love you, Lou, and they want the time with you, pamper you a bit. The doctors say it helps if you can stay calm and positive and take care of yourself and it'll take your mind off the wait. I think you should go.'

I thought about it some more. There were still things to be said, questions to be asked. I needed them to know things and to help me with all the loose ends.

'Hey, Ginger,' I said as she picked up the phone. 'This weekend in the hotel? I'm in.'

Fifty-one

Ginger

The St Kentigern Hotel, Glasgow. Saturday afternoon, 3 pm

'Oh, my head hurts,' I groaned. I moved my wrist in and out in front of my face as I tried to focus. 'Shit, it's three o'clock.'

Where had the day gone? God, I felt awful. The whole point of this weekend had been to pamper Lou, take her mind off Monday, give her some support and what had I done? Slept through most of it. Fuck, I was hopeless. What kind of crap friend was I?

'Lou, I'm so sorry. I've missed the whole day.'

'Don't worry about it.' She smiled. I could see that she and Lizzy had been crying. It didn't take a genius to work out what that was about and that made me feel even worse. Where had I been when my pal needed me? Wiped out, sleeping off a hangover.

I knew Lou wouldn't mind – she was the most accepting, forgiving friend ever and God knows I tested that often enough. But that wasn't the point. *I minded.*

I forced myself up to a kneeling position and tried not to

301

fall back down when the world started spinning around me.

'What can I do to make it up to you? Anything. Except my handbag collection because that's way too expensive.'

'Actually there is something,' she said quietly.

'Anything.'

'I want you to stop drinking.'

Of all the things that could possibly have come out of her mouth at that moment, I didn't expect that one.

'What?' I could feel my defensive barriers kicking in. I didn't drink too much. It was sociable. Part of my job and my image. A bit of fun. I could stop anytime. Anytime at all.

'I told you that you drank too much when you were in the hospital and you took no notice, so I'm telling you again. And this time I want you to stop.'

'Don't you dare tell me what I should do!'

Noooooo, this wasn't how today was supposed to go. This was supposed to be a fun day of girlie bonding not a mass blowout. But somehow I couldn't stop my outrage from taking control.

'Why?' she asked calmly. Wow. This was a side of Lou I'd never seen before. Usually she'd roll her eyes or back down or just ignore me but now she was actually challenging me and by the sound of it she was just warming up.

'Why do you think you've got a right to tell me what to do, to give your opinion of everything we say or do, yet we can't be honest with you? Forget it, Ginger. We've stood back and watched you abuse yourself with drink for years. It almost killed you once and if you are the person who is going to look after my daughter then you need to be fucking alive. I might not have a choice in this but you still do and you're a selfish cow if you don't realise that you're drinking yourself into an early grave and there are people around here who need you.'

Stunned. I felt like I'd been punched in the face. The

302

tension in the room was excruciating yet no one said anything. Not a word. Lou looked absolutely fucking furious and I was just . . . stunned.

Because she was right.

I knew it.

I'd known it for a long time and never bothered doing anything about it because that's who I was. Ginger, the party girl. The rock chick. Hard-core hedonist.

'Lizzy?' I suddenly wanted to know if Lizzy felt the same. Her sad nod told me that she did.

'I'm sorry, Ginger, but she's right. I'm only saying it because I love you.'

I felt sick, but at the same time seemed to have lost the power to move.

'Actually, Lizzy, while we're being honest because we love each other . . .' Oh, shit, Lou was off again.

'You need to stop hiding and doing everything for everyone else. This is your life. Yours. I know it's scary and you hate change and new challenges but you owe it to yourself to get out there and make a life on your own terms – you're not here just to facilitate the lives of everyone around you – because if you don't you're going to look back one day and really regret that you didn't find your own happiness.'

Oh for fuck's sake, what was going on here? Lou was possessed. This was so unlike her. So random. Yet . . . again she was right.

'And both of you – you need to remember everything we've talked about this weekend.'

'What do you mean?' I asked, slightly scared of the reply.

'All the reminiscing, the stories from the past, the most important moments of my life, because if I don't get through this then you need to tell Cassie all of them so she'll know. I want her to understand that every single moment that mattered had you guys in it. Because I want her to truly understand that how great your life is depends on your friends. And she has to know how to pick great ones . . . because I did.'

Fifty-two

Glasgow General Hospital. Monday Morning

'Budge up, Bruce Lee, and give me a seat.' Ginger, clutching two plastic cups of Starbucks skinny lattes, dished out the orders to Josie, who sat there, dressed head to toe in black – polo-neck jumper, wide-leg pants, black patent boots. I had no idea why. She'd been dressing like this since she spent a rainy afternoon watching back-to-back fifties movies. I think she was going for the dark, classic style of Audrey Hepburn, but instead she looked like a ninja warrior from a Jackie Chan movie.

'Ginger, you're not too old for me to slap the back of those legs,' Josie warned her. 'And the wobble of that cellulite could destabilise the Earth's core.'

Ginger immediately switched gob to outraged. 'I do not have cellulite!'

'Do.'

'Don't.'

'Do.'

I zoned them out. The clock made an extra-loud click as it hit the hour. Two o'clock. My appointment was running an hour late, but I didn't mind. Over the months that I'd been coming here I'd realised that if the schedule had been pushed back, it often meant that bad news had been delivered to someone earlier on the conveyor belt, jamming up the finely tuned machine. Good news equals a happy patient who is swift to exit. Bad news means tears, strategies, plans and questions.

'Mrs Jones?'

The nurse hadn't even got the whole word out before I was on my feet, Josie and Ginger just a split second behind. OK, I was ready. I could do this. I was prepared to go and no matter what the verdict was we'd deal with it. Let's go. Let's do this. Let's . . .

'I'm so sorry, Mrs Jones, but clinic is running terribly late today. We'll be with you as soon as possible.'

Let's wait a little longer.

Slowly, we all sat back down and if Josie's and Ginger's hearts were racing like mine, it would take us a few moments to recover.

Bloody hell, this was excruciating.

For a second I regretted not telling Red that I was getting the results this morning, but he'd been offered a week on the road doing a pictorial for the biggest rock band ever to come out of Scotland. He'd headed off last night as soon as I got back from the St Kentigern.

It was the gig of his career. Five cities over seven days with the possibility of photographs that could become iconic images of the future. Yet, I knew he'd give the whole lot up in a heartbeat to be here. So instead of admitting the truth, I'd told him that my appointment was next week, when the most exciting thing he had scheduled so far was a tourism push on the Isle of Mull.

If the news was bad we'd have plenty of time to get used to the idea so there was no point in disrupting his life yet, whether it was what he wanted or not. Besides, if the results didn't go the way we needed them to then I highly doubted he'd believe it anyway. Illness wasn't an option as far as he was concerned.

My reality was a little different.

The initial mole had been removed, a biopsy done and the doctors could see that they hadn't removed all the affected tissue.

More skin was cut away, checked, still cancerous.

And so it went on. Seven times in all. Each one getting closer and closer to the possibility of a sinister diagnosis: the spread of cancer to the lymph nodes. Or worse. The liver. The kidneys. The bones. The brain.

My heart started beating faster, sweat beads formed on the palms of my hands, on my forehead, in all the little crevices of skin that could no longer tolerate the sudden switch of my internal temperature to 'white hot fear'.

More blood tests, scans and the biopsy on my lymph nodes had been done two weeks before and now I was waiting to find out if I was going to be in and out in five minutes or if I was going to be one of today's patients who would have questions, require strategies and plans.

'Yeah, well at least I'm not dressed like the last of the samurai,' Ginger's voice cut through my thoughts.

'You're right, my love, much better not to be dressed at all. Do the words "mutton" and "lamb" mean anything to you?'

A woman further along the row of plastic orange chairs, her chin almost hitting her chest with astonishment, looked from Josie and Ginger, then at the two perfectly behaved children that sat next to her. I could tell what she was thinking. Josie and Ginger, aged eight and a half.

They'd been like this for weeks, both of them highly strung and bickering. I kept hoping they'd go for strong, heroic and dignified in the face of adversity but apparently a running commentary of insults and abuse won out in the battle of the coping mechanisms.

I'd half expected Ginger not to turn up today after everything I said to her at the hotel, but she was here. It made me love her even more.

My heart accelerated even further as another patient appeared from inside a consultation room, tears streaking her face, being supported in every step by a tall man who had devastation written all over his face. Inhale. Exhale. Inhale. Exhale.

Happy place – it was time for the happy place.

Immediately after diagnosis, Ginger had appeared with the evidence that she'd dealt with the metaphorical kick in the melanoma bollocks in the same way as she did everything else: shopping. Apologies to anyone else in the West of Scotland who is seeking comfort or information on the subject of cancer, because the entire literary stock of the nation was now on my kitchen table.

Somewhere in amongst that pile of fact and fiction, I'd discovered 'the happy place' – a concept that I'd have dismissed as being psychobabble tosh only weeks before became my lifeline. When the situation got too much, the book said, imagine a place or event in your past, somewhere safe and warm, close your eyes and go there until you feel ready to deal with reality again.

Right now I was dealing with terror, dread, a hospital waiting room, green walls, orange chairs, a ninja warrior and a former pop star turned music mogul who was threatening to twang said ninja warrior's bra until she squealed.

I wanted to be anywhere else but here.

Fifty-three

The clock on the wall clicked at the half-hour and I watched as this time a young, blonde-haired girl, perhaps twenty-one or twenty-two, exited one of the consultation rooms, her beaming smile and joyful demeanour telling the world that she'd had good news.

I wanted to hug her, to tell her to get out of there, slap on the factor fifty, and enjoy every minute of her life because . . .

'You weren't going to tell me?'

Red slipped into the seat next to me and nudged my knee with his. The playful gesture was at odds with the tension in his voice and the sweat on his frowning forehead. He'd obviously been running, rushing to get here.

I looked across to Josie and Ginger, both of them heads down, unwilling to meet my gaze. 'Which one of them cracked?' I asked him.

'I can't say. They said if I told you they'd have to kill me.'

A hand slipped into mine. 'I'm just glad I got here in time. You don't have to deal with this without me, Lou. I'm not some kid who needs to be protected.'

'I know. But you were so adamant about refusing to accept that the results might not go our way that I didn't want to burst that bubble. I get it, Red. I get the positive thinking and I know that's how you deal with everything, but I deal with things differently. I need to know all the options and prepare myself for the bad stuff too. And I am. Prepared.' I took a deep breath. Then out. I would not cry in the waiting room. I would keep it together. And when I got in there I would deal with whatever was dished out. Cancer in the lymph nodes wasn't a death sentence. They could be removed; I could have radiation, possibly chemotherapy. And if today's results suggested that it had spread further then there would be more scans, different treatments, further curable actions that could be taken. So even if we didn't get the verdict that we wanted there was still a massive possibility that I'd be OK. Today wouldn't come with a large signpost warning of the end of the road.

Surgery. Radiation. Chemo. Options. The worst thing about it all would be having to tell Cassie. Until now, all she knew was that Mum had a funny spot on her back that the doctors had to cut off. If things progressed then . . . we'd handle it. Last night after Red had fallen asleep I'd slipped into her bed and held her for the rest of the night, letting the calm rhythm of her breathing tick away the hours as I made bargain after bargain with God. I'd never been religious, but somehow I felt the urge to give it a shot, just in case.

Please God, let me be OK. I feel like I've finally found where I'm supposed to be so please don't take that away from me yet. I want to cherish what I have – love my husband, watch my daughter grow up. And I'll do anything, God, anything at all. Just name it and – as long as it isn't illegal or involving heights – I'll do it. Just let me get through this. I'll stop and smell the coffee. I'll stop sweating the small stuff. I'll make the most of every day. I'll conform to every single one of those life-enhancing proverbs and sayings. I'll do voluntary work, become a missionary, wean Josie off the caramel logs – anything, God, I'll give you anything at all if you will just get me through this.

Cassie's calm, measured breathing didn't provide a response from on high.

But I knew that's what I had to do now – stay calm, just keep on breathing. Just keep on breathing.

'Mrs Jones?'

The nice nurse was back, clutching her clipboard, her tone apologetic.

'So sorry you had to wait all this time. If you'd like to come through, Doctor Callaghan will see you now.'

Red stood up to come with me and I looked over at Josie and Ginger.

'We'll stay here,' Josie said quietly. 'Just shout if you need us.'

The nurse led us into a tiny room, with a desk and computer in one corner, and examination bed against the back wall. Sitting on a grey wheeled chair Doctor Callaghan studied the file in front of him. Oh shit. Was that the results? Why wasn't he looking up? My heart thumped like a hyperactive drummer on speed.

After a couple of seconds that dragged on for at least a week, he finally acknowledged our presence and reached over to shake our hands. I'd researched him on the internet and the general consensus of opinion was that he was an expert in his field. Somewhere in his mid-forties, with dark wavy hair and little round glasses, he looked like that bloke from *Grey's Anatomy*'s slightly less attractive but more intelligent brother. He was Dr McDreamy Lite.

'OK, Lou,' he started, his voice a low baritone of practised reassurance. 'Let's get straight to it.'

I tried to read his expression but got nothing. No relief, no joy, no disappointment, no sign that he was about to impart good news or bad. They must teach that in medical school.

311

Just keep breathing. I could deal with this. Whatever it was I could deal with it. I just had to stay strong, keep breathing.

'As you know, we carried out two procedures a fortnight ago. We took another layer from the cancer site and we took a biopsy from the sentinel lymph node.'

I nodded. The sentinel lymph node. It sounded like another of those characters from *Star Wars*.

'Sentinel Lymph Node, would you prepare your troops and ready the ship for take off.'

Focus, Lou, focus.

He referred back to the file in front of him as if checking what it said there. Was that good? Bad? Please, please hurry up or I'll need a transfer to the cardiac ward for resuscitation. Red's grip on my hand was now cutting off the blood circulation to my fingers.

'And it's good news, Lou.'

'Yes!' That was Red, who jumped from his chair, sending it flying across the tiny room as he punched the air.

I didn't move. I was still staring at the doctor's face, trying to absorb what he was saying.

'The lymph node is clear, the blood work was good, and we finally got a clear perimeter on the sample we removed from the mole. It looks like we got it all out, Lou.'

They got it all out.

No cancer.

No. More. Cancer.

Just life.

'I want to keep an eye on you though. I'll see you again in six months, just to check that there hasn't been a recurrence. After that, at least once a year, just to be on the safe side. But for now, it's all good.'

'Lou?' Red's voice reached me and I slowly looked up to meet his quizzical stare. 'It's going to be OK.'

From somewhere deep inside, I finally found the strength

to speak. 'Are you going to say that you told me so?' Nothing could stop the tears or the ecstatic smile that had suddenly taken possession of my face.

He nodded, reached down, pulled me up and swung me around the room, taking out two boxes of rubber gloves and a blood pressure monitor.

We were going to be fine. All of us. My whole family. Me, Red and Cassie, Josie, Ginger and Lizzy.

Lizzy.

A thought struck me and I knew that there was one more vital question that I had to ask Doctor Callaghan, right after I thoroughly mortified him by enveloping him in a very non-medical bear hug.

'Doctor,' I whispered, praying for the reply I was looking for, 'are you single?'

Fifty-four

Lou

2010 – Aged 40

It had taken me ages to find my old key to my parents' house, but I'd finally located it in the junk drawer in the kitchen in amongst old stamps, paper clips, miscellaneous instruction books, rolls of sticky tape, scissors and my passport from when I was twelve.

I let myself in and the first thing I noticed was the silence. The second was that everything was perfectly in place, every cushion at the right angle on the couch, every fold of the curtain perfectly straight. It must be exhausting keeping up this level of perfection.

Heading up the stairs, I got a flashback of Ginger, Lizzy and me when we were teenagers, sneaking in, sneaking out, crawling up step by step after too many drinks, falling back down them because we were wearing heels the size of a Mini Metro.

My wonder years may not have been perfect but they were interspersed with moments of brilliance.

This was no time for nostalgia though. Everything that had

happened had made me realise that I wanted to preserve everything I had for Cassie. We'd had good news and it felt like a victory. But if I'd learned anything I realised that life is unpredictable. Who knew when something terrible could happen? I'd done everything I could to make sure that Cassie would be taken care of if anything happened to me, but I'd also realised that there was something else I could give her so that she would always have me there no matter what – my teenage diaries and notebooks. I knew exactly where they were. They were in . . .

I opened my bedroom door and stopped in my tracks.

Some supernatural force appeared to have beamed up my bedroom and left a gym in its place.

'Your dad changed it into a gym and sports room years ago.'

Shit! The surprise of my mother's arrival startled me. 'Hey, Mum,' I managed when I regained power over my vocal cords. 'I didn't think you were in.'

'I was just having a sleep,' she told me, gesturing down at her cream silk robe, wrapped around a caramel-coloured lace nightdress underneath. Perfectly painted toenails. Perfectly manicured nails. 'Your dad and I are going out to dinner tonight, so I just wanted to get some rest so that I'd be looking my best later.'

Why did that comment raise the hackles on the back of my neck? It was great that she still took pride in the way that she looked. She was still an attractive woman, always impeccably dressed and as stick slim as she'd always been. Because that's the way my dad liked her.

Maybe that was it. Maybe I just still couldn't get my head around the fact that she still lived her life entirely for him, bending to his will, doing exactly what he wanted, believing everything he said and accepting that he always knew best. Allowing him to act like a spoiled, narcissistic brat who demanded 100 per cent of her time and attention and had a tantrum when he didn't get it, even if the source of the distraction was his own child. She deserved better. If she'd met another man, a more decent family guy then her life could have been so much richer.

Don't say anything. Do not say anything. I'd managed to go almost forty years without a full-scale showdown and there was no point in starting now. Besides, this was what made her happy. She was as completely besotted by him as she had always been.

'How did you get on at the check-up?' she asked.

'Fine. Still all clear. I go back again this time next year unless I notice any changes before then.'

'Good.'

Awkward pause. That happened with us sometimes.

'I was just, er, looking for all my old notebooks. Did you keep them?'

She nodded and I followed her to the big walk-in cupboard in the hall. 'They're in there.' She pointed to a large box, one of about six, on the top shelf. 'If you're ever looking for any old documents or paperwork, bank stuff, anything like that, it's all up there.' There was another pause. 'Or you could ask Josie. She always seemed to be able to get her hands on things when she needed it.'

Was that a hint?

I peered at her quizzically and I could see by the glimmer of a smile around her lips that she knew exactly what she was implying.

'You knew? All those years ago, you knew about the bank books?'

'The bank sent me a letter, acknowledging that I'd guaranteed your business loan.'

At that moment, if Tom Cruise had walked in wearing his *Top Gun* flying suit, I wouldn't have been more stunned.

'But why didn't you say anything?'

'Because your father wouldn't have approved and sometimes it's better not to rock the boat.'

That statement said everything. That my dad was the kind of guy who wouldn't cross the street, never mind put his name to a piece of paper to help his kid. That my mother knew that. That, as always, she hadn't wanted to go against his wishes. It absolutely astounded me that on this one occasion, she'd done it anyway.

I just didn't understand . . . 'Why?'

Another awkward silence, before she started a sentence with a sigh. 'I know you don't understand my relationship with your dad, but it works for us. That doesn't mean that I don't love you, Lou, because even though I might not have shown it, I always have.'

'Just not as much as you love him.' The words were out before I could stop them. She didn't argue. We both knew it was true and that was the choice she had made before I even had a say in the matter.

I thought about arguing, about shouting, telling her how outraged I was, but really, what was the point?

They would be happy together, in their own little co-dependent, intense, obsessive bubble and they didn't need or care for anyone else. It was their choice.

Despite a tug of sadness that she would never know what she was missing, I kept quiet, took my box and left. One day, the sad reality was that one of them would die and the other would be left with absolutely no one in their life. But that was up to them.

Another thing I'd learned over the last couple of years was that there was no point worrying about tomorrow, because the only way to get the most out of life was to live for today.

And today I was late for a very important occasion.

Fifty-five

'Have I missed anything? Have I? Have they started?'

Everyone in the green room spun around to face me as I stormed in and, in true Lizzy style, wobbled on my ankle, staggered, and crashed into a table of savoury snacks. I knew borrowing Ginger's eight-inch Louboutins had been a bad idea.

There was a second of stunned silence before a wave of hysterics descended.

'That was some entrance, Lou. I might try that when I walk on stage.' Ginger laughed, before Lizzy interrupted her with, 'I taught her everything she knows.'

Cassie just slapped her hand to her forehead in mortification.

She looked so beautiful, my girl, although not dressed in the most traditional contents of a young girl's wardrobe. Yes, I would have loved her to be sitting there in a pretty pink taffeta skirt, a little white cardi and red patent shoes, but as she'd announced when I was attempting to shop for her outfit for tonight (in full volume, in the middle of Marks & Spencer's changing rooms), she was eight now, not four and planning to visit the Wizard of Oz.

OK then. Sometimes she slugged right in there with a forceful reminder that she was Ginger's niece.

Instead of being dressed for the evening in the style of Judy Garland, she was wearing black leather biker boots (brought back from New York after Ginger's last business trip), a vintage Motley Crue T-shirt (also Ginger), white skinny jeans and a long silver cardigan that looked like it had been spun from a spider's web. It was either a prodigious sign of a flair for edgy fashion or a really scary warning sign that her teenage years were going to be interesting. I blew her a kiss and she rolled her eyes while the two little friends who sat next to her giggled. Since the day she'd started school, they'd been an inseparable little band. Tilly was sweet and shy, always making house and baking, when she wasn't up at A&E with a bump/breakage/cut that she'd managed to obtain while running/swinging on a rope/roller-skating/falling in a puddle. On the other side of Cassie, best friend number two, Roxy, was busy nodding her head to the beat of a song on her iPod and trying to look as grown up as possible. I made a mental note to check all the local pubs on a nightly basis as soon as they looked old enough to pass for eighteen.

I grabbed a glass of something with bubbles from the hospitality table and kissed Red, before plonking myself down on the edge of his chair, loving the fact that his arm automatically snaked around my hips.

'What time are you on at?' I asked my sister-in-law.

'Six o'clock.'

Tonight they were taping an episode of the *Music Biz* show for Channel 4 and Ginger was one of the guests. The request had come after an unusual event even by her standards. Yes, she'd achieved semi-major fame as a singer in the nineties. And of course, she had gone on to be a regular face in the music mags and showbiz sections of the newspapers due to her flamboyant character and the fact that she managed a variety of successful acts, culminating in her present role as chief honcho for one of the biggest boy bands in the country.

However, she'd only become a truly household name when she'd been caught on camera in the first-class lounge of an airport, telling a very famous diva singing star to 'get the stick out of your arse and stop being so fucking rude to everyone, you jumped-up cow. I remember when you were a waitress and you'd let punters grope your arse for tips.'

The exchange had been caught on a nearby teenager's mobile phone camera, posted on YouTube and Ginger had become an overnight sensation. Said diva was last seen stomping off in outrage in the direction of her lawyer's office.

Meanwhile, the offers had come flooding in to Ginger's company. Journalists wanted to interview her, TV shows wanted her on board, and she'd even been tentatively approached about becoming a judge on a new talent show that was all about finding the next big rock god.

The most bizarre thing about it all? She'd done the whole lot sober.

Completely sober.

In the most touching act of love since Red got three speeding tickets trying to make it to the hospital for the results of my lymph node biopsy, my sister-in-law, the diehard boozer, hadn't touched a drink since the day we checked out of the hotel.

It had taken us a while to notice because to be honest, as witnessed by the obnoxious superstar diva, she was just as outrageous when she was sober as she was when she was pissed. Also, she didn't make a big deal out of it. She just quietly came to terms with the fact that if she carried on drinking the way that she always had, then Cassie could be faced with the possibility of losing two people that she loved far sooner than she should. She'd locked up the metaphorical drinks cabinet and thrown away the key. In news that wasn't of course in any way connected to the fact that they didn't have to give her free drinks any more, the Carriage Club had just reported record profits over the last twelve-month period.

Miraculously, abstinence had also brought out her long lost maternal side. Yes, she now had a miniature shih-tzu that went everywhere with her in a Louis Vuitton case.

Suddenly, Josie rushed into the room in a fairly accurate reconstruction of my entrance. There was no getting around genetics.

'Have I missed anything? Has it . . . for Christ's sake, Ginger, I can almost see your kidneys!'

Ginger wriggled her pelmet-length skirt down a couple of centimetres. On any other forty-year-old woman, I'd have said it was indecent. On Ginger it looked spectacular. Although, there was no doubt now that Josie would walk directly behind her to prevent passers-by getting a flash of her buttocks.

'Is it always like this?' the dark-haired guy sitting next to Lizzy asked with just an edge of fear in her voice. Yes, Lizzy had a man. And not just any man. No, it wasn't Doctor Callaghan – much to my disgust, he claimed it breached medical ethics to allow me to set him up on a date with my pal.

Nor was it the very funny warehouse manager that I'd taken home to meet her after he'd walked into the salon for a cut and blow-dry. Or the cute joiner that had come to fix my warped back door and been sent straight round to Lizzy's, with express authorisation to ask her out if he fancied her in the hope that she'd say yes, they'd fall madly in love and live happily ever after in a home with superior woodwork. He did. She didn't. They never would.

Over the black leather sofa, Lizzy turned to her recently acquired boyfriend and grinned. 'Your brother is married to my ex-husband and your new girlfriend had a baby for them and you think *this* lot are a bit unusual?'

Yes, Lizzy's boyfriend was Alex's brother John, recently returned to this country after being posted abroad with the navy for the last ten years. They'd met at Alex's birthday party last month and hit it off immediately. She claimed she'd not yet asked him to wear his white uniform and sweep her off her feet but given the way she was looking at him, I wasn't so sure.

Life was good. Life was so, so good and sitting in the green room of a Glasgow television studio I felt an overwhelming surge of happiness. Elation. Gratitude. Right now, there was nothing that could make a dent in this joyous state of unadulterated bliss.

'Miss Jones?' I automatically looked up, before realising that the young girl with the clipboard and earpiece standing at the door was talking to Ginger. In typical Ginger style, she hadn't changed her name when she married Ike, so we both had the same surnames. 'We're just about ready to go, so if you could follow me please.'

Ginger pulled herself out of her chair and stood up, ignoring Josie, who was holding her cardigan up so that it covered Miss Jones' crotch area.

If any of the television producers in this building were looking for inspiration for their next sitcom, this sixty-something, caramel-log-loving ninja would be a great place to start.

'Your friends can either wait here and watch the show on that monitor, or there's room for one or two of them at the side of the stage.'

I was on my feet beside her before you could say 'pushy pal'. What was the point of having a best friend who was an international celebrity if you didn't get to witness the glamorous, exciting stuff first hand?

'Is it safe to leave you here with this lot for half an hour?' Lizzy asked John with a teasing smile.

He put on an admirable show of bravado. 'Lizzy, I've taken on the Taliban. I think I might just make it through this.'

We decided not to point out that he'd just broken into a sweat.

We were shown to our places, where we watched the little girl from Weirbank with the massive shrub of bright red hair, spend half an hour being so indiscreet, funny and completely irreverent that the audience were in stitches from beginning to end.

Just when Jack Jardine, the presenter, was winding up, Lizzy slipped her arm around my waist and gave me a squeeze. 'This is so brilliant,' she said with a moist glint in her eye. 'I'm happy, Ginger's doing great, and you're . . . you're . . .' I felt her hand curl around my hip and pause when it came into contact with my stomach. Then move up. Then down. Then across one way. Then back. Then . . . '. . . pregnant! You've either swallowed a very large pie or you're up the duff again.'

I thought I'd disguised it with my flowing tunic and water-fall-style cardi, but I hadn't reckoned on my inappropriately tactile pal.

'Pregnant,' I whispered, gleefully. 'But don't say anything because this is Ginger's night and we're going to announce it at the weekend after our next scan. The docs say everything looks fine though, and there's absolutely no reason for us not to have ten more. Apart from the fact that Red would leave me for a supermodel because I'd be surgically attached to the washing machine.'

'Oh, Lou.' Lizzy hugged me. 'That's the most amazing news ever. I'm so happy for you.'

'Ladies and gentlemen, a huge round of applause for the absolutely bloody marvellous Ginger Jones.' Jack Jardine got to his feet and kissed Ginger on the cheek before waving her off stage. We reached out to envelop her in our cosy little hug-in but she reacted like we'd just told her we had fleas. Public displays of affection would never be her thing.

323

'And now, ladies and gentlemen, another guest who hails from this part of the world.' Jardine was lining up the next guest. 'Shall we go or stay and watch?' Lizzy asked and was met with simultaneous shrugs.

'I don't mind,' I said. 'Do we have any idea who it is?'

'He's loud, he's proud, back in the nineties he had hit records all over the world and had ten – count them, ten – number one singles,' Jack continued. 'And now he's still racking up the hits as one of the most successful producers in the charts today . . .'

Oh no,' Ginger murmured, before spinning around, grabbing Lizzy's arm and mine, and taking a step towards the exit.

I stood my ground and refused to be moved. 'What is it? What's the problem? Who is . . . ?'

'Yes, ladies and gentlemen, it's Glasgow's very own indie hero, Mr. Gary. Collins!'

'Fuck. Fuckety fuck,' I mumbled.

Right on cue, with the young girl with the clipboard and what looked like an agent of some kind leading the way, Gary Collins, wearing an impeccably cut black suit over a charcoal shirt, materialised through the door directly in front of us and strutted in our direction.

'Against the wall! Against the wall!' Ginger hissed, trying to move us out of his direct path. 'The injunction is off my record now and I don't want another one.'

All those years ago, after she tipped a bucket on his head in front of a live audience at an awards show, his lawyers had shot off a warning that if she came within a hundred feet of him she'd be shot. Or something like that.

Now, faced with the man who publicly humiliated me all those years ago, I just wanted to disappear, to be anywhere but here.

I allowed Lizzy to pull me into the wings, into a dark

enough shadow that, in the flurry of activity going on around him, he'd never notice we were there. He'd just walk right on by. Right. On. By.

'Gary Collins?'

Who was that? Who was speaking to him?

Nooooooooooooo. It was me.

'Oh fuck,' Ginger muttered as she realised it was too late to pull me back in.

Clipboard girl looked terrified and the bloke in the sharp agent's suit looked furious and moved to push me out of the way.

'Don't. You. Dare.' Oh shite, why was I using the tone that I usually only reserved for school bullies and the bloke down the road that kept nicking my wheelie bin?

Gary Collins, the former love of my life, stepped into the full light and squinted a little as he stared at me, clearly trying to work out how he knew me.

'Gary, we really need to move,' the suit told him.

Gary swatted the words away. 'It's OK, it's recorded. They can do it again in a minute.'

Wow, Mr Big Shot. What must it be like to know that you can keep a whole TV show waiting until you decide to honour them with your presence?

'Lou, I . . .'

Now it was my turn to swat away Lizzy's interruption.

But it was too late – something in Gary Collins' memory clearly made a connection.

'Lou? Lou Cairney? Oh my God, Lou Cairney?'

Hold on, this was unexpected. Yes, he looked incredulous but he also looked strangely *pleased* to see me. 'Wow, you still look . . . I mean, you're still gorgeous!'

Still gorgeous. Right then. So I may well have been gorgeous back then but that didn't stop him telling the whole world that I had the sexual skills of a concrete slab.

And no, I would not admit that he was still the best-looking guy that I'd ever seen. I wouldn't. Definitely not.

'What are you doing here?'

Ginger stepped forwards and I gained a slight satisfaction from seeing him register her presence and flinch.

'I'm here with Ginger. I'm married to her brother, Red. He was in your year at school.'

You see, I'm married! said the voice in my head. A man had sex with me and liked it so much that he actually married me. And he says I'm good at it. And we do it all the time. In fact we do it so often that I'm pregnant right now. Yep, right now. So stick that in your pop star pipe and smoke it, you big prick.

'Yeah, yeah, I remember him,' he answered in a voice that made it completely obvious that he didn't. I felt Ginger tense up beside me as he kept right on talking. 'So listen, I'm up here for a few nights – do you fancy hanging around and we can go for a drink afterwards? It would be great to catch up again and you know . . .'

You know what? What the fuck was he talking about? Did he not hear me say that I was married? Did he not remember that he made a whole fucking career out of mortifying me? Did he seriously think he could just flash that perfect, chiselled, designed-by-the-angels face and I'd just melt into his arms. Did he? Is that what he thought of me?

'Or how about we do something a little different?' I purred, to his clear delight. 'How about something a little more . . . physical.'

'Now you're talking,' he flirted back.

'I was thinking I could just . . .'

Fifty-six

The three of us trooped back into the green room in silence, and were met with a solid wall of open-mouthed astonishment. Eventually, it came down to my ever-bold daughter to speak up first.

'Mum,' she said, her tone that of someone using extreme caution. 'Did you just punch Gary Collins?'

'How did you know?'

Every head in the room swivelled towards the screen, where Jack Jardine was keeping the audience going with babbling chat while they still awaited the arrival of the next big star.

'There was a camera following him as he approached the stage. It caught everything,' Red clarified.

Oh crap, he must be furious. I'm sure he was probably already calculating how much he'd need to pay me in child support if he packed up and took off right now.

'The conversation too?' I asked warily.

Everyone nodded. Bloody hell, what kind of woman was I? I'd spent my whole life avoiding being the centre of attention and now here I was, in front of a god-forsaken camera crew, losing the plot and decking one of the biggest celebrities of our generation.

'Red, I'm so sorry. Really, I didn't mean to do it, I just . . .'

'Sorry?' He got to his feet and walked towards me. 'Lou Jones, you are the most magnificent woman I have ever known.'

The drum roll started with Josie's feet and gathered pace around the room. It even almost drowned out Jack muttering something about being safer with the Taliban.

Red leaned down and kissed me hard and long.

Right on cue, Ginger spoke up. 'Will you two stop that?'

'I know, I know – you hate the whole PDA thing,' Red groaned.

'No, it's not that,' she argued. 'It's just that security said if we're not out of here in ten minutes, they're calling the police.'

'Our house? A little celebration?' I shouted to our extended brood.

'Celebration of what?' Cassie asked.

I ruffled her hair. 'Just everything, love. Let's just celebrate every single thing.'

Acknowledgements

As always, the wonderful Sheila Crowley was the best agent (and friend) an author could have – especially in times of author panic and hysteria. Also at Curtis Brown, Katie McGowan, Tally Garner and Sarah Lewis have been fantastic. Thank you all.

Joanne Dickinson is not only an incredibly talented editor, but showed patience and support way above and beyond . . . Thank you.

Huge gratitude to the rest of the team at Little, Brown for being consistently stellar. And to the wonderful Emma Beswetherick who started it all off.

This book is all about friendship, gossip, scandal, disaster, drama and bendy activities. Some incidents may or may not have been inspired by this merry band of fabulous friends: Frankie Plater, Jan Johnston, Lyndsay MacAlister, Gillian Armstrong, Janice McCallum, Linda Lowery, Gillian Miller, Wendy Morton, Pamela McBurnie, Sylvia Lavizani, Mitch Murphy, Carmen Reid, Gemma Low, Emma Vijayaratnum, Isobel Cook, Sadie Hill, Rosina Hill, Liz Murphy and my darling Fairy Crean.

Thank you once again to all the journalists, booksellers and bloggers who said such nice things about my previous books.

Friday Night with the Girls is my ninth book and I'm eternally grateful to all the readers who have supported me throughout the years.

And finally, to my gorgeous, funny, adorable menfolk (one large, two small) – thank you, thank you, thank you. I know how incredibly lucky I am. But no, just because there's another book doesn't mean we're buying a spaceship.

Love,
Shari x